continued . . .

Twist and Shout Murder

A MURDER A-GO-GO MYSTERY

Rosemary Martin

A SIGNET BOOK

SIGNET
Published by New American Library, a division of
Penguin Group (USA) Inc., 375 Hudson Street,
New York, New York 10014, USA
Penguin Group (Canada), 90 Eglinton Avenue East, Suite 700, Toronto,
Ontario M4P 2Y3, Canada (a division of Pearson Penguin Canada Inc.)
Penguin Books Ltd., 80 Strand, London WC2R 0RL, England
Penguin Ireland, 25 St. Stephen's Green, Dublin 2,
Ireland (a division of Penguin Books Ltd.)
Penguin Group (Australia), 250 Camberwell Road, Camberwell, Victoria 3124,
Australia (a division of Pearson Australia Group Pty. Ltd.)
Penguin Books India Pvt. Ltd., 11 Community Centre, Panchsheel Park,
New Delhi - 110 017, India
Penguin Group (NZ), cnr Airborne and Rosedale Roads, Albany,
Auckland 1310, New Zealand (a division of Pearson New Zealand Ltd.)
Penguin Books (South Africa) (Pty.) Ltd., 24 Sturdee Avenue,
Rosebank, Johannesburg 2196, South Africa

Penguin Books Ltd., Registered Offices:
80 Strand, London WC2R 0RL, England

First published by Signet, an imprint of New American Library,
a division of Penguin Group (USA) Inc.

First Printing, April 2006
10 9 8 7 6 5 4 3 2 1

 REGISTERED TRADEMARK—MARCA REGISTRADA

Printed in the United States of America

PUBLISHER'S NOTE
This is a work of fiction. Names, characters, places, and incidents either are
the product of the author's imagination or are used fictitiously, and any resemblance to actual persons, living or dead, business establishments, events, or
locales is entirely coincidental.
   The publisher does not have any control over and does not assume any
responsibility for author or third-party Web sites or their content.

If you purchased this book without a cover, you should be aware that this
book is stolen property. It was reported as "unsold and destroyed" to the
publisher, and neither the author nor the publisher has received any payment
for this "stripped book."

To Cynthia Holt-Johnson: My equally high-maintenance friend, my partner in crime in shopping, and my best pal since high school. Martinis on me.

Acknowledgments

A big thank-you to my agent, Harvey Klinger, aka the Wonder Agent. Love ya, baby!

Thanks to WBP for the inspiration.

Thanks to Donna Andrews, author extraordinaire.

I couldn't possibly write without the support of my family: Tommy, Rachel, and Alana. I love you all so very much.

Twist and Shout Murder

Chapter One

New York City
April 30, 1964

I closed the door to my apartment building on East Sixty-fifth Street and zipped down the steps to the sidewalk. The glow I felt because Bradley Williams, my dreamy boss, had given me a generous bonus to follow him to his new assignment as head of Ryan Modeling Agency kept my spirits high despite what I called my Problem with Bradley. I hoped that today matters would improve. Otherwise, I might have to kill someone.

I'd saved some of my bonus money, but the rest I'd given to Darlene, my stewardess roommate, to shop for me on her next layover in swinging London. I had shortened all my Jackie Kennedy–style suits two inches above my knees so Bradley could admire my legs. But fashions from London! That would catch his eye.

Yesterday the box had arrived. Darlene had shopped on Carnaby Street! She sent me short, mod dresses in vibrant colors and some daring miniskirts. If Daddy saw me in them, he'd go ape and drag me back home to Richmond, Virginia, even if I was twenty-two years old. But what was a girl to do? I was proud of my legs, which made up for my 34-As and narrow hips.

To wear with the shorter skirts, there were light tan

"tights" that looked like stockings with underwear. Darlene had pinned a note on these saying, *No more girdles!*

Giving me dictation was going to be a whole new experience for Bradley.

At the bottom of the box, Darlene had packed the most groovy item of all: a pair of white go-go boots! I loved those boots! I tried them on and danced around in front of my full-length mirror, feeling happy and a little naughty. If anyone had seen me, they'd have thought I was nuts.

I might have to refrain from wearing the boots to the office, though Ryan Modeling was cool. Maybe one day if I felt particularly daring. . . .

"Hey, there, Miss Sweet Face, don't you look . . . different this morning," called Harry, the wino who slept across the street behind St. Vincent Ferrer Catholic High School. In the almost two months I'd lived in New York City, I had never been able to figure out why Harry didn't clean up and get a job and a decent place to live. But Harry had proved himself a friend, and I dashed over to see him, digging in my purse for quarters.

"Good morning, Harry. Do you like my new look?" I twirled around for his inspection. I had on a double-knit, A-line dress with three-quarter-length sleeves. Diagonal hot-pink, white, and black stripes made up the body of the dress, which ended about four inches above my knees.

Harry scratched his gray hair. Then he stroked his scraggly beard. "Kinda short, isn't it? I mean for a nice girl like you."

I laughed and handed him two quarters. "No, silly. This is the new look from London. You know, in England where the Beatles come from."

"Bugs?" Harry said, looking around, confusion making his wildly bristling eyebrows come together.

"Oh, Harry, you make me sad that you don't even know who the Beatles are. They were on *The Ed Sullivan Show* in February, singing and making every girl fall in love with them. You should get into the world again. I'll help you," I assured him.

He began to move away. "Bebe, I like my world. Takes away the pain. Thanks for the dough."

I walked down to Lexington Avenue, putting Harry's troubles aside for the time being. Now that I had finally mastered the subway, I made my way to the nearest station and dashed down the steps. I smiled as several people turned to look at me in my cool dress.

I rode the train down to 199 Lafayette Street, where Ryan Modeling, second only to Ford Modeling, had offices on the seventeenth floor. On the eighteenth floor we had a studio for photo shoots and making commercials, and where we leased space for a live TV show.

Riding along with the occasional jolt, I thought back over the past few days of my new job.

Bradley and I had taken a tour of our new quarters. The agency's décor was the height of modern, even in the typing pool, where brand-new Selectras were on every desk. The supervisor, Mrs. Seeds, assured me that I could call her if I needed any help with typing or covering the phones during lunch.

On the eighteenth floor, we looked at three large shooting areas separated by steel walls; the makeup room; dressing areas; and a holding area for clothing sent over from stores or clients. And then we met Gina Simmons, the woman responsible for dealing directly with the models. A former model herself, now a well-maintained woman in her forties, Gina looked at us with hard eyes. She had portfolios spread out on her desk and replied to Bradley's introduction with a chilly, "I look forward to working with you."

We had moved over to the leased space.

Bradley said to me, "I've heard that Debbie Ann's a perfectionist, gossipy, and a bit opinionated, but she's had a rough life."

"Oh?"

"Her husband committed suicide, leaving her with a boy just out of high school."

"How terrible," I said, shocked.

"It gets worse. Her son left her not long after that to join the army and fight in Korea. Later, she learned he was killed there," Bradley said.

"A double tragedy."

He nodded. "I'm only telling you this so that you'll be patient with Debbie Ann."

"I promise I will. I watched her show last Friday at four o'clock. I'm eager for an introduction."

Inspired by Julia Child's successful program on cooking, Debbie Ann aired *Fun in the Kitchen with Debbie Ann*.

Debbie Ann Allard was a well-groomed woman in her fifties with brown hair (dyed?) swept back from her forehead and ending beneath her ears in rows of flipped-up tight curls. She wore a shirtwaist dress and an apron with colorful flowers on it. With natural charm, a constant smile, and nonstop chitchat (I didn't know how she managed all three), she demonstrated how women could whip up easy, delicious meals that were much less complicated than Julia Child's.

Advertised as Every Homemaker's Friend, Debbie Ann began each show promising that the viewer could follow along and have a scrumptious meal waiting for her husband when he came home from work. A grocery list for the following week's dishes was posted on Friday afternoons before the show started, so that women could shop for upcoming recipes.

I was amazed seeing "the kitchen" set.

Debbie Ann's set featured a modern kitchen complete with a new Philco Galaxie range in turquoise. The "walls" were covered in a cheerful wallpaper of turquoise and orange stripes with small yellow flowers between the lines. A new Presto mixer, Deluxe toaster, a set of orange Tupperware, and a copper planter with artificial buttercups gave the set a homey feel.

It was about two in the afternoon, and Every Homemaker's Friend scurried about, checking off items for the day's show on deviled chicken. A harried-looking girl I thought must be her assistant helped.

Debbie Ann saw us and, as fast as a rocket, she came shooting over, all smiles and charming greetings.

"Did I mention, Mr. Williams, that *Fun in the Kitchen with Debbie Ann* has consistently drawn a wide audience since the day we first went on air? I remember it well," Debbie Ann said in a nostalgic, sweet voice, one hand over her pointy bosom, not giving Bradley a second to speak. "I showed women how to make crabmeat Norfolk with Harris's crabmeat. For only ten cents' postage and a label from any Harris can, one could get an adorable reusable seashell for baking and serving crab dishes. Women loved the idea!

"After that first show aired, I received hundreds of grateful letters from housewives. In fact, while I don't want to seem immodest, my fan mail has grown into the thousands. Today's busy homemaker needs all the help she can get. I'm so proud to assist them," Debbie Ann finished, finally out of breath.

Bradley smiled, looking as if he wished Debbie Ann didn't chatter so. "I know you are, Debbie Ann. The show is very popular, according to the figures I've seen. Advertisers love it."

"I'm so glad. When she doesn't have to spend long hours in the kitchen, a woman has time to dress and look her best for her man. My true aim, you see, is to help the ordinary woman please her husband when he comes home from the office."

I felt sorry for Debbie Ann. Clearly she was trying to please the husbands of New York City, because she'd failed to please her own and he'd committed suicide.

Jolting to a stop, the train I rode picked up more passengers. I couldn't wait to get to Bradley—er, work. I thought with pleasure of my Danish Modern desk and credenza with its direct view into Bradley's spacious executive suite. He'd had his furniture from our stint at Rip-City Records moved here: Arts and Crafts desk and seating arrangement, lovely rugs done in blue, cream and rust, and his bar, hidden away in a cabinet.

When we'd moved in on Monday, I couldn't stop grinning. My desk offered a complete panorama of Bradley's gorgeous self, affording me many opportunities for covert visual delight. All I had to do was lift my gaze from whatever I was typing on my Selectra, and there he'd be at his desk, working hard, his St. Louis Cardinals mug waiting to be filled with fresh coffee.

And he could see me, too. My desk didn't have a front, so my legs were fully visible as I sat there, oh, so innocently trying to drive him insane with desire.

While that was terrific, this arrangement also afforded me a front-row seat for something I didn't want to see: the Problem.

The train stopped, cutting off any further musings. I ran up the subway steps and hurried to Ryan. Arriving breathless in the office, I put my purse in my credenza and immediately began to brew coffee. Bradley was in his office, wearing a medium-blue suit with a hint of iridescence. My favorite. Of course, there was also his navy suit, his gray one, and his black one . . . Ooops! Here was my chance to show off my dress.

Not *exactly* posing, but close to it, I stood in Bradley's doorway, smiling. "Good morning, Mr. Williams."

Bradley looked up from his newspaper. His gaze slid slowly down the dress to my legs, where it lingered, before he raised his eyes to mine.

I held back a giggle. It seemed he was concentrating on what was right in front of him, ready for the taking—*after* we were pronounced man and wife, of course.

In an instant, though, his normal unflappable demeanor was back in place. One thing about Bradley: He was always cool.

"Coffee—I need coffee, kid."

"I have a pot brewing. It'll be ready in a minute," I replied cheerfully, though I wished he'd stop calling me by that stupid nickname.

Couldn't he see I wasn't a kid? Okay, maybe there was about eight or nine years' difference between us. So what? Lots of women married slightly older men. Mama told me it was because men didn't mature as fast as women.

"You're ever efficient, Miss Bennett," he said, giving me a wide smile that made me completely forgive him for the "kid" remark.

"Thank you, Mr. Williams," I said, reeling.

"By the way, Miss Bennett, your title here at Ryan Modeling is executive secretary," he told me. "I'm the boss, and I feel you've earned the promotion."

My heart filled with pride. The training I'd received at Charlotte Marie's Secretarial School, my jobs back home in Richmond, and my hard work at Rip-City Records had paid off! "Thank you, Mr. Williams. I'm very pleased."

"I am too," he said. "You're an excellent secretary. One I wouldn't want to lose for any reason."

"I'll get your coffee now." I walked out of his office floating on a cloud. A bonus, an increase in pay, his appreciation of my legs, and now the title of executive secretary! Just wait until I told Darlene—especially that remark about not wanting to lose me!

My parents would be so proud. I wouldn't tell them the part about my legs. Maybe now Daddy would get off my back about living in the big, bad city.

At lunchtime, humming "One Fine Day" by the Chiffons as I went about my work, I heard the elevator ding. The person who got off had me crashing back to earth.

The Problem arrived in a low-cut, orange-sherbet-colored minidress a good two inches shorter than mine. Without a glance at me, she swept directly into Bradley's office as if she owned the place.

Struggling not to let her bug me, I sat at my desk with its sunny yellow blotter, and tried to study the memo I had been typing for Debbie Ann's weekly grocery bill.

It was useless. I looked at the woman in the mini-dress. *She* was the one giving me nightmares: Suzie Wexford, the agency's top model, a star whose every new photo shoot was eagerly anticipated by the whole country.

"Bradley, darling, it's utterly lovely and so feminine. How did you know Tiffany's is my favorite little shop?" exclaimed Suzie, loud enough for me to hear. *She* was the stunning blond model Bradley had taken out *every night this week,* breaking his own rule of dating a girl only *once.*

That's what really had me scared, worried to the point that I was grinding my teeth in my sleep. Surely Bradley was not ready to give up his bachelorhood, his key to the Playboy Club, his nights out with a string of blondes, his man-about-town reputation. Surely he wasn't prepared to settle down, with a model, no less.

When he decided to marry, *I* was supposed to be the pure girl he turned to with a Tiffany's engagement ring. And my dreams were not groundless. A few weeks ago Bradley and I had shared a flaming-hot kiss, even though he apologized for it afterward and said there could be no office romances in his life. Suzie was repped by Ryan, but I guessed he didn't consider her an employee.

"Tiffany's is the only jewelry store for someone as exquisite as you, honey," came Bradley's low-timbered voice. "Here, let me put it around your delicate wrist."

Suzie pressed her tall, skinny, orange-clad body against his and held out her right wrist. From the side, she looked like a Creamsicle. Bradley kissed her temple, then focused on clasping the gold bracelet on her like a mark of possession.

I sat with my right index finger pressed down hard on the *M* key on my Selectra. Little *M*s for *murder—*

ooops! I meant little *M*s for Bradley's and my *marriage*—ran across the paper.

Gossip about the new boss and his preference for the famous model had flown around the office since Tuesday. Apparently Suzie had dropped a word here and there about how "taken" she was with Bradley. Her frequent trips to his office—sometimes with the door shut!—confirmed their relationship.

While I had unpacked a box of file folders earlier, Nellie, Debbie Ann's mousy young assistant, had stopped by my desk. About my age, Nellie was plump and had medium-brown hair in need of a good cut. She wore glasses, but still squinted.

She gabbed about famous celebrities before gossiping about Bradley and Suzie. I'd heard all the details of their candlelit dinner at the 21 Club (Bradley's fave) Monday night, a Broadway play Tuesday night, dinner at the Rainbow Room followed by a stroll around Rockefeller Center last night.

I had ended up with a knot in my stomach.

Now here was Bradley handing Suzie an expensive bracelet.

How she had managed to twirl him around her manicured pinkie with seemingly little effort was a mystery. I'd give up all my Beatles pictures and records to find out how she did it.

I reminded myself that Bradley was too intelligent to spend his life with a model whose looks would fade and who, most likely, had no conversation or morals.

Suddenly it hit me that they were talking about Tiffany's. I took a deep, frustrated breath. Tiffany's was *my* jewelry store, had been ever since I saw *Breakfast at Tiffany's* back home in Richmond. The movie had played a big part in my desire to move to the city of my dreams.

In fact, one of my dreams was to have breakfast in front of the exclusive store with its blazing, glittering, perfect diamonds displayed in the heart-shaped window. Diamonds that made a girl dream of the man she loved.

I guess you could say I fell in love with Bradley at first sight, though that love had grown as I'd come to know him. He had interviewed me for the position of secretary after he had run through half a dozen other secretaries in the previous months. At first I couldn't figure out why he'd had so many, but after working with him for a while, I thought I understood. They all wanted him, his sexy build, his dirty-blond hair, his full lips, and the icing on a delicious cake: his incredible blue eyes.

Apparently Bradley had gotten in trouble for dallying with them. Then he had hired me. The kid.

Darlene had left me a copy of Helen Gurley Brown's *Sex and the Single Girl*. Wide-eyed, I'd read the book, but nothing in it had changed my views. I wanted Bradley for keeps, and I wouldn't get him if he thought I was easy.

Bradley came out of his office, Suzie in tow.

"Miss Bennett, have you met Ryan's top model, Suzie Wexford?"

Be nice, I told myself. "Why, no, Mr. Williams, I don't believe we've been formally introduced."

"Suzie, this is Miss Bennett, my secretary—er, my executive secretary, I should say," he said, smiling at me.

I smiled back, then reluctantly turned to Suzie and held out my right hand.

Suzie took a step away like I'd offered her a spider. "Is that typewriter-ribbon ink on your hand?"

I withdrew my splotched fingers. "Sorry, the ribbon got off track." I blushed, an embarrassing habit of mine.

My gaze was drawn to the bracelet, sparkling like the water at Virginia Beach on a sunny day.

Suzie turned away from me. "Bradley, I'm starved," she said, her arm on his.

"Just a second, Suzie," he said, pulling something out of his suit pocket. "Here, Miss Bennett, this is for you."

I accepted a richly engraved ivory-colored envelope,

anxious to know what was inside. I lifted the smooth
vellum flap and saw it was an invitation to the gallery
showing by famed photographer Pierre Benoit. It was
for tonight and, I knew, a highly anticipated and publi-
cized event.

"Thank you, Mr. Williams. How exciting!"

Suzie rolled her eyes.

Bradley grinned at me. "My invitation stated I could
bring a guest. Since Suzie has an invitation of her own,
I thought you'd enjoy the show. You can take the rest
of the afternoon off to get ready if you like. I know
how ladies like to primp."

"What a good idea, Bradley," Suzie said, her voice
dripping with sarcasm. "I'm certain Miss Bennett
could use the extra time."

The witch! I tilted my head at her, and the little
devil on my left shoulder made me say, "You're so
right, Miss Wexford. Unlike you, I don't have a team
of people trying to make me look good. I have to
manage all on my own."

Suzie glared at me.

Bradley coughed behind his hand, and the two
walked to the elevators.

I began cleaning off my desk. I had a dress to buy!

Chapter Two

Suzie and Bradley stood together at the gala showing. He wore a black tux and looked debonair holding a martini glass, living up to his swinging reputation. She wore a black designer number that made her body look like a string of black licorice.

I glanced away, telling myself it was a sheer joy to be fresh, young, and female in the big city. I forced myself to radiate good cheer and straightened to my full five feet seven inches while I took in my surroundings.

The large room was the utmost in understatement, the brick walls painted black, the wood floor dark. I guessed the idea was for the black-and-white photographs on the walls to mesmerize the viewer without distraction. Each photograph had its own individual light above it. The only other light came from round tables scattered throughout, draped in black and decorated with lit votive candles in silver holders.

I stared at a stunning candid shot of Brigitte Bardot walking down a Paris street at twilight looking lonely. You had to give Pierre credit: He had a way of capturing celebrities in photos that revealed something personal about them.

"Great shot, isn't it?" a deep male voice beside me said.

I looked up to see a young man about my age. At least six foot two, he bore a slight resemblance to Bradley. Full lips, blue eyes, high forehead, but his hair was light brown, and the shape of his face more angular. "Yes, it is a lovely photo of Miss Bardot."

"I'm Tom Stevens. I haven't seen you around," he said, a twinkle in his eyes.

"Oh, I'm not really part of this crowd," I said.

"No? But you're here. I don't mean to be forward, but I'm fairly new to all this"—he waved his hand expansively—"and would like to get to know more people."

Give him your name, I told myself. *He's good-looking and friendly, and that voice is incredibly sexy.* I opened my mouth, only to see Lauren Bacall approach us, smile at me, and take Tom's arm.

"Tommy, darling, come with me. I want to introduce you to a friend of mine who can help make you a star on Broadway."

Tom looked at me ruefully. "Will you excuse me? I'll try to find you later, if that's okay."

"Sure," I said, flabbergasted that beautiful Lauren Bacall had just stood right in front of me, and happy that such a good-looking guy had made a pass at me. He'd made me feel more confident. I wore a black silk Audrey Hepburn–like halter dress with a low back topped by a satin bow. Pierre's invitation had specified black attire only. I'd spent the afternoon shopping at Macy's, digging deeper into my bonus money, but surely, in the classy feminine formal, Bradley would notice that I was a woman, not a "kid." I'd even had my dark hair, which normally fell to my shoulder in a flip, done in an Audrey upsweep.

I tried to appear cool as celebrities strolled through the crowd, but it was an eye-popping group. I watched as Henry Fonda, Joan Fontaine, and Vincente Minnelli roamed the room, puffing on cigarettes, kissing cheeks, the men slapping each other on the back. A new gentleman arrived, causing heads to turn. It took me a minute to realize he was Gregory Peck. What a party!

Trying not to stare at the celebrities, I made myself focus on the photographs lining the walls. The Beatles

began singing "I Want to Hold Your Hand" on the
mono, which made me look at Bradley in his classic
tux. He was the type to make a girl swoon, and maybe
lose her head, the type Mama and Daddy always
warned me against. Military man that he was, Daddy
wanted me to marry someone like the brand-new GI
Joe doll that had just come on the market. Only
human.

Bradley hardly looked unhappy with Suzie draping
herself all over him, darn it. In fact, he had his left
hand on the back of her neck, under her just-to-the-
chin perfect blond hair, massaging away any tension
she felt.

"Don't you just want to kill her?" asked a voice
with a Jersey accent.

I looked at the woman, who could apparently read
minds. Shorter than me, she had dyed her dark hair
blond. I could tell because the roots showed. I had
once considered dying my hair blond, but quickly realized I'd look like a ghost.

"I'm Gloria Castellano, Suzie's makeup girl," the
woman explained. In contrast to her frizzy hair, Gloria's makeup was perfect, the latest style of heavily
lined eyes and pale pink lip gloss expertly applied. She
wore a lovely black sheath dress that went to the floor
and featured a side split with matching black bows
running from the split up to her hips. "You do a great
job with your makeup. Your brown eyes look huge
with that black liner and those thick lashes," she said.

"Thank you. That's quite a compliment coming
from someone who specializes in cosmetics. I was
thinking the same thing about your makeup. I'm Bebe
Bennett, Bradley Williams's secretary at Ryan."

I had moved on to a photo of Natalie Wood. Since
there were no chairs, Gloria and I stood in front of
the photo, to the right of where Bradley and Suzie
were murmuring to each other.

Gloria nodded wisely. "Geez, no wonder you have
that tortured look on your face. You must be in love
with him."

Startled that my thoughts flashed like a traffic caution light, I tried again to adopt a calm, cool air like the rest of the crowd. I rarely drank, but I snagged a crystal flute of champagne from a waiter dressed in white. Champagne was the only alcoholic drink I liked, not that I'd tried them all. With celebrities all around and Bradley misbehaving, I needed something.

"What Mr. Williams does out of the office is hardly my concern. We have a professional relationship," I recited, lying through clenched teeth.

Gloria snorted. "Yeah, right. Listen, I just got here. What's the scene? Lots of pretty faces around."

"Isn't it exciting? You'd think everyone's being in black would make for a funereal tone, but instead, it's very elegant."

"Black is all Pierre Benoit ever wears. I've known him for years and have never seen him in anything else," Gloria confided.

We walked together along one wall, examining shots of Marilyn Monroe, Judy Garland, Cary Grant, Rock Hudson, Dean Martin, Lola—the legendary model represented by Ryan—Suzie—I averted my eyes—and, to my surprise, the Beatles! I was in the same room with someone who had photographed the Beatles. How fabby!

We lingered in front of that photo. "I wish I could have been there the day Pierre took this shot. He really is a gifted man. Just look at that soulful gaze in Paul's eyes."

"You like Paul?" I asked.

"Mm-hmm. And you?"

"John."

I had plenty of pictures of John and the rest of the Fab Four on the walls of my bedroom, but to my mind, Pierre had captured the boy inside John. The shot was like no other I'd seen. Magical.

We moved to where a plaque hung prominently in the center of one wall of photographs. Pierre had written a short biography of himself, the letters printed in gold on a black background. Gloria and I read silently.

Pierre had a tragic childhood. His mother, a model, and his father, a photographer, were killed in a car crash in their native France when Pierre was thirteen.

Afterward, for years he moved from place to place, working odd jobs and passionately learning his father's profession of photography before coming to America in his twenties. He was an immediate success, and currently, in his late thirties, stood at the pinnacle of his career.

"What a sad beginning," I remarked to Gloria, "but with an impressive recovery and now all this success."

She snorted again. "Yeah, but does he use his power for good or for evil?"

I wondered what she meant, but chose not to pry, enjoying her company. Darlene had been flying all over the country, leaving me to my own devices at night. I could use a new friend.

The Dave Clark Five's "Glad All Over" played. The upbeat tune had me groovin' to the music. Admiring looks flashed my way, including one from Tom, the young actor. He winked at me and shrugged. I smiled at him, not really blaming him for trying to advance his career by hanging with the big shots.

All of a sudden, I saw Stu, Darlene's boyfriend, talking with a man I didn't know. I'd have to go over and speak to him when he wasn't busy.

With Gloria, I made my way down the line of photos. I drank more champagne, and my darn gaze went back to Bradley. On the positive side, maybe his attention to Suzie was simply to reassure her that, as the new head of the agency, he understood her value. Yes, that might be it, I fibbed to myself. I reached up to twirl a piece of hair, only to realize my long dark hair was pulled up out of twirling reach.

"Hello, Bebe, are you still with me?" Gloria took another glass of champagne from a waiter.

"Sure. I'm admiring what a genius Pierre is with a camera. Just look how vulnerable Marilyn appears."

"Right. If you say so, but I think you're still mooning over your boss." She leaned closer and whispered in my ear, "I'll arm-wrestle you for who gets to kill Suzie first."

We fell to giggling.

"You don't like her either?" I asked.

"God, sweetie, the stories I could tell you. I wouldn't know where to begin, and they'd burn your young ears. But if it's any comfort, I can say that right now Suzie probably isn't enjoying your boss's attention as much as she makes it look."

"Really?" I asked, burning to know more.

"Really," Gloria confirmed. "I'm sure she'd rather be stalking the room for prey."

"What do you mean?"

Gloria nodded knowingly. "Suzie *loves* movie stars, if you get my drift. And that's a Pauline Trigere couture evening gown she's wearing. She's looking boss, and she knows it. All the better to reel the stars into her web of lies."

I took a minute to admire the cut of Suzie's black wool crepe gown. Simply elegant, it reminded me of the 1920s styles, sleeveless with hundreds of rhinestones over the upper bodice, covering the straps and forming a bow in the front. A pretty dress, but in it she looked as skinny as an exclamation point. "Doesn't everyone love movie stars?"

Gloria finished a swallow of champagne and seemed to consider saying more, then let out a deep sigh. "I mean she screws them, Bebe. If they appear on a movie screen, Suzie's in their bed for a wild night or two and, most important, is always 'accidentally' photographed with them. Constantly thinking about ways to raise her profile in the world, that's our Suzie. She's a user, and she employs her body for power. She's sleeping with Pierre, has slept with, gosh, I don't know how many of the people at this party, and has an old flame who follows her around for the times when she's into nostalgia. She has to be careful, though, because Pierre's got a temper. She counts on him to make her photos perfection. Heck, after some of her crazier nights, she'd be in big trouble without my special under-eye concealer. Anyhow, in the past Pierre hasn't minded Suzie straying for a one-night stand, but lately he's pulled in the reins big-time. Frankly, I'm glad. Pierre's the one who made Suzie a star, but she's not worth his love."

"Wait, back up a minute," I said, trying to take it all in. "You mean Suzie is sleeping with Pierre and movie stars to get ahead—" I broke off and swung around to look at Bradley. His gaze rested on Suzie while his hand had shifted to her lower back. No! Surely Suzie wasn't doing *that* with Bradley!

I turned to Gloria, frantic, hoping she'd reassure me.

She shot me a look of pity. "Don't think about it. I only told you so you wouldn't feel bad about your boss. You new to town, Bebe? You don't mind if I call you by your first name, do you? I hate it when people call me Miss Castellano. Which, of course, Suzie does. I'm here tonight just in case Miss Suzie Wexford should muss her lipstick or a lash from her false eyelashes should fall onto her perfect cheek," Gloria said in a sarcastic voice.

My head spun at the very thought that Bradley would . . . But, stupid me, wasn't that what all men did? It was okay for a man but not a woman, who was expected to come to her marriage bed a virgin. I forced myself to focus on Gloria.

Poor thing, I thought, getting the impression that Gloria must lead a life of misery under Suzie's hands. "Bebe is fine by me, Gloria. As for Manhattan, I've been here for almost two months. I love being a single girl in the big city. Everything is so exciting, and there's energy in the very air. There's so much I want to do and see. I can't wait to go to the World's Fair. I've been too busy this week settling into the new office, but maybe I'll go Saturday."

Gloria nodded. "I'm happy for you. I've lived here ever since I turned eighteen. I'm twenty-seven now. I consider myself a New Yorker, but the city doesn't hold charm for me anymore," she said in a world-weary voice. "Though I'll probably have to be at the World's Fair. Suzie is introducing that new Ford, the Mustang, on Saturday."

"That's a plum job."

"It is," Gloria confirmed. "A lot of the other models are very jealous, especially Lola."

"I know she's one of Ryan's, but I haven't met her."

"She's over there, the blonde standing next to Norman Mailer."

I saw a familiar-looking, beautiful woman with enormous smoke-gray eyes who appeared to be a few years older than Suzie.

"Lola was Ryan's number one model until Suzie deviously pushed her aside and drove her to booze," Gloria said. "Before you could blink, Suzie was the new star. Don't let all the air kisses here tonight fool you. It's all an illusion. I'll bet Pierre gives the guest list to the newspaper so they can print it in the society section, furthering *his* reputation."

"I guess everyone is out for themselves."

"You betcha. Suzie is also almost a shoo-in for the next Breck Girl, a job Lola's had for two years. She's up for contract renewal, and Lola will scratch Suzie's eyes out if Suzie takes that Breck deal away from her."

That's why Lola looked familiar. I'd seen her in Breck ads. I decided right then never to use Breck shampoo again if Suzie took over as model. "Suzie must keep you busy. Do you do makeup only for her?"

Gloria's mouth pursed. "No. I'd never be able to cover my bills with what that blond she-cat pays me, when she pays me. Since I make Suzie look good, I get a lot of referrals and requests from other models, sometimes stars. I got called to do Bobby Vinton's makeup before he went on *The Ed Sullivan Show* back in January."

"Bobby Vinton! How thrilling!" I almost squealed, but restrained myself. Then I flashed back to a night not long ago when I shared a dance with Bradley to

Bobby's song "Blue Velvet." I started to remember how it felt to be so close to him, smell his lime aftershave, feel his strong arm around my waist while his other hand held my hand. . . . I drew myself up and called myself to order. "Tell me about Bobby."

"He was real nice," Gloria said, one side of her mouth curving. "His regular makeup girl fell sick and couldn't make it. Bobby cracked jokes with me the whole time and left me a big tip. He's great."

"That's too bad about his makeup girl, but at least you had a neat opportunity."

"Yeah." Gloria had turned her attention to Suzie.

My gaze followed hers. To my horror, I saw Suzie reach up and kiss Bradley right under the small, crescent-shaped scar under his left eye. The scar I constantly wanted to trace with my finger.

Gloria grabbed my arm, forcing my attention away from them. "Look, I know we just met, Bebe, but you seem like a really nice person. Sweet, which is something you won't find much of in the modeling biz. You said you love being a single girl in the city. Let me give you some advice: *Be* a single girl in the city. Bradley Williams isn't the only male around."

I couldn't speak.

Gloria shook her head. "A beautiful girl like you— what are you, nineteen?"

"I'm twenty-two."

"You should be dating! Digging the guys, having fun, going to nightclubs, shows, not pining over one man."

"Yes, you're right," I said, wondering what it would be like going out on the town with a cute guy like the young actor. Shoot, he was leaving with a group of Broadway stars. I didn't think Bradley would be taking me on a date anytime soon.

"Uh-oh," Gloria said, pointing at Pierre with her glass.

I saw a dark expression mar his face. With obvious anger, he had finished greeting guests and noticed Suzie and Bradley close together.

Luckily he was distracted by the arrival of Frank

Sinatra and his friends. My jaw dropped. Mama would have died and gone to heaven had she been there.

Gloria was unimpressed. I supposed she'd seen it all.

She persisted: "You think about what I said, Bebe. Lots of men would find you attractive and want to take you out. But you have this sign on your forehead that says, 'Taken.'"

"Do I?"

"Yeah. Stop thinking about Bradley so much. You have to get out more— Oh, damn, I see Suzie motioning for me." She fished in her purse. "We'll see each other at the agency. I'd love to hang out with you, and help you meet some cool guys."

"Okay, Gloria. Maybe I'll see you Saturday at the World's Fair." I put her card in my purse.

Then Gloria spoke from behind her hand. "Oh, and Bebe, as far as killing Suzie goes, I think we'd have to stand in line for the honor."

We shared a laugh; then I watched as she quickly made her way to Suzie's side and they disappeared into a back room together.

I thought I'd have a chance to talk to Bradley, but Pierre snagged him. The tension between the two men was obvious, as Pierre's hands balled into fists, while Bradley leaned against the wall looking like a cat ready to spring.

A man I didn't recognize reached Pierre, capturing his attention.

Bradley appeared as cool as ever when he sauntered over to Lola's side. She giggled and smiled up at him.

Then I heard laughter coming from the doorway. To my utter surprise, Darlene made a grand entrance, sexy red curls shimmering even in the low light.

Attached to her arm was a handsome older man, maybe in his early sixties, dressed in a black tux and wearing a black Stetson.

My gaze was drawn to three things: Darlene's big grin, her very low-cut black gown, and the impossible-to-be-missed necklace glittering around her throat.

I glanced across the room to where her boyfriend, Stu, eyed her with a wounded expression before turning away.

Darlene, still grinning from ear to ear, began moving in my direction with her date.

What had Darlene gotten herself into this time?

Chapter Three

"Bebe, honey! What a blast seeing you here," Darlene called out above the crowd, beaming, still holding the older man's arm.

Up close, I felt the need for shades, her rhinestone—it couldn't be diamond—necklace was so alive with light. Made of round stones, each the same size, the piece lit Darlene's face. That it drew attention to her low-cut gown was not lost on some men in the room, who were openly ogling petite but busty Darlene.

We managed to hug while she held on to her date. I whispered furiously, "Just who is this guy? Stu's here. He'll be mad. And how did you get into this party? Bradley gave me my invitation."

"We're crashing, honey. No one will notice. And I'm finished with Stu," she announced with a pout.

"What! What happened?"

"Never mind, I'll tell you later. Looks like you've got your own problems." Darlene shot a look to where Lola was draped over Bradley like a tarantula. They stood away from Pierre, who was talking to—and obviously brownnosing—Frank Sinatra. Darlene raised her eyebrows at me.

In her Texas drawl, which always managed to get attention in New York, she said, "Where are my manners? Bebe, let me introduce you to Cole Woodruff. Cole owns a big oil refinery in Texas. I met him on my flight from Los Angeles to Dallas. I had a little

layover, and Cole was sweet enough to drive me down
to his ranch."

I shook hands with Cole. "Nice to meet you, Mr.
Woodruff."

Gosh, he was older than Daddy. He did have nice
brown eyes and a rugged look about him, but what
was Darlene thinking? She already had much younger,
much better-looking Stu, heir to the Minty-Mouth
Breath Mint fortune, hanging on her every word, taking her on trips, buying her clothes, and Lord knew
what else.

"Please call me Cole, Miss Bennett. When Darlene
had to come back to New York, I wasn't about to let
her go without me. She told me all about you, saying
you were another Southern belle. I see my lambkin
was right," he said.

Darlene giggled and snuggled against him.

Heat rose to my cheeks. "Cole, please call me Bebe.
I don't know what Darlene said, but I assure you *none*
of it is true," I said with a smile.

Cole's eyebrows rose. "Is that so? Well, now, maybe
I'll have two fillies on my arm tonight."

"I mean, everything Darlene told you *is* true," I
said hastily.

The three of us laughed.

"I can tell from your accent you're not from Texas
like Darlene," Cole said, as if it were a cardinal sin.

"No, Cole, I'm from Virginia."

"Never been there."

I didn't think Virginia's beaches, horse country, and
mountains would impress him, so I turned back to
Darlene. "Darlene, that's a striking rhinestone necklace. I've never seen you wear it before."

She looked up adoringly at Cole, touching the
stones at her throat. "Cole gave it to me, and
they're diamonds."

I drew in a sharp breath.

Cole spoke as one instructing a student. "Now,
Bebe, a woman should always know the difference
between rhinestones and diamonds. Diamonds can cut

glass. If a man gives you a diamond, you can make sure it's real with that little tip. Darlene likes sparkly things, don't you, lambkin?"

I stood with my mouth open. What had she done to make Cole give her a diamond necklace?

I didn't want to know.

Darlene fluttered her lashes up at the older man and said, "Not as much as I like you, Cole."

"See you around," Cole said to me, and led Darlene away. I noticed he was bowlegged.

I felt queasy. In fact, I couldn't stay at Pierre's gala another minute. Between Bradley and Suzie, and now Darlene and Grandpa—I mean Cole—I'd had enough.

I looked around for Stu, remembering I wanted to say hello. He was gone. *Oh, Darlene, what have you done?*

Before I left, I was determined that Bradley see me all dressed up. Suzie was still in the back, and Bradley remained at Lola's side.

I walked up to them and said, "Excuse me, Mr. Williams. I don't mean to interrupt, but I wanted to meet Lola, our most famous model."

Lola turned unfocused eyes toward me. Now that I was in front of them, I could see that Bradley had his left arm firmly around Lola's waist, holding her upright. She was drunk.

"What a nice thing to say, Miss . . . ?"

"Miss Bennett, my executive secretary, who has a knack for appearing precisely when I need her."

I stood with a neutral expression, while Bradley looked over my bare arms and sophisticated hairstyle. When I dropped my clutch purse—accidentally on purpose—and bent to retrieve it, I could feel his gaze burn over my exposed back.

I stood up, giving him a demure smile. There was an expression in his eyes I hadn't seen since that time he'd kissed me. Softly, he said, "I like your hair better down."

Darn, it was hot in that room.

However, I wasn't going to let Bradley know the

effect he had on me. "What can I do for you, Mr. Williams?" *Massage your back? Kiss you for an hour? Turn back your bed covers and be waiting for you between the sheets? Oops!*

Bradley cleared his throat. "Lola is leaving, and I thought she could use some company on the taxi ride home," he said, tilting his head meaningfully at the inebriated model. He pulled some money from his pocket and palmed it to me for the taxi.

"I'd love to accompany her," I said.

Lola lurched forward. Between Bradley and me, we managed to keep her upright while we edged toward the door. She said, "I'm not that blitzed."

"Don't you have a meeting tomorrow morning, Lola?" Bradley asked. "The one for your Breck Girl contract."

She squinted her eyes. "Oh, yeah."

"A girl needs her beauty rest, even one as lovely as you," I said.

"Beauty rest, yeah. Let's go, Miss . . ."

"Call me Bebe," I said.

Bradley and I escorted her to the door, acting as if nothing were amiss, even when Lola stumbled into a passing waiter, sloshing champagne onto the white cloth covering his tray.

I smiled to further cover Lola's embarrassment, not that she seemed humiliated.

The outside air hit us like a cold blast. The temperature had dropped considerably while I was at the party, and goose bumps rose on my exposed flesh.

Bradley hailed a taxi, then practically inserted Lola into the backseat. "Move over for Miss Bennett, Lola."

While Lola struggled to gain her seat, Bradley turned to me. The white of his shirt seemed very bright. "I appreciate this, Miss Bennett. I hope you enjoyed the party."

"I did," I said casually, as if I saw celebrities every day. "Thank you again for the invitation." I wanted this moment to last, Bradley and I formally dressed against the backdrop of Manhattan. I imagined that we were getting in the taxi together, off to dinner and a show. Thinking about it, I wasn't cold anymore.

"Well, thanks, kid."

The temperature dropped again. Without looking at him, I gracefully entered the taxi and slammed the door closed. I kept my gaze straight ahead, though I knew he was still standing there. "What address, Lola?"

"Sutton Place," she mumbled, her hand on her stomach.

Hoping Lola wouldn't be sick, I gave the taxi driver the location and asked him to drive slowly. I braced myself as we sped away from the curb. I'm proud to say, I did not look back at Bradley.

I turned my attention to Lola, who was slumped against the far door. "How are you feeling?"

She shrugged and lit a cigarette. "I'm all right. I party a lot, and it never does any harm. I've got some pills for a hangover."

Her slack face and signs of wrinkles under her bloodshot eyes told me a different story. If she kept up this pace, she'd soon have a hard time getting modeling gigs.

"Rest well, and I'm sure at the Breck Girl meeting tomorrow they'll be handing you a pen to sign your new contract. I've seen your ads, and they're beautiful," I said, trying to be encouraging.

She sat up straight and blew out smoke. "I'm gonna lose the contract."

"What do you mean?" I asked, although Gloria had already hinted as much.

"That slutty bitch Suzie Wexford, she's gonna get it. She's ruined my career. I hate her!" Lola's voice poured out venom.

"Why do you say that?"

"Suzie's a clever schemer," Lola said, turning in her seat to face me. "She followed me around, and she learned where I had contracts. Then she'd show up at a shoot before I got there, saying the agency sent her

because I wasn't feeling well. By the time I'd arrived—
so I was a little late—Suzie would already be trying
on the dress I was supposed to model, her makeup
artist, that New Jersey cow, in tow."

"How could she get away with that? Wouldn't the
client call Ryan to confirm that you were ill?"

"Oh, come on, get with it," Lola scoffed, then took
a long drag on her cigarette. "You've seen Suzie oper-
ate firsthand. She's been hanging all over your boss
since he took over the company. Suzie always beds
the president of the agency. She screws anyone she
thinks will make her more famous. If the client had
called our old boss, Dirk Snellings, Dirk would have
confirmed anything Suzie said."

Now I thought *I* would be sick. Bradley's behavior
with Suzie, Gloria's insinuation, and now Lola flat-out
telling me that Bradley and Suzie were doing *that* . . .
I forced myself to look out the window and admire
the skyscrapers, trying to wash away the dirty picture
forming in my mind.

Lola went on: "The fact that Dirk was married with
a baby didn't stop Suzie. She seduced him, and he
became obsessed with her. Rumors flew that they were
doing it in his office sometimes more than once a day.
He was her puppet."

I turned back to Lola. "How awful! I mean, him
being married—"

Lola let out a bitter laugh. "Things like that don't
mean anything to Suzie, and to a lot of other men
either. Suzie is the only thing that matters to Suzie. It
took me a long time to build my career; then she just
waltzed in, cast her spell over Dirk, and slowly took
my clients away from me. She spread rumors about
me too, like that I was an aging alcoholic, so I couldn't
go to another agency." Suddenly Lola's voice rose. "I
hate Suzie Wexford! I could kill the bitch!" She
stubbed her cigarette out viciously in the little metal
tray. "If she takes that Breck contract from me, I'll
strangle her."

The cab came to an abrupt halt, and I paid the

driver. I had to get out so Lola could exit the car on the curb side.

"Thanks for seeing me home, Deedee."

"It's Bebe."

She slammed the cab door, removed her high-heeled shoes, and limped up the steps to her building, disappearing inside.

Beside me, the cab took off, leaving me standing on the sidewalk without a way to get home.

And with less of my innocence.

I walked down to the cross-street and put my hand in the air. Several cabs flew by in a streak of yellow, but finally one stopped for me, and I got in. "138–140 East Sixty-fifth, please," I said, just wanting to go home.

Once in the apartment, I went straight into my bedroom. Stripping to my slip, bra, and girdle, I carefully hung my dress in the back of my closet. I took down my hair. It went off in wild directions from all the teasing and spraying, so I put it back in a ponytail.

I like your hair better down.

Throwing on my pink chenille robe with the big coffee-cup design, I headed for the kitchen and the consolation of a box of Hershey's bars. When I couldn't decide how many to eat, I took the whole box into the living room and flopped down on the pink sectional facing the fireplace and the white-painted brick wall.

Swell, I thought, biting into the chocolate and staring at the wall. That was exactly what I was up against in my quest to win Bradley's heart: a brick wall.

The thought of Bradley being with Suzie in *that* way haunted me. I took another bite of chocolate and chewed, the melting sweetness comforting me. In the back of my mind I'd always known Bradley didn't have his man-about-town reputation for nothing. But those women had been onetime dates. Suzie was different.

If I were going to make it at Ryan, I would have to tamp down my feelings for Bradley. For all I knew, he was a confirmed bachelor and would never marry. He certainly wouldn't care if his "kid" secretary went out on the town, as Gloria suggested. I ripped open another Hershey's bar and took a big bite.

Brace yourself, men of Manhattan. Bebe Bennett is officially available.

Chapter Four

The next morning I headed straight for the kitchen and coffee, but my stomach warned me not to eat anything, after I had devoured three Hershey's bars the night before.

I peeked into Darlene's room, but she hadn't come home. Shocked, I realized she'd spent the night with Cole. Maybe he had a hotel suite, and they'd slept in separate bedrooms.

Opening the front door, I retrieved the newspaper and, while drinking my coffee, fumbled to find the society column, a section I never read.

The first thing that met my eye was a picture of Bradley and Suzie with their arms around each other, smiling for the camera. That must have happened after I left. I wondered how Pierre felt about it. There, as predicted, was a list of the gala's attendees, minus my name, though I had signed the guestbook. I threw the paper down in disgust.

During my shower—the hot water came and went with bursts of freezing cold in between—I thought the decision I'd made about dating and trying to control my feelings for Bradley was very mature. How did I know he was really the one for me if I didn't play the field?

I hadn't dated much. There'd been one guy, Jim, who worked with me at Philip Morris, the cigarette manufacturer in Richmond. But a girl can listen to only so much about an ex-girlfriend and how badly she treated him. Then there was Mike, whose idea of a date was watching TV at his parents' house, where he lived. He never took me out for a meal, although once he broke out a bottle of beer and poured it into two paper cups, putting me off beer for life.

I'd done the blind-date deal too, where the guy—I couldn't even remember his name—kept talking about pine nuts and how healthy they were for you.

As I got ready for work, I told myself again—just to drum it into my head—that I shouldn't wait around for Bradley to come to his senses. I needed to broaden my horizons, I decided, while making sure my hair was perfect, applying an extra coat of mascara to my false eyelashes, then dipping my little finger into a pot of pearly pink Mary Quant lip gloss and smoothing it over my lips.

Back in my room I grabbed the first thing I saw on my clothes rack. That it was a pink-and-white-checked A-line miniskirt meant nothing. I was pulling a pink cashmere sweater over my head when I heard the key in the lock to the apartment. I smoothed my hair and the tight-fitting sweater, then dashed into the living room just as Darlene entered, smiling. "Good morning, Bebe. Hey, aren't you late for work? I love that outfit on you. Sexy."

"Thanks." Me? Sexy? Why, I hadn't given my appearance a second thought, had I? I glanced at my watch and saw the time had somehow gotten away from me. "Yes, I'd better hurry. But before I go, I want to talk to you, Darlene Roland."

At that moment Cole walked through the doorway as if he were astride a horse. He carried Darlene's suitcase. "Hello, Bebe. Off to work?"

I shot Darlene a look. "Yes, I am."

She grinned. "We'll have plenty of time to catch up, Bebe, since I have a two-week layover in New York."

"Two weeks! We'll have a blast," I said.

"You can put that suitcase down, Cole," Darlene said. "Yeah, two weeks. You see, Skyway has had one of their planes on display at the World's Fair since it

opened last week. The company wants to convince
people how safe flying is, and show what the inside of
a plane looks like. So far the exhibit hasn't drawn
many people."

Cole took up the story. "So the Skyway folks decided they'd do better by showing off their prettiest
stewardesses to hostess the exhibit. Naturally, they
picked my lambkin."

If Cole called Darlene *lambkin* one more time, I
thought I'd rip his Stetson off his head and smack him
in the face with it. Then, being a good Catholic girl,
I'd go to confession.

"I'm proud of you, Darlene," I said. "I'll be going
to the fair tomorrow, and I'll be sure to come by and
see you. It's great having you home."

Darlene sighed. "I'm happy too, but you know you
can't keep me on the ground for long. I do want to
show Cole around New York before I get my next
flight assignment."

Cole looked at his watch.

Ah, that was my cue to leave before Cole called
Darlene *lambkin* again. I'd have to wait to find out
what on earth had happened between Darlene and
Stu. "I'd better go. I'll just grab my purse and be out
the door."

"Good-bye, Bebe," Cole said cheerfully.

I gave them a little wave and closed the door behind me.

Darlene and I would have to have that talk real
soon. Cole Woodruff didn't like me, and I didn't like
Cole Woodruff. There was no real reason for it, just
woman's intuition, and a nagging conviction that Cole
wanted Darlene all to himself.

Finally arriving at the Bleeker Street stop, I was the
first one out of the train and raced up the stairs to
the street. Knowing I was late, I dodged people on
the crowded sidewalks and was almost panting when
I reached the steps that led to a paved area outside
the building.

I ran straight into Bradley. Well, there was no body

contact; we stopped short of that by two inches. He
looked down at me with an amused expression, a take-
out cup of coffee in his right hand and his briefcase
in the other. He wore a dark gray suit, white shirt,
and a blue-and-gray tie. He looked so gorgeous with
the sun shining on his dirty-blond hair, I had to fight
to keep my knees from buckling. I would be dating
soon, yes, going out with a man other than Bradley.
Many men. I'd forget all about my boss.

"Good morning, Miss Bennett," Bradley practically
sang, taking a step backward. "Did you run all the
way here?"

Devil. I decided to match his tone. "I find walking
fast energizes me for the day," I chirped, and gave
him a killer smile, hoping the sun would shine on my
lip gloss.

"In that case," he said, giving me the once-over,
"you must be full of vigor."

"I am. Being a single girl in the city fills me with
energy."

That made the smile disappear from his face. "Er,
good. We've got lots of work to do today. Shall we?"
he said, motioning me to go before him up to the
brass revolving doors. I hoped he would enjoy the
look from behind when I sashayed in front of him.

But we were stopped in our tracks before we could
get to the door.

"Sarge! Hey! Sarge! Is that you?" shouted a male
voice somewhere behind me.

Bradley looked past me and froze. He dropped the
coffee cup he held, splashing hot liquid on the pavement, his trousers, and my shoes and tights. I yelped,
but my curiosity regarding Bradley's reaction held me
at his side.

He said, "Miss Bennett, I'm terribly sorry about the
coffee. I'll meet you upstairs." He pulled out his handkerchief and briskly wiped the coffee from my shoes
and tights. A shiver went from where the handkerchief
touched me to the pit of my stomach.

I'm not going anywhere. Something's rattled you, and I wouldn't miss seeing what—or who—it was. Without answering him, I turned and saw a dark-haired man in a cheap suit striding toward us at a brisk pace.

"Miss Bennett, go on ahead," Bradley tried again.

But it was too late. The other man had reached us. He grabbed Bradley's newly freed right hand and began shaking it for all he was worth. "I can't believe it's you, Sarge, after so many years. This here your wife? She's mighty pretty."

"No," I said, starting to explain—while secretly loving every minute of this—when Bradley spoke at the same time.

"No, er, she's not."

A playful look crossed the man's face. "Not your wife? Or not pretty? Couldn't be the latter."

Heat rose to my cheeks.

Bradley looked like a little boy on the playground scuffing his foot in the dirt. "She's not my wife; she's my executive secretary. I'm not married. Let me introduce you. Miss Bennett, this is Jerry Mitchell. We knew each other years ago. Jerry, Miss Bennett."

"Nice to meet you, Mr. Mitchell," I said.

"Call me Jerry," he said enthusiastically, and then laughed. "Sarge here makes it sound like we were in a croquet tournament in school. Did he ever tell you that we fought halfway up to China together?"

Bradley rubbed his forehead with the heel of his hand and sighed.

Alarmed, all I could think of was my beautiful Bradley fighting in . . . why, it must have been Korea, where Debbie Ann's son had died. Suddenly all of Daddy's stories about World War II came flooding back to me, and I realized the danger Bradley must have faced. "No, he never told me, never said a word," I answered faintly.

"And we'll keep it that way," Bradley said, as if that were an end to it.

Luckily Jerry showed no sign of shutting up. "Let's move over out of the way of these folks trying to get into the building."

I walked with Jerry, Bradley following like an eighteenth-century French aristocrat being led to the guillotine.

Jerry had our attention and a flair for drama. "Miss Bennett, this guy saved my life."

"Jerry, for God's sake—" Bradley said.

"Come on, Sarge, you got yourself a nice Bronze Star and a Purple Heart out of it."

"What!" I cried out, completely forgetting that I wasn't in love with Bradley anymore. "A Purple Heart means—"

"The past is the past, Jerry. Leave it back where it belongs," Bradley interrupted.

But no one was going to stop Jerry. He addressed me in the manner of one about to embark on a long and exciting story. "Sarge and I were in the army infantry. We blitzed up into North Korea after Mac-Arthur landed at Inchon. The advance was lightning-fast up a river gorge. We had nearly gotten to the Chinese border when the Communist Chinese began to overrun the United Nations forces."

"Jerry!" Bradley tried. "I'm sure Miss Bennett is bored by this old story."

I turned innocent eyes toward him. "Not in the least, Mr. Williams. In fact, I'm totally intrigued." At Bradley's frown, I turned and smiled at Jerry. "Please, do go on."

"Where was I?" Jerry thought out loud. "Oh, yeah, so the American supply lines were stretched real thin because the advance had been so fast. Miss Bennett, some of the GIs were without food or ammunition when we began a forced retreat."

"How awful," I said, imagining a skin-and-bones Bradley, possibly without a gun.

"Oh, it was. Picture this: The Chinese soldiers flanked us; then they surrounded us; killing some of my buddies right before my eyes, taking others prisoner. We were humiliated by our retreat, and we were scared. The Chinese had taken the high ground along the river gorge. Land mines could be found anywhere from the middle of the road to the rocky hillsides."

"Land mines?" I gasped, horrified.

"You better believe it. Sarge here was barely in his twenties, but they had given him a field promotion to sergeant. He was leading the platoon through the gauntlet. I was standing next to him when I took a step forward and heard the worst sound of my life: the distinct sound of a pressure mine being activated."

"Oh, good Lord!" I exclaimed.

"You bet I said a prayer. I knew if I took my foot off the top of the mine, it would explode, killing me. That's when Sarge saved me. He told me not to move, and he got the other men away. He even appointed someone to take over in case he got killed trying to rescue me."

Jerry looked at Bradley, admiration shining in his eyes.

I put my hand on Jerry's sleeve. "Go on; I must hear the rest."

"Okay," he said, wiping his eyes real fast. "Sarge's plan was for the men to build a circle of boulders and large rocks around me, which they did. When they were done, the men stood back and Sarge told me to jump over the rocks. I tell you, Miss Bennett, I was sweating despite the freezing temperature. I was a coward. I couldn't move."

Bradley said, "You weren't a coward. You were an eighteen-year-old with his foot on a land mine. Anybody in his right mind would be terrified."

Jerry paid no attention. "All the men had backed off, but Sarge stayed close. I-I was crying by then, thinking I was gonna die. Then, all of a sudden, Sarge pointed at a spot in the distance and yelled, 'What's that?' When I looked, Sarge grabbed me and hurled me over the circle of rocks."

I felt tears burn the backs of my eyes. What a brave, selfless thing to do. I took a deep breath so I wouldn't cry.

Jerry said, "The mine exploded, but we landed safely except for Sarge's left eye. A piece of shrapnel had hit the left side of his face, but it was his eye that was injured. We got to a MASH unit, and they evacuated him to Tokyo."

I stood speechless, trying to keep my chin from trembling and the tears from falling. The scar under his left eye. The one I always wanted to trace with my finger and kiss. The one I had always assumed was from a childhood accident in a baseball game or some other boyhood mishap.

"What happened then, Mr. Williams?" I asked.

"Yeah, Sarge, you look all healed now. I can just see the scar now that I look for it," Jerry said, peering up at him.

Bradley spoke in a low voice, one I could barely hear over the street traffic. "They thought I was going to lose the sight in my left eye, but that was hogwash. I had a hard time seeing the pinup girls, but after a month, the eye cleared."

I felt sure he was making light of what must have been a frightening time.

"I'm relieved to have run into you, Sarge," Jerry said. "They sent me home, an honorable discharge. Heck, they thought I'd gone off the deep end. Did take me a long time to stop having nightmares about what went on over there, especially my stepping on that mine. I guess it's the kind of thing that never leaves you. When I think of those boys over in Vietnam . . . well, let's just say I ache inside for them."

"Yes," Bradley said. "I know what you mean."

We all stood silent for a moment.

Then Bradley said, "It was good seeing you, Jerry. Are you doing all right now as far as a job goes?"

"Sure! I'm a bank manager in Jersey, just came into the city for a big meeting at headquarters later today. You're doing well yourself, I can see."

"I'm running a modeling agency for my great-uncle."

"Oh, yeah, I remember you mentioning him. He's the rich guy who doesn't have a son to leave all his companies to, right?"

"Yes. I've got two cousins vying with me to be the one Uncle Herman appoints to take over after his death."

Jerry hit him playfully in the arm. "I have every confidence you'll be the one." Then he turned to me. "Miss Bennett, it was sure nice to meet you."

"You too, Jerry."

With a last grin at Bradley, Jerry walked on down the sidewalk.

"Mr. Williams," I said, looking up into his blue eyes, "I'm proud to work for a man who fought for his country and saved another man's life at risk to his own."

He frowned. "Don't put me on any pedestals, kid. Because the way I live doesn't merit any medals."

He strode ahead, but pushed the revolving door for me and stepped aside. Over my shoulder, I said, "I'll put a fresh coffeepot on right away."

"Good," he said, as we entered the crowded elevator and faced front.

My heart beat fast simply because I stood close to him and breathed in his lime aftershave. *Darn you, Bradley.*

Just when I thought I could toughen my feelings against him, I found my heart reaching out to him more than ever.

Chapter Five

After I'd made coffee and poured some into Bradley's St. Louis Cardinals mug, I returned to my desk. I still didn't have the files in the credenza behind me arranged to my satisfaction. I bent over as modestly as I could in my miniskirt, a tricky maneuver. By lunchtime I felt quite pleased with the organization of the files, and slid the last one into place.

"Miss Bennett?" Bradley said from the other side of my desk.

I stood—how long had he been watching me?—so fast that I knocked over the new lamp with the circular paper shade. It fell to the floor, and the hot lightbulb hit the paper, which burst into flame.

"There's a bit of fire there," Bradley said with amusement.

I grabbed my own full coffee mug and threw the contents on the flame. An icky burning smell came from the once-fashionable lamp, and there was a brown stain on the hardwood floor. Bradley tamped out the last burning ember with the tip of his shiny black shoe.

I looked at him, certain I was blushing, and said, "I'll clean this mess, and you can deduct the price of the lamp from my paycheck."

"I've never seen you act so uncoordinated, Miss Bennett. You're not ill, are you?"

"If you hadn't sneaked up behind me and scared me half to death, maybe I wouldn't have jumped like that. You usually use the phone to buzz me when you want something."

A smile played about his full lips. "Do I really? You see, Miss Bennett, I saw you bending over by the files and didn't want you to have to get up to answer the phone. I was thinking of your comfort."

So, in other words, he had enjoyed the view long enough to come out to my desk and get a closer look. I smiled to myself. In a smooth tone, I said, "What can I do for you, Mr. Williams?"

"I need you to call the florist and have a dozen roses sent to Suzie Wexford," he said. "You have her address, don't you?"

Bradley Williams had real talent when it came to playing Ping-Pong with my emotions. I turned my gaze from him to a lined pad on my desk. "Yes, I do. What color roses do you want sent?" I bit my tongue. If I hadn't asked, I could have sent Suzie all black roses, assuming the florist had such a thing.

"Red, long stemmed."

I made notes on the pad. "Will there be a card to go with the flowers?" Something like, *I never want to see you again.*

"I positively don't know what I'd do without you, Miss Bennett. You're so efficient."

I glanced up at him, eyebrows raised into my bangs. "Is that what you want written on the card?"

He threw back his head and laughed. "Efficient and with a sense of humor. Ah, let's see. Just have the florist` write, 'I'll pick you up at seven for an early dinner.' And have them sign my name."

"Very well, Mr. Williams," I said, as my heart pounded in my chest. Another date with Suzie!

"Thanks, kid. I'm going out to lunch now."

"Bon appétit!" I said, and watched him stride toward the elevator.

He turned around, caught me looking at him, adjusted his cuffs, and said, "Oh, and kid, don't worry about paying for the lamp. The company will cover it."

"I'm very sorry—"

The elevator dinged. He pointed at me. "Be sorry for nothing."

Then he was gone, leaving me with my emotions all stirred up like they'd been through an electric mixer.

First I phoned in the order to the florist. Then I cleaned away all traces of the burned lamp. When I felt Bradley would be safely away from the building, I took the elevator downstairs and went outside. The weather was glorious, springlike on this first day of May, with the promise of new adventures in the air. I dashed down the sidewalk to the corner hot-dog vendor.

"Hi, Marv! How's your wife today?" Eating a hot dog and drinking a Coke for lunch were my guilty pleasures. I'd found Marv on Monday, and I'd been down to his stand every day since. He had a wife who was expecting their first baby any day.

"Not too good, Bebe," he said, fixing my order, remembering I liked my hot dog with mustard and relish—no onions. The smell of the hot dogs made my stomach growl.

As he passed me my order, I handed him some money. "What's wrong?"

Marv had a big heart when it came to his wife and was suffering right along with her during her pregnancy.

I waited while Marv served another customer, then another. Finally he turned to me, wiping his hands on his stained white apron. "Her back is killing her, she tosses and turns all night trying to get comfortable, and she keeps sending me out for pineapple."

"Oh, Marv, I'm sure all this is normal. Just stock up on canned pineapple."

"Betty only wants fresh. The doctors don't have a certain date for the delivery. They say it can be any-time between now and the next two weeks. I'm losing my mind." He shrugged, starting to refill the ketchup from the big jar of mustard.

"Marv," I said, touching his arm. "You've got the mustard there. . . ."

He looked at what he was doing and shook his head. Deep circles under his eyes told me he wasn't getting much sleep.

A group of women approached the stand, and Marv snapped to attention. I couldn't help but laugh.

As I strolled back toward the Ryan building with my hot dog and bottle of Coke, I enjoyed the sunny day. What would it be like, I wondered, to be carrying Bradley's baby? The thought sent a tingle through me. One of the goals in my life was to have first a boy, then a girl. I imagined lying in a hospital bed holding a baby Bradley. Big Bradley would come in, grinning, clutching a bouquet of red roses.

My fantasy screeched to a stop. Big Bradley had just sent red roses to Suzie!

I headed back to the office, where I found a man seated in the reception area. He stood when I walked in.

I smiled, put my food on my desk, and said, "Hello." I gave a quick glance to the sign-in sheet that we used to keep track of arrivals and departures. All I could make out was that a new name had been scrawled at the bottom.

"Nice lunch you've got there," he said, and grinned.

Surely he was a model. Striking green eyes looked at me from a face that was all angles and topped with shiny black hair worn in the same style as John Lennon's. His teeth were very white, he seemed about Bradley's height, and he had a vaguely European look about him. He wore a black suit and white shirt with a narrow paisley tie.

Suddenly, I felt shy. "I'm Bebe Bennett, Mr. Williams's secretary."

He held out his hand, and I took it. He gave it a tender squeeze, then said, "I'm Louis Kinnaird, Miss Bennett. Nice to meet you." He'd pronounced his first name *Lou-ee*.

"Thank you. Are you here to see Mr. Williams? Because he's at lunch right now." I walked around my desk and got out Bradley's calendar.

"Oh, I don't have an appointment," Mr. Kinnaird said.

Was there a hint of a Scottish accent in his voice? "I see. Well, when Mr. Williams returns, I could ask him if he has time to meet with you. That is, if you want to wait."

"That's very kind of you. I have to be upstairs soon, but I do want to wait. Here, okay?"

Well mannered, charming, good-looking. I slanted a quick look at his left hand: free of any ring. *Hmmm.* "Please do. May I get you some coffee?"

"No, thanks. I'm not much of a coffee drinker. And don't let me keep you from your lunch."

I smiled. "Okay." I settled in my chair and took a bite of my hot dog. Then I looked up and saw that he had moved one of the metal-legged, light brown chairs from the waiting area over to my desk. I took a swallow of Coke and used my napkin, suddenly wishing for my lip gloss.

"You're a very pretty girl, Miss Bennett, but I'm sure you're told that often. Do you model?"

Was he flirting with me? "Thank you, and no, I don't model. In fact, I know only a couple of the models here. And please call me Bebe."

"I'm Louis. I understand Mr. Williams took over this week. I landed a print campaign for Burma-Shave shave cream. I'm hoping to do well enough for them that they'll give me TV ads too."

"I've never heard of Burma-Shave, not that I keep up with men's shave cream."

He chuckled. "The company was established in the 1920s, but over the years sales haven't been increasing. Last year Philip Morris bought them out and is hoping to attract a younger crowd. They're starting a whole new advertising campaign."

"Philip Morris? Out of Richmond, Virginia?"

"Yes, I believe so."

"I worked for them for a while before moving to New York."

He smiled and lounged in his chair. "Really? So that explains your sweet accent."

Here came the heat to my face. "You have a bit of an accent yourself."

"My dad's from Scotland and my mom's Swiss, but I was born on American soil. They live in Rochester now."

"Your parents have the same ancestry as James Bond!"

He laughed. "I like James Bond movies."

"Me too."

Just as I was about to ask him how he got started in the modeling business, Gina, the agency's scheduler, came striding from the elevators. An ex-model, she was tall, still trim, and in her late forties. She wore her blond hair in a tight chignon. She nodded at me, then pinned her gaze on Louis. "You must be Mr. Kinnaird."

He stood. "Yes."

"Come along then, and let's get you into makeup," she said in a brisk tone.

"I'll be right there," he told her. She stood to one side, tapping her foot. To me, Louis said, "Will you still be here when I'm finished?"

A little flutter went through me. "I'll be here until five."

"Good." He smiled and then allowed himself to be whisked away by Gina.

I stared off into the distance. Slowly I picked up my hot dog and resumed eating. Louis was an attractive man. Did he have a girlfriend, or was he potential dating material? My hand reached for the cold Coke bottle, and I took a long swallow. Would I really be able to go out with someone other than Bradley?

"Dreaming, Miss Bennett?" Debbie Ann asked, bringing me back to reality. She removed a pair of large shades, reached for the clipboard that held the sign-in sheet, and used the pen tied to it with bright orange ribbon (my choice) to sign her name. Today she had on a red plaid cotton shirtwaist dress. Her brown hair was immaculate. Her face, almost bare of cosmetics now that she wasn't on air, appeared very pale and lined against the red lipstick she wore.

I smiled at her, determined to treat her with kindness because of her tragic past. "What's on the menu today, Debbie Ann?"

"Vegetable juice, breaded fish fillets, tartar sauce, parsley potatoes, Harvard beets, coleslaw, and raisin rice pudding," she replied. "A much healthier meal than hot dogs, I might add. In fact, I never recommend serving hot dogs. Do you know what they are made from?"

"Uh, no, but they're very American," I said, borrowing a line from Daddy. "And I'm sure you know Coke was provided free to American soldiers during World War Two." I almost clapped my hand over my mouth. Her son had died in the Korean War.

"Just because hot dogs are popular does not mean they are good for you. And that soda you're drinking is unhealthy as well, regardless of its history," she lectured without losing her smile. "A homemade tuna-salad sandwich, an apple, and a Thermos of milk would be a better choice, and less fattening. I must go upstairs. Think about what I said, won't you, dear? I'm only thinking of what's best for you. You'll never catch a husband if you put on weight."

She smiled back at me from the elevators, and I managed a weak smile and a thank-you in return. The elevator didn't dare keep her waiting, though, so I was saved from further dietary advice. Debbie Ann was the bossy type, but I could not find it in my heart to dislike her.

I looked at the hot dog in my hand. My mind formed a mental image of my waistline expanding, of my wearing housecoats—like Mama—at home, while I slowly became known as a spinster with a penchant for hot dogs, eating six of them at a time.

That would never do. Mama and Daddy wanted

grandchildren. I suspected Daddy, a gun collector, was dying for a little boy whom he could show his fallout shelter to, tell all his military stories, and give his first Red Ryder BB gun.

Telling myself my hot dog was cold, I threw the remains in the trash. I kept my Coke, though. Darlene had started drinking Tab, which was Coke without the calories. Maybe I'd try it.

The phone rang, interrupting my thoughts.

"Ryan Modeling Agency, Miss Bennett speaking."

"Are you that Southern girl who sits outside Bradley's office?" a female voice demanded.

"Yes, I am. How may I help you?" I tried to keep the irritation from my voice. At Charlotte Marie's Secretarial School in Richmond, we were taught to be polite to callers, no matter how rude they were.

"This is Suzie Wexford. Put me through to Bradley."

With evil pleasure, I said, "I'm terribly sorry, Miss Wexford, but Mr. Williams is out to lunch."

"How inconvenient," she barked. "Have him call me immediately when he returns. I can't see him tonight after all. I feel a case of the sniffles coming on and need to rest. I know he'll be devastated."

She hung up before I could say a word.

What a shame they wouldn't be getting together tonight, I thought, then grinned.

I hummed "My Guy" by Mary Wells while typing a letter Bradley had dictated, fielded phone calls, and made another pot of coffee (Bradley usually liked a cup when he returned from lunch).

My timing was perfect, as the elevator pinged, announcing his return. He looked as if he had just stepped out of the pages of a magazine himself, not a blond hair out of place, carrying a bag from B. Altman's, the department store for which we were scheduled to do a photo shoot next week.

"Everything in order, Miss Bennett?"

"Oh, yes, Mr. Williams. I put your phone messages on your desk."

"Excellent," he said, and flashed me a blinding smile.

I smiled back with equal enthusiasm, knowing he wouldn't be seeing Suzie that night.

He put the bag from B. Altman's on my desk. "I've purchased this Pucci scarf for Suzie," he said, pulling a stunning pink-lavender-yellow-and-white confection from the bag. "But I didn't have time to have it wrapped. The clerk gave me a box and some gift paper." He piled those on my desk as well. "Would you be so kind as to wrap it for me?"

"Why, of course I will!" Darned if I would let him know how I felt, which was jealous. "Shall I have it sent over to Miss Wexford?"

Bradley turned to enter his office, speaking to me over his shoulder. "Don't bother, kid; I'll be seeing her tonight."

Oh, no, you won't, I thought happily. I counted the seconds until I figured he'd read the phone message from her.

"Dammit!" he exclaimed, then got up from his desk and closed his door.

His phone line lit up. A measure of satisfaction carried me through wrapping the scarf—not before I tried it on and looked at myself in the mirror that hung above my credenza.

Just as I finished wrapping the scarf, Louis returned wearing pancake makeup, and stood in front of my desk.

"Had your picture taken?" I asked.

"Yes, many times. I can't wait to go back to my studio apartment and wash my face. I don't like the soap they have here, or the towels," he replied. He leaned closer. "Bebe, could I persuade you to have dinner with me tomorrow night? I know it's short notice, but I'm hoping you might be free."

My heart jumped in my chest. A handsome man was asking me for a date! I had told myself I would date, and now opportunity was not only knocking at my door, it was standing right in front of me.

I looked at the wrapped box containing the expensive scarf Bradley had bought for Suzie. I remembered them cuddling at Pierre Benoit's gala. I thought about the times Suzie had been in Bradley's office with the door closed.

Then I turned back to Louis. Not only was he asking for a date, but a *Saturday-night* date, the most important date night of the week! On the heels of this came Mama's voice in my head, telling me a girl should never be too available.

I crossed the fingers of my left hand behind my back. "I'd like to, Louis, but I'm afraid I already have plans for Saturday night." I said it with just the right encouraging note so that he might ask for another night.

"How about Monday night?" he persisted, as I'd hoped.

I spared a thought for Bradley's rule of no office dating, but quickly decided that models obviously didn't count in his book.

"That would be lovely."

"Do you like to dance, Bebe? I was thinking we could go to the Phone Booth. They have great food and an orchestra."

I repressed a gasp. The Phone Booth was one of *the* cool places to be seen in New York City. It was also expensive and dressy. "I'd love to go there, Louis. What a good idea."

He beamed. "Great! I'll pick you up at seven Monday night."

I wrote down my address, and he was pocketing it when Bradley's door flew open. The annoyed look on his face told me his conversation with Suzie had not gone his way. And I thought he'd seen Louis pocket that piece of paper with my address on it.

Too bad, I thought, and stifled a giggle.

He sauntered over and took Louis's measure. "Have we met?"

Louis held out his hand. "No, Mr. Williams, but I was hoping for a chance to introduce myself. I'm Louis Kinnaird, the new Burma-Shave guy."

"Yes, Gina told me about you. You were hired before I came on board," Bradley replied while he shook Louis's hand, looking from him to me.

I had on my most innocent expression.

Bradley looked fierce. I guess Louis picked up on it too, because he did not press him for a meeting. He said, "I'd better go. It was good to meet you, Mr. Williams. I plan to do the best job I can with the print ads, so that maybe the execs at Burma-Shave will want a TV spot. I also wanted to let you know that Burma-Shave doesn't have an exclusive on me. So I can do other assignments for you."

"I'll keep it in mind, Kinnaird," Bradley said.

Louis knew a dismissal when he heard it, and made for the elevators, turning once to wink at me. I smiled.

I turned back to Bradley and saw that he was eyeing me with an expression I couldn't read. He picked up the neatly wrapped gift for Suzie.

"Would you like a cup of coffee, Mr. Williams?" I asked, my tone professional.

"Sure, kid, bring it in."

When I did so, he said, "Thanks. Got any big plans for the weekend?"

I set the coffee cup down carefully, my fingers shaking. Was he finally going to . . . going to . . . ask me out? Or was he fishing about Louis and me? "I'm going to the World's Fair tomorrow," I managed.

He took a sip of coffee. "Be sure to come by and see Suzie's introduction of the Mustang. I'll be there. Oh, and thanks for wrapping the scarf. I'll give it to her tomorrow night."

So the two were going to be at the fair together; then they had a date for Saturday night. I needed chocolate. "I'll see if I can work the Mustang display into my schedule. There are so many things to do and see at the fair, you know."

"True, but I hope you come by, kid. Tomorrow night will be a celebration for Suzie. She landed the Breck Girl contract."

My feelings deflated even more. "Does Lola know?"

"Yes, I called her after I returned Suzie's phone call. I don't know what I'm going to do about Lola. She's under contract with us, but she cursed at me when she heard the news, and I won't have that."

"I'm sure she was upset," I said, thinking back to Lola's drunken prediction that she would lose the contract and that she'd kill Suzie if she did.

"Lola's done it to herself," Bradley said. "Her drinking is out of control. I don't know how many assignments I can give her. Advertisers are clamoring for Suzie."

"I feel bad for Lola," I said, then turned and marched back to my desk.

I looked up Lola's phone number in the company's talent directory, wrote it down, and slipped it into my purse. I'd call her tonight and try to encourage her, though she probably wouldn't remember me, or take any advice from me.

While I finished my work, I tried to concentrate on what I would wear for my date with Louis. But my mind kept wandering to Suzie and the part she'd played in Lola's career slide.

And Suzie's date with Bradley tomorrow night.

My enthusiasm for going to the World's Fair dimmed.

Chapter Six

Standing in front of the Unisphere while the Waldwick High School band marched by, I realized there was too much to see, more than I could ever fit into one day.

The Unisphere, sponsored by U.S. Steel, was twelve stories tall and 120 feet around. I gaped at the steel representation of Earth, which I read in my fair guide was the size of the Earth if you viewed it from space, six thousand miles away.

The Unisphere alone was worth the long subway and bus ride I'd taken into Queens, and the dollar-and-eighty-cents admission.

I'd dressed comfortably but—since I knew I would see Bradley—fashionably. My dress was a sleeveless sheath, one side black with white polka dots, and the other white with black polka dots. I had on low-heeled T-straps in black to save my feet.

Last night when I got home from work, Darlene wasn't there. I'd tried calling Lola to offer comfort, but got no answer. Going to bed early seemed like a good idea, so by nine I'd turned back my black-and-white daisy bedspread and fallen fast asleep. Darlene hadn't returned this morning. I *had* to talk to her.

Past lunchtime, I felt my stomach grumble. I stopped at a booth selling pizza for twenty-five cents a slice. With pizza in hand, I saw a vendor for Fizzies. Delighted, I ordered the root-beer flavor. I watched as the man dropped the tablet into a cup of cold water, causing the water to fizz, bubble, and turn brown. Yummy.

I sat down for a moment with my lunch and map and, while eating, planned what I would do next. I wanted most to see the *Pietà*, Michelangelo's 469-year-old masterpiece carved in marble, on loan from the Vatican. Pope John XXIII himself had granted permission for the precious piece of art to be displayed. It had never been taken from the Vatican before, and was said to have been created by Michelangelo when he was only twenty-four years old.

Once I found where the *Pietà* was located on the map, I looked for the Ford Pavilion, where I'd see Bradley, Suzie, and maybe Gloria, and then the Skyway exhibit, where I'd see Darlene. They were right around the corner from each other.

Throwing away my trash, I decided to walk to the *Pietà* at R10. On the way, I stopped at the New York State display, where they were having a fashion show, and also a display of paintings of the Hudson River. Then it was on to the Vatican Pavilion.

The pavilion was an oval-shaped building topped by a cross, with a curving wall extending from the entrance. You had the option of being carried past it on three moving platforms at different heights, or staying on a walkway and visiting at your own pace. I chose the latter and stood in awe of the expression on Mary's face as she held a dying Jesus. It touched me deeply.

Reluctantly I moved on, turning right around one corner, then left to an avenue that would take me to the Ford and Skyway pavilions.

Ford was first, so I took a deep breath and entered.

There she was: Suzie lovingly stroking the Mustang's white hood while a male voice over the speaker system proclaimed the advantages of owning the car.

People gathered around the Mustang and Suzie. A burly man stood near her, obviously to protect her from overzealous males. She wore an extremely tight strapless cocktail dress—which showed off the ivory

column of her neck. The black and white sequins
formed a harlequin pattern, and Suzie had topped the
dress with a light, airy piece of white fluff that covered
her shoulders. Naturally, it kept slipping. She wore her
blond hair in an upsweep, with a band that ended in
front with a black velvet X topped by four white feath-
ers. A rhinestone—or maybe diamond—clip held the
black X in place. Even I had to admit she was stunning. Reporters thought so too, as flashbulbs went off
again and again.

While Suzie smiled and elegantly pointed out the
car's features being announced over the speaker system, I looked around for Bradley. When I navigated
my way to the area behind Suzie, I spotted Gloria
standing on high heels away from the crowd, arms
crossed in front of her chest.

I hurried over. "Gloria! It's me, Bebe."

She gave me one of her half smiles. "Hi, Bebe, nice
to see you."

"What's going on? You look bent."

"You don't want to hear about it."

"Don't be silly! Of course I do."

Gloria drew in a deep breath. "I swear I'm going
to kill Suzie Wexford."

I tried for a playful tone. "Gloria, we already decided we had to stand in line to kill her, remember?"

Gloria's expression radiated anger. "I mean it. I've
been trying to fly low around her, but I'm about to
explode. Between last night and today, man, I can't
handle it."

"Can we sit down and talk?"

"No. In case you haven't noticed, there is no place
to sit down back here. Suzie said it wouldn't look good
for me to be sitting around. So I'm stuck here for four
hours, standing on these heels—because she insisted I
look fashionable—with only my big makeup case for
company. This is all for *her* convenience, *her* image.
She doesn't give a snap of her fingers for anyone
else."

Wow, Gloria was really worked up. "What is Suzie doing? Coming back here for touchups?" I asked.

"You got it. I wouldn't mind that at all; it's my job. But Suzie is just plain cruel making me stand here. Other models I work with still have some human decency and make sure I have something to drink, a place to sit until I'm needed on a photo shoot. Suzie's got some flunky bringing her water every fifteen minutes."

"Can I go get you a drink? It's hot in here with all the crowds. You might dehydrate." She looked pale.

Gloria's gaze darted to Suzie, then back to me. "Maybe if you pretended the drink was yours . . ."

"I'll be right back."

"Take your time. I'm not going anywhere."

I darted in and around the crowd until I found a vendor selling Coke. I bought the largest one he had, then rushed back to Gloria.

Positioning my body in front of her, where Suzie couldn't see what was going on, I handed Gloria the drink. She sipped from the straw, took a breath, and sipped some more, then passed me the cup.

"Bebe, you're a lifesaver. I can't tell you how thirsty I was."

"We'll hang together back here, talk, and you can drink some more," I assured her. "Now, start with yesterday. What happened?"

Gloria narrowed her eyes at Suzie. "I hate her."

"Don't look at her. Look at me. Remember, like you told me the other night," I said.

"First thing yesterday morning, I had to go to her place and do her makeup so she could go down to the Breck offices looking perfect and sign the contract she stole from Lola. Then she told me to be back at her apartment no later than five, because she had a dinner date with Pierre and needed to change from daytime makeup to evening makeup."

A dinner date with Pierre! Suzie had told me—and probably Bradley—that she felt "the sniffles" coming

on and needed to rest. Liar! But why would she want
to get out of a date with Bradley?

These thoughts flew through my mind, but I said
nothing to Gloria. "So she and Pierre were together
last night?" I asked.

"Yeah. When he summons, she obeys. I think he
knows all her dirty secrets."

"What dirty secrets?"

Gloria shrugged. "I don't know the specifics, but
I'm sure she's got even more of a lurid past than I
told you about at Pierre's showing. Can I have another sip?"

I passed her the cup. "It must bother Suzie that
Pierre has this hold on her."

Gloria handed the cup back to me. "I've been
thinking about that. Now, with the Breck Girl contract
under her belt, this Mustang assignment, and an offer
to appear on the cover of *Redbook,* Suzie is chafing
at Pierre's control. She had a tantrum while getting
dressed for her date with him."

"Suzie is going to be on the cover of *Redbook*?"

"Yeah, Pierre told her at dinner last night. He got
her the assignment. You'll probably be getting the
paperwork at Ryan soon. But here's the big news,"
Gloria said, and glanced around to make sure no one
was listening. "Pierre asked Suzie to marry him, and
she said no."

I gasped. "But I thought they were lovers, and he
made her what she is today with his photography
and—"

Gloria held up a hand. "Bebe, you've forgotten
what I told you about Suzie sleeping around to further
her career. The last thing on her mind is being tied
down to Pierre for the rest of her life. She wants to
be known as a swinging model and play around as
much as she desires without answering to anyone. She
told me she might even reel in a bigger fish."

Not Bradley! "Pierre must have been furious."

"Oh, yeah, you got it. While I was doing Suzie's
makeup this morning, she gabbed on and on about

how the poor man was broken. I swear, she was brag-
ging. She said that Pierre threatened to reveal all regarding her sleeping around—even with your boss."

"What else did she say?" I asked, blotting out the
part about Bradley.

"Suzie thinks nothing can touch her now. She
laughed in Pierre's face. The way she acted this morning, she thought the whole thing was one big joke,
regretting only having to pass up the four-carat diamond engagement ring Pierre had bought her."

"Maybe she thinks that Bradley—I mean Mr.
Williams—will take care of her career."

"I didn't want to mention it, Bebe, but that thought
crossed my mind."

"It's okay, Gloria. I know how things stand between them."

"Remember, she's only with him because he's the
head of Ryan."

"Right, I know." But the realization didn't ease the
pain. Besides, who could resist beautiful Bradley?
"Did she say whether or not Pierre was still going to
photograph her? I mean, he's so brilliant with a camera, what will she do if he refuses to work with her
now that she's turned down his marriage proposal?"

"He's still going to photograph her. Suzie thinks he
won't give up on getting her to marry him. Suzie always has her bases covered. Oh, here she comes,"
Gloria said, and opened up her big white makeup case
in preparation.

"I'll come back later, Gloria," I said. "I have news.
You'll be so proud of me."

"I'm done at five."

I tossed the empty Coke cup in the trash, and
walked briskly away into the crush of the crowd. I
actually wanted to see the new Mustang, so I forged
my way through until I was at the front.

"Hello, Miss Bennett," Bradley said.

I turned to find him squeezed next to me. We were
so close, I had to turn slightly and raise my head to
speak to him. "Mr. Williams. What a surprise to see

you here," I said in a tone laced with sarcasm. *Oops!*
That just slipped out.

I tried a recovery. "Are you thinking of purchasing
a Mustang?"

"I believe I will. I already have a Triumph Spitfire
garaged, but I like the look of the Mustang," he said.
"Variety is my thing, so it would be nice to have a
choice in cars when I decide to leave the city."

Smelling his lime aftershave, being in a position to
reach up and stroke his cheek—*Stop!* I told myself.
Hadn't he just said "variety is my thing"?

"It'll be groovy if you get a Mustang. They'll probably be popular for years to come," I said casually.

He looked down at me. "I like that dress and the
other outfits you've been wearing lately."

"Thank you. They're just a few things Darlene
brought back from London."

He raised his right eyebrow. "London fashions? I
approve. I have an order in for three suits from
London."

We were ruthlessly cut off from further conversation by the reappearance of Suzie. She flashed me a
scornful look before taking Bradley's hand and giving
it a squeeze.

"I should be finished here soon, darling," she cooed.
"I'm looking forward to our dinner date." She gave
him a sultry smile, one that promised things I could
only imagine.

The wretch grinned at her.

I turned on my T-straps and marched out of the
Ford Pavilion without saying good-bye. Bradley's eyes
were on Suzie anyway, so what did it matter?

I soon found myself at the Skyway exhibit. The huge
Aeroflyer, white with its signature large blue stripe
going from nose to tail, dwarfed the people standing
around it. Beautiful women in bright sky-blue suits
with matching pillbox hats smiled and waved to the
crowd with white-gloved hands. Men ogled the
women, as it was a well-known fact that every guy

wanted a stewardess on his arm. They were so glamorous, so worldly, so sexy.

One stewardess who was not as tall as the others, being only the required five feet three inches tall, shone among the others: Darlene.

I spotted Cole in his Stetson watching her with possessive eyes, but it took a moment longer to see Stu sulking with his arms crossed over his chest. *Uh-oh.*

The area around the plane was roped off, but Darlene let the cord fall near a sign that indicated tour times. I scrambled to get a place in line, hoping for a word with her. With relief, I noticed that neither Cole nor Stu intended to take the tour.

Darlene smiled at me, then began talking to the crowd about the luxury and safety Skyway Airlines afforded its customers. Men eyed her, rather than the plane, but being Darlene, she kept her wide Texas smile in place, enjoying the attention.

"The Captain's Special offers a seven-course meal served on china and includes caviar and hors d'oeuvres," she said. "We also offer Dover sole and prime rib prepared in our galley ovens."

As potential passengers admired the spotless galley, I caught up with Darlene. "You've got to talk to me," I whispered. "What happened between you and Stu?"

She kept her enthusiastic expression, but muttered under her breath, "I found out from one of the other girls that he had a wild weekend of sex with a chief stewardess in Paris."

Darn! "Have you asked Stu about it?"

"No, why should I? He's a free man, able to do just as he pleases," she replied airily.

"But Stu loves you!"

Darlene kept tabs on the visitors. "Ssshhh, Bebe. He's never said so. It just seemed like fate had taken a hand when I met Cole. He's so comfortable to be around."

"Since when have you liked being comfortable?" I asked.

Darlene went on with her spiel, her audience hanging on her every word. "Let's go down into the belly of the plane, shall we, ladies and gentlemen? This spiral staircase leads to a plush sit-down bar. . . ."

Frustrated, I turned against the tide of the crowd and made my way out of the plane. Cole was there, waiting for his "lambkin," and I was forced to nod at him. He tipped his hat at me, but I kept walking. Stu was leaving the exhibit, and I hurried after him.

"Stu!" I called, out of breath.

He turned and gave me a lazy smile. Tall, with dark hair, he was handsome and rich. While I could see other women would flock to him, I didn't for a moment believe Stu wasn't devoted to Darlene, even if he did have a penchant for stewardesses in general.

"How are you, Bebe? You're looking good in that boss dress."

"Thanks." Now that I had Stu's attention, I was suddenly at a loss for words. Then I thought of Cole Woodruff. "Stu, I know it's none of my business, and just stop me if I'm really out of line, but I'm worried about you and Darlene."

His shoulders slumped. "Hey, she has someone new and looks happy."

"Stu," I said gently, touching his arm, "was there a misunderstanding between you two? One that could easily be cleared up with a frank talk? You see, I like you both, and you seemed so right for each other."

He looked off into the distance, and I feared I'd gone too far. Then he turned to me and gazed directly into my eyes. "Bebe, sometimes Darlene gets an idea in her head and nothing can dislodge it. There's a lot of competition among the stews, and someone wanted Darlene to get bent out of shape."

"So what she's, er, been told about, um, Paris, is not true?"

"Absolutely not. There's no other gal for me but Darlene. Sure, I like looking at stewardesses, but Darlene's my doll. I tried to tell her that Peggy—she's the one who says she slept with me—was making things up because I hadn't accepted what she offered me."

"A woman scorned," I said.

"I'm afraid so. Thing is, I thought there was some trust between me and Darlene, but she wouldn't even listen to me and went ahead and believed the lies. Now she's with that Stetson-wearing lecher."

"I don't like him either," I added quickly. "There's something about him that's not right."

"Yeah, what's not right is that he's got my girl. I'm gonna split now, Bebe. I just came to see her, that's all. You're sweet for trying to help."

He moved away before I could say anything else, leaving me more determined than ever to pin Darlene Roland down on our pink sectional and make her talk to me.

I wandered around the fair for a while longer, but began to feel tired from the exercise, the heat, and the crowds. Gloria, Suzie, and Bradley were all gone when I returned to the Mustang exhibit. I must have lost track of time, and felt bad about not seeing Gloria. I wanted to tell her about my upcoming date with Louis.

I waited in long lines for both the bus and then the subway—there were thousands of tourists to contend with—and it was after ten in the evening when I let myself into my apartment.

No sign of Darlene.

I put on a pair of blue nylon pajamas, washed off my makeup, and went into the kitchen for a glass of milk. I was so beat, I couldn't even bring myself to think about Bradley being out with Suzie.

Finishing my milk, I yawned, then lay down on my bed to read the rest of the latest issue of *Look* magazine.

Bradley sat in the seat next to me on the Skyway plane. We were holding hands, and he leaned over to kiss my temple. His full lips felt warm against my skin.

A big Tiffany's diamond solitaire with a matching platinum band on my left ring finger sparkled like the ocean below. Darlene carved prime rib for us. I smiled, but something began pulling me away, while I groaned in protest. The scene evaporated, and I opened my eyes with a start, squinting at the light I'd left on the night before.

The phone. The phone screamed at me from the kitchen.

I scrambled out of bed, slipped on the magazine that had fallen during the night, and barely caught myself by gripping the side of the bed before my nose hit the floor.

Trying to get my bearings, I saw that the clock read twenty after five! The phone demanded my attention, and I stubbed my toe on the bottom of my dresser before making it into the kitchen and grabbing the receiver. This had better be good.

"Hello?"

"Miss Bennett?"

"Yes."

"Bradley Williams here."

"Mr. Williams! Are you at the office at this hour?"

"Miss Bennett, I need you to get me a lawyer."

"A lawyer? You mean Ryan's corporate lawyer?"

"No, a criminal lawyer."

"Cri— Where are you?"

"In jail, Miss Bennett."

"What! Why on earth—"

"Suzie Wexford was murdered last night, strangled with the Pucci scarf I gave her. I found her body, and the police think I did it."

Chapter Seven

Wide-awake without benefit of coffee, I took a five-minute shower with my hair in a plastic cap, put on my makeup in record time, and threw on a bright yellow Jackie Kennedy suit.

I had trouble remembering numbers in general, so I resorted to the worn notebook I kept in my purse to retrieve Stu's phone number. I couldn't spare a thought for what he might think about my calling him. Stu was the most powerful man I knew—next to Bradley—in New York City. He would know the best criminal lawyer, and he would keep quiet about what I told him.

Stu picked up on the seventh ring. "Hello," he said groggily.

"Stu, this is Bebe Bennett. I'm awfully sorry to wake you, but this is an emergency."

"Is it Darlene?" he asked, alarmed.

"No, Stu, she's fine; I didn't mean to scare you that way. It's my boss, Mr. Williams. He's in trouble, and I need you—well, not you exactly, but your connections, and I have to have them fast."

"Bebe, Bebe, slow down; you're not making any sense."

Tears burned at the backs of my eyes. I took a deep breath. "Mr. Williams called me from jail. The model he's been dating, Suzie Wexford—"

"Yeah, I know who she is. What happened?"

"Someone murdered her last night with a scarf that

Brad—I mean, Mr. Williams—had given her, and he
was the one who found the body. The fuzz think he
did it." My voice rose on the last few words.

Stu let out a low whistle. "How can I help?"

"I need you to get in touch with the best criminal
lawyer in New York City and get him down to the
jail and straighten out this mess!"

"Calm down, Bebe, okay? I'm going to help you.
What precinct has Bradley been taken to?"

Oh, God, my trouble with numbers! Bradley had
told me, but I forgot. But wait, he'd said he'd seen
my "friend," Detective Finelli. "Stu, I don't know the
number, but it's the one where Detective Finelli—you
remember him—works."

"Yeah, I sure do remember him, after what he put
Darlene through a few weeks ago. I know just the
lawyer to call, but before I get him, I want you to
promise me to try to calm down. I'm sure there's an
easy explanation as to how Bradley came to be found
with the body."

My empty stomach lurched. "Hurry, Stu. I'm going
down there now to see what I can do."

"Bebe, no—"

I hung up, grabbed my purse and gloves, and raced
out of the apartment and down the stairs. I tripped
on a child's red truck on a step and almost fell head-
long to the ground. Telling myself I had no time to
break my neck right now, I grabbed the rail, righted
myself, and continued down.

Outside, the morning chill hit me, and a quick
glance at my watch underneath the building's light
said it was five forty-five. The streets were dark, and
I imagined Harry asleep behind the Catholic high
school across the way. A couple of young men stood
loitering at the corner I had to pass.

I didn't care. I had to get to Bradley.

As I walked briskly over to Lexington, catcalls
greeted me, but I kept going at a no-nonsense pace.
I paused long enough to hail a taxi, opting not to take
the subway, and slid into the backseat.

"I don't know the exact street and number," I told the taxi driver, wishing I'd remembered to get them from Stu, "but I'll guide you there."

"Okay, lady. It's your dime."

We sped off, with the Four Seasons singing "Big Girls Don't Cry" on the cab's radio. By the time I arrived at the police station, dawn had turned the city sky a pale lavender. Trucks were delivering goods to stores and restaurants, garbage trucks noisily took care of the city's trash, and lights dotted the windows of apartment buildings.

I ran up the steps and entered the police station.

The uniformed desk clerk, a balding, paunchy man in his forties, eyed me suspiciously. "Help you?"

I clunked my purse down on the desk. "Yes, please. You see, my boss, Mr. Williams, has been arrested, and I'm here to get him out of jail, because it's all simply a terrible misunderstanding. If you would show me to where he's being held, we can be on our way."

"You his lawyer?" he asked with heavy sarcasm, bushy eyebrows raised.

"Well, no, but I'm his executive secretary!"

He riffled through some papers, then looked at me with total unconcern, head cocked. "Nobody but his lawyer's allowed to see the Williams guy."

Anger rose up in me for this man who obviously cared nothing about Bradley. I read his name tag and said, "Listen, Mr. Lonegan—"

"That's Officer John Lonegan," he interrupted.

"Very well, *Officer* Lonegan, Mr. Williams is a very important man. He runs a company! His uncle owns a conglomeration of entities across the United States. Mr. Williams doesn't belong here in this rather unclean building."

"Does if he strangled a broad and left her naked except for a fur coat, like this report says he did."

Naked? My voice rose. "Mr. Williams did not kill anyone! I give you my word on that."

Officer Lonegan had the nerve to chuckle. "Your word? Tell it to the judge."

My temper snapped. "Don't you dare treat *me* in such a condescending manner, mister. I'm here to see Mr. Williams, and I *will* see Mr. Williams, and I want you to take me to him right this minute and stop wasting my time and his, or I'll report you to Detective Finelli!" I yelled, pounding my fist on the desk for emphasis.

The officer narrowed his eyes at me and began to walk around the desk. "Lady, maybe you need to be clapped in the slammer for being insolent to a policeman."

"Don't even think of laying a hand on me," I commanded, ready to kick him where it hurt.

"Did I hear my name? And your voice, Miss Bennett?"

Detective Finelli, glowering, came out from the depths of the station house. I scurried past the mean desk clerk and hastened over. Detective Finelli and I had become acquainted—although he hadn't liked it—on a previous murder case I had managed to solve.

Reaching him, I barely refrained from grabbing the lapels of his gray suit. "Detective Finelli, they've got Mr. Williams locked up for something he didn't do! Get the key and release him."

"I can't do that." The detective ran a hand back and forth across his brown crew cut, a gesture of frustration I remembered well.

"Why? You know he's innocent."

"I don't know anything of the kind, Miss Bennett. I was at the scene a few hours ago, and your boss was the one with the dead body. I'm sorry, but it looks clear to me that he killed her, though I will investigate the crime."

"You'll investigate? That's a good idea. Then you can find out who really did Suzie in."

"Miss Bennett, Miss Wexford was a celebrity known across America for her modeling. Her personal life was public knowledge. For instance, there was a picture of her and Williams at that photographer's party in the *Times*."

"That's just gossip," I tried.

"Are you saying to me, an officer of the law, that you have no knowledge of Bradley Williams and Suzie Wexford having had a personal relationship in addition to their business relationship?"

"No," I said.

The detective spread his hands. "Williams had the opportunity—we found him crouched over the body— and as for a motive, maybe a lovers' quarrel. I'll find out. Meantime, no visitors."

Oh, dear God! In a calm, reasonable voice like Mama used when she wanted to guilt someone into doing something they didn't want to do, I said, "Detective Finelli, Mr. Williams called me, and I'd like to see him, please. I'm aware that what I'm asking you might be against the rules, but because I know you to be a good man, I'm asking you to bend the rules a tiny bit, since I assisted your department in bringing the Philip Royal murder investigation to a successful conclusion." I took a really deep breath and waited.

"Catholic girl, aren't you? You sound exactly like my mother," he said. "Come on, but just fifteen minutes, do you understand me?"

"Yes, thank you."

We walked down a dingy beige hall; then another officer let us into the cell area with a key.

Detective Finelli turned to face me, his voice low. "I've told you more than I should have regarding this case, but I did it for a reason. You're not going to get mixed up in this, are you, Miss Bennett? No breaking and entering, no questioning of suspects, no putting yourself in danger?"

"You seem to think you have the killer already, so how could I be putting myself in harm's way?" I asked, eyes wide.

"Don't give me that innocent look. I know what you're capable of."

"Aw, you flatter me, sir," I said, exaggerating my Southern accent.

Detective Finelli patted the white handkerchief he always had tucked in the breast pocket of his suit. "I want your promise, Miss Bennett, that you will not interfere with police matters like you did before. Otherwise I won't let you see your boss."

Naturally, I crossed my fingers behind my back. "I won't interfere like I did before." *Because this time will be different.* That was an effective way of putting it to the good detective, I thought, though I knew I'd have to jot this lie down in my notebook under the "Confession" section.

"I'll hold you to that statement, Miss Bennett," he said with a skeptical look. "Mr. Williams is in a holding cell with lots of company. I warn you, it won't be hearts and flowers."

I gasped. "Do you mean you've got him locked up with common criminals?"

"Unless his lawyer can call in a favor with the judge on a Sunday, Williams will be our guest." Throwing open yet another steel door, Detective Finelli entered first, holding the heavy door for me. "Not a place for you, Miss Bennett," he tried one last time.

That made me determined to show him I could be tough. I marched inside like I had a gun strapped to my garter, like a James Bond girl would.

In a large square cell, men in varying degrees of dirt and quality of clothing slumbered on the cement floor, some snoring. The room smelled like sweat and alcohol and maybe something else. *Eeewww.*

And there, in the middle of the filth and stench, standing against the back wall wearing an expensive slate-blue suit, white shirt, and narrow tie, was Bradley, a swan among the ugly ducklings. His rumpled hair, five-A.M. shadow, and fingers massaging the bridge of his nose were the only outward signs of any distress. I fought back tears. Bradley needed me to be strong.

I heard Detective Finelli say he would sit in a chair and remain during my visit "for your own protection."

"Mr. Williams?" I said, going up to the iron bars.

He raised his golden head and looked at me.

I was shocked at the grief in his eyes, never having considered that he would be feeling the loss of Suzie.

But of course he would, I mentally kicked myself. They had been . . . involved.

At the sound of a female voice, two of his cell mates woke and began saying vulgar things to and about me. Bradley pushed himself away from the wall and growled, "Leave her alone unless you want a shiner."

That shut them up, but they still stared at me. I didn't care.

Bradley came up to the bars until we were mere inches apart. His eyes were red, probably from lack of sleep.

In a low voice he said, "Miss Bennett, what the hell are you doing in a place like this? I called you to get me an attorney, not to come down here looking as fresh as a daffodil and about as innocent."

Innocent! Maybe it was time to start changing Bradley's view of me. I flung my arms through the bars, wrapped my hands around his neck, and pulled him toward me. I pressed a kiss on his forehead and then brushed my lips softly over the same spot.

As if nothing had happened, I released him, over the cries and whistles of the other two inmates who were awake. "Are you going to treat me like an adult and tell me what happened, so I can help you out of this mess you've gotten yourself into?" I kept the pitch of my voice completely professional.

Bradley's normally cool composure stayed in place. Still keeping his voice low, he said, "You are the sweetest, most adorable little pain in the neck I've ever known."

I smiled. "Why, thank you."

"Did you call a lawyer?"

I rolled my eyes. "Of course I called a lawyer. Or rather, I called Stu Daniels; you remember him—"

"Yes."

"I figured he would know the best criminal lawyer in the city."

"Good thinking, Miss Bennett."

"Stu promised to get someone over here quickly."

"Excellent. I could use a cup of your coffee." He

tried to smile, and when he did, I felt a powerful urge
to tell him I loved him and that everything would be
okay. Fortunately, I got hold of myself before the
words came out. Besides, what if everything didn't
turn out okay? Dear God!

"I'd certainly like to make you a pot of coffee. You
look like you could drink the whole thing. Want to
tell me what happened, since I'm here?"

Talking to the floor, Bradley said, "We went out to
dinner at the 21 Club. Suzie was tired from standing
on her feet all day, so we skipped dancing. Instead we
lingered over dinner, discussing her future plans with
the agency. I officially gave her the Durden account—
you know, the important swimsuit shoot set for the
Virgin Islands next week?" He glanced up at me.

"Yes." Boy, was that another plum assignment!
Suzie would make thousands off that job—or she
would have if she had lived. I wondered if Lola had
been hoping for the job.

"We'll have to find someone else now," Bradley
muttered.

"Don't worry, Mr. Williams; I'll start on it today.
What happened after dinner?" I managed to ask without my voice breaking.

He hesitated. "We went to Suzie's place for, er, a
nightcap." He glanced at me again, and when I kept
my expression neutral, he looked at the floor again
and went on. "The hours went by, and Suzie asked
me to go out for something."

"What?" I asked, wondering what she could want
at what was surely by then two in the morning.

He straightened and looked me in the eye. "Miss Bennett, I don't know that I should be telling you all this—"

"Don't be silly. What did you go out for?"

He mumbled something.

"What did you say?"

"Chocolate syrup."

I tilted my head. "So you were making sundaes;
what's wrong with that?" Then my brain flashed back
to something Darlene had told me once when we were

talking about guys. *Ooooh!* I made a mental note: Once Bradley and I were married, I'd keep Hershey's in business.

Bradley ran his right index finger down the side of my left cheek. "Nothing, kid. Anyway, when I got back to Suzie's apartment, I found her on the floor of the living room. The killer had strangled her with that Pucci scarf you wrapped for me."

"Yes, I remember."

"Someone had called the police, a neighbor. Maybe Suzie screamed. . . . God, I could use that coffee."

"And that's when the police found you with her?" I asked, remembering that the officer had told me Suzie had been naked with a fur coat thrown over her.

He nodded. "Yes. I just don't get it, kid. Who would want to kill Suzie?"

Oh, boy, could I give him a laundry list of people, but now was not the time. I heard the big door to the cell area open, and Officer Lonegan entered with a tall, thin gentleman carrying a briefcase. He reminded me of illustrations of the character Jeeves from the P. G. Wodehouse books I'd read, with slicked-back black hair, a fair complexion, and very dark brown eyes. I hoped he was as clever as Jeeves.

Officer Lonegan said, "Williams, here's your lawyer, Mr. Pickering."

"That's David Pickering, Esquire," the lawyer intoned with an English accent, looking down his long nose.

My mouth dropped open. He was English! Maybe he *would* be like Jeeves and have Bradley out of jail in the blink of an eye. Stu wouldn't have sent just any lawyer.

Mr. Pickering eyed Bradley, nodded as if he would do; then his gaze dropped to me before he settled his attention on Detective Finelli.

A grim expression crossed the detective's face before he stood, shook hands with the lawyer, and said, "Mr. Pickering, nice seeing you again."

"Good morning, Detective Finelli. How is your family?"

"Fine, thank you. The boys are a trial for the wife."

Mr. Pickering allowed a faint smile to cross his lips. "Boys of five and seven *will* do that to a woman."

This was new information for me. I had suspected that Detective Finelli possessed a family, but he'd never mentioned sons. I guessed that Mr. Pickering and Detective Finelli had been on opposing sides previously, and, from the look on the detective's face, he had not always been the winner.

"You will, of course, provide Mr. Williams and myself with the privacy of a conference room, so that I might become acquainted with him." He turned to Bradley. "That is, if you are amenable to the plan, Mr. Williams."

"Mr. Pickering, I'm amenable to anything that will get me out of here," Bradley said.

I looked at him and smiled, trying to broadcast the message that this man was here to help and now was not the time for masculine competition.

With a start, I realized Mr. Pickering had turned his sharp gaze on me. "I see from your bare left hand, miss, that you are not Mrs. Williams. May I ask who you are, and what you are doing here?"

Bradley spoke before I could answer. "I'm not married. Miss Bennett is my executive secretary and the friend of Stu Daniels who contacted him."

"Nice to meet you, Mr. Pickering," I said, and turned to Bradley. "Mr. Williams, I'll be at the office working on plans for that photo shoot we discussed. You can reach me there once you've been released." These last words were directed at Mr. Pickering.

Officer Lonegan led me from the room, back down the hall, and to the exit.

"Looks like your boyfriend will get out after all," the officer said. "Pickering will arrange bail. He's a big shot at the courthouse and knows all the judges."

With my hand on the doorknob to freedom, I said, "Mr. Williams will be released and cleared because he didn't kill anyone."

"Tell it to the judge, lady."

Chapter Eight

Stepping out of the police station, I felt drained. Heat rushed to my face when I remembered how I had brazenly kissed Bradley. Funny, though, he hadn't chastised me for it, or given me a lecture on office romances. And he had called me "the sweetest, most adorable pain in the neck" he'd ever known.

Remembering that made me smile, but I couldn't dwell on it now. First I had to get some coffee in me, since I hadn't had anything to drink or eat yet today. I felt a headache coming on, and needed aspirin and caffeine. There was a Chock Full o' Nuts near the Ryan building, so I whistled for a cab (Darlene had taught me how).

Later, as I sat at my desk munching doughnuts between sips of coffee, the thought crossed my mind that meddling Debbie Ann would not condone my breakfast. No doubt she'd lecture me about my figure while writing down instructions for making oatmeal. Luckily, since it was Sunday, she was not around.

Sunday! I clapped a hand over my mouth: I'd missed the early-morning Masses at St. Patrick's, and had told Bradley I would be at the office, so I couldn't leave now to attend the later Mass. Groaning, I pulled my notebook out of my purse, turned to the current "Confessions" page, and wrote down my transgression.

Then I got up and put on a pot of coffee for when

I'd finished my take-out cup. I still couldn't think straight, so I decided to call Darlene.

To my surprise, she answered on the second ring.

"Darlene, I didn't think you'd be home."

"Then why'd you call, silly?" she asked, and laughed. "Where are you?"

"I'm at the office, and I need to talk to you."

"Honey, I know we haven't had any time together, but we will tonight, I promise."

"Really? You mean you won't be with Cole?"

"Now, Bebe, I know for some reason Cole has rubbed you the wrong way—"

"He doesn't like me either!"

Darlene chose to ignore that. "I'm working the Skyway exhibit at the fair from noon until five today. Cole is coming with me, but he's tuckered out, and is gonna stay in tonight at his hotel."

"Can't keep up with you, huh?"

"Plus, Miss Cynical, I need time to do chores like washing my stockings, redoing my nails, and trying on some of the clothes I brought back from London."

"Great, we can talk while you're doing that. But, Darlene, I need you now for a few minutes. Something terrible has happened."

"Well, why didn't you say so! What is it?"

"Suzie Wexford was murdered—strangled—last night, and they've got Bradley in jail for it." Somehow saying this out loud to Darlene turned out to be my breaking point. I started to cry.

Darlene sneezed like she always does when she's upset. "Oh, my stars! I just saw the bitch yesterday at the fair. She was shouting orders to her makeup girl."

"Gloria," I said, tears running down my face.

"Whoever. Did you say Bradley is in jail?"

Another sob. "Yes! I mean, when I left him he was. He called me from there about five this morning, wanting me to find him a criminal lawyer. I called Stu, you know, *your boyfriend,* and he helped. A Mr. Pickering—he's English—came down to the jail."

"Wait a minute. You were at the jail with Bradley?" Sneeze.

"Uh-huh. You don't think I'd leave him there all alone?"

"No, of course not. I don't know what I was thinking. Why do the fuzz think Bradley killed her? I thought he and Suzie were, uh—"

"That's okay—you can say it; I'm a big girl," I said, wiping my eyes. "They were having an affair. Bradley had given Suzie a Pucci scarf. Then they had dinner last night and went back to her apartment for, well, a long time. Suzie asked Bradley to go out and get some chocolate syrup. . . . Darlene, are you okay? You sound like you're choking."

"I'm fine, Bebe, I just swallowed some coffee the wrong way. Did Bradley tell you all this?"

"Yes, through the bars at the jail," I said grimly. "Bradley came back, and he found Suzie dead, strangled with the scarf he'd given her. She must have fought her attacker and screamed, because someone, probably a neighbor, called the police. Bradley said they got there and saw him with the body, and Darlene, Suzie was naked except for a fur coat."

"Classy way to go," she muttered.

"And you'll never guess who brought Bradley in and put him in a cell with criminals."

"Oh, please. Not Detective Finelli."

"Bingo."

"Lord have mercy, that man gets under my skin."

"Well, since he once thought you murdered someone, I guess so." For a while Darlene had been a prime suspect in the Philip Royal murder investigation.

"Why are you at the office now, Bebe?"

"I left Bradley with Mr. Pickering, hoping the lawyer will be able to get him released. I told him I'd be here. We have all this rescheduling of modeling shoots to do now that Suzie is . . . dead. God, Darlene, I just remembered that I wished her dead!"

"Honey, that doesn't mean anything!"

"Yes, it does. I feel awful that I kept thinking I'd like to murder her, and now someone's gone and done it. Even Gloria and I talked about how there'd be a line of people waiting to kill her."

"Bebe! Who all did you tell you wanted to kill Suzie?"

I thought for a moment. "I guess just Gloria, Suzie's makeup girl."

"Don't mention it to anyone else, you hear? You don't want the fuzz thinking you did it."

"That thought never occurred to me; my head's been in such a whirl since Bradley called."

"Think of it now, and be on your guard. There's no reason you can think of why Bradley might have killed her, is there? I mean, in the heat of passion and all."

"Darlene Roland! Bradley would never kill anyone. I want you to apologize right now for even thinking such a thought."

"I'm sorry. Who do you think killed her?"

"That's what I'm going to consider next. I need to talk to some people—"

"Bebe, you're not going to get involved— Oh, what am I saying? You're going to try to find the killer, aren't you?"

"Darlene, have you come unhinged? The man I love is in trouble. If he's charged—God forbid—or even if he just remains a suspect, of course I'm going to find out who really did it. And you're going to help me."

"Yes, Lucy."

"What? Are you comparing me to Lucille Ball?"

Darlene snickered.

I drew in a deep breath. "If anyone is Lucy, it's you with your red hair."

"Okay, Ethel."

"I'm hanging up now. My head is clear, and I've got work to do."

"See you tonight. By the way, what are you wearing?"

"One of my Jackie Kennedy suits, the bright yellow one."

"Have you got on your white sleeveless shell underneath it?"

"Yes, why?"

"Take your jacket off in case Bradley comes in, and remember to cross your legs. He needs that right now."

"I'm already one step ahead of you. I kissed him through the bars in the jail."

"What a hussy you are!"

"Tell you about it tonight," I teased, and hung up the phone.

There was work to be done, and I was a list maker. First I pulled out my daisy Mary Quant compact and touched up my face, then covered my lips in pink lip gloss. Next I pulled out a lined pad and began working in two sections. The one in front was Ryan Modeling Agency business. Toward the back I wrote, *List of Suspects.* I decided to work on the latter first.

Number one: Pierre Benoit. The photographer had made Suzie famous, and the two were having an affair. According to Gloria, Pierre had grown increasingly possessive of Suzie, culminating in his marriage proposal, which Suzie refused. Had there been a furious fight when she said no? Pierre knew she was seeing Bradley. Had he been mad enough to kill Suzie, using the old male logic that if he couldn't have her, no one else would? Would a man in his position really throw his life and carefully built reputation away over one model?

Number two: Lola. I rolled my head, getting the kinks out of my neck. Lola sure had a motive. Although part of it was Lola's own fault that her career was faltering, Suzie *had* been devious in snagging Lola's clients, if one believed what Lola said. And if you did believe her, did that mean she was serious that night in the taxi? That she would *strangle* Suzie if she took the Breck Girl account away from her? Suzie *had* taken the Breck Girl contract. Suzie *was* dead.

I tapped my pen on the paper, thinking about how

Lola had been drunk when she'd made her threats. Were her vows to kill Suzie just a way of expressing her anger?

Number three: Gloria. I chewed my bottom lip as I wrote her name. I liked Gloria, but what did I really know about her? Our conversations had been limited to guys and our mutual dislike of Suzie. Gloria had said we'd have to stand in a line of people who wanted Suzie dead. Yesterday, at the fair, Gloria had been very angry at Suzie, even said she could kill her. She hadn't hung around waiting for me after I'd told her I had news—my accepting a date with Louis. . . .

My pen slipped from my fingers. How was I going to go out with Louis now when Bradley needed me? Well, I just would, that was all. Canceling the date would be plain rude. Besides, what had really changed in my relationship with Bradley? He'd called me a sweet, adorable pain in the neck, not the sweet, adorable love of his life.

Back to my list of suspects: I decided I would find a way to speak to each of them as soon as possible, face-to-face to get their reactions to news of Suzie's murder. Someone had been watching her apartment; yes, that sounded right. And when Bradley came out, he or she decided to go up and kill her. I closed that section of the lined pad with that notation.

Reaching around to my credenza, I picked up the black spiral notebook that served as a schedule list for upcoming photo shoots and TV commercials and the models involved.

Flipping to Monday, I saw the biggest projects were *Fun in the Kitchen with Debbie Ann* at four, and a TV commercial for Fuller Brush to be filmed at one.

Skipping through to Tuesday, I saw we had our big photo shoot for B. Altman's department store at the brand-new fountain outside Lincoln Center. Eight models, four women and four men, were set for that. Suzie had not been hired for that one, the department store having felt that her going rate was ridiculously high.

Problems didn't start until Wednesday afternoon, when Pierre, a crew, Bradley to oversee, and Suzie to model, were all set to fly to the Virgin Islands for the Durden swimwear account. Durden wanted Suzie photographed in lush, tropical settings wearing their daring new bikini.

I twirled a strand of hair. We certainly didn't want to lose the lucrative Durden account to Ford Modeling, so we had to come up with another famous model. Could Lola do it? Would Bradley approve?

Over the next couple of hours I made lots of notes of things to do for Ryan, and made plans for Suzie's murder investigation.

Finally the elevator pinged, and Bradley walked in, apparently straight from jail, as he still wore his suit and tie from the night before.

"You really are here, kid," he said, as he sat down behind his desk.

I hurried after him, steno pad in hand. "Did you ever get any coffee?"

"Coffee? No? Liquid tar? Yes."

I grabbed his mug and returned a minute later with the hot beverage.

Bradley drank some, then leaned his head back against his chair. "At least I'm out of that place."

"What happened? How did the meeting with Mr. Pickering go? Did you have to appear before a judge?"

He raised a hand. "I met with Pickering for about an hour, and he called a judge he knew and got me released. Pickering's got a brilliant mind, but he seems focused on my future trial and how to prepare for it, not on looking for the killer."

"Does that mean you've been charged with murder?" I asked, feeling an awful sinking sensation.

"No. I expect Pickering is thinking ahead." Then he said, "We need to plan a memorial for Suzie. I think Wednesday morning at the Cathedral of St. John the Divine, followed by a reception at the Legends Hotel would be good. Write that down, please, and place a notice in the *Times*. Detective Finelli informed

Suzie's parents in Omaha, and they're flying in to take her body back home."

Gosh, he'd been doing some planning. "How sad for them."

Bradley puffed out one cheek and blew out air. "Sad for a lot of people."

I guess he was including himself.

"Look, I'm beat. I need sleep. I'm going home, and I think you should too. Tomorrow is going to be a very busy day."

He stood and so did I. "Mr. Williams, what is Mr. Pickering going to do?"

"This is my mess, Miss Bennett, and I'll handle it."

He began to go past me, but I stopped him in the doorway.

"Why won't you tell me—"

Looking down at me through red-rimmed eyes, unshaven, and with an air of melancholy, he said, "A woman I've been involved with has been murdered. I'm the prime suspect. I don't have time for chitchat right now."

Ouch! "As your secretary, I was trying to help you, and I don't think I deserve to be snapped at."

"Trying to help me? See, that's exactly why I'm not going to talk to you about this anymore. You did your job by finding a lawyer for me. Let Pickering and me handle it. We're doing well so far. I'm out of jail."

"But I can help! I have information—"

He pointed at me with his right index finger and spoke in a stern voice. "No. You are not to get involved in this like you did with the Philip Royal murder, do you understand me? I won't have it, Bebe, and that's my final word."

I crossed my arms over my chest, watching him walk to the elevator. His final word indeed. Did he think he could stop Bebe Bennett?

I'd help him whether he wanted me to or not.

As he stepped into the elevator, leaving me alone, I wondered if he realized he'd called me by my first name.

Chapter Nine

Deep in thought, I wandered around Fifth Avenue, window-shopping aimlessly; then I went home.

Darlene greeted me at the door wearing an apron. "You're just in time for my famous tuna-and-macaroni-and-cheese casserole."

"Since when have you become so domesticated?" I said, taking my jacket off and throwing it over the pink sectional.

"I caught a few minutes of *Fun in the Kitchen with Debbie Ann* the other day. That woman comes across like a real kook about food, but she inspired me to do some cooking."

"They shoot the show at Ryan. I've met Debbie Ann. She's not a kook, but she likes to mother everyone."

"Come on, honey, I bet you're hungry. Sit down, and I'll get everything."

Too tired to do anything else, I obeyed, taking a seat at our tiny table in the minuscule green-and-white kitchen.

"So, clue me in, Bebe," Darlene said, putting hot plates of food in front of us and taking the seat opposite me.

"Bradley came back to the office for about ten minutes. The lawyer got him released from jail." I took a bite of the casserole. "This is good. You even left out the peas. Thanks, Darlene."

She waved a fork. "I like tomatoes in my tuna casserole anyway. Has Bradley been charged with Suzie's murder? And what's this about you kissing him?"

"He's not been charged yet, but don't ask me for any other details. He refused to tell me anything except to say, 'Stay out of it and let me handle everything.' He's such a . . . such a—"

"Man?" Darlene supplied.

"I guess that's it."

"And the kiss?"

I shrugged. "I don't know what came over me. He looked so bummed and vulnerable, I kissed his forehead, that's all."

"Hmmm. Did he get all professional on you?"

"No. He called me a 'sweet, adorable pain in the neck.' "

"I can dig it!"

"Yes, but he's miserable."

"He's probably in shock. I mean, he finds his easy lay—I mean date—dead, strangled with something he gave her, and the fuzz are all over him. He doesn't know what he's doing right now. Think he's grieving?"

"Some. I don't know. Bradley is always so in control, so cool." I swallowed a bite of macaroni. "He did slip and call me Bebe."

Darlene grinned. "You've got him running hard. First this thing with Suzie, who was nothing but a slut—"

"Darlene! Don't speak of her that way now. She's dead."

"Still. Playing loose like he did with Suzie is the final step a man takes before he settles down for good. His last hurrah." Darlene nodded wisely. "I'll bet he's having more and more thoughts about you, and they aren't the pure type."

"What's this sudden insight into my relationship, huh? Let's talk about you and Cole."

Darlene sighed, rose, retrieved a pitcher of iced tea from the fridge, and poured us each a glass. "Cole's from Texas, like me."

"So it's a 'Texas thing'?"

Darlene looked at her plate. "It's comfortable being with an older man. I feel like I can trust him."

"Isn't he old enough to be your father?"

"Man, let's not talk about my father," she said.

I reached across the table and took her hand. "You never talk about when you were growing up. Can't you even tell *me* about it?"

Darlene sneezed. She pushed a red curl behind her ear. "Oh, it's a common enough story, happens all the time. My father worked on an oil rig; Mother was a barmaid in town. When she got pregnant, they married and had me. I guess I was an ugly little girl, all red hair and freckles, because he took off when I was three."

"I'm sorry, Darlene, and I'm positive it had nothing to do with you. Don't think those kinds of thoughts."

"Don't be sorry; that's what men do. Leave. Mother got all religious after he split, and I don't mean like you being a Catholic. She's a fanatic, raised me so strict I couldn't go out on a date until after I'd left home and landed the job at Skyway. I was always having to pray or read the Bible or do my chores. I didn't have any friends, because my parents were *divorced*. You know how cruel kids can be."

"How did the job at Skyway come about?"

"Wasn't easy. My father never came back, never sent money, and most of the money my mother made waitressing at this little diner, Mason's, she gave to the church. When I got old enough to babysit, she forced me to give money to the church, only I lied about how much I'd made and started saving." Darlene looked at me. "I'm going to hell for that, aren't I?"

"No! God knows the reason you saved part of the money was for your future. You might want to tell Him you're sorry for lying, that's all."

Darlene sneezed twice, so I knew her opening up to me this way was hard for her. "What were you saving for?" I prompted.

"From the time I was fourteen I wanted to be a

stewardess. Just thinking about that glamorous job and getting to fly all over the world made me the only babysitter in our small town who would take care of the Tyler twins. Lord, those boys were terrors. Anyway, I knew that once my senior year came, I'd find my way to the airline recruiter in Dallas, fifty miles away."

"So you had to save up for the bus money?"

"Yeah, but that wasn't all. I had no decent clothes. By the time my senior year came, I'd managed to save enough to buy a white blouse, a navy-blue skirt, navy pumps, and some cheap lipstick and mascara. I couldn't afford a purse, so I just put the lipstick, mascara, and some money into my bra."

I giggled, and Darlene smiled.

I said, "I'll bet they hired you on the spot."

She nodded. "I had to break the news to Mother that I was going to stew school. She never has spoken to me since. In her mind, being a stewardess is like walking the streets."

"That's not fair. I know you get lots of attention from men on your flights, but you work hard preparing and serving meals, making sure the passengers are comfortable, dealing with crying babies."

"Honey, you don't have to tell me."

An idea formed in my head, and I chose my words carefully. "Darlene, I don't want to sound like that Freud guy, but a couple of things make sense to me, now that I know what you went through growing up."

"Like what?" Darlene asked, getting up from the table and taking down the bottle of whiskey she kept in the cupboard. She poured a small amount into a shot glass and drank it.

"Your father leaving like he did, which was really crummy . . . well, maybe that's left you wanting an older man in your life. Cole enters the picture, appearing to adore you; he's from Texas. . . ."

"My relationship with Cole is hardly one of father and daughter," Darlene said.

"I know, but think about it. Plus, Cole strikes me

as being very possessive, have you noticed? He's hardly left your side since you met, and doesn't even want you to be around me."

Darlene held the bottle of whiskey to her forehead and closed her eyes. "Cole just wants to protect me, keep me safe."

"The Darlene I know likes adventure. She likes trying new things, dancing all night, exploring the cities she flies to."

"I have to think of my future. The mandatory retirement age for stews at Skyway is thirty."

"Darlene! You're not going to be thirty for five more years. How old will Cole be in five years? Sixty-five?"

She pushed away from the counter. "I don't want to talk about it, Bebe."

"That's fine," I said, and got up and gave her a big hug. "You know I'm here if you ever change your mind. I'll just say one last thing: I saw Stu at the World's Fair. He was watching you at the Skyway exhibit."

Darlene looked at me. "He was?"

"Yes. We chatted for a few minutes, and he said how much he misses you."

She snorted. "He should have thought of that before he spent that weekend screwing Peggy, that chief stewardess." She put the whiskey back in the cupboard and started to leave the kitchen.

I followed. "Did he really do that?"

She swung around. "Of course he did. All men cheat!"

"Mama told me the good ones don't. I think Stu is a good one," I said. Then, seeing a flush come up Darlene's throat, I thought it best to drop the subject. "Hey, *The Ed Sullivan Show* is about to come on. Gerry and the Pacemakers are supposed to be playing! Why don't we do our nails while watching the show. I'd like to try the new Cutex Hot Pink you have."

"Just as I thought. You're turning into a hussy," Darlene teased.

"That's me, all right. Kissing men. Going out on dates with models."

She gasped. "You have a date with a model?"

"I sure do. I would have had a date with a cute actor if he hadn't been caught up with some very famous people. Let's get settled in front of the TV, and I'll tell you all about it."

Monday's *Times* splashed the news of Suzie's murder across the front page. A picture of her looking fresh and innocent headed an article titled, "Top Model Suzie Wexford Murdered."

I cringed when I read . . . *police found the body after a neighbor reported screams coming from Miss Wexford's apartment. Upon their arrival they found Bradley Williams, head of Ryan Modeling Agency, crouched over Miss Wexford's dead body.*

The article went on to say that the coroner pronounced Suzie dead due to asphyxiation. The time of death was noted as *somewhere between two and two thirty in the morning.* Sitting at my desk at Ryan, I decided Bradley did not need to see the newspaper, and threw it in my trash can. Coffee brewed while I finished routine work before Bradley arrived.

He came in an hour later wearing a dark gray suit and black tie. "Damn photographers. Hello, Miss Bennett, we need to get busy."

"Yes, Mr. Williams." I stood up, smoothing the skirt of my bright green, pink, and white horizontally striped minidress.

Before I could collect steno pad and pencil, Bradley bolted back out of his office and filled his mug with coffee. This was a first! He always asked me to get his coffee. For a moment I stood in shock, then managed to follow him into his office. He sat in his high-backed blue leather chair.

"Shut the door, Miss Bennett," he said.

With the door closed, the room seemed more intimate, more conducive to an exchange of confidences.

Plus, even in these circumstances, I loved being alone with him.

"All right, first, I want you to get me the phone number of the blonde in the Bernat Yarn dealer ad. The ad ran in the March issue of *Woman's Day*. Her name is Evelyn something, and she's one of our models." He pulled open his middle drawer. "Here's the key to the models' personnel drawer in the large filing cabinet over there," he said, pointing to my left.

I accepted the key. "Do you need her for a shoot?"

He sat lounging back in his chair, holding a pencil between two hands, a gesture I knew well. "No, I'm going to ask her out for tonight."

My mouth fell open. "But, Mr. Williams, won't that look bad for you—I mean, so soon after Suzie's death?"

"I'm following Pickering's advice. I have a reputation around Manhattan, and my lawyer thinks I should maintain it. Continuing to date will demonstrate that my relationship with Suzie was casual, not something worth murdering her over."

That did make sense, darn it. "Do you know Evelyn?"

"No, but she'll accept; they always do. I'm rich, I run the company, and I'm easy on the eye."

Humble, too!

"At any rate, it's only for show. I assume you saw the newspaper this morning?" At my nod, he continued, "If you think about it, I'm sure you'll agree with Pickering's strategy. Now, on to Suzie's memorial service. Mr. and Mrs. Wexford arrived in New York late last night. Ryan is putting them up at the Legends Hotel. Neither of them was willing to speak to me. I want you to call them right away and get their approval for the plans you and I discussed yesterday for Suzie's memorial. I'm counting on you, Miss Bennett, to arrange everything; the best flowers, the best music, the best photo of Suzie—get with Pierre Benoit about that—the best food at the reception, got that?"

Writing furiously, I said, "Yes, Mr. Williams."

"I have to spend the morning calling clients and
reassuring them I'm not a murderer, and offering sub-
stitute models for their needs. Although I went over
the portfolios when I landed the assignment here, I
need to do it again. Run up to the eighteenth floor
and see if you can find Gina. She might be able to
help suggest which models are popular."

"I will. Mr. Williams, I checked the schedule for the
week, and we have the B. Altman department store
shoot at the Lincoln Center fountain tomorrow. Everything is set for that, as long as it doesn't rain."

"Good."

I took a deep breath. "The other assignment is the
Virgin Islands shoot for the Durden swimwear
account."

Bradley dropped the pencil to his desk. "I'd completely forgotten."

"What do you think of Lola doing it? I know we've
had some problems with her, but I was thinking of
talking to her, woman to woman. You see, I think
she's been drinking because . . . well, um, because
Suzie took away Lola's accounts."

"Only because Lola couldn't professionally fulfill
her obligations. Suzie told me that she only wanted to
help Ryan by going on those shoots when it seemed
Lola wasn't going to show."

Yes, I'll bet that's what Suzie told you. "I think we
should give Lola another chance. Besides, the Durden
people are expecting a star. We don't have anyone
other than Lola who fits the bill. We don't want to
lose the contract to Ford Modeling."

"Maybe you're right, kid. By Wednesday afternoon
the police will have lifted this ridiculous order that I
not leave town, so I'll be there to supervise as
planned."

"So, Detective Finelli *did* tell you not to leave town.
You remain a suspect," I said.

"Finelli is investigating. There's to be a grand jury

hearing on whether or not the police have enough evidence to charge me. I'll be cleared then."

"When is the grand jury hearing?" I asked, my throat dry.

He sat up straight in his chair and leaned forward, elbows on the desk. "Oh, no, Miss Bennett, you're not going to drag information out of me about my personal business. Don't forget what I told you yesterday."

"This is not just your personal business, Mr. Williams," I countered. "We need to know who will oversee the Virgin Islands shoot if you are still under police orders not to leave town."

That seemed to strike a chord. "Perhaps."

"I think I should be the one. Will you authorize me to purchase an airplane ticket for the flight the Ryan people are taking? My roommate is working the flight as a favor to another stewardess."

Bradley's expression reflected utter surprise. "You? You, oversee a shoot for an important client? You're barely twenty years old."

Fury swept through me, as well as a good measure of hurt. "Mr. Williams, I am twenty-two years old and have excellent organizational skills. I like to think I deal well with other people. In addition, I can keep an eye on Lola, and," I finished, raising my chin, "since I'm a woman, and Durden is targeting women with this campaign, I might also be able to offer creative suggestions."

"Pierre Benoit won't listen to a word you have to say."

I raised my eyebrows into my bangs. "Would he listen to you?"

Bradley stared at me. "This is crazy. You're not going to the Virgin Islands on that shoot, Miss Bennett. I am and that's final."

"Whatever you say," I replied. "I have a lot of work to do, so I'd better get started. Do I have your approval to give Lola the assignment?"

"Yes," he said, then turned in his chair and stared out the window.

Internally fuming, I moved over to the file cabinet, unlocked it, and began looking for Evelyn's contact information.

The dunce! Didn't he know by now that Detective Finelli was like a dog with a bone once he got an idea into his head? Bradley would never be free to supervise the Virgin Islands shoot. I'd have to wrangle a seat through Darlene.

In the meantime, I definitely would be in touch with Pierre Benoit regarding Suzie's photo for the memorial.

And her murder.

Chapter Ten

After finding Evelyn Miller's phone number in her file—she was rather ordinary, if her headshot was anything to go by—I put it on Bradley's desk and left his office, closing the door behind me. We hadn't exchanged another word.

I threw my steno pad on my desk in a gesture of hurt, frustration, and fear. Maybe Darlene was right in thinking that Bradley was in shock. He certainly was irrationally confident that he would be cleared in the next few days.

Considering the problem of Pierre Benoit, I decided it would be better to ambush him at his studio rather than phone him. That way I could see his face, ask questions. Flipping through my Rolodex, I found an address for him and wrote it down.

Although I dreaded doing it, I had to call the Wexfords to get their approval for the memorial service. Dialing the number to the Legends Hotel, I thought it best not to introduce myself as Bradley's secretary.

"Good morning, Legends Hotel," a male voice said.

"Please put me through to Ralph Wexford's room."

A ringing; then a gruff male voice said, "Hello."

"Mr. Wexford?"

"Depends. You're not another lousy reporter, are you?"

"No, sir. I'm Miss Bennett from Ryan Modeling, and I'm calling to get your approval regarding Suzie's memorial service. I know you're planning to take

Suzie back to Omaha, but she had so many friends here in the city, we thought a service and reception here would be welcome."

"Ryan footing the bill for this?"

"Yes, sir."

"They damn well should after the head of that place killed my little girl!"

I decided to ignore that. "Let me take this opportunity to offer you and your wife my sympathy. I knew Suzie." *God, what a hypocrite,* I thought, but then realized I did feel sorry for Suzie's parents, even though I hadn't liked her.

"What kind of memorial are you talking about?"

I quickly outlined our plans, which Mr. Wexford grudgingly agreed to.

"I'll make all the arrangements, Mr. Wexford. Unless you hear different, expect the memorial to start at ten in the morning on Wednesday."

"Fine. Then we can book a flight out of this crime-ridden city for later Wednesday. None of this would have happened if Suzie had married Jeff," Mr. Wexford said.

"Jeff?" I asked, pressing the phone closer to my ear.

"Jeff Granford, star quarterback. He and Suzie were high school sweethearts and were supposed to marry, until Suzie sent her senior picture to that bum of a photographer."

I started taking notes. "You mean Pierre Benoit?"

"No, somebody Roberts. Forgot his first name. He was the one who told Suzie she could be a model, and enticed her to this heathen city."

"Oh, I see. Is Mr. Roberts still here?"

"I don't know. Look, the wife's crying again. I hope they fry that Williams fella for killing my little girl. You can tell him I said so."

With that, Mr. Wexford hung up.

I thought for a moment and remembered Gloria telling me that Suzie had an ex that she slept with occasionally for old times' sake. Could that be Jeff Granford? Had he followed her to New York? Maybe

Gloria could point him out to me if he attended the memorial service. There was always the possibility that he, too, was jealous of Suzie's other lovers, and got fed up enough to kill her. I needed to talk to Gloria.

I found her phone number and dialed. A service answered for her, so I left my name and both work and home phone numbers with a request that she call me.

Making the arrangements for Suzie's memorial took longer than I thought, even with an unlimited budget. It was around eleven when I took the elevator up to the eighteenth floor.

The door to Gina's office stood open, but I knocked anyway.

The former model wore a pale gray Chanel-inspired suit—or maybe it was the real thing—and gave me a chilly look. "What can I do for you, Miss Bennett?"

"Mr. Williams wants your opinion about our female models."

She smirked. "What does he intend to do with the next one?"

I kept my calm. "I believe he's wondering if there's anyone in particular whom you have been grooming for bigger assignments. He'd like their portfolios."

Gina lit a cigarette. "You and your boss have been here only a week, and our top model, a star in the industry, is dead. I think I should be talking to the owner of this company before I turn over any information to Mr. Williams."

She hadn't invited me to sit down, so I placed my palms on her desk and leaned forward. "First of all, Mr. Williams had nothing to do with Suzie's death. Second, he already has all the girls' contact information in his office along with headshots. He simply requested your opinion as to who might be a rising star. Finally, Mr. Williams's great-uncle owns this company, among others. I'm surprised you didn't know that, Gina. You impress me as being a woman who does her homework."

She breathed out smoke through her nostrils and,

without another word, went to a big filing cabinet behind her desk. I watched with approval as she began selecting, then stacking, several portfolios.

"There you are," she said coldly.

"Thank you very much," I replied in my sweetest voice.

Lugging the portfolios onto the elevator, I blew air into my bangs. Was this the way Bradley would be treated around the agency from now on? I had to find Suzie's killer!

Bradley's door was shut when I reached our office suite. Glancing at my phone, I saw that his line glowed red. The portfolios began slipping out of my arms, so I decided that since he was on the phone, I'd quietly place them on one of his chairs. I opened the door to hear him saying, "That's wonderful, Evelyn. I'll see you tonight."

He ended the call as I was leaving.

"Have you talked to the Wexfords?" he asked.

"Yes. Mr. Wexford approved of our plans, and I've made all the arrangements."

"Very good. What was Mr. Wexford's attitude?"

Oh, boy. "They are grieving the loss of their daughter. Mr. Wexford was, understandably, not in a good mood."

"Thinks I killed her, doesn't he?" Bradley asked.

"He'll find out he's wrong. I'm sure Mr. Pickering has hired a private detective," I said, fishing.

Bradley drummed his fingers on top of his cluttered desk, ignoring my comment. "Have you spoken with Lola yet?"

Talk about pigheaded! "That's next on my list."

"I won't keep you. Close the door behind you, please."

I did as he asked, thinking it best if he remained ignorant of my plans to investigate, though at the same time I hoped Mr. Pickering *had* hired a private detective. As Bradley's lawyer, it was his duty to make sure Bradley's name was cleared.

I sat down and called Lola at home.

"Hello," she said, her voice level and clear.

Encouraged, I said, "Hi, Lola. This is Bebe Bennett from Ryan."

"I remember you," she said in a sunny tone. "I had too much to drink at Pierre Benoit's showing, and you were nice enough to take me home."

Surprised by how chipper she sounded, coupled with the fact that she actually remembered me, I thought that maybe the Virgin Islands shoot would work out after all. Meanwhile another part of me mused that Lola might be in a good mood because Suzie was now out of her way. Permanently. Strangled, as Lola had threatened.

"I'm sure you've heard that Suzie Wexford has . . . er, passed away."

"You mean somebody finally bumped off the bitch," Lola said. "The paper made it sound like the killer was our princely leader at Ryan. God, I hope not; he's too choice to waste away in some prison cell."

"I can assure you that Mr. Williams had nothing to do with Suzie's death."

"Glad to hear it. I pictured him boning her, and afterward them getting into a fight. She probably had plans for him, and he didn't follow along."

"What makes you say that?" I asked, pencil poised over my lined pad.

"Nothing in particular. Just that Suzie was such a schemer, I think she figured she'd bring Bradley to the altar. He's rich, handsome, runs the agency—she'd be set for life."

Gloria had expressed a similar theory about Suzie's plans for Bradley. "Lola, Mr. Williams and Suzie had known each other for only several days. I doubt he had marriage on his mind," I said.

"I guess you're right. He was getting the milk for free—why buy the cow, as the saying goes."

I wanted to ask questions, lots of them, but it had to be in person. "Lola, the reason I'm calling is to offer you a bikini photo shoot in the Virgin Islands.

The client is Durden swimwear, and we're leaving Wednesday night. Are you interested?"

"Are you kidding!" she exclaimed. "I've heard that Durden is really going all-out for this campaign. The bikini is supposed to be racy. I'll be in the magazines again. Count me in!"

"I'm glad to hear that." I put as much authority as I could into what I said next. "Woman to woman, Lola, between now and when we leave, you should stay away from alcohol. It makes a girl look bloated, and you're so pretty, we wouldn't want that to happen. I went to bat for you, and don't want to come off looking like a fool."

"I get your drift, Bebe. I'll stay off the sauce, no problem. Now that Suzie's croaked, I think my life will be taking a real good turn for the better."

We went over the details of the trip, and Lola was easy to please on every issue and thrilled that she'd be working with Pierre again. The whole time I talked to her, I couldn't help thinking about how much Lola had to gain from Suzie's death and how different she acted now that Suzie was dead.

At lunchtime I thought it best to bring over one of the girls from the typing pool to cover the phones. I intended to go by Pierre's, and I didn't know how long I'd be gone.

I called Mrs. Seeds, who was in charge of the girls, and put my request to her.

"Let me check and see who is available, Bebe. Hold on one moment."

I sat with the phone propped up to my ear, tidying papers on my desk and laying out a fresh telephone message pad.

Finally Mrs. Seeds came back on the line. "Sorry to keep you waiting. Girls can get such crazy ideas in their heads. Danielle will be right over."

"Thanks," I said, and hung up.

Bradley was still behind closed doors in his office.

He must be reassuring clients. I'd bet he'd also called his uncle Herman.

My thoughts were interrupted when a tiny young woman walked slowly down the hall until she reached me. She wore a modest white blouse and blue skirt and had pretty dark hair. She said, "I'm Danielle. Mrs. Seeds said I was to come here and answer the phone for you while you're at lunch."

"Thanks for coming, Danielle. There are just three lines," I said, showing her the phone. "These two are for general calls to the agency, and the third is Mr. Williams's private line. Don't use that one if you need to use the phone. If any calls come in that sound like reporters, anyone asking about Suzie, don't give them any information. Your reply should be that Ryan has no comment on Suzie Wexford's death other than to express sorrow for her loss. Okay?"

Danielle's hazel eyes widened. "Yes." She looked over toward Bradley's door. "Is he . . . in there?"

Obviously she'd read the newspaper and come to the conclusion that Bradley was a cruel murderer, roaming the halls of Ryan Modeling looking for fresh young girls, like a scene from one of those paperback slasher books.

"Danielle, Mr. Williams is a good man, and he didn't kill Suzie. He was just in the wrong place at the wrong time. You'll see when the police arrest the real killer," I said, and smiled.

Danielle nodded and took her place in my chair.

Just as I was about to leave, the phone rang. Looking ruefully at Danielle, I said, "Here, I'll get that one.

"Ryan Modeling Agency, Miss Bennett speaking."

"Bebe, it's Gloria."

"Hi, Gloria, I've been trying to get in touch with you," I said, turning and making sure Bradley's door remained closed.

"I've been busy doing makeup for Edie Segwick. Did you know she dyed her hair silver to match Andy

Warhol's? Hey, what was that news you were going to tell me at the fair? A date?"

"Yes, I'm going out tonight to the Phone Booth with a male model I met, but I wanted to talk to you about Suzie's death."

"Good riddance!" Gloria said, and laughed. "You can't live wild like she did without putting yourself in danger. Wonder who killed her? Do you happen to know?"

"No!"

"You don't have to yell in my ear," Gloria complained. "I'd like to shake the killer's hand, even though I'll lose some money not working for Suzie, but I'll make it up."

"I don't know who did it," I said, noting that a second person on my suspect list sounded cheered by Suzie's murder.

"Guess Suzie's secrets died with her. Bet it was one of those very secrets that got her killed," Gloria said.

"I love juicy secrets," I said, thinking about Jeff, the high school sweetheart, and Roberts, the photographer guy. "When can we get together and grab a burger?"

"Gee, I'm booked all tomorrow; then Wednesday we're going to the Virgin Islands."

"You'll be at the memorial service for Suzie, won't you?" I asked, not wanting to tell her that I would probably be on that flight with her.

"Gloria? Are you still there?"

"Yeah, Bebe, I guess I'll come. Some of her clients will likely attend, and I don't want to make them wonder why I'm not there. Otherwise there's no way I'd go."

I gave Gloria the memorial service information, ended the call, and said good-bye to Danielle.

I took the elevator downstairs and hurried to the corner. The day had turned cloudy with drizzling rain. Marv didn't have his usual line of customers at the hot-dog stand. I managed to place a hand on his arm and ask about Betty.

"The doctors don't know when the baby will come. Betty's switched from fresh pineapple cravings to peanut butter. She's eating it right out of the jar."

"Easier on you, Marv! Just stock up on Peter Pan. I gotta run, but I just wanted to say hello before I get a cab."

"Good luck in this weather."

Marv was right. While my hair turned into a frizzy ball, taxi after taxi went by without stopping, all full.

Finally a cab pulled over, and I gave the driver Pierre's address on East Forty-fifth street. The cab raced away from the corner, causing my usual slide and bump in the backseat. From my purse, I pulled out my black daisy Mary Quant compact and surveyed the rain's damage. The Dippity-Do I'd applied to keep the ends of my hair flipped up was fighting a valiant battle against the moisture in the air. I ended up powdering my nose and refreshing my lip gloss, while my stomach rumbled with hunger. I'd have to wait to eat: Questioning Pierre took precedence over lunch.

My thoughts turned to Lola and Gloria. Both women had reason to want Suzie dead. Both women would have had the opportunity to kill her. Suzie would have let either of them into her apartment, even at that late hour.

Arriving at Pierre's, I paid the cabdriver, then ran up the steps and rang the buzzer. And waited. I rang the buzzer again. "Who is it?" a male voice demanded.

I pressed my finger down and spoke into the intercom. "Mr. Benoit, it's Bebe Bennett from Ryan Modeling. I need to talk to you about a photo of Suzie Wexford for her memorial."

A minute passed, during which I wondered if he would answer me, then, "Come on up to the second floor." The door gave a distinct click, and I pulled it open. The first level was a short but elegant hall with a door to the right marked, A.

"Up here," Pierre said from the landing above, scaring me to death.

I climbed the steps and followed him into what turned out to be his studio. On one side were hardwood floors with no carpets, a squarish black leather couch and matching chairs, and a white square cube as a coffee table. In the middle of the room stood a camera set up on a tripod, a huge umbrellalike thing, which I knew from photo shoots helped with the lighting, a set of lights, and a black lounging chaise.

But it was the walls around the high windows that captured my attention. Pierre had covered them in aluminum foil. On the closest wall I saw a distorted view of myself. No photographs were in evidence until one looked up to a winding iron staircase where the foil ended and brick walls lined with photographs began. The glass inside each frame had been shattered. Every photograph was of Suzie.

A chill went through me. Had Pierre done this in a fit of temper when Suzie refused his proposal?

"Does it meet with your approval, Miss Bennett?" Pierre said in an overly polite tone, his voice carrying a French accent from his earlier years. He wore his customary black, but as I took a few steps closer to him, I could see that his face around his goatee was bloated, and his eyelids were swollen.

"Excuse me for gawking, Mr. Benoit. It's just that I've never been in a photographer's studio before," I said.

"Call me Pierre. Mr. Benoit makes me feel old. You're a very pretty girl—what did you say your name was? And that dress would look better with go-go boots."

"Thanks. I have some boots, but haven't worn them yet. My name is Bebe Bennett. Please call me Bebe. I'm sure you don't remember, because you had so many famous people at your elegant gala showing, but I was there. I admire your work."

"Thank you," he said in a mournful tone. "Now that my star is gone, I don't know how I can take another photograph."

Saying this, he broke into loud sobs.

Here was my cue. I took a step closer and said,

"Suzie will be missed by many. I know you and she were close."

He wept openly now. "Never. Been. So hurt."

I had to get him to calm down enough to have a conversation. "Can I get you a glass of water?"

"No. Tissues upstairs," he mumbled, collapsing onto the chaise.

I hurried up the spiral staircase, my heels clanking on the metal.

Pictures of Suzie on the walls, all smashed.

Big bedroom with a huge, unmade bed.

All the window shades pulled down.

Clothes scattered, all black.

Photo on the dresser of a young boy and his parents with mountains in the background.

Framed photographs stacked against the walls. None hung.

Where were the tissues? I looked around and found a box on the dresser. I grabbed it, turned on my heel, and started to make my way out of the room, feeling uncomfortable being in a man's bedroom.

I stopped. There had been a bracelet on the dresser. Aware of the sound of my heels on the hardwood floor, I tiptoed back into the room. Sure enough, it was the bracelet Bradley had given Suzie. Evidence of his relationship with her. Evidence she had been in Pierre's bedroom since Bradley had given her the bracelet. I pocketed it, mentally adding "stealing" to my list of sins, tiptoed out of the bedroom, and went carefully back down the spiral staircase.

Pierre was where I had left him, tears falling silently now.

"Here," I said, offering him the tissues.

He accepted and blew his nose. "I apologize for my display of emotion. What can I say; I'm French."

"There's no need to apologize, Pierre. Everyone has feelings."

"Ah, but it is weak for a man to show his. She always did bring out the weakness in me."

How I wanted to ask him about the shattered pic-

tures of Suzie, about the bracelet, about their last dinner together, but there were just the two of us in the
studio, and he was not in control of himself. What if
he confessed to killing her, then killed me?

"I know you're grieving. When was the last time
you saw Suzie?" That seemed a safe enough question.

He paused. Reaching for another tissue, he wiped
his face with it, then got up and walked over to where
a few pretty glass decanters sat with glasses on the
white cube. "Would you like a drink?"

"I appreciate it, but no. I don't drink much, and I
haven't eaten lunch yet."

"I'd offer you something, but I have my meals ordered in, or I eat out. This is only wine; are you sure
you won't partake?"

"I'm sure, even though I know that as a Frenchman,
you must have the best wine. Maybe another time?"

He stared at me. "Yes. I would like that."

"About Suzie. . . ."

He poured wine into a glass and almost drained the
liquid in one swallow. "I saw her last Friday night.
We had dinner together here."

"How lovely. I'm sure she enjoyed it."

His expression darkened, and his gaze went from
my shoes to my eyes. "What position do you hold
at Ryan?"

Uh-oh. "I'm Bradley Williams's executive secretary."

With all his might, Pierre threw the glass across the
room, where it crashed against the wall and fell to
the floor in pieces. My heart beat fast at this display
of temper.

"Your boss is filth! He treated my Suzie as a play-
thing, not as the goddess she was!" he shouted.

"I-I don't know much about their relationship," I
lied.

"Believe what I tell you then, because it is the truth.
Williams tried to come between Suzie and me, but the
two of us had a bond that could not be broken. She

toyed with him, since he was head of the agency, but felt nothing for him. Nothing!"

I did not reply to this, as the uneasiness I felt in Pierre's presence increased. But that didn't stop my head from reeling. Gloria had been right when she said Pierre was possessive of Suzie. I could easily imagine him having the motive and the opportunity to kill her, but didn't he love her too much? Even if he didn't, he'd spent his life building a name for himself. That wasn't something he would throw away easily, would he? If only I could get him to talk about what happened at that dinner, but now was not the time.

I said, "Would it be too much for you to select a photograph of Suzie for the memorial Ryan is planning for her?" I quickly filled him in on the details, trying to bring some normalcy to the conversation.

"This photograph would be on loan, no?"

"Oh, of course. I'll personally make sure it's returned to you."

"I know all of the photos I've taken of Suzie by heart. There is one that will be perfect." He walked over to the far side of the room, near where the glass lay shattered, to a large group of framed pieces. He picked one out and began stroking the frame with his fingertip.

Several minutes passed before I cleared my throat. "Is that the one?"

He looked at me as if he'd forgotten my presence. Carrying the large silver-framed photograph, he handed it to me. "Yes."

I accepted the heavy piece, which was about two feet high, and gazed at it. The setting was summer in Central Park. Suzie sat on a blue blanket, a wooden picnic basket beside her. She wore a red-and-white gingham shirt, tied at the waist, and white shorts with no shoes. She was about to take a bite out of a hamburger. Her delighted look at being photographed screamed Mom, apple pie, and baseball.

She looked nothing at all like the Suzie I knew. I wondered if it was one of the earliest snaps Pierre had taken of her.

"You see the innocence in her, Bebe? How she speaks for the typical American girl? That is how I will always think of my Suzie."

Everyone was entitled to their delusions, I thought. "This will be perfect. Thank you, Pierre, for loaning it to Ryan. I'll make sure it's displayed in the front of the church, where everyone will see it."

"I'll bring it myself," he insisted, taking the photo back from me.

I nodded in agreement, too afraid of him to argue.

Suddenly it appeared he wanted me out of the apartment. He led me to the front door. With one foot out in the hallway, I turned and said, "I could get another photographer if you feel you can't do the B. Altman's shoot tomorrow."

He ran a hand across his forehead. "No, I'll be there."

I smiled. "Your reputation as a real professional is well deserved, Pierre."

He shrugged. "You're correct. My work is my life. I must continue or go mad."

"Perhaps time in the Virgin Islands will help. You remember the photo shoot for Durden swimwear?"

His eyes narrowed. "That is to go on? Who will we use as a model? There's no one who can do it but Suzie, and she is lost to us."

I took another step away so that I was fully in the hallway. "I understand your sentiment, believe me, but this is business, as you know. We've decided to use Lola."

Pierre's face went red. "That drunken, washed-up bitch who hated my Suzie? If your Mr. Williams didn't kill Suzie, then without question Lola did!"

Chapter Eleven

I headed back to Ryan in a cab with the windows rolled down. The sun poked out of the clouds, and the radio blared the Temptations' "The Way You Do the Things You Do." As usual, the driver had to snake his way through the crowded streets. He loved his horn, and used it frequently, but I tuned it out, thinking of my last words with Pierre.

After he'd made his proclamation of Lola's guilt, I'd had to soothe him by assuring him that *he* could make Lola look fabulous, and that Ryan had no choice but to use her, since she was known as a star model.

Pierre hadn't liked it, but the businessman in him won out, and he went along. I started praying Bradley would be cleared in time for the Virgin Islands trip, as I predicted Pierre would be hard to handle, but logic told me otherwise. I wondered if Detective Finelli would come to Suzie's memorial. Probably, if he really was investigating and had not just decided Bradley was a murderer.

I had the cab drop me at Marv's corner, but I was out of luck. Marv had packed up after lunch. Glancing at my watch, I was shocked to see it was almost two thirty! My growling stomach insisted on food and drink. I needed something fast, so I could relieve Danielle, who had probably developed ulcers from the stress of working for a suspected murderer.

I caught the elevator and punched eighteen. Maybe Debbie Ann had a piece of fruit to spare.

An hour and a half before showtime, Debbie Ann was already in makeup. She wore a turquoise shirt-waist dress with a white-and-turquoise apron. Her assistant, Nellie, took notes while Debbie Ann talked nonstop.

I walked onto their set. "Hello, ladies. I apologize for interrupting, but I've come to beg a favor."

Nellie squinted at me through her glasses. "Wow, that's the shortest dress I've ever seen, except for in the magazines."

I pasted a smile on my face. "This length is all the rage in London, Nellie. For the first time in memory, London, not Paris, is setting the trends. Isn't it groovy?"

"Um, no," Nellie said, nose in the air. "I wouldn't wear it, especially in this office, where you might catch the attention of a killer."

Debbie Ann piped up before I could set Nellie straight. "Nellie is right, Bebe. A dress that short might be popular in London, and I admit I've seen it here in New York, but I don't think the trend will last. Women will not embrace the idea of showing as much leg as a prostitute."

Heat burned my face.

Debbie Ann went on: "Frankly, I'm surprised to see you here, Bebe. Aren't you frightened, working for someone the police consider their chief suspect in Suzie Wexford's murder?"

I opened my mouth, but she was quicker. "I think the entire affair is a horrid reflection on our company. The two of them should never have been dating. Office romances rarely end well, except for the amazing instances when the man actually marries the woman. Obviously the two had a falling-out—perhaps Suzie demanded an engagement—and Mr. Williams lost his temper in a deadly way. I admit, I was taken in by the man, charming and attractive as he is. But a little birdie told me that a replacement for Mr. Williams is on his way. We must hope the man arrives swiftly, before any damage can be done to my show's ratings."

Debbie Ann paused for breath, and Nellie broke in.

"I'm so very happy Mr. Williams never showed any personal attraction for *me*," she said.

Every Homemaker's Friend opened her mouth, but this time I cut her off. "Debbie Ann, who told you Mr. Williams is going to be replaced? And what makes the two of you so certain that he killed Suzie Wexford?"

Nellie rolled her eyes.

Debbie Ann focused a stern gaze on me. "Bebe, I hope you haven't been blinded by a handsome face. Do not permit yourself to be alone with him under any circumstances."

Outnumbered, I decided to play along. "All right, I won't," I said, fingers crossed behind my back. "But, Debbie Ann, you still haven't told me who the 'little birdie' is."

"That's because I know how to keep a secret. All I'll say is that when Mr. Williams killed Suzie, I had to make sure my position and reputation would be protected. Otherwise I would have to entertain offers from other studios that would want me to broadcast live from their facilities."

Translation: Her agent told her. Was it true? Would Bradley's uncle really send in a replacement? God, please not that awful Drew, Bradley's cousin and competitor, whom I'd met last month. I dismissed the thought from my mind, deciding it was pure gossip, and Bradley had nothing to worry about.

Debbie Ann glanced at her watch. "I'm glad you came to visit, but I have only an hour before my show starts, so—"

"I'll go. I really came up to see if you had any food to spare for a secretary who missed lunch." And now wished she'd suffered in silence.

"Bebe!" Debbie Ann exclaimed, her tone one of severe disapproval. "One should never skip a meal; it's simply not good for your body. I thought you were going to take my suggestion and pack a tuna sandwich, an apple, and a Thermos of milk for lunch every day. What happened?"

"I've been busy, and—"

"That's no excuse for bad nutrition." She went to the refrigerator and began pulling out the makings for a sandwich.

"Oh, no, Debbie Ann, please. One of those apples and, um, a glass of milk would be fine, thank you. I'm going to have a big dinner. Honest." I wanted to be nice to her, despite her lecturing and her feelings about Bradley. After all, her husband had committed suicide, and then she lost her only son in Korea.

Debbie Ann sighed theatrically. "All right, it's your health, your future." She meticulously washed an apple, scrubbing it so hard I thought all the skin would fall off, poured me a glass of milk, and gave them to me.

"I really do appreciate this. It won't happen again."

"I hope that's a promise you'll keep, Bebe," Debbie Ann said, then turned her attention to that evening's show, enabling me to make my escape.

Rather than take the elevator, I took the steps to the seventeenth floor. As I approached my desk, Danielle picked up the phone and said, "She's back, Mr. Williams." Pause. "You're welcome."

With that, Danielle gave me a guilty smile, then bolted in the direction of the typing pool.

Bradley's door flew open.

"Where have you been, Miss Bennett? Do you know what time it is?"

He was as mad as a hive of bees Daddy once disturbed when mowing our lawn. I looked at my watch. "It's just a minute or two past three."

"I repeat, where have you been for the past three hours?"

Mrs. Seeds from the typing pool moved our way, probably wanting to speak to me. Instead, Bradley's loud, angry voice must have dismayed her, as she turned on her heel and hurried back the other way.

"Mr. Williams," I said calmly, "there's no need to shout. I didn't leave for lunch at noon. I was too busy."

He pointed at the apple and the glass of milk in my

hands. "And apparently you were too busy to eat when you did leave."

I placed the food and drink on my desk. When I turned around, he was motioning me to come into his office. I followed him, and he closed the door and loosened his tie. "I want a straight answer. Where have you been?"

"I didn't realize my job description included having to report my activities outside this office—"

"Oh, for the love of God!"

"All right! I went to Pierre's studio."

Bradley looked so adorable, I wanted to forget he had me on the grill. "Pierre Benoit? *His studio?* Why did you go there?"

Uh-oh. "I thought it important to go in person and pick out the photograph of Suzie we'll be using at the memorial."

"You could have called Pierre and asked him to bring one."

"I—"

"I don't see the portrait in your hands."

"Pierre decided he'd bring it himself."

"He picked it out by himself too, I'll bet."

I knew where this was going, and I didn't like it. "Actually, Pierre did select it. But I had no way of knowing that before I went to his studio."

"Alone, in a man's apartment, possibly Suzie's killer."

Remembering the uneasiness I'd felt at Pierre's, I blushed.

"That! That pink on your face tells me what I want to know. You went there, even though it could possibly have been dangerous, and you asked questions about where Pierre had been when Suzie was murdered. Isn't that what you did, Miss Bennett?"

Darn him! "It might have happened that way. But I also had to talk to Pierre about the B. Altman's shoot, and the Virgin Islands shoot, and calm him down when I told him we'd be using Lola! And it wasn't his apartment; it was his studio."

"If I'm not mistaken, he lives at his studio."

An image of that big bed upstairs at Pierre's flashed in my brain. "I guess."

"You were poking your nose into something that doesn't concern you."

"It does too concern me," I shot back, feeling like a five-year-old arguing with another five-year-old.

Bradley scowled. "I've told you, this is my mess, and I'll take care of it. You are not to get involved. Now, I'll ask you again: Why did you put yourself in a chancy position over my affairs?"

Because I love you, you fool! "Because you're my boss, and I don't want to lose my job if they throw you in jail for something you didn't do."

That gave him pause. He stared at me to see if I were telling the truth. I stared back.

He lowered his voice to a deadly calm. "You will lose your job, Miss Bennett, if you investigate Suzie Wexford's murder and I find out about it."

"What?"

"I've told you not to do it, so you'd be going directly against my orders. Have I made myself clear?"

Men and their pride! "Why must you feel this way? I solved that other murder. I can help you."

"You almost got yourself killed with your investigating, if you recall. I won't have you put your life in danger again. I don't *need* you to help; do you understand?"

My body felt as if it were shrinking into itself. He didn't need me. "Yes, I comprehend what you're saying, Mr. Williams. If I may go, I do have work to accomplish."

He opened the door. "Good idea. Drink your milk and eat your apple too, kid."

I couldn't decide whether the itching in my hands meant that I wanted to smack him, choke him, or thrust the scissors Danielle had left out into my own heart.

I decided Bradley had already done the latter, threatening to fire me, and took a big crunchy bite out of my apple.

Chapter Twelve

Bradley was irrational, I reminded myself, stricken with shock and grief. I mustn't hold it against him that he was behaving like the most pigheaded, willful, stubborn mule I'd ever come across.

The phone rang.

"Ryan Modeling Agency, Bebe Bennett speaking."

"Now that's a pretty name, Bebe Bennett. Miss Bennett, how'd you like to make a lot of cash, fast? All I need are your thoughts on the man who killed Suzie Wexford—"

I cut him off. "Since I don't know who that man is, I cannot help you. Please do not call here again." I hung up.

The phone rang again.

I jerked it to my ear. "The agency is grieving Miss Wexford's death, and we have no further comment—"

"Bebe! It's me, Darlene."

I sighed. "Hi, Darlene. I thought you were another reporter."

"Been calling all day, have they?"

"Yes, although I was out part of the afternoon, so I don't know exactly how bad it's been."

"You sound like you're in the dumps."

I lowered my voice in case Bradley should sneak up on me. "Bradley chewed me out for going over to Pierre's studio. I had a valid reason to go, but of course I did a little snooping."

"What'd you find?"

"Some very interesting facts. Pierre was a mess, sobbing his heart out. He asked me to go upstairs to the bathroom to get some tissues. Get this: Smashed framed photos of Suzie lined the wall, and I found her bracelet—the one Bradley gave her—on the bathroom vanity."

"Suzie's pictures were smashed? Sounds like someone has quite a temper. What about the bracelet? Did you five-finger it?"

I patted the pocket in my dress to make sure the bracelet was still there. "I did."

"Good girl!"

"I like to think I'm *borrowing* a piece of evidence."

"That's right. Pierre didn't need it. You'll look better wearing it. It proves Suzie was in Pierre's upstairs bathroom."

"We already know they were having an affair, and I'm not going to wear the bracelet. At some point I'll return it to Bradley."

"At any rate, we'll talk about Pierre later. I took the liberty of going through your clothes to find something for you to wear tonight on your big date."

I chuckled. "Okay, Edith Head. What did you come up with?"

"The perfect dress: your royal-blue chiffon, the one with spaghetti straps, fitted waist, flirty skirt, and folds of chiffon around the bust area to, er, fill you out."

"I haven't been brave enough to wear that one yet, but I will tonight. A problem might be the shoes—"

"Covered. You've got a sexy pair of silver sandals with kitten heels, and I've got the clutch to go with them."

"Oh, Darlene! That sounds pretty."

"Correction, honey. It sounds sexy."

"Darlene, it's my first date with Louis," I reminded her. "I don't want to come across as fast."

She laughed. "Don't worry; you won't. You'll look gorgeous. Don't forget what I told you about men and royal blue. They can't resist a woman wearing that color."

I laughed. "If you say so. I'd better leave work right at five, since I got caught in that drizzle and my hair is a mess."

"Lots of Aqua Net hair spray will do the trick. Oh, and I left out a tube of lipstick that matches the hot-pink nail polish you have on."

"Thanks, but does this mean you won't be home when I get there?"

"Cole's taking me to dinner. He doesn't know it yet, but afterward we're going down to the Village for a Bottom Painting. It's all the rage," she said, and giggled.

"A Bottom Painting?" I asked in disbelief.

"I don't know if I'll see you tonight or not, but we'll catch up and I'll tell you all about it. Bye."

"Bye." I hung up, thinking that Darlene might stay overnight with Cole. How could I get her back with Stu? I'd puzzle over that one later.

The rest of the day flew, and at quarter to five I knocked on Bradley's door.

"Come in."

I found him in the process of pulling on his suit jacket.

"Mr. Williams, I'll be leaving in a few minutes. Is there anything you need before I go?"

"No, thank you. I'm headed home myself." He pulled his London Fog raincoat from his personal closet, dropping a navy-blue wool scarf in the process. "Just close the door behind you when you leave. I'll see you later."

"Good night." I eyed the scarf, then peeked out the door. Bradley entered the elevator, and the doors closed behind him.

I picked up the scarf, held it to my face, and breathed in. My fingers trembled as I smelled his lime aftershave, and apparently my heart thought it was running from Dracula, because it was beating so fast.

Looking both ways to be sure the coast was clear, I darted from Bradley's office to my credenza and slipped the scarf into my purse. I was becoming quite the kleptomaniac, but I assured myself that I was simply *borrowing* the items and would return them. Bradley had no need for a wool scarf in this spring weather, and Suzie wasn't going to miss her bracelet now.

I didn't know why I wanted to keep Bradley's scarf for a little while. It seemed such a pathetic, childish thing to do, like a toddler with a favorite blanket. In my own defense, I *was* going out with Louis tonight, taking a step away from my adoration of Bradley. Yet my conscience tweaked me. Was it fair to go out with Louis while feeling the way I did about Bradley?

Deciding to continue this internal debate on the subway, I gathered my things and headed toward the elevator.

The phone rang.

I stopped in my tracks and then, sighing, I went back to answer it.

"Ryan Modeling Agency, Miss Bennett speaking."

A male voice said, "I tried to call Gina, but she must have gone for the day."

"And you are?"

"Jack Norton. I'm supposed to be at the photo shoot—"

"Yes, I remember. The B. Altman's shoot at Lincoln Center tomorrow morning."

"I can't make it."

"Why not?"

"Gee, you sound just like Gina except with a Southern accent. I'm sick."

"You don't sound sick. What's wrong?"

"Hey, I don't need some hayseed holding my toes to the fire, okay, lady?"

I clenched the receiver. "And I don't need a model, who is supposed to be a professional, canceling out on this agency at the last minute without a darn good reason."

His voice rose. "I'm going on a barge party off Long Island tonight, and I expect to be boozed and passed out somewhere in the Hamptons at ten in the morning. That a good enough reason for you?"

The nerve of him! "Very well, Mr. Norton, I'll leave Gina a note. Before I keep you from your party, can you give me your trouser and shirt sizes?"

"Thirty-two-inch waist, size fifteen shirt." He hung up without saying good-bye.

I leaned against my desk. Darn it! There were four girls and four guys in that shoot. I'd have to find someone else, and quickly.

My thoughts turned to Louis. I'd ask him tonight if he would like the assignment. Perhaps if Bradley observed me handling this situation competently, he would let me go on the Virgin Islands shoot in his place.

Unless I caught a break in the case.

Poor Louis. The man wasn't going to have the full attention of his companion tonight.

Waiting for the elevator, I still couldn't help but wonder how Bradley would feel if he knew his "kid" secretary had a date with a handsome male model.

Chapter Thirteen

Once home, I tried to take a quick bath, but all the water kept running out of the tub despite the plug. I gave up and took what Mama called a kitty-cat bath, using the washcloth. While drying off, I spotted a note from Darlene next to a perfume bottle.

The note read: *Don't turn your nose up at this classic man-killer. Wear it tonight!*

The perfume was My Sin. I gasped. I couldn't wear that! I knew the fragrance had been around for years, but the very name made me blush. . . . I hesitated. I could smell it and see what it was like, I rationalized, turning the cap. A heavenly but sexy odor wafted to my nostrils.

It smelled even better dabbed behind my ears. I had put the bottle down and turned to leave the bathroom when Bradley's voice played in my head, saying he did not need me to help him. I applied perfume on my wrists and, closing my eyes, between my 34-As.

I armed myself with a can of Aqua Net and went to work on my hair. Next I freshened my makeup and smoothed Darlene's hot-pink lipstick on my lips. Taking a step back from the mirror to see the results, I had second thoughts. Much brighter than the usual pale pink Mary Quant lip gloss I used, the hot pink made me seem . . . well, older somehow. Deciding that might not be such a bad thing, I went into my bedroom and dressed.

Passing the yellow vinyl chair I call the Banana, the

one I had obtained while doing some curbside shopping soon after moving in with Darlene, I looked at myself in the full-length mirror on my closet door. *Oh, my!* Even with the pearl necklace and earrings Mama had given me when I graduated from secretarial school, the dress and the lipstick and the silver sandals made for a sexy look. Was it too sexy? I looked at the Banana chair—more specifically, to Bradley's wool scarf I'd put there. Suzie's bracelet was under the seat of the Banana along with my New York to-do list—the latter I had sadly neglected.

I ran back to the bathroom, tissued off the hot-pink lipstick, and applied the pale pink. Then I headed back to the full-length mirror. *Darn!* Some of the hot-pink lipstick lingered, making the gloss turn an ugly shade. Back in the bathroom, I cleaned my lips again and reapplied the hot-pink lipstick. Nodding at myself in the mirror, I dropped the lipstick, my daisy Mary Quant compact, a few dollars (Mama always said to be prepared to take yourself home from a bad date), and my apartment keys.

At quarter to seven, I turned on the black-and-white TV Darlene had recently found a stand for, sat on the pink sectional, and watched the end of the news. President Johnson was making a speech on what he called "the war on poverty." He also addressed the Civil Rights Bill before Congress, saying it would be passed by the end of the summer. A 102-year-old man, Edward Everett Cauthorne, prepared to be the guide when he and twenty-nine of his fellow residents in a Rockaway Beach retirement home toured the World's Fair. No rain was expected for tonight or tomorrow, which, I thought, was good news for the B. Altman's shoot.

The intercom sounded promptly at seven. I leaped off the couch, then took a deep breath before answering the summons.

"Hello?"

"Bebe?"

"Yes."

"It's Louis; are you ready to go?"

"I'll be right down, Louis."

Throwing a soft, short silk cape in merging shades of blue around my shoulders, I grabbed the clutch Darlene had loaned me and headed down the stairs, carefully avoiding trash that could make me slip, and toys I could trip over.

Once outside, I smiled at Louis. "Hello."

"Wow!" he exclaimed. "You look beautiful."

"Thank you." He didn't look bad himself. Dressed in a navy dinner suit, with a white shirt, white pocket handkerchief, and a navy-and-red striped tie, Louis looked every inch the model he was. My anticipation for the evening grew.

"Here, I have a cab waiting for us," he said, and I followed him to the curb. He gestured for me to get in, saying, "I already wiped the seat with my spare handkerchief."

Using tricks Darlene had taught me about entering and exiting a cab while wearing a dress, I managed to keep my modesty.

Louis followed, gave the cabbie an address, and turned to me. "That's a nice perfume you're wearing. It smells good on you."

The back of the cab suddenly felt like an intimate setting. I felt myself getting nervous. I didn't want to tell him the name of the scent, so I mumbled my thanks, thinking this would never do. Once again, Mama came to my rescue. She always said to get the gentleman talking about himself. That way he'd find you interesting.

"Louis, how long have you been modeling?" Just as the words came out of my mouth, I realized I still had the key to the personnel file and could have investigated him. *Darn!*

"My mother kind of pushed it on me when I was young. I was in ads for cereal, bicycles, a macaroni-and-cheese recipe, and my career grew from there. I have Mother to thank for any success I've had."

"Was it hard making the transition from doing kids' ads to landing the Burma-Shave account?"

"No, actually it wasn't. Mother had built contacts over the years, and I kept doing ads through my teenage years. I did a portfolio a year ago with a great photographer, Scott Roberts, and— Oh, we're here."

While Louis paid the driver, my mind began spinning. Was Scott Roberts the same Roberts who'd taken Suzie's initial photos? How many photographers named Roberts were in New York City? Could I get information out of Louis regarding the guy?

I slid out of the seat, knees together, and smiled at Louis when he offered his hand to help me out. His hand felt soft and warm. He probably had to take really good care of his face and body. I tried to concentrate on him and our surroundings, but my brain was like a broken record saying, *Scott Roberts,* over and over. I'd wait until we were seated and had ordered food before I began the third degree.

Inside the Phone Booth, a full band, dressed in tuxedos, played the current favorites. A talented young man belted out "Hello, Dolly!" while Louis gave his name to the maître d'. On the dance floor lots of couples dressed in cocktail attire were gyrating to the music. We had to wait only a minute before we were shown to a white linen-covered table.

"Is this all right, Bebe?" Louis asked me.

"Oh, yes, of course."

We were seated and presented with the wine list, but my attention was caught by the fancy phone positioned to one side. It was black and ivory with faux gold trim, and a "hold" button. What was the polite etiquette if someone called to dance with me . . . or Louis?

Louis took charge. "Would you like me to make a suggestion about the wine?"

I leaned forward. His green eyes were almost hypnotic, and his black hair shone. "To tell the truth— like the TV show says—I'm not a big drinker."

"Perhaps it wouldn't be wise to order a whole bottle of wine then?"

"Gosh, no, not for me. I like champagne, can't stand beer, and tried whiskey once or twice. I'm not a high-ball girl."

Louis smiled. "I find your freshness charming, Bebe. How does this sound: I'll order a champagne cocktail for you, and I'll have a vodka tonic. We'll have water with dinner, unless you prefer a soda."

"I approve your plan, sir," I said cheerfully. "Thank you, Louis."

The room became smoke-filled as more couples crowded into the restaurant. It occurred to me that Louis was not a smoker, which pleased me. Bradley didn't smoke either— *Stop!* No thoughts of Bradley.

When the menus came, I immediately noted that mine did not have the prices listed. I didn't know Louis's financial situation, so I thought I'd play it safe and order a chicken entrée. Our drinks had arrived, and I'd already had a third of my champagne cocktail. Giggles tried to force themselves out of my mouth, but I kept them in, fearing an all-out gigglefest. I grooved a little in my seat when the band broke into "Love Me Do."

Louis looked at me over his menu. "Like the Beatles, do you?"

I grinned. "I looooove the Beatles, especially John. Which reminds me: Your hair is fab, long that way."

"I have to keep up with current styles as part of my reputation as a model. I'd much prefer to wear it short. What do you say we order the beef Wellington for two?"

"That sounds delicious!" Apparently Louis was willing to spend his money on a girl, which was swell. He avoided saying anything about the Beatles, though. If he didn't like them, that would be the end of it. I couldn't bear to be with someone who would frown at me for listening to my favorite band.

I took another sip of champagne. "Louis, tell me

more about Scott Roberts, the photographer you said did a good job on your portfolio."

Louis drank some of his vodka tonic. "Not much to say. At the time his rates were low and he did a great job. Scott's reputation grew after he claimed he was Suzie Wexford's first photographer."

"Oh, was he?"

"Apparently so. The story he told me was that Suzie sent him her senior high school picture, along with a few candid shots. He was so impressed, he encouraged her to come to New York from Oklahoma—"

"Omaha," I corrected.

He peered at me, then shrugged. "I try to retain only important information. Scott got Suzie right off the bus, and took her to his studio apartment. She, uh, stayed with him for a while, until she caught the attention of Pierre. Just like a woman, Suzie dumped poor Scott for a bigger name, but I think he has some early photos of her. Er, many female models pose for pictures they later regret."

The waiter arrived and Louis took care of everything, stopping only to ask if well-done was okay for our beef. I would have preferred medium, but my mind was on other things, so I nodded absently.

First, I hadn't liked Louis saying, "just like a woman." And was he putting me down when he said, "I try to retain only important information"? I told myself that I had gotten something out of him: that Scott Roberts might have naughty pictures of Suzie. Was Roberts blackmailing her? Did Suzie refuse to pay? When was the last time Roberts had seen Suzie? Was it a volatile relationship? Could he have killed her?

"Where's his studio now, Louis?"

His green eyes met my brown ones. He said, "Scott's moved since I saw him last."

At that moment the phone at our table rang, startling me. Louis picked up the receiver. I tried to signal him that I didn't want to dance with anyone, but then

I heard him say, "Yes, Mr. Williams. I'm sure she'll be happy to. We didn't see you when we arrived. Yes, I'd be happy to dance with Miss Miller. Okay."

No! No! Bradley couldn't be here with Evelyn Miller. It would be too much of a coincidence. I tried to keep my composure, but mentally, my mouth hung open and my eyes popped out of my head.

"I accepted for you because he's your boss," Louis said, downing the rest of his vodka tonic. "And he could get work for me. I'll put the phone on hold now, so we won't be disturbed again."

"It's all right," I replied, a sneaking suspicion coming into my mind. I removed the cape I still wore, causing Louis's gaze to drop to my chest.

Bradley and Evelyn walked up to our table. Louis stood, and the two men shook hands. Bradley wore another somber suit, dark gray with a dreary tie. His "mourning for Suzie" look. As usual, my heart jumped when I saw him. Without question, he was the most handsome man in the room. Not that I'd looked at every man, but I didn't have to.

Evelyn Miller's blond hair was in a short bob, one side tucked under, a low side part sweeping the rest over, ending in a flip. She had on a shimmering, cream floral brocade cocktail dress with gold and pale green flowers. Cut low, the front of the dress was finished off by a matching cream brocade bow, trimmed with sequins, directly under her ample bust.

She held on to Bradley's arm, bringing out the green-eyed monster in me.

Introductions were made, and Evelyn shook my hand, saying, "So you're Bradley's secretary. I didn't realize he was helping the area high schools."

Bradley coughed.

I made myself laugh. "Oh, my, what a sense of humor you have, Evelyn. Why, I'll bet you know all the latest bon mots."

She narrowed her eyes at me.

The band tuned up, and Bradley held out his arm. "Shall we dance, Miss Bennett?"

"That was the purpose of your call, wasn't it, Mr. Williams?"

"It was indeed."

Louis led Evelyn away.

Bradley smiled at me, making me dizzy. He pulled my arm through his and walked with me to the dance floor. When we turned to each other, he looked me up and down and said, "Your dress is very flattering. That shade of blue is my favorite color."

"Thank you." I would not melt, I would not faint, I would not tell him my favorite shade of blue was the color of his eyes; I would stand my ground.

The band played the opening notes of Peter and Gordon's new song, "A World Without Love," a slow number. Bradley held me closer than was proper. I loved every second, but blinked a few times to overcome the hazy cloud that threatened to turn me into a gooey marshmallow at a campfire.

Gathering my strength, I started the attack. "What a coincidence that you're here tonight, Mr. Williams."

"Are you wearing My Sin?"

"Yes, I am. How predictable that you should be familiar with women's perfumes. Danielle, the girl from the typing pool, told you I would be here tonight with Louis, didn't she?"

Bradley raised his eyebrows. "You're a good guesser, but I can't applaud your taste in fragrances. My Sin is for a more . . . er, worldly sort of woman."

"What makes you think I'm not worldly? And, in my opinion, you were overbearing, drilling that poor girl from the typing pool. She was frightened—" *Oops.* I hadn't meant to say that.

Bradley chuckled. "Yes, she was. I'm a monster, you know. Killing young girls. You shouldn't be dancing with me, but you see, that only goes to show how unworldly you are."

I looked up into his blue eyes, and the haunted look I saw there almost made me back down. Almost. Darn if I was going to show him how I felt. "On the contrary. You followed me here. You phoned my table.

How could I refuse a request from my boss? That would have been foolish. I have my job to consider."

A muscle worked in his jaw. "What's foolish is you here with that preening model Louis."

Was he jealous? Was he?

I feigned surprise. "Surely you aren't going to tell me that it's against office policy for employees to date models."

"That wasn't fair," Bradley said. "Besides, I am the head of the company, not an employee."

"A fine distinction, don't you think, Mr. Williams? So you followed me here to keep an eye on me and my date?"

He dodged the question. "That lipstick you're wearing is not your style, Miss Bennett. It's too . . . too *disturbing* for someone your age."

I felt my temper rise. "I am a *woman,* Mr. Williams. What is *supposed* to be my style? Ankle socks with lace trim and patent-leather shoes? Little white dresses with smocking and rosebuds—"

"You've made your point," he said through gritted teeth.

Was it my imagination, or had he pulled me closer, just short of up against his chest? Something was making it difficult to breathe.

"You still haven't explained why you followed me here," I said, moving my left hand from his shoulder to the back of his neck. I guess I kind of stroked him.

Without warning, he put a bit of distance between us. A sheen of perspiration appeared on his forehead. Got to him, didn't I?

"I don't understand it myself, kid. I guess I feel a need to protect you."

"That's funny," I said, softening my voice and looking up at him, happy I had applied an extra set of false eyelashes. "I have that same feeling about you. Now that you understand what it's like, perhaps you'll tell me what Mr. Pickering's investigator has uncovered."

"I don't think Pickering has hired a PI yet. Uncle

Herman has given me ten days—" He broke off. "I shouldn't have said that."

"Your uncle is going to make you leave the company in ten days if we don't find out who killed Suzie? And Pickering hasn't hired a PI yet?"

"Lower your voice, Miss Bennett; we don't want people here thinking I'm strangling *you*."

I complied, but held back from revealing what I'd learned in my own investigation so far. "I didn't know your uncle could be so cruel. You must tell your lawyer to get busy. What's he waiting for anyway? Money? A sign from above? A message on his bathroom mirror written in shaving cream?"

Bradley laughed. "We're not going to discuss this, Miss Bennett, remember? And speaking of shaving cream, I think your date wants you back."

The music had ended without my noticing. I could have screamed, so great was my frustration at being shut out of the formal investigation . . . and Bradley's arms.

Before I turned to Louis, I whispered furiously at Bradley, "Just make sure Pickering does his job and gets you cleared, or else I'll—"

The angry look that flared on Bradley's face stopped me.

He grabbed me by the arm and leaned close to my right ear, growling, "Or else you'll *do nothing*. Am I understood? And don't ever wear that damn perfume again."

Mentally I vowed to buy the biggest bottle of My Sin I could afford. "Bully," I hissed at him, and pulled myself away. "Louis, I'm hungry. I hope our dinner is ready."

Transferring Evelyn back to Bradley, Louis said, "If it's not, would you like another glass of champagne, Bebe?"

In a voice I knew would carry, I said, "I'd adore one! Oh, and I have something I want you to do for me, if you're willing."

"I am at your service," he said.

It took every ounce of restraint I had not to turn around and see what effect these words had on Bradley. As it was, I struggled to regain my composure, and vowed not to look at him for the rest of the night, a vow I kept. Unfortunately, that didn't prevent the place on my arm where Bradley had grabbed me from tingling all evening.

Dinner proved to be delicious. The beef was too well-done for my taste, but I didn't mind. Louis was not pleased with a spot he found on his fork, which he promptly sent back to the kitchen, or our cherries jubilee, which he didn't think flamed long enough.

I found myself nervous around him. He just wasn't the sort a girl could feel comfortable being with. I told myself the uneasiness stemmed from the fact that I hardly knew him. On the cab ride home, while the radio played Dionne Warwick's "Walk on By," I thought of how Louis hadn't liked the towels or the soap at Ryan. He made me feel like I should check my makeup or look down at my dress to be sure I hadn't spilled anything.

Even so, he had been truly delighted when I offered him the B. Altman's shoot. His size even matched that of the model we were to use before he called in "sick." Louis thanked me profusely.

When we reached my building, he said, "I'd like to take you out again, Bebe. Would you say yes if I asked?"

Again I felt nervous. How could I rudely say no? "Sure, Louis, and we'll see each other tomorrow at the shoot. Thank you for the lovely dinner."

Just when I was about to go up the steps, Louis leaned down and brushed a light kiss across my lips. I didn't have time to react, because he didn't want to keep the cab waiting. He entered it and the cab took off, the breeze moving my layered chiffon skirt.

I stood there, my fingers to my lips. I felt absolutely nothing from his kiss. *Uh-oh.*

From across the street Harry the wino yelled, "Is he the one you're in love with?"

I looked around to make sure no one was in ear-shot. Then I yelled back, "No. Do you need money?"

Harry shook his gray head. I thought I heard him say, "You women, break a fella's heart every time." But he'd been stumbling down to the corner, so I couldn't be sure.

Upstairs, I opened the door to my apartment and found Darlene on the pink sectional, crying. Nearby, a canvas showing a naked derriere in blue paint stood against the white brick wall.

I sighed and went to fetch the whiskey.

Chapter Fourteen

Darlene, clad in her purple lounging pajamas, was curled up on the sofa, arms hugging a lime-green pillow to her face. Her sobs were muffled.

I sat down next to her on the floor, my dress pooling around me. "Darlene, what's wrong?"

More sobs.

"Darlene, have some whiskey."

Sniffles. A sneeze.

"Come on now, talk to me. What happened? Did you go out with Cole tonight?"

She brought out a tissue she'd been clutching in her right hand, moved her hair out of her eyes, and blew her nose.

"Here, swallow a bit of this whiskey, for medicinal purposes," I said in a nurselike voice.

She managed a tiny smile and followed my instructions. "Bebe, I'm in a terrible mess."

"I'm here for you," I said, unstrapping my silver sandals and kicking them away. "Where did the, um, painting come from?"

"I took Cole down to the Village. There's a supergroovy place there called Patty's. You know they do bottom paintings because there's a discreet black-and-white-sign with a lady's legs and—"

"Okay, I get it. So you went, and that canvas propped up over there is your . . . behind."

"Uh-huh. I thought it was fun!"

"Let me guess: Cole didn't." I tried not to imagine

what Cole's painting would look like, but thank the
Lord, he wouldn't have done one.

"Yeah, and we got into a fight. Well, it really wasn't
a fight; more like he gave me a stern talk. He practically frog-marched me out of Patty's, once I'd gotten
my clothes back on. He acted like an overbearing father, telling me I would tarnish my reputation doing
things like that. He said I was a mature woman, not
a youngster like . . ." She flashed me a look.

"Like me. That's okay, Darlene. I know Cole
wouldn't cross the street to talk to me." The thought
occurred to me that one day, when I was much older,
I'd be grateful that people mistook me for being
younger. "What did you say to Cole?" I asked, wondering how often the oil man had called Darlene
lambkin.

"I figured he was probably right," Darlene mumbled.

Right! This was tricky. While I didn't approve of
this bottom painting, I didn't want Darlene's lively,
fun personality squashed. Especially by stuffy Cole.
"Do you think Cole will continue to act like a father
during your relationship?"

"Maybe not," she said slowly. "On the other hand,
maybe that's what I need to be happy."

"I don't think that's true at all," I said. "Darlene,
you need a guy whose personality complements
yours."

She just shook her red curls.

"We talked about this before, remember? Are you
really going to continue dating a guy who's more than
old enough to be your father, to let him *be* a father
figure for you?"

"I guess so," Darlene said. She sat up on the
sectional.

"But you were happy with Stu. The two of you had
all kinds of fun together. I thought you loved him,
and I know he loves you."

"Look where it got me! He cheated on me," she
cried.

"You don't know that for sure, Darlene, because you never would talk to him about it. All you're going on is gossip. Why don't you listen to Stu's side of the story?"

Darlene's eyes filled with tears. Her voice wobbled. "Honey, I can't. I can't talk to Stu about it now. I miss him, but in time I'll have to get over him."

"Why on earth can't you talk to Stu?" I asked. I got up off the floor and sat next to Darlene. I put my arm around her and squeezed.

"B-because of this," Darlene said and broke into fresh tears. She held out her left hand.

My jaw dropped. On the fourth finger of her left hand, Darlene wore a huge round diamond solitaire.

"Oh, my God," I muttered, as she wept. "Darlene, get ahold of yourself. Drink the rest of this whiskey, and tell me this isn't an engagement ring."

She used the tissue again, then took the glass and flung her head back, polishing off the whiskey. She looked away before speaking, as if she were remembering the evening. "Cole took me out to dinner first, a beautiful, romantic place, Valerie's, that served French cuisine. After we ate, he told me how much he loved me, how he wanted me to be his companion in life more than anything in the world. He said that I was special, and more beautiful than a perfect diamond. Then he slid a black velvet box across the table to me, and got down on one knee."

"Oh, my, Darlene," I said, mentally wondering how the bowlegged old coot got back up.

She continued the story, her attention on me. "When Cole asked me to marry him, I felt like a princess. The one thing that ran through my mind was that he represented security and a place in Texas society."

Darlene was going to leave New York City, the place she loved? What evil spell had Cole cast over her?

Darlene took up her story. "When I have to retire from Skyway in a few years, I won't have to work.

Cole wouldn't cheat on me. I don't really want children," she added, then paused, as if she were considering that last statement. "Anyway, I said yes, and the people in the restaurant cheered when Cole kissed me."

"Gosh," I said. "But now you've had second thoughts, right? Isn't that why you're crying your eyes out?"

"All I can think of is Stu," she confided. "If only I knew he hadn't cheated on me . . . but it's too late now."

I thought fast. "What are you doing tomorrow?"

"Cole's taking me shopping for new clothes. He wants to honeymoon in Paris, and he thinks I need some different outfits to wear, more conservative pieces."

"What honeymoon? You have to plan a wedding first."

Darlene looked down at the turquoise fur rug. "Cole said that since Mama doesn't talk to me, and all his family are gone except for a sister in Oregon he hasn't seen in years, we might as well just get married at City Hall."

"City Hall! Darlene Roland!" I exclaimed, standing up, my hands on my hips. "You will *not* exchange wedding vows in some poky hole-in-the wall wedding at City Hall! Haven't you dreamed about being married in a beautiful white—or, um, ivory—dress in a church filled with flowers, with bridesmaids, all your friends, a wedding cake, and champagne toasts? What about all that?"

"Girlish dreams, nothing more."

Darlene got up and made her way into the kitchen. She reached for the whiskey bottle, but I said, "How about some ice cream?"

"Sounds good," she said, then slumped at the tiny table, looking all of twelve years old. Without makeup, her freckles stood out across her nose.

I scooped generous amounts of chocolate ice cream into two green bowls, got out the spoons and napkins,

and sat across from her. All the while, my head spun.
I didn't believe for one second that Darlene thought a
nice wedding with all the trimmings was just a "girlish
dream." But that was not the critical point. First I had
to pour more doubts into her head about this crazy
idea of marrying Cole. Ever since she'd met him, he'd
tried to change her, mold her into something she
wasn't. Darlene needed to be who she was.

I passed her her bowl, spoon, and napkin, and said,
"So you'll be busy on Tuesday. Then on Wednesday
you're working the flight to the Virgin Islands. Maybe
in the tropical setting, you'll be able to think over this
engagement."

She took a tiny bite of chocolate, then dropped the
spoon into the bowl. "Cole bought a ticket for the
flight. He said that way we could consider our honeymoon in two parts: one in the hot sunshine and beach,
and the other in the cool spring of Paris."

"With the City Hall stop-off somewhere in between," I said sarcastically.

Darlene rose. "Listen, I can't talk about this anymore. I need to lie down. Would you come in my
room and talk to me? I want to know how your investigation is going, not to mention your date."

An idea came to mind. Darlene would hate me,
maybe even smack me or tear my hair out, but one
day she'd be on her knees thanking me.

"All right, let me get out of this dress, and I'll be
right in. You're not going to fall asleep on me, are
you?"

"Honey, don't be silly. It's only ten thirty. I'm not
at death's door." She moved into her room, and I
went into mine.

I shut the door, peeled off my dress, girdle, and
stockings, and flung on my pink chenille robe, the one
decorated with big coffee cups. Looking widly around
my room, I spotted the purse I'd taken to work that
day on the Banana chair. I grabbed it, opened it wide,
and retrieved my trusty little notebook. Flipping
through the pages, I found what I needed. I made a

quick trip to the kitchen, noisily putting the dishes away, then strolled into Darlene's bedroom.

She reclined on her bed, a box spring and mattress on the floor. Red chiffon material formed a tent that gathered at the top over the bed. On a narrow, rickety table sat a phonograph and a collection of albums. Darlene had Patsy Cline playing. I closed my eyes, thinking of how we'd lost dear Patsy just last year in that awful plane crash. Her magical voice sang the words to "Why Can't He Be You." I was sure Darlene had thoughts of Stu on her mind, just as I couldn't get Bradley off my brain. From the attention of the young actor at Pierre's gala showing and my date with Louis, I felt my confidence growing.

Darlene scooted to the far edge of the bed. "Come on, honey, tell me about your date."

I lay down next to her. We both stared at the top of the red, see-through chiffon. "I will, but don't think I've finished talking to you about Cole. You're just getting a break."

"You're the best, Bebe."

I poked her left arm. "Bradley was there."

She gasped, rolled to her side, and propped herself up on her left elbow. "On your date? How in blue blazes did he manage that?"

I rolled on my side to face her. "He got the information out of this sweet girl from the typing pool who took over for me at lunch. Can you believe it? Then he showed up at the Phone Booth with a model he'd had *me* help him contact."

Darlene shook her head and smiled. "I'm telling you, Bradley considers you *his*; otherwise he never would have followed you like that! I've been in the Phone Booth. Did he come up to your table, or—no, don't tell me—he called you for a dance."

"All right, I won't tell you, but that's what he did," I said, and grinned.

Darlene and I fell to giggling.

"Get this," I said, "he recognized the My Sin perfume and told me never to wear it again!"

Darlene burst into laughter. "Lord have mercy! That man is trying so hard not to act on his feelings."

"I don't know about that, but he also told me never to wear that hot-pink lipstick again." I snickered.

"You can have my tube. It doesn't look right on me. As for the My Sin—"

"I'm buying a big bottle."

We laughed, and I felt a surge of happiness that Darlene thought Bradley considered me his.

Then Patsy started singing "Crazy" and the smile faded from Darlene's face.

"Do you want to know about my date with Louis?" I asked, hoping to keep her mind off the "engagement."

"Yeah, how was he?"

I looked down at the red bedspread. "He's handsome, polite, paid for a very nice dinner—"

"If that's all you have to say about him, he was dull."

"He kissed me, kinda, and asked me out again."

"How was the kiss?"

"It was a first date; I couldn't expect much."

"Dull. Did he dance with you?"

"Gee, no. I hadn't even thought of that, but he didn't. I danced with Bradley; then Louis and I had our meal. I'll go out with Louis again if he asks. I hardly know him, though he seems hard on himself and others. I gave him a modeling assignment, which he appreciated."

"I'll bet he did. Bebe, I think you do know him, but go ahead and give him another chance."

"I'll be seeing him tomorrow on a photo shoot for B. Altman's. What's better is that Bradley will be there—"

The sound of the intercom buzzer cut me off. I said, "Here, Darlene, hand me your engagement ring."

With her brows together, she did as I asked, then said, "Why do you want the ring? The buzzer for downstairs went off. Didn't you hear it? Someone's here to see one of us."

"I'll give you back the ring." Now I was shaking. Should I really be meddling in Darlene's life like this? Was I turning into Debbie Ann, well-meaning but intrusive?

This time didn't count. I sprang out of the bed, scrambled to the intercom, and buzzed for Stu to come up. I knew it was him, because I'd called him and told him to come over. I couldn't let Darlene marry Cole without her hearing Stu's side of the story.

Darlene was right behind me. "Who is it, Bebe?"

I held up my hands as though I were being arrested, and put the pink sectional between us. "Now, Darlene, don't get mad. This is for your own good."

Her eyes popped. "Tell me you didn't call Stu."

I stood mute.

"Tell me!"

She tried to come to my side of the sectional, a look of fury in her eyes, but I dodged her.

"I'm going to kill you, Elizabeth Bennett," she hissed at me.

A knock sounded on the door.

Darlene ran into the kitchen, came back into the living room with a pen in her hand, and scrawled *Bebe* on the bottom painting.

"Darlene! You can't do that!" I cried.

"That's just the beginning of what I'm going to do to you for calling Stu," she promised.

I finally made it to the door and flung it open. Stu, dressed in a midnight-blue evening suit, his dark hair styled like a movie star's, strolled into the room.

He looked at Darlene with concern blazing in his brown eyes. "Darlene, are you all right? Bebe called me and said you were sick. That I should come right over."

She shot me a look that might have felled the Empire State Building. Then she gazed at Stu for a long moment, her arms crossed over her chest.

No one spoke.

Finally I said, "Stu, I love Darlene, and I'm very fond of you. I wanted the two of you to talk, but if you don't want to, maybe you could just watch TV together. Oh, look at the time, all the stations are off the air. I guess you'll *have* to talk."

Stu said, "Hey, if I'm not wanted here—"

Darlene interrupted. "Bebe, will you excuse Stu and me?"

"Yes," I said, and dashed to my room. I closed the door behind me, then mentally kicked myself for doing so. I wasn't going to hear them well with the door tightly shut.

That didn't stop me from sitting on the floor, my right ear pressed to the wood.

Darlene started the attack. "You spent the weekend with that stewardess Peggy in Paris. Why did you come here?"

"Bebe said you were ill, that's why. And if you would only listen and *trust* me, I can explain why the rumor of my so-called infidelity got started."

"Start talkin', buster," Darlene instructed. I could picture her, arms crossed, glaring at Stu.

I could still hear Stu's voice, but not enough to make out what he was saying. I remembered him telling me when I saw him at the World's Fair how Peggy, a chief stewardess, had made up the story of a fling with him, wanting to make Darlene jealous. I figured he was explaining this to Darlene.

She stayed quiet while he spoke, thank heavens.

When it was her turn to talk, she spoke too softly for me to hear, much to my frustration.

At least they were talking, I thought. I hoped Darlene wasn't dumb enough to tell Stu she was engaged to Cole.

Suddenly Stu must have walked around the sectional, closer to my door. I heard him say, "Okay, doll, if you want to think about it, that's fine by me. I'm damn glad we talked. When you get back from your trip to the Virgin Islands, give me a call. You know I'll be waiting for you."

Another little spell of silence; then I heard the

apartment door open and close. I crawled over to my albums, pretending to look through them.

Darlene knocked on the door, and I said, "Come in unless you're going to kill me."

She opened the door and stuck her head around it. "I don't like your tactics, Bennett."

"It was for your own good, Roland."

We smiled at each another.

"Well, do you believe Stu now?" I asked.

"I told him I'd think it over," she replied. "Toss me that rock of a ring. I'll need it tomorrow."

I complied and Darlene caught it in one try. I said, "Did Stu kiss you?"

She licked her lips, then shook her finger at me. "No more information for you, Miss Nosy."

"Stu did kiss you, or you wouldn't have licked your lips."

Darlene came around the door. "We never talked about the murder investigation."

I shrugged. "It's really late. I need to get to bed. But I will say there are three, maybe four suspects on my list right now: Pierre, Gloria, Lola, and a photographer named Scott Roberts. Plus, Bradley's uncle is going to kick him out of the company if the killer isn't caught within ten days."

"That's nice of him. What can I do?" Darlene said, yawning.

"Nothing tomorrow. Come to Suzie's memorial on Wednesday and help me check people out. When we get to the Virgin Islands, hopefully we can nail the killer."

"So you're sure the police won't let Bradley leave town by Wednesday afternoon?"

"I'm sure, but I'd love to be surprised."

"And you think he'll let you go in his place?"

"He'd better."

Darlene yawned again. "Whew, crying takes a lot out of a body. I'm going to bed." She turned to leave the room, then peeked back at me. "Stu said he knew the bottom painting was of me. I wonder how we could get Bradley to see it and get his opinion."

She closed the door before I could fling a slipper at her.

"Oh, and your daddy called," Darlene yelled. "You'd better call him back."

I put my head in my hands and groaned.

Chapter Fifteen

Tuesday morning at Ryan, I sat at my desk typing letters for Bradley. His door stood open, and when I'd brought him his coffee he hadn't said a word.

Before I'd gone to sleep last night, I'd called Daddy back, deliberately not reversing the charges so he'd have to be quick. I suspected why he wanted to talk to me, and I was correct.

"What in tarnation is going on up there, Bebe? I told you that Williams fella was nothing but a playboy. Now look what he's gone and done, murdered that cute girl. Tell me you're not working at that place anymore—"

"Daddy!" I interrupted. "Mr. Williams didn't kill Suzie Wexford. He hasn't been charged with her murder. It's only a misunderstanding."

"There won't be any misunderstanding when I come up there and carry you to the train! Your mama's been pale as a snowdrop, worried sick about you."

"I'm sorry. Give her my love," I said, and yawned.

"What are you doing awake so late? You haven't been out at night in that heathen city, have you?"

"Daddy, I had a date with a young man who's a model. He took me for a nice dinner."

"A male model? Don't you know all them are queer?"

I rolled my eyes. "Daddy, I need to get some sleep, okay?"

"All right, Little Magnolia. Next time reverse the

charges. And don't get mixed up with that Williams
character, you hear me?''

I hadn't made any promises.

I sipped my coffee. Eight models were upstairs getting into makeup and the clothes from B. Altman's.
Gloria had come in before I did, according to the
talent sign-up sheet on my desk.

There was no sign of Pierre, who was supposed to
be shooting the ad.

A few minutes before ten o'clock, the models
started straggling downstairs and lounging in chairs.
They were beautiful! The girls were decked out in
fashionably striped long culottes—in shades of pink,
white, pale blue, red, orange, and tan—with strawberry-
pink halter tops trimmed with large front bows. They
had on big, pink plastic earrings and plastic bangle
bracelets on their arms. Simple tan sandals were on
their feet.

Gloria had done a dramatic look with their makeup,
and the girls' hair had been teased high. B. Altman's
promotional material had said the outfit was smart for
home entertaining or seaside sunning.

The men wore tan slacks with striped shirts that
matched the girls' culottes, along with strawberry-
pink ties.

Gloria came up to my desk carrying a big white
makeup case. She set the case down and said, ''Boy,
that was one hell of a job getting everyone done, but
the money will be rockin'.''

''You did a fantastic job on the models, Gloria. I
feel out of place in this sleeveless purple sheath.''

Gloria snorted. She leaned closer. ''The models are
jumpy because of your boss. They all think he killed
Suzie. Even Gina wouldn't come down here where
'the murderer' is.''

''That's ridiculous, Gloria. We know Bradley didn't
kill Suzie. The question is, who did?'' As soon as the
words were out of my mouth, I noticed that Gloria's
expression changed.

"My mind is gone right now," she said, checking her nails for chips in her red polish.

Gloria wasn't her usual friendly self toward me. I tried for some conversation. "I had a date last night with Louis Kinnaird."

Gloria rolled her eyes. "He is prime, but a perfectionist. Very picky with his makeup, and, if I'm right, he's still upstairs trying to get his tie flawless."

I sighed. "You know, I got that impression, but figured I needed to get to know him better. He took me to the Phone Booth for dinner."

Gloria's brown eyes grew wide. "Choice place. Do you think Louis could change your mind about Bradley being the love of your life?"

The question surprised me. The truth was worse: I didn't think there was *any* man who could take Bradley's place in my heart. "Like you told me at Pierre's showing, I should be dating and having fun."

She looked at me for a long, unsettling moment. Then she nodded. "As long as you're just having fun with Louis, I can give you the gossip on him, if you want it."

"Tell me."

Gloria looked at Bradley's door to make sure he hadn't left his office. "Louis used to work for Models, Inc.—you know, the agency that is Ryan's biggest competitor, with Ford being over both?"

"Yes, I've heard about them. Didn't they try to steal Suzie away from Ryan at one point?"

"Yeah, but Ryan offered her better assignments, and there were some other factors. Anyway, Louis is very ambitious. Though Models gave him lots of assignments, it was never good enough for him. He jumped ship and came here for the Burma-Shave gig, but"—here Gloria paused dramatically—"that's not what he's really after."

"I know he told Bradley he was hoping Burma-Shave would be so pleased with his print campaign that they'd use him for a TV spot."

Gloria nodded. "That's not surprising. But what he really wants is to be the 'Us Tareyton smokers would rather fight than switch!' guy, and Ryan holds the account. Louis wants to have his face in magazines across the country, on billboards, become a recognizable face to America. A star."

"But we already have a very popular guy doing those. I know, because when we went over accounts one day, Bradley told me the Tareyton people were extremely pleased."

Gloria shook her head. "You've still got a lot to learn about this business. Think of it: Louis comes in here, gets in Dutch with Bradley . . . and you. You've already given him an assignment. Maybe it takes a while, but soon Bradley and Louis are hangin' together, and the next thing you know, boom! Louis is getting the prime assignments and gets in with the Tareyton people, convincing them their guy is looking stale."

"That's quite a plan."

"Ruthless models do it all the time, Bebe. Remember Suzie? I know you must," Gloria said, staring at me in a peculiar manner before moving to the models. Her look indicated suspicion. But of what?

I thought about what she had said about Louis. If true, Louis was *using* me. I decided to reserve judgment.

Right then, Louis himself came out of the elevator and walked straight to my desk. "Good morning, Bebe. You look lovely."

"Thank you, Louis. Are you all ready to go?" A movement out of the corner of my eye alerted me to Bradley, coming out of his office, his eyes on Louis and me.

Louis answered. "Bebe, you made me happy giving me this assignment." He bent down and whispered, "And your lips taste sweet."

I know I went red.

"Good morning, everyone," Bradley said, standing right behind Louis.

Louis turned and faced him. "Good morning, Mr. Williams. We're ready for a great photo shoot."

Bradley glanced at me, ignoring Louis, his gaze going over the other models. To my dismay, some of them looked at him with barely concealed disgust, though they all returned his greeting.

Bradley turned to me. "Miss Bennett, where is Gina?"

"She called me earlier and said she wasn't feeling well enough to attend the shoot. I called Danielle from the typing pool. She's going to cover for me so I can come and help out."

Bradley raised an eyebrow at me. The eyebrow said that he hadn't given permission for me to go. I stared back at him with a bland expression.

Danielle stood at the edge of the reception area.

"Where is Pierre?" Bradley asked.

From across the room, Gloria said, "I talked to him on the phone this morning. He'll meet us on location."

"Well, then, what are we waiting for? Miss Bennett, since you're coming along, I'll put you in charge of getting cabs."

"Yes, Mr. Williams," I said, smiling sweetly. I grabbed my bag and the B. Altman's order and nodded at Danielle.

I swept past everyone and entered the elevator, my finger on the stop button. For a second no one moved, afraid to get into the elevator with the murderer. Then Gloria got in, followed by Bradley and Louis.

The doors closed and Gloria said, "Bebe, is that My Sin you're wearing?"

Bradley turned his head an inch and glowered at me.

Louis looked at me and winked. "So that's what it was."

I put my chin in the air. "Yes, My Sin is my favorite perfume. I just discovered it, and I won't wear any other scent." I kept my gaze straight ahead until we reached the lobby.

In the lead, I marched across the concrete in front

of the building, down the steps, and to the corner. I flung my hand in the air. I repeated this until everyone, including me, was on the way to Lincoln Center.

The Lincoln Center fountain had opened only recently, and this was my first visit. In the center of a large place, there was a large, sparkling pool from which many sprays of water shot upward. A slight breeze fluttered our way, bringing a mist to my face. I turned toward the sun and smiled, happy to be outside in the city of my dreams on this keen day.

The models gathered to one side, laughing, giggling, and hamming it up.

Gloria stepped over to them, ready for touchups.

One person was missing: Pierre.

Bradley, wearing a cool pair of dark shades, walked over to where I stood admiring the fountain. "Where's Pierre?"

"Um, I'll ask Gloria and see if she knows any more," I replied, and dashed away.

"Gloria, where is Pierre?" I asked. "I thought you said you talked to him."

"He's always late. Lay off him, would you? He likes to make an entrance." She powdered a male model's nose.

Sure enough, about ten minutes later Pierre arrived in a huge black Cadillac. Daddy once told me Cadillacs cost around six thousand dollars!

Pierre emerged from the long car dressed in his usual black, complete with beret. A male assistant carried a huge silver-and-black transistor radio with an antenna. Pierre gingerly lugged a big, sturdy bag that I assumed held his cameras and accessories.

All at once two things happened: The female models ran to flock around Pierre, and he spotted Bradley. Blowing kisses to the models, Pierre left them and stormed over to my boss.

"What are you doing here?" he demanded in his French accent.

Bradley said, "Are you addressing me, Pierre? I'm head of Ryan Modeling."

"Good morning, Pierre, it's me, Bebe Bennett," I tried. He nodded at me but his focus was on Bradley.

Pierre's face became as purple as my dress. "I will not work while Suzie's murderer stands free instead of in jail where he belongs!"

Bradley sighed. "You'll do this photo shoot unless you want to be held in breach of contract."

"Not while you are here!" Pierre yelled, his voice carrying over the noise of the street traffic, over the sound of the fountain, making the models huddle together. They had a stake in this, after all.

Bradley remained unruffled. "I don't have all day. Let's get busy."

"I tell you, I will not!"

"Pierre," I said, and was gratified when he turned to me. "Did you hear that Jack Norton bowed out of the photo shoot just last night?"

His brows came together. He seemed to notice me for the first time since his arrival. "He's not here, Bebe?"

"No. He had the nerve to call the agency right at five and say he'd be partying on a barge off the Hamptons and expected to be too hungover to attend. Can you believe it?"

"I won't photograph him again," Pierre said, looking toward the models.

"Don't worry, though, Pierre; I found a replacement: Louis Kinnaird. He's so excited to be working with you," I said with enthusiasm.

Bradley muttered, "Your boyfriend."

I'd savor that comment later. I put my arm through Pierre's and guided him over to meet Louis. All the models fawned over Pierre, including Louis.

Pierre's ego seemed to be sufficiently stroked. "Bebe, you did well. I'm impressed with you," he said, rubbing my back.

I scooted out of reach and shouted, "Is everybody ready?"

A chorus of yesses sounded.

"Come on, Pierre; I want to watch you work," I

said, excitement in my voice. "That's a groovy radio. What station are we going to play, WABC?"

I made sure to block Pierre's view of Bradley while the photographer painstakingly adjusted one camera, then discarded it back in the bag for another.

It wasn't long before a series of upbeat pop tunes filled the air, and Pierre was shouting directions and encouragement to the models, who posed over and over again by the fountain.

"Swingin'!" Pierre shouted over "Can't Buy Me Love."

He dashed around taking shots from all angles, his assistant supplying him with fresh rolls of film.

"Gear! Tammy, give me that haughty tilt of your head."

After an hour it grew warm, and I thought it best that everyone have a cool drink.

"Mr. Williams, I don't know how much longer Pierre is going to keep shooting, but I thought I'd go out and get some Cokes for everyone."

Bradley's gaze was on the street.

I turned to see what he was looking at, and my mouth dropped open. Detective Finelli cruised slowly by in his Pontiac Tempest. He came to a stop and looked our way. I didn't know how Bradley felt, but goose pimples rose on my arms.

Then, just as slowly, the detective moved his car back into traffic.

Bradley acted as though nothing had happened. "Drinks . . . a good idea, Miss Bennett. But I think I'd be the better person to go. You seem to be able to charm men into doing what they don't want to do. Pierre, for example. I dare not continue the shoot without you here to keep him calm."

"Is that your way of saying thank-you for replacing a model at the last minute and stopping Pierre from leaving?" I asked, miffed that he hadn't thanked me, Though he hadn't really had a chance.

"I've always said that I consider you a valuable secretary, Miss Bennett. I did promote you."

Before I could reply, he headed toward the street.

A valuable secretary.

I'd show him exactly how valuable I was, and not just as his secretary, but as the woman who proved he hadn't killed Suzie Wexford!

Chapter Sixteen

About an hour after Bradley returned with a box filled
with cold cans of Canada Dry's Tahitian Treat, which
he asked me to hand out, Pierre told the models they
were fabulous, gear, beautiful, and he kissed every one
of them—and me!—on both cheeks, the French way.
He had the shots he needed and seemed in a rush
to leave.

After Pierre's display of temper, he did not interact
with Bradley again during the shoot. Just before he
left, he looked at Bradley and spat on the ground.

Bradley ignored him.

"Miss Bennett, can you organize everyone in cabs
back to the agency? I need to go and thank the people
in the center."

"Yes, Mr. Williams. I'll see you back at the office."

"Okay, kid," he said, leaving me standing there
watching the impressive back view of him.

I managed to get everyone, including myself, back
to Ryan. Outside the building, Gloria told me she had
another assignment and took off immediately. I
frowned. I had thought she and I might grab lunch,
but she vanished before I could make the suggestion.
I puzzled over her marked change in attitude toward
me.

Deciding to hit Marv's hot-dog stand and get a Tab,
I dashed down the crowded street to his corner and
stood in line. A quick glance at my watch told me it

was almost one o'clock, the height of the lunch rush for Marv.

I didn't mind the wait. I spent my time thinking about who had the strongest motive to kill Suzie. Lola? Pierre? Scott Roberts? Gloria? I hated to think it might be Gloria. She had been so angry at Suzie, though, an anger that had built over a period of time. At the World's Fair, she had threatened to kill Suzie. I wondered if Gloria had yet another motive. Much to my regret, I would have to study Gloria at the memorial tomorrow. The service would reveal a lot; I could feel it in my bones.

Finally it was my turn for a hot dog.

"Hi, Marv. You sure are busy. I'll have the usual hot dog but with a Tab. How's your wife? How are you?"

Marv didn't even look up. "Wife's miserable. I'm miserable. Instead of the doctor, I want to be the one who spanks the kid's bottom when he or she enters the world."

I laughed. "Marv, you know they don't let fathers in the delivery room. Soon you'll be showing off—"

A loud screech of tires at the curb directly behind us made me and everyone else in line turn our heads. A checkered cab stopped short of running into a crowd of people.

The cabbie screamed out his window, "Hot-dog man! Your wife's in labor! She won't go to the hospital without you. Get in the cab! Now! I don't want no woman delivering a baby in my cab!"

From the back window, a pretty, dark-haired lady, crying and looking frightened, called, "Marv," in a voice barely audible over the traffic.

Marv grabbed me. He took off his apron, put it over my head, spun me around, and tied it tight. All the while he yelled, "I'm coming, Betty! Hold on!"

"But . . . what . . ." I tried, sputtering.

Marv eased me behind the stand. "Bebe, just help me out for a while, please. Betty and I need the money bad. I'll call my cousin to come down and then you can go. Won't be but twenty minutes, tops!"

Me? Run the stand?

"Free hot dogs for life, Bebe!" Marv shouted as he got into the cab. The driver gunned it. Horns honked when the cab dived into the nearest lane.

I stood alone behind the hot-dog stand.

An older woman wearing a pillbox hat said, "Miss, I don't have all day. I want a hot dog with ketchup. No mustard. No relish. And certainly no onions. Do you understand me?"

"Yes, ma'am," I said, grabbing a hot-dog bun. I used the tongs to get the hot dog out of the steaming water, but the darn hot dogs were slippery. I finally got one in a bun, squirted ketchup on it, and handed it to the woman.

Then I had to take her money and give her change, which she carefully counted, making the people behind her more impatient.

I went on in an endless world of hot dogs: mustard that flew on my cheek, ketchup on my apron that made me look like a gunshot victim, and bits of relish and onion that covered my hands. Would the line never end? Where was Marv's cousin?

Finally I thought I had a break when a man in slacks and an unbuttoned pale orange shirt walked up to me. Marv's cousin? I smiled.

"Give me the money, cookie. Wouldn't want to add blood to those ketchup stains." He revealed a long, deadly knife hidden under his open shirt. One he could use on me, and then run away through the crowds. The smile died on my lips. I trembled.

Give him what he wants, one side of my brain screamed.

Then the other side took over.

Marv's money.

The baby.

I took a deep breath. "Okay, mister, it's underneath the hot dogs in a tray. I'll get it for you; please don't hurt me," I said, having no trouble acting afraid.

"Make it snappy," the crook said, looking from left to right.

I bent down to the extra mustard-filled plastic bottles, and picked one up. My heart raced in my chest. I thought it would explode at any moment.

The next few seconds blurred together.

"Hey, Scarlett O'Hara, what's taking so long?"

I jingled the cash box. "I'm getting it all together for you."

"You've got five seconds before— Aaaaaaahhh!" The crook yelled when I jumped up and squirted a stream of mustard right in his eyes.

"Help! Someone help!" I screamed.

People walked by, fear on their faces, steering clear.

I hated to run and let the crook get Marv's money, but I had to or this guy was going to stab me, kill me maybe. Even now, he was using his shirt to clear his eyes.

The knife came out. I saw the crazed look in the man's reddened eyes. *Run! Run!* I commanded myself.

But my feet were frozen to the ground, I was so terrified. It was like a dream when you want to run, but find you can't move.

I shut my eyes. "Dear Jesus, please forgive—"

The sounds of a scuffle made my eyes fly open.

Four men were holding the crook down on the pavement. Another man said he'd call the police and ran off to find a phone booth. A crowd gathered.

My breath came in strained gasps. I was going to live—I was alive! There were good people all around me. The others who had turned away had been too afraid, that was all.

Suddenly I went cold. The tall buildings around me started to sway.

"Bebe! Oh, dear God, Bebe!"

That husky voice . . . those strong arms coming around me, hugging me tight.

"Bebe, Bebe, are you all right?" Bradley asked in a panicked tone I'd never heard him use. He held my head against his chest with one hand. The other stroked my hair.

"Bradley," I mumbled, and threw my arms around him, never wanting to let go.

"Sshh, you're safe now, sweetheart," he whispered. "I've got you; go ahead and cry."

"I'm not gonna cry," I said, and sniffled. "I'll ruin my eye makeup."

I felt rather than heard his deep rumble of laughter.

"That's more like it," he said, continuing to stroke my hair. "You're going to be fine."

Sirens announced the arrival of the police.

Bradley eased me away from him, much to my regret. He said, "Let's deal with the police; then I want to know what in hell you were doing working a hot-dog stand."

That had the effect of throwing cold water on me. What had happened to *sweetheart?*

Uniformed officers swarmed the area. They secured the crook in the patrol car while an officer asked me if I was hurt.

"No, sir, this is ketchup on my apron. I'm okay."

"You sure?" the young cop asked. "You look pretty shaken up. I don't want you going into shock. How about a check at the hospital?"

"No, thank you. I'm rattled, but it'll pass."

Bradley said, "I know Miss Bennett, and I'll watch her for the rest of the day."

I felt better already!

The officers shooed away the crowd.

My officer took a statement from me, detailing what had happened. Out of the corner of my eye I noticed that Bradley, standing nearby, listened intently. The cop told me I would have to go down to the station house and sign the statement once it had been typed up. I agreed, and the officer turned his attention to Bradley.

"Sir, may I ask your name, and can you tell me about your involvement in this incident?"

Bradley hesitated. "My office is on this block. I

came out to get some lunch, and stopped when I saw what was happening. The other men here are the heroes. I just happened by and saw Miss Bennett after the fact."

"So you weren't a witness to the crime?"

"No," he said.

"All right, then. I suppose there's no need to involve you. Miss Bennett, you'll be notified when to present yourself at the precinct. The two of you are free to go."

The four men who saved me came over to shake hands. I hugged each one. I kept trying to thank them, told them they'd be in my prayers, but they said they'd done what anyone would do. Gradually they drifted away.

"Would you like a soda?" I asked Bradley.

"No," he responded in a terse voice.

Uh-oh. Using a bottle opener, I took the top off my Tab and drank, liking the soda as much as Coke. I took a napkin and daintily wiped my lips. Then I used more napkins to clean my hands. I removed my apron, folded it carefully, and tucked it away.

"All right, that's enough, Miss Bennett," Bradley said.

So we were back to last names. "I'm sorry, Mr. Williams; I seem to have gotten mustard all over the front of your suit. Do I have some on my face?"

He looked down, saw the huge yellow stain on his tailored suit coat, and took it off. "Yes, you do."

Outside in the bright sun, I could see he didn't have an undershirt on. I wanted to stare through his white shirt, but had to refrain. Bradley had a fierce look on his face. I knew I was in for it.

I took another napkin and wiped my face. "I think your suit coat is ruined. I don't know what men's suits cost, but you can take it out of my paycheck."

"My suit jacket is the least of my concerns right now. I—"

A man walked up to the stand.

Bradley barked, "Closed."

The man looked at me. "Hey, are you Bebe? I'm Mickey, Marv's cousin."

"I'm so glad to see you!" I had to explain everything that had happened all over again. To my surprise, Bradley remained.

Mickey listened, horrified by what I told him. "Thank God you're not hurt, Bebe." He came around to my side of the stand, leaned down, and said, "Marv has a permit for a gun. He's been robbed before. Here's the gun right here."

"Oh, please! Don't bring it out! My father has a collection, and I'm afraid of guns," I pleaded.

Mickey put the gun back and stood up. "Don't want to spook you. You and your boyfriend go on. I'll take care of this. Marv will be so grateful. Free hot dogs for life!"

"Marv already told me," I said absently, thinking Debbie Ann wouldn't approve.

"Let's go, Miss Bennett," Bradley said.

We walked back toward Ryan. I carried my Tab. "Mr. Williams, I'm really—"

"Don't talk to me yet," he ordered. "I'm not in control of myself at the moment."

I took a swallow of Tab instead of smiling. Bradley was out of control? Instantly I felt like doing a twirl in the middle of the sidewalk.

We climbed the steps to the area in front of the door to our building. Bradley took me lightly by the elbow and guided me to one side. I remembered standing in that spot with Jerry, the soldier who told the story of Bradley's heroism.

Bradley removed his black shades and looked me in the eye. "Miss Bennett, the responsible part of me says I should call your parents and tell them how much trouble you've gotten into since your arrival in New York."

I gasped, thinking of what Daddy had said on the phone. "Don't you dare!"

He held up a hand. There was a spot of ketchup on

it. "Since I'm no gallant gentleman, I won't. I've had a difficult time keeping a secretary—"

"We both know why that's so," I interrupted.

He peered at me with those gorgeous blue eyes. "I didn't think the gossips would keep their mouths shut, but then, I do have a reputation to maintain. However, after the last secretary, I figured I'd do better in Uncle Herman's eyes if I kept my . . . activities . . . out of the office. That's all I'll say about those days. But *you* . . ." He pointed his right index finger at me. "*You* are the most vexing, exasperating, provoking, nosy, maddening, walking magnet for trouble I've ever known!"

I raised my chin. Then I batted his finger away from my face. "Number one, you have ketchup on your right hand. Number two, I am a valuable secretary— your words. Number three, I'm smart and capable, and, unlike you, I care about people."

He blinked at that last part. Then he retrieved his handkerchief and wiped his hand. Once finished, he looked at me again, angrier than before, if that were possible.

"I do care about people, but that's not the topic now. You are the topic. You defended yourself against a knife-wielding criminal with a bottle of mustard, for the love of God!"

"It worked!"

"No, it did not work, Miss Bennett. From what I heard, the man had the knife out, ready to cut you, stab you, do whatever he wanted with you, and you stood there like a deer ready to be run over by a truck."

"How would you know about deer? You live in Manhattan."

He wiped his forehead with his handkerchief, leaving a thin line of ketchup. "I grew up in Oklahoma and Missouri. I know about deer. Don't try to change the subject. I want you to immediately, and I mean *immediately,* stop putting yourself in danger."

"By not helping people?"

"No! Yes!"

"I'm sorry; that's not in my nature. What happened today won't be repeated. Marv and his wife are at the hospital. Mickey will take over until Marv decides to return."

"Good, but there's more. Don't think it's escaped my notice that you are writing things in your notepad in a secretive manner."

Devil!

"Nor have I been in the dark about your going to Pierre's, getting chummy with Lola, whispering with Gloria, all people who could be suspects in Suzie's murder."

"Aha! You agree with me then that they're suspects."

Bradley lost it. "What did I tell you about not getting involved in Suzie Wexford's murder investigation? God, I should have known you couldn't keep out of it. You make me want to strangle you, Miss Bennett!"

Inside, I smiled, happy to have gotten him worked up. I *did* have some power over him, after all. Who knew where that could lead?

Unfortunately, I saw Bradley's gaze swing toward the street.

There, listening to us arguing, stood Detective Finelli, leaning against his car and taking notes.

Without a second's thought I ran over to him. "Mr. Williams didn't mean that last part. We were kidding around, that's all."

Detective Finelli ran a hand over his crew cut. "Thanks for the explanation, Miss Bennett. I can't tell you how relieved I am to hear it."

"You're making fun of me, Detective, and I don't like it. Nor do I like your following Mr. Williams around. He hasn't done anything wrong."

"Love is blind," he replied, looking at me sharply.

I whipped around to see if Bradley had heard that, but he'd vanished, thank heavens.

"My personal life is none of your business, Detective." I tried for a steely gaze.

Detective Finelli's expression remained neutral. "So, I'm correct. You *are* in love with Williams."

"You tricked me!"

"Doing my job, Miss Bennett. Although I think I've got the man who killed Suzie Wexford, I have to cover every base. You have quite a strong will. I wonder how jealous you were of the attention Williams showered on Miss Wexford."

Without giving me a chance to reply, he got into his car and drove away.

Chapter Seventeen

By the time I reached my desk, it was almost four o'clock, and I was beat. Bradley's door was closed, serving as a blockade to any further sparring.

Danielle's pretty face appeared much more relaxed today.

I said, "I can't thank you enough, Danielle, for helping me. Was everything okay while I was gone?"

"We had lots of calls from reporters again, Bebe. I'm beginning to recognize their voices," she said, and chuckled. "And I'm happy to cover for you. Mrs. Seeds says I'll get extra money in my next paycheck."

"You deserve it. Danielle, can I confide in you?"

"Sure, I can keep a secret."

"You know I'll be attending Suzie's memorial tomorrow, but there's more. A strong possibility exists that I'll have to go out of town tomorrow, and won't be back until Saturday. Would you be willing to cover for me again? You'd have to do a little more than answer the phone, I'm afraid. There's some typing to do on the Dictaphone, Debbie Ann's weekly grocery bill invoice—"

"Bebe, I could use the extra money, and I'm used to typing." She paused, then added, "I'm not afraid of Mr. Williams anymore."

I squeezed her hand. "I'm pleased to hear that. He *is* innocent of Suzie's murder. There are other people who wanted to see her dead."

Danielle looked around, then said, "Nobody liked

Suzie, even Debbie Ann, who preaches that we should all be good to one another. I don't know how the police are going to figure out who killed her."

"Debbie Ann didn't like Suzie?" I asked, puzzled.

"No, and Suzie hated her. She told Debbie Ann to her face that her style of cooking would make people fat."

"Gosh, I'll bet Debbie Ann didn't take that well."

Danielle shook her head. "Debbie Ann told Suzie that she was so skinny, if she stood sideways and stuck out her tongue, she'd look like a zipper. They frequently exchanged insults."

"I didn't know any of this."

Danielle nodded. "They were downright mean to each other. You know Debbie Ann wants to know everything about everybody and doesn't hesitate to make her views known, even to Pierre."

"Pierre?"

Danielle chuckled. "He's a hotshot, but when he comes to Ryan, Debbie Ann finds out from her assistant and watches whatever shoot Pierre is doing. I'm telling you, Bebe, no one is spared from Debbie Ann's eagle eye. When she signed in today and saw me sitting here, she asked if I had brought my lunch. I always do pack my lunch, but the phone kept ringing, and I didn't have a chance to go back to my desk and get my brown bag. Debbie Ann went and got it for me. She's really concerned about everybody's personal life and diet, but lots of times she'll bake cookies and send them around."

"That's sweet of her. She's scolded me about eating hot dogs," I said, flipping through legitimate phone messages to see if there was anything urgent.

Danielle laughed. "Never let Debbie Ann know you eat hot dogs. She has a whole speech on what they're made of, and it's gross."

After today, I doubted I could eat another one. Too bad, since I could get them free for life!

"What do you know about Gloria?"

Danielle shrugged. "I haven't been around her,

though I know who she is. . . . Oh, wait, I just remembered something. Gossip went around the typing pool about three months ago that Debbie Ann had given one of her lectures to Gloria about her weight. Gloria mouthed off to Debbie Ann, calling her a lonely old busybody with no life of her own. Word is Debbie Ann was hurt, maybe because it's kinda the truth. They're not friends."

"Interesting." Danielle and I switched places, and I thanked her again for helping me.

At a few minutes before five, Bradley's door remained closed. I knew I should stay late, but I thought it more important to go home and pack. I didn't see how on earth Bradley would be on that plane to the Virgin Islands tomorrow evening, unless he was keeping something to himself about Mr. Pickering. Maybe the lawyer would pull a rabbit out of a hat, the rabbit being Suzie's killer.

Wednesday morning, at precisely fifteen minutes before ten, I arrived at the Cathedral Church of St. John the Divine on Amsterdam Avenue. The day was overcast and windy. Dark clouds raced across the sky above the gothic exterior of the church.

Wearing my black suit, black gloves, and a black pillbox hat with netting over my face, I entered and found a seat near the back. That way I could see who was crying and who wasn't.

I overestimated my abilities. About eight hundred people had decided to attend Suzie's memorial service. More would be at the reception at the Legends Hotel. There, I told myself, I would have better luck at seeking people out.

To my surprise, four NYPD officers in dress uniform were positioned at the front, standing next to Detective Finelli.

Darlene was here somewhere with Cole.

Celebrities arrived at the last minute and were ushered to the roped-off section in the front pews. I had to hold back a gasp as Truman Capote, the author of *Breakfast at Tiffany's,* arrived.

Lola came in, followed by Edie Sedgwick—wearing a tiny black vinyl miniskirt—who made an entrance with Andy Warhol.

Bishop Donegan began the service promptly at eleven.

While he spoke of Suzie's humble beginnings, I noticed that Pierre had made good on his promise. The silver-framed photograph of Suzie had been placed on a high stand for everyone to see.

When the bishop finished speaking, Pierre took the microphone. "Ladies and gentlemen, friends of Suzie, I am at a loss for words to describe my grief over the cruel way my fiancée has been ripped from my side," he began dramatically. Pierre had every ear in the church.

Into the silence, a man yelled, "No!"

A general gasp came from the people assembled, including me. Gloria had told me that Suzie had turned down Pierre's proposal. Suzie had been out with Bradley the very next night. Someone was lying.

Pierre carried on. "The night before her brutal murder, Suzie had agreed to become my wife."

The photographer droned on about the couple's love. I couldn't believe what I was hearing. Whispers went around the church like the soft sound of a light breeze ruffling new leaves.

Pierre kept at it for thirty minutes, his words punctuated by bouts of sobs. Finally, overcome, he stumbled back to his seat.

A series of people took the microphone and briefly expressed their sentiments. One of them introduced himself as Scott Roberts. Suzie's first photographer was a slim man of medium height with very light blond hair.

"I suppose you could say that I'm the person responsible for Suzie's rise to stardom. She sent me candid shots—"

An older man in the first pew rose and shook his fist at Roberts. "Suzie would be alive today if you hadn't lured—"

He broke off when Bishop Donegan stepped to his side, speaking to him and guiding him gently back into his seat next to a gray-haired lady. The Wexfords.

Scott Roberts heaved a sigh, then surrendered the microphone to a husky man who promptly burst into noisy tears. Everyone waited.

"My name is Jeff Granford. I'm from Omaha. Suz and I were high school sweethearts, and she was engaged to *me*," he declared. In his early twenties, the ex–football quarterback still retained a muscular build and must have been over six feet tall.

He continued in a high voice that didn't match his beefed-up body. "We were homecoming king and queen. The two of us planned a wedding; then she sent those pictures to you, Mr. Roberts. You ruined our lives! I hate you and what you did to my Suz! I could punch your light out right here!" he yelled. "And wait until I get my hands on you, Bradley Williams!"

Police officers marched over and restrained Jeff Granford, taking him with them to the side of the church.

Bradley took the microphone. I held my breath, fearing a physical attack on him

Dressed in a sleek black suit, white shirt, and black tie, he did not introduce himself. "We at Ryan Modeling are in mourning for our star model. Miss Wexford was a consummate professional, a beauty and talent that come to light only once in a decade. We are grateful that she chose to shine her light through the assignments our agency easily obtained for her. To say that she will be missed would be an understatement. Thank you."

My gaze darted to the Wexfords for a reaction, but there was none, perhaps out of respect for the bishop.

Pierre, however, shouted, *"Menteur!"*

At that moment, the choir began singing "Amazing

Grace," drowning out any further outbursts. I didn't understand what Pierre had said, but I could feel the anger behind the word.

I slipped out of the church and whistled for a cab. I wanted to get to the Legends and make sure everything was in order before the crowd arrived.

Thank goodness I had arranged for a dozen of the hotel's security staff to be on hand.

Chapter Eighteen

I rushed into the Grand Ballroom of the Legends Hotel. The hotel had a long, glamorous history, including famous star guests. The brown-and-gold décor was up-to-the minute in fashion, the hotel having been renovated the previous year.

The large double doors to the elegant Grand Ballroom stood open, a mistake I corrected immediately.

"Bebe!" a female voice called from behind the long buffet table, which was covered in creaseless white linen.

"Maria!" I answered, and hugged her across the table. "How have you been?"

The last time I'd seen the dark-haired girl, she'd been in a lot of trouble with a bad boyfriend. When Bradley and I had been working at Rip-City Records, I'd arranged for Maria to have extra waitressing work at the Legends to help her out.

"I'm so happy I can see you in person and tell you how much you changed my life," Maria gushed.

"I hardly did anything," I said.

"I took your advice. I never saw that man I told you about again. The Legends likes my work so much, they give me plenty of hours. And I moved back in with my parents."

"How is that going?"

"Fine. They're wonderful people, Bebe. I was just man-crazy and wanted to get away. Now I see it's better for me to stay home a little longer." Her brown eyes lit from within. "I'm going to school in the fall."

"That's fantastic!" I exclaimed.

"I want to be a secretary, like you," Maria said. Then a sad look crossed her face. "I wanted to go to the best secretarial school, but they don't take people like me."

"What do you mean . . . ?" I started; then it dawned on me. Maria meant they didn't take Puerto Ricans. "That's shameful, Maria."

She smiled. "I'll show them by being the best student in my school."

"Good for you! How's the buffet coming along?" I asked, observing other waitresses bringing out food. Large crystal chandeliers throughout the ballroom threw prisms of light on the silver platters.

"This is quite a feast," Maria promised. "The chef has been a lunatic ordering his assistants around."

Together we walked down the line, passing cold antipasto platters, smoked-salmon rolls with cream cheese, imported cheeses with crackers, all manner of cut fruit, miniature crab cakes, shrimp cocktail, and even steak tartare—the latter I thought was icky. The next long table contained the desserts. Cheesecake, chocolate cake, apple pie, an assortment of fancy cookies, and even a selection of ice cream. Women in brown-and-gold uniforms lined up behind the tables, ready to serve the guests.

On the opposite side, behind a table holding a huge roast beef, a man in a chef's hat waited. Four free bars were next. I had suggested we serve only wine, but Bradley had scoffed at me. Another table contained soft drinks.

Small round tables with the hotel's signature L embroidered in gold on brown cloth were scattered throughout the room, holding ashtrays.

"This is decadent, Maria," I said, and laughed.

"Don't worry, Bebe; you could stand to put on a few pounds."

"Are you kidding? I'm drinking Tab now, watching my figure like a hawk— Oh, Maria, I see the security guards coming in that back door. I need to speak to them."

"Anything you need me to watch out for? I think you're more than a secretary," Maria said, giving me a knowing look.

I laughed. "Not really, but . . . I don't know if you remember my boss, Bradley Williams. He's tall and lean, with dirty-blond hair and—"

Maria held up a hand. "Who could forget a man who makes every woman's knees weak?"

We giggled.

"Is he yours yet?" Maria asked.

I stopped giggling. "No. I'm still working on it. Anyway, he's in trouble for something he didn't do. There may be people here who want to hurt him. If you could keep an eye on him—"

"Oh, keeping an eye on that one would be a pleasure."

"Thanks. See you later. Oh, can I leave my hat with you? Just slip it under the table, okay?"

"Sure."

I glanced at my watch. Shocked to see it was almost one, I turned in my tracks and scrambled across the ballroom. I threw open the doors and gasped.

"Miss Bennett, I wondered how long you would keep me locked out," Bradley said. Looking as sleek as an ice cube in a pitcher of dry martinis, he entered the room. "Any problems?"

"That's why I came early and kept the doors shut. I didn't want to allow people inside until I was satisfied the Legends had followed my instructions."

"Good work, kid," he said, then went directly to the bar.

Curious, I edged closer. Bradley gave the bartender instructions for a martini. I held back a smile. Was he a James Bond fan like me? If he told the bartender he wanted his martini shaken, not stirred . . . The bartender shook the stainless-steel pitcher. I giggled. Well, James Bond Bradley wasn't, no matter the drink, since he was leaving the darn murder investigation to Mr. Pickering! Though Bradley was much more handsome than James Bond.

I blew out a breath of air and strode over to the

security guards. I introduced myself, told them what I wanted, and discreetly pointed out Bradley. We had only a few seconds, as people began streaming inside.

I sprinted back across the room so that I could talk to Jeff Granford before he got drunk. I had a feeling everyone was going to be sloshed before long.

I saw Jeff and followed him to the bar, leaning up against it casually. "I'll take a whiskey, straight," Jeff told the bartender.

While waiting for the drink, he looked to his right, and then to his left, and bingo, there I was.

"Oh, is that you, Mr. Granford?" I asked innocently.

He gave me the once-over. "Yeah, it's me."

I gazed into his reddened eyes and said, "The way you talked about Suzie at the memorial positively made my eyes fill with tears." I had a more pronounced Southern accent when I was playing a role.

"Call me Jeff," he said, accepting his drink and downing half of it in one swallow.

His huge body made me feel like an elf beside him. And if he drank like that all the time, Scott Roberts had probably saved Suzie from a rough life. Jeff's face was more than rugged; he looked like a boxer. There was something about his nose. Maybe it had been broken.

"Thank you, Jeff. Suzie and I didn't know each other," I lied, fingers crossed behind my back, "but I thought she was a beautiful girl. Your heart must have been broken when she left Omaha."

Jeff finished his drink and flashed the empty glass at the bartender for a refill. He waited until he received it, took a gulp, and looked into the liquid, as if seeing something there other than whiskey. "I followed her to New York immediately. I've been here all along trying to convince her to come home with me, have a houseful of our babies. She said she would, that I just had to wait."

"When was she planning to go back to Omaha?" I asked softly so as not to break his concentration.

"We didn't know for sure. Suz told me that models

have a shelf life like food. When she couldn't get work anymore, we'd have plenty of money to take back with us to buy a big house."

Suzie? Leave New York? *Ha!* Only for London or Paris. "Did you see each other often?"

His meaty face turned red. "Whenever she could get away from that son of a bitch Scott Roberts. He rented a room to her. I wanted her to stay with me, but Suz said it would be better for her career if we kept our relationship a secret. When she got her own place, we were together whenever she didn't have work or business dinners. Suz worked so hard; she never had more than an afternoon or evening here or there to spend with me."

"You have those times to remember," I said, thinking back to what Gloria had told me about Suzie keeping an old boyfriend around for nostalgia's sake. Looking at the man in front of me, I couldn't imagine Suzie doing anything for "nostalgia." Jeff was more like bad news that wouldn't go away. Maybe he was one man Suzie couldn't control.

"I can't believe we won't have our family now." He gulped the rest of his second drink, turned from the bar, and burst into tears. My purse was jammed with tissues for this reception. I pulled one out and handed it to him. Although he accepted it, great, wrenching sobs came from the big man.

"Jeff? Jeff, dear," said an attractive woman with pretty gray hair and fine features. A man accompanied her, one I recognized from the church service. The Wexfords.

Jeff turned at the sound of her voice and enveloped her in his arms. "Mom, Dad, I did everything I could, and I failed."

I walked slowly away. I didn't want them to know who I was, lest they start in about Bradley. Jeff had never asked my name either. Good. He frightened me, with his ham-sized hands, his anger, his sobs, and his delusions. Did he really believe that Scott Roberts "rented a room" to Suzie?

Obviously, until the day Suzie died, Jeff was convinced that he would marry her. He even called her parents "Mom" and "Dad." Was it possible that Suzie *had* accepted Pierre's marriage proposal? That she told Jeff she was marrying someone else? I could imagine her leading him along, saying that it was for her career, and that her heart belonged to him.

But what if he didn't like the scheme? What if Jeff went to her apartment that night—she would have let him in—and he found her—I squeezed my eyes shut for a second—in whatever state she was in that told him she'd been with a . . . a lover?

Yes, I could easily picture him losing all control and strangling her.

"Bebe?"

"Oh, Gloria. I'm sorry; I was lost in thought and didn't see you." I glanced around and noted the ballroom was at capacity.

"That's okay," she said coldly. "I saw you talkin' to Jeff. He's a dope," she proclaimed. "Believed every lie Suzie fed him. Have you seen Pierre?"

"No, not yet. What does Jeff do for a living?"

Gloria didn't meet my gaze. She had a plate of food in her hands, and popped a salmon roll in her mouth. Speaking around it, she said, "Teaches teenagers how to box down in the Bowery."

"He looks like he's taken a few hits to the face," I said.

"Bet on it. One of Suzie's secrets, finally out in the open after Jeff's performance at the memorial."

"Didn't you tell me that the morning you did Suzie's makeup for the Mustang display, she bragged that she'd refused Pierre's marriage proposal?"

"What she told me," Gloria answered, her gaze finally meeting mine.

"I see. I'm glad you came to the memorial, Gloria."

She shrugged. "Business. Lots of Suzie's clients were there. Now they're here, so I've got to hang loose with the execs. I'll see ya."

"Wait! Gloria, have you seen Dirk Snellings, the old boss at Ryan? Is he here?"

"Yeah, I saw him a few minutes ago." She craned her neck. "You can't miss him. Very tall, dark hair, kinda a classic American look—there he is. He's the one with the red rose in his lapel over by the steak tartare."

Gloria edged away before I could say thank you. It seemed she didn't want to talk to me except for a brief chat now and then.

Why?

I couldn't think about it now. I needed to question Snellings. The steak tartare was at the end of a long buffet table, before the desserts.

Boldly, I walked back to the bar and ordered like a female James Bond. "I'll have a martini, shaken, not stirred."

The bartender looked at me and snorted. "I guess you're of age. Nobody at this function is underage."

The nerve! I accepted my drink and looked down my nose at him before walking away. Immediately some of the liquid spilled over the edge onto the gold carpet. I held the martini glass slightly away from me, then bent and took a gulp. *Wow!* That was some wicked drink, burning its way down my throat and making my eyes water. I guess I shouldn't have taken such a big swallow.

I elbowed and squeezed my way through people, more of the martini sloshing over the top of the glass, until I reached Dirk Snellings. Mr. Snellings, husband, cheater, and liar, was good-looking in a choirboy way. How ironic.

"Mr. Snellings?"

He turned and looked me over. "Hey, chickie, do I know you?"

I took a quick peek at his left hand and noticed he wasn't wearing his wedding ring, but an indentation on the appropriate finger gave his game away. *Jerk!*

I smiled. "We haven't been introduced. You might say I know you by reputation."

He popped some of that raw steak into his mouth. I was so grossed out, I took another sip of my martini.

"By reputation, you say. Now, how's that?" he asked, taking a sip of his amber-colored drink.

"I'm Bebe Bennett, the new secretary at Ryan."

Again the once-over, then, "You looking to be a model? Because, chickie, I think I could set you up."

"No, she's not looking to be a model; are you, Miss Bennett?" Bradley said, nearly making me fall into Dirk Snellings's arms when he bumped my back before strolling to my side.

I gave Bradley a blinding smile. "Of course not, Mr. Williams. You know I enjoy my job as your executive secretary."

"And you were just bringing me this martini," he said, taking the glass—complete with pink-lip-gloss stain—right out of my hand, darn him.

"Exactly! Listen, you two should know each other," I said cheerfully. "Mr. Williams, this is Mr. Snellings, the former head of Ryan."

The men shook hands.

If I had judged Snellings correctly, nature would take its course. Bradley had unknowingly handed me an opportunity, and what was about to happen was for his own good.

Right on cue, Mr. Snellings broke into a laugh. He said to Bradley, "Funny we should meet here, Williams. How'd you like Suzie chickie? She was the best lay—"

Mr. Snellings stopped and looked at me. "I'm not offending you, am I, Bebe?"

"Me? Not in the least, Dirk," I said, taking the liberty of using his first name. "I've been around the block." I smiled at Bradley and snatched the martini glass back. "Just a sip," I told him in my best Marilyn Monroe voice.

Bradley pretended to drop his napkin. On his way down to retrieve it, he muttered for my ears, "Only blocks you've been around, kid, are wooden with the ABCs printed on them."

I kinda kicked him. Discreetly. He took the martini back.

I moved closer to Dirk. "What a lovely red rose you're wearing."

Dirk gave a hearty laugh. "I wore it in honor of our Suzie. Always demanded red roses the whole two years she was mine. She do that to you, Williams?"

Oh, how this needed to be done, even though Bradley might experience pain. Maybe the scales would drop from his eyes and he'd get over Suzie once and for all. I shifted my gaze to him.

Bradley looked at Dirk intently. "Yes, she always asked for red roses."

Dirk gobbled another bit of steak tartare from his plate, and laughed around it. "I knew it. Suzie never changed. Slept with whoever could advance her career. Lived life to the limit. Hell, I'm still paying off Tiffany's!"

Bradley drank my martini in one shot. He appeared to be his normal, cool self, but I could see his full lips tighten, indicating anger. I hoped he was angry at Suzie, not Dirk.

"So, Dirk, did she drop you like a hot potato when Mr. Williams took over the agency?" I asked, flipping one side of my hair back and giving Dirk a big grin, Darlene style.

"She sure did, Bebe. I never saw her again once it was announced that you were the new man, Williams."

"Is that so?" Bradley said in a neutral tone.

"Yeah, but, hey, no hard feelings. I'll bet she got to know you real well the very first day you were on the job. But, buddy, I had her for two years. True, I had to share her with Scott, then Pierre, but hell, I didn't mind." He leaned closer to Bradley and me. "I've been married the whole time, and I've got a cute chickie at my new job in advertising. Christ, it's not like Suzie ever said she loved me."

Dirk straightened and glanced around. Bored with the conversation and looking for greener pastures, I thought.

Quickly, I said, "Lola is here."

Dirk pointed at Bradley with a cracker. "Lola was wild in the sack, but when Suzie came along, I only saw Lola every once in a while. Hey, buddy, tell it like it is, or was. Suzie didn't say she loved *you,* did she? Kinda hurt a guy's pride if she did."

"No, she didn't," Bradley said in that same calm tone.

"Now that you've mentioned Lola, Bebe," Dirk said, "I think I'll go say hello. Nice meeting you both. Here's my card, Bebe, if you ever want to get in touch."

He winked at me, then started to walk away. I followed him a few paces, then reached out my right hand and grabbed him by the sleeve. "Dirk, have you got any idea who might have killed Suzie?"

Suddenly I felt my left hand, holding Dirk's card, being pulled so hard my arm stretched out.

Dirk glanced over his shoulder at me and said, "Not a clue. Suzie not only had lots of lovers; she also had lots of enemies."

I couldn't thank him, because he kept going through the crowd, and finally the pain in my left arm caused me to surrender to Bradley.

Tripping in my pumps, I managed to right myself. He dropped my arm, taking Dirk's card from my hand. His well-manicured fingers tore the card into tiny pieces and let them fall to the floor.

Bradley's fierce gaze burned holes in my eyes. "Dammit, what kind of game are you playing, Miss Bennett? Because you're in way over your head."

"I don't know what you mean," I said, wishing that someone, anyone, would appear wanting a conversation. Bradley's body was practically touching me, since we were near the hordes of people waiting to get food.

Bradley cocked his head, his gaze never faltering. "Yes, you do know what I mean. Don't *you* lie to me too."

Oh, dear God. "How dare you suggest that I would lie to you the way Suzie did!" I may have told him a fib here and there, but that wasn't the same.

"Because that's what women do. Lie. Which is why I now regret spending time with Suzie. Once with any woman is quite enough for me."

"Don't you think that depends on the woman?"

"I haven't met one yet who's been different."

Was I included in that statement? My chin trembled, and I felt that painful burning behind my eyes. I would *not* cry.

Bradley said, "Did you set me up for that meeting with Snellings?"

"How could I do that? I was talking to the man who was your predecessor, and *you* walked up to us." I had taken full advantage of the situation, though, knowing it would hurt Bradley.

He looked furious. "That's because I saw you with a martini in your hand, and I didn't want to have to carry you out to a cab."

"You needn't worry about me!"

"No? Good. I suppose you know what kind of impression you made with that ass. Is that what you want? To be the type of woman Suzie was?"

I opened my mouth to deny it when Bradley moved so close to me I could feel his breath on my face.

"If that's what you want, we can go upstairs to a room right now, and I'll be sure word gets around afterward," he said.

Tears threatened again at the idea of Bradley doing *that* with me the way he suggested, as if I were another girl just good for one night. I raised my hand to slap his face, but he saw it coming and caught my fingers in a strong grip.

I forced myself not to cry. "You're angry because you thought Suzie was special, and now you've found out she was just another floozy! Don't take that anger out on me, Mr. Williams. I'm *not* that kind of girl, and you damn well know it!"

My voice shook, but I managed to snatch my hand out of his. I bolted through a gap in the buffet tables, and walked behind them to Maria.

"Hi, Maria. I wanted to see how you were doing," I said, my voice low and quavering.

She froze in the act of placing fancy toothpicks into small squares of cheese. "Bebe, you look like you're going to faint. You're trembling. Take a deep breath."

I did so, realizing I had been taking shallow gasps of air. "Something upset me, that's all. I'll be okay in a minute."

"It was *him*, wasn't it? You need some ginger ale." She raised her hand and waved until she caught the glance of one of the waiters at the soda table. Maria mouthed the words *ginger ale* to him and he nodded.

"Hey, you've got some power in this place," I said, as the young man hastened to do her bidding.

"Ah, he's another one who makes big promises," she said under her breath. "Thank you, Carlos."

The young man grinned, then winked at Maria.

She handed me the full glass. I drank it down, feeling cooler, more calm. I began helping her with the toothpicks. "Maria, do I look fast to you?"

She burst out laughing, causing people around us to glance our way. "No, Bebe. You look like what you are, a beautiful woman inside and out."

I lowered my head. "Thanks. I needed that right now."

She regarded me sharply. "Your man didn't try to—"

"No," I told her, and smiled. I gave her a brief hug. "I didn't mean to upset you. He just found out that he'd been grieving for something that was never there. He's hurt and angry, and took it out on me."

"Men. They are wretched things."

I patted her shoulder. "Now, where have I heard that before?"

"Bebe! What are you doing behind the buffet table? Checking the food? Because, you know, I'm the expert at that."

Debbie Ann, dressed in a black shirtwaist dress and a small black pillbox hat with a red feather, had arrived.

Chapter Nineteen

"Just a sec, Debbie Ann, and I'll come around to talk."

I murmured my excuses to Maria, and found my way to Debbie Ann's side. Remembering what Danielle had said about how Debbie Ann and Suzie didn't get along, I wondered for a moment why she was here. Then it dawned on me: the gossip!

"How are you, Debbie Ann? Did you go to Suzie's memorial?" I asked, reaching her side.

"I'm fine, thank you," she said, then took a deep breath. "I always enjoy good health because of my diet, Bebe, and yes, I did attend Suzie's memorial. I can well imagine what her parents are going through, having lost a child of my own. I went out of respect for the Wexfords and Pierre, though I never understood what he saw in such an immoral person," she said, talking nonstop. "But never mind about me. I saw you with—I cannot speak his name—your boss. You looked upset. Are you all right? Because if you're not, I'll take you to my home and give you something good to eat, and we'll think about getting another job for you."

"No, no, I'm okay, but thanks for the offer," I hastened to say. "And I'm so very sorry for your own loss. It must have been agony."

"I try not to think about it or discuss it. Bebe, I worry about you," Debbie Ann said. "You are young and vulnerable. Your boss has quite a reputation and is almost ten years older than you."

Boy, was I sick of people commenting on my age. Before she could go on, I said, "Debbie Ann, I'm twenty-two years old and capable of taking care of myself. People underestimate me. As for Mr. Williams, I don't believe for a second that he killed Suzie."

Debbie Ann smoothed her hair. "That's not what the rest of us think, dear, including the police. I even told that nice detective that I think Bradley Williams is too handsome for his own good. Use reason, Bebe. If he didn't kill Suzie, who did?"

At that moment I spotted Pierre's beret-covered head over by the bar. I wanted to talk to him.

"Bebe?" Debbie Ann said, following my gaze.

"Oh, I'm sorry," I replied absently. "I don't know yet who killed Suzie, but I can assure you it wasn't Mr. Williams. You're a kind person. Please give him the benefit of the doubt."

"Bebe, forgive me for speaking to you like a mother. I sense you don't have much of a social life. Perhaps you might have a crush on your boss that's clouding your judgment. Mr. Williams and Suzie were having an affair. I think she pushed him away, and he killed her in a moment of passion. Men used to getting their way can snap when they don't. That's what I told the detective."

Darn her for talking to Detective Finelli! There was no way I was going to be able to change Debbie Ann's mind about Bradley, and I didn't want her to know my feelings for him. I shook my head. "Oh, no, you're mistaken about me, Debbie Ann. I'm a single girl, enjoying the single life in Manhattan. I have no illusions. Don't worry," I said, and smiled. "If you'll excuse me, I see Pierre Benoit, and I desperately want to speak to him."

"Pierre? You're not talking to him about Suzie's death, I hope. He's grieving," Debbie Ann went on.

"Before all this happened, I tried to point out to Pierre that your boss had won Suzie's affections—"

"Agency business; excuse me," I broke in. "I'd love to hear your thoughts on the food here. I'll find you later." I dashed away.

I was so mad at Debbie Ann for being Mrs. Nosy Homemaker, going to Finelli, I could remove all the food from her kitchen set and replace it with hot dogs! Debbie Ann intruded in everyone's life.

Then I felt bad. She didn't have a family of her own. Maybe her meddling was just her way of trying to be helpful. I would try to find her later, and I'd listen to a sure-to-be-long speech on the evils of the buffet food.

I scooted through the crowd toward the bar. About halfway there, I saw Pierre with a militant look on his face, talking to Lola.

I barged right in and interrupted them. "Hi, Pierre, Lola," I said, and gave Pierre a quick kiss on the cheek. I noticed his eyes were red, his nose swollen, and that he held a drink, probably not his first, and a handkerchief in his hands.

"Bebe, are you responsible for this reception?" he asked.

"Um, yes. Is everything okay?"

He took my hand and kissed it. "Magnificent, my *chérie*. Elegant and fitting for my Suzie. As a Frenchman, I do regret the lack of wine, but I'm enjoying my bourbon."

I noticed he didn't call Suzie his "fiancée," as he had at the memorial. How could I bring that up now? Besides, I couldn't ignore Lola.

"Lola, you look beautiful," I said, and meant it. The blonde had on a black bouffant dress, tight through the bodice, the skirt puffed out, and her hair was swept into a beehive. Even better, her smoky gray eyes were clear.

"Thank you, Bebe. I was just telling Pierre that I haven't been drinking. I took your suggestion about alcohol, and I've been exercising, eating well, and get-

ting plenty of sleep. I think I'm in top form," Lola
concluded.

"And you are going to continue this behavior, and
not fail me in this cursed photo shoot in the Virgin
Islands?" Pierre asked, a strong hint of mockery in
his voice.

Lola kept her temper. "Yes, I am, Pierre. Because
I am Ryan's top model now that Suzie is dead, and I
intend to regain the Breck Girl contract, magazine
covers, and all the plum assignments I lost to her. I
hope you'll be my photographer, Pierre, since the best
should work with the best."

Uh-oh.

Pierre's face turned that shade of purple I saw on
Daddy when he was about to explode with anger. He
hissed words at Lola. "How can you speak in such a
selfish way?"

To my surprise, Lola did not let Pierre's anger affect
her outwardly. But then I thought I understood: Lola
needed Pierre to make her look her best. She would
not make an enemy out of him. Maybe she even
wanted to take Suzie's place in his bed. She needed
to watch her mouth about Suzie, though.

"Pierre," Lola said in a consoling tone. "I'm sorry.
You're right. I've been thinking of my own future. I
know the great love you and Suzie shared, and I don't
mean to diminish it in any way. Remember, you even-
tually healed after Kiki. You're a young and attractive
man. There will be someone else. A new lover is what
you need."

Who was Kiki? More important, Lola was stroking
Pierre's ego like I stroked my first pet kitten when I
was six years old. She was one determined woman.
Suddenly I remembered what Gloria had told me
about the lengths to which models would go for stardom. Again I remembered that night in the cab, when
Lola had said she'd strangle Suzie. And her alibi was
that she'd been with a friend.

In that instant, Lola rose to the top of my suspect
list.

Pierre addressed Lola but looked at me. "Maybe you're right."

She reached out and gave Pierre a hug, all the while rolling her eyes at me.

"There," she said. "I'm going to make my way out of here, boys and girls. We leave at seven tonight for the Virgin Islands! Being in such paradise will take our minds off our troubles. All right, Pierre?"

He paused for a moment, then nodded. "I'll see you on the plane, Lola."

"Groovy!" She beamed and walked away. Both Pierre and I watched as she smiled and hugged people—clients, I guessed—on her way to the door. Lola was the happiest girl at the reception.

Why shouldn't she be? Lola had the most to gain from Suzie's death. If she was the one who pulled the Pucci scarf around Suzie's neck, strangling her, she had no qualms about Bradley taking the heat. I decided that Lola and I were going to be the very best of friends, *confiding* friends, in the islands.

Past two o'clock, the crowd thinned.

I spoke to Pierre. "You made sure to get your photograph of Suzie back from the church?"

"Yes, I had my assistant take it back to my studio," he said. "Will you join me for a drink, Bebe? You've been kind, and I appreciate a woman of your beauty, your intelligence."

Uh-oh. Could Pierre be thinking of Lola's advice to take another lover? Me? Surely not.

I placed my hand on his sleeve. "Do you think that's wise, Pierre? I'll bet you haven't been able to eat anything. Why don't you wait until you're on the plane to drink? I have it on good authority that you're going to be pampered on your flight."

He smiled. "I suppose you arranged that too."

I smiled back. "Of course I did."

Pierre sighed. "You're right; I haven't eaten anything all day. I wish you were coming with us tonight, such a charming thing as you are. Who is going to be in charge of the shoot? Not that murderer, your boss, of that I am certain. You should come to work for me, Bebe. Your kindness warms my heart."

First Dirk, now Pierre. "How sweet, Pierre, thank you. Your tribute to Suzie at the memorial was so moving. You know, I didn't even realize the two of you were engaged until you called her your fiancée."

He looked away. "If you don't mind, Bebe, I don't wish to speak of it at length. Let us say that we had a lovers' quarrel over the time Suzie spent with *that man*. You must have noticed when you came to my studio that I had broken the glass of a few photos."

"I really didn't pay much attention," I fibbed.

"When one is French, one does things out of passion." He shrugged. "I have my temper just like anyone else. Suzie came to me Friday night. She told me how much she loved me, and she accepted my ring."

"That's a wonderful story—I mean memory—that you'll always have," I said, wondering what really went on Friday night. Was that when Suzie left her bracelet in Pierre's bathroom? Was Pierre lying to save face in society?

I glanced around for Bradley and found him standing alone against the far wall, drinking. Security men patrolled the room, most of them in Bradley's direct vicinity.

I needed to get Pierre out of here, before he saw Bradley and caused a hideous scene.

"Pierre, have you paid your respects to the Wexfords?"

His mouth formed a sneer. "They were unwilling to talk to me. They are provincials who wanted to keep Suzie from the world. The fools would have let her marry that barbarian Jeff Granford."

"Luckily Suzie came to New York," I said. I put my arm around his shoulder. "You must be exhausted. Why don't you go home and rest for a while before the flight. Order in a meal. You mustn't neglect yourself. Suzie wouldn't have wanted that."

"Is it what you want, Bebe?"

"Of course."

He put his arm around my shoulder, and I walked him to the door. I had a moment of fear when I saw Scott Roberts nearby, but Pierre had his gaze on the floor. I also saw Darlene and Cole. I held up my left index finger, and Darlene nodded. She knew I wanted to talk to her.

Pierre and I exited the ballroom, and he turned me toward him. "What can I do to convince you to be on that flight tonight, Bebe? I want you with me."

"I'll see what I can manage. You promise to get something to eat?"

"Yes, my *chérie*," he said, and kissed me on both cheeks.

I waited until he was out of sight, then turned back to the ballroom to find Darlene. Scott Roberts and a man I didn't know were coming straight toward me.

On impulse, I said, "Mr. Roberts, may I introduce myself?"

The man had the lightest blond hair I'd ever seen. "What's it about?" he asked, his pale blue eyes cold.

"I want to talk to you about doing some modeling," I blurted.

Disdain was written across his small features.

"Come on, Scott, give her a chance," his companion said. He was an older man, maybe in his mid-fifties, with dark hair liberally streaked with gray. His nose bore the signs of a heavy drinker, but he had a twinkle in his brown eyes. He reached out his hand for me to shake. "I'm Tony Arturo from Thom McAn shoes."

"Hi, Mr. Arturo," I said, shaking his hand. "I'm Bebe Bennett, and I love your shoe line."

"See there, Scott?" Mr. Arturo said. "A lady with taste."

Scott let out an impatient sigh. "Miss Bennett, the models I work with are mostly blondes, taller than you, and—"

Mr. Arturo broke in. "Scott, you might be able to use her as a foot model. She's got great legs."

I smiled at Mr. Arturo, feeling like a horse at auction, then said to Scott, "Mr. Roberts, all I want is fifteen minutes of your time. As I'm sure you know, all of America loves Luci Baines Johnson, and she's a brunette."

"Miss Bennett's right, Scott," Mr. Arturo said with a laugh. He stepped outside the ballroom and lit a cigarette.

My words didn't sway Scott, but I thought Mr. Arturo's did.

Scott pulled a card from his inside suit pocket and jabbed it in my hand. "This is my address. It'll have to be next week."

"That's fine," I said eagerly.

"I have a shoot on Monday at five. You can come a few minutes before then, and we'll talk while I'm setting up."

"Thank you," I said, but he joined Mr. Arturo, and the two walked away, resuming their conversation.

About a hundred people remained in the ballroom. The Wexfords, with Jeff by their side like a son, were still accepting condolences.

Debbie Ann was talking to Maria and pointing at the remaining food on the buffet line. I caught Maria's eye and shook my head. She smiled.

I wished everyone would leave. I glanced at my watch and saw it was two thirty. Another half hour to go.

Darlene and Cole were over by that awful steak tartare. Darlene wore her sleeveless black silk sheath. She had her arms folded over her chest. Cole's attention was on the steak tartare.

As I walked up to them, I heard Cole say, "I can't believe you won't eat any of this, lambkin. All Texans like a good piece of beef, doesn't have to be cooked. And why aren't you drinking?"

"Because as a stewardess I'm not allowed to drink for twenty-four hours before a flight," Darlene answered crisply.

Cole laughed. "You're not going to follow that silly rule."

"Bebe!" Darlene exclaimed.

I gave her a hug, whispering in her ear, "We've got to talk. Now."

Cole saw me. "Hello, Bebe. I guess you know our good news," he said, putting a possessive arm around Darlene.

"I heard some news, yes," I replied, feeling the gloves were off between Cole and me.

Darlene broke away from Cole's embrace. "Excuse me, Cole, I have to speak with Bebe."

He narrowed his eyes at me, creating at least twenty more lines around his eyes. With his almost-bald head and that peering look, he could have been an American bald eagle.

Darlene and I walked about twenty feet away from him.

She said, "What have you found out? I've seen you buzzing around here like a bee going from flower to flower."

"Too much to tell right now. It'll have to wait for when we're in the Virgin Islands."

"Like Cole is gonna leave my side," Darlene said.

"He'll probably fall asleep on the plane. Maybe we can talk then—"

I froze.

"Bebe, what's wrong? Oh, no!" Darlene exclaimed, turning in the direction of my gaze.

Detective Finelli and three uniformed NYPD officers had walked into the ballroom.

My heart raced.

Without looking my way, Detective Finelli marched up to Bradley, who had never moved from his place by the far wall.

Everyone in the room fell silent, all eyes on the police.

I broke away from Darlene and dashed over to Bradley's side.

Detective Finelli said, "Bradley Williams?"

He remained cool. "You know who I am. Somehow I think it didn't go my way at the grand jury hearing this morning."

Detective Finelli was all business. "Bradley Williams, you are under arrest for the murder of Susan Ann Wexford."

"No!" I cried. "He didn't do it!"

"Miss Bennett, please," Bradley said.

Without looking at me, Detective Finelli said, "Do you wish to confess to the crime, Miss Bennett?"

For a split second I actually considered it. Finally I said, "What about Mr. Pickering? Why is he allowing this to happen?"

"That's enough, Miss Bennett," Bradley said.

"You know what I think?" I asked Finelli, then didn't wait for a reply. "I think Pickering's a bastard who hasn't investigated this case properly. And neither have you, Detective Finelli. The two of you looked pretty chummy that day at the jail."

"Miss Bennett!" Bradley said through gritted teeth.

Detective Finelli ignored me and brought out a pair of handcuffs. He turned Bradley around and snapped the cuffs on him.

The sound of that click made tears run down my face.

"You son of a bitch! You killed my daughter! I hope they fry you!" screamed Mr. Wexford. Mrs. Wexford held her head high, staring at Bradley with a frigid expression.

Security guards rushed to Mr. Wexford, making sure he stayed in his place.

Without warning, Jeff Granford charged toward Bradley, emitting a horrible, animalistic howl. Three police officers restrained him, putting Jeff in handcuffs too. Still, with three men holding him down on the floor, Jeff yelled, "I'll kill you, Williams! I swear I will!" Two other security guards ran over to assist the police.

Detective Finelli said, "Let's go, Williams."

Bradley said, "Give me three minutes with Miss Bennett."

I drew in several breaths, wiped my face with a tissue pulled from my purse, and glared at Detective Finelli.

"Three minutes, and I'm not moving," the detective grunted.

Bradley said, "Could you turn around?"

Finelli held Bradley by the handcuffs and shifted position, so that Bradley faced me. I moved closer.

"Stop crying and listen to me, kid," he said in his husky voice.

"Yes," I said, but my tears had a will of their own.

His gaze locked with mine. "I'm sorry for what I said earlier about you and me going up to a room. I was way out of line—"

"You don't have to apologize."

"Will you be quiet and let me say what I have to say? Because my hands aren't free to throttle you."

I let out a half laugh, half sob.

"I know very well that you aren't that kind of girl." He looked away. "I, ah, live my life the way I do because . . . well, dammit, because although I believe in marriage, I've become jaded over the past ten years. I don't know if I'll ever change. This thing with Suzie didn't help."

"You need to pick the right woman," I said, then wished the words back, afraid I'd said too much.

But Bradley only nodded. "Someday. Maybe."

He looked at me again. "I know you're ready to take over the shoot in the Virgin Islands."

More tears. He *did* believe in me.

"Make me proud, kid."

"I will," I managed.

"And don't let the words *bastard* and *damn* come out of your pretty mouth again. You're not the kind of girl who swears."

I could only nod, drowning in his eyes.

"No more of that perfume you've got on again today despite what I—"

"Let's go, Williams," Detective Finelli demanded.

"Hang on a second," Bradley told Finelli. Then to me, "No more crying. Pickering will get me out on bail."

"He'd better!" I said fiercely.

Bradley smiled. "That's my girl."

Detective Finelli led him away.

The officers took Jeff with them.

I watched until Finelli escorted Bradley out of the ballroom.

Debbie Ann, standing a short distance away, said, "I did try to tell you, Bebe."

I collapsed into Darlene's waiting arms.

Chapter Twenty

Darlene had a tight grip on me. A good thing because, as she led me through the ballroom, the gold-colored carpet kept rising up and down.

From behind us, Cole said, "What's the matter with Bebe? Why is she so upset about a killer being arrested?"

Darlene said, "He's her boss, Cole."

"Not anymore."

Darlene halted our progress long enough to turn her head and say, "Cole, shut up."

Then I heard Maria's voice. "Bebe, the truth will come out. Keep that knowledge close to your heart."

I nodded and accepted my black pillbox hat from her. "Maria, would you tell the management that Ryan will settle the bill on Monday?"

"You know I will."

Outside on the sidewalk, the street noises of honking horns and crowds of people talking jolted me. A cool wind brushed my face. I raised my head and took a deep breath. Thank goodness there were no photographers around. Still, I felt sick, overwhelmed, and frightened. And dark clouds remained over the city.

Darlene said, "Cole, Bebe and I are taking a cab home."

"But I thought the two of us were going to Bonwit Teller to buy those shoes you liked, then get your suitcase and go to the airport."

Darlene tapped her stiletto on the sidewalk. "Those plans have changed. I'm going home with Bebe—"

"Please, you don't have to," I said softly.

"See there," Cole said. "No reason to ruin our—"

Darlene went on as if no one had spoken. "And Bebe and I are going to change our clothes. My suitcases and Bebe's are at the apartment, so we'll get a cab to the airport together. You can meet us at the Skyway gate."

"What?" Cole said, his voice tinged with anger. "Bebe's coming with us on what's supposed to be the first part of our honeymoon?"

"Bebe is running the photo shoot for Ryan now that her boss is temporarily inconvenienced," Darlene said impatiently.

Cole laughed. "You have to be joking."

Before I could gather the strength to sock Cole a good one, Darlene said, "No, I'm not joking, Cole. Bebe was the only reason I did another stew a favor by working this flight. You're the one who turned it into part of our honeymoon. I'll see you on the plane."

With that, her arm still linked with mine, Darlene walked us to the street and whistled for a taxi. We got in, and I stared sightlessly out the window the whole way home. Bless her, she left me in peace.

Arriving at East Sixty-fifth, we got out of the cab.

Harry lounged on our front stoop. "Who died? The two of ya look like old crones . . . uh, crows."

Boozed again. "A woman we knew, Harry," I said.

"Let's go, Bebe," Darlene commanded.

I opened my purse, and a tissue flew out. Digging into my wallet, I said, "Harry, I'm going away for a couple of days." I reached out to hand him a dollar. "Please get some food and coffee."

Darlene tried to block my hand that held the money. A struggle ensued. I almost fell to the stoop, but I was determined that Harry not beg on the street. In a fast move, I ducked my arm under Darlene's, and Harry got the money.

"Thank you, Miss Sweet Face," he said. A bleary eye gleamed at Darlene. "Redheads. Nothing but trouble."

"You take advantage of her kindness," Darlene shot back.

Now I was the one leading Darlene as we passed Harry, entered the building, and walked up the steps to our apartment.

"I don't know why you give that bum money," Darlene complained, closing the door behind her.

"He needs help," I replied. "One day I'm going to find out why he lives on the streets."

"Because he's a wino, that's why," she said. Then, "Oh, honey, let's not argue. I know it was horrible watching Bradley being taken away by that stubborn mule Detective Finelli. But you have to be strong for Bradley now. We'll find the killer."

"I think *Lola* killed Suzie. She had the most to gain, that I know of. At the reception, Lola was almost giddy with happiness."

Darlene raised a brow. "Really? Then it's just peachy that she'll be along for the trip. We need to talk about this."

"We will. You're my best friend, Darlene, you know that. Thanks for taking me home. But once we get on that plane, I'm going to be Lola's best friend."

Darlene smiled. "I like it when you think deviously." Then, "Honey, no offense, but your face is a mess. We need to change clothes and freshen up fast. Being a stewardess, I have to be at the airport no later than five to sign in and get the plane ready."

"Hey, check it out! I wanna fly with you, sweetheart!"

"Baby, tell me where you're going so I can buy a ticket."

"Red! Over here! Coming home to the city? I can show you a good time. I've got lots of money to spend on a gal like you."

And so it went, all through the airport. Darlene smiled at the guys, but kept walking, me by her side.

I had on my prettiest pink suit, but I couldn't compare to the striking picture Darlene made in her Skyway uniform of a bright, sky-blue suit, dyed-to-match high heels, white gloves, and a tall sky-blue pillbox hat, which she had placed on her red curls at a jaunty angle.

"So this is what you meant by stew-bums?" I asked.

"Airport johnnies, hostess-hoppers, stew-bums, whatever you want to call them, they're always around. That's how Stu and I met."

"Have you talked to Stu?"

"No. I told him I'd speak to him when I got back," Darlene said stubbornly. "You know that, Bebe."

"It's not exactly a secret that I want the two of you back together again."

As we walked on through the airport, the guys continued their catcalls.

I said, "I see you're not wearing your engagement ring."

"I'm not permitted to. Stewardesses are supposed to be swinging singles. We're not allowed to marry, and if we get engaged, we get six months' notice and we're out."

"Gee, that means if you marry Cole—"

"Whew! We're here right on the dot. I have to sign in, Bebe. I'll be just a minute." Darlene went behind the long Skyway counter and through a door, dodging my remark.

I stood holding my light blue suitcase, forcing that scene of Bradley being led away in handcuffs from my mind. Instead I focused on what had been New York International Airport until last Christmas Eve. On that day, in honor of our assassinated president, the airport was renamed John F. Kennedy International Airport.

Lots of people were flying these days. Darlene had told me the latest figures showed almost nine million people—more than the total population of New York City!—used an airplane for travel.

Oh, it was no use. All I could think of was Bradley. *Someday.* Wasn't that what Bradley had said? Someday he'd choose the right woman. I'd wait for him, even if he didn't want me to. What alternative did I have? I loved him. In that instant I thought of Louis. I couldn't go out with him again.

Other Skyway stewardesses arrived, including a harsh-faced, tight-lipped busty stewardess with brassy blond hair, but I didn't think any of them could hold a candle to Darlene.

I realized I needed to check my suitcase with the Skyway clerk and did so.

A few seconds later Darlene emerged and came to my side. She wasn't smiling. "Let's make tracks, honey. We need to go to the gate. I'll board the plane, but you'll have to sit in the waiting area," she said in a tight voice.

"Darlene, what's wrong? You've got a murderous expression in your eyes," I said as we walked along.

She adjusted her features. "Did you see the bottle blonde bursting out of her Skyway uniform who came in after me?"

"Yes, I did notice her."

"That bitch is Peggy. I can't believe my luck, Bebe! She's chief stewardess on our flight. Keep the knives away from me."

"Oh, gosh, Peggy's the one who claims to have had a fling with Stu in Paris," I said.

"You got it, honey."

"Stu wouldn't have such bad taste," I assured her. "Darlene, you're not going to beat Peggy up, are you?"

"I'm not making any promises. Here's the seating area. I see from your empty hand that you got your suitcase checked. Make yourself comfortable, and I'll come out and get you when the plane is ready."

Darlene disappeared through the boarding door.

I sat trying not to think about the weather. The dark clouds over the city had finally let loose their contents. Rain poured down outside the large window. Tonight, after an emotional day, my nerves were on edge. Did airplanes have windshield wipers?

Around six Cole arrived, his legs spread as if he were riding an invisible horse. He sat directly opposite me, one leg crossed over the other, a black Stetson on his head. At his side was a leather briefcase, obviously custom-made. He folded a newspaper and began to read.

Neither of us spoke.

Next to arrive was Lola. I knew before I saw her from the flashbulb lights going off. My eyes popped at the sight of her printed silk minidress in oranges, pinks, grays, and black. Wild, concentric circles danced on a geometric background. The dress had cutout armholes and a folded down collar. On her feet were mid-calf black patent-leather boots.

People stared. Lola's appearance screamed *high-fashion model*. Looking at those black boots, I mentally chided myself for not daring to wear my white go-go boots. As soon as I got home, I would be sure to correct that mistake.

"Hello, Bebe," Lola greeted me in a chipper tone.

Remembering my determination to be her new best friend, I replied, "Come and sit next to me, Lola. You look stunning. Where did you get that groovy dress?"

"Oh, a friend in Italy sent it to me. Emilio Pucci. You might have heard his name," she said.

"I have. His designs are so different, they explode with life," I said.

"Don't you think wearing Pucci right now is in bad taste?" Pierre said, appearing in his entirely black uniform of pants, shirt, sports coat, and beret. He carried a large bag that probably contained his cameras. "It was a Pucci scarf that was used to strangle Suzie."

Lola lit a cigarette. "Was it? I didn't pay attention to the details of the murder. I only know she was strangled. Forgive me, Pierre."

He gave her a brief nod, put his bag down, and took a seat on my other side. Claiming both of my hands in his, Pierre said, "Ah, you never disappoint me, Bebe. How did you convince that monster of a boss that you were needed on this shoot?"

I smiled as Pierre released my hands, but when I opened my mouth to give him the explanation I'd planned, Cole spoke: "She's in charge of the shoot, if you can believe that. At the end of the reception, the Williams guy was arrested for murder and hauled off by the police in handcuffs," he said, tipping his Stetson back on his head.

Darn him! I had hoped to keep the news of Bradley's arrest a secret for a while.

Pierre jumped out of his chair and began to pace. "There is justice! I can never have Suzie again, but the one who took her life will be punished."

Lola blew smoke from her nostrils. "Damn. I wish Bradley hadn't been the one arrested. He's so handsome. I hope he's replaced by someone reasonable. I wonder if I should approach Ford."

"Ford Modeling won't take you," Pierre said with a grimace.

Lola tried for a hurt expression. "Pierre, I thought we had decided to be friends."

"And as a friend, I'm telling you, Lola, Ford will not put you on their talent list."

While Lola seethed, Pierre turned his attention to me. "You are in charge of the shoot, Bebe? Nothing could make me happier."

"Thank you, but I'm sure I won't have much to do. Everyone is a professional," I said, wishing I were correct and didn't have egos to juggle.

Lola put out her cigarette in the metal tray fixed in the armrest of her chair.

Pierre took my right hand and held it.

I began to hope a storm would hit Saint Thomas, the island chosen for the shoot, so the whole thing could be canceled without any blame on my head.

I could kill Cole.

I needed chocolate.

Gloria walked up to our sullen group carrying her big white makeup bag. "Somebody else die?" she cracked, placing her case on the seat next to Cole and sitting in the following seat.

Lola said, "No, but Bradley Williams has been arrested for Suzie's murder."

Gloria's brown gaze flitted to me, then to my hand in Pierre's before she answered Lola. "Mr. Williams? I didn't peg him for the killer."

"Who did you think strangled Suzie?" Pierre asked sharply.

Gloria was in the hot seat, and I for one waited for her answer.

She hesitated, then assumed a rebellious air. "I don't wanna say. The police know what they're doing, I guess."

Her words hung in the air.

"If you don't think Bradley did it," Lola said, "then maybe you should voice your opinion as to who did."

"Maybe I already have," Gloria shot back.

Darlene joined the group. "Everybody ready to jet down to the island?" she asked cheerfully.

We all rose, Darlene giving me a "what's wrong" look.

I shook my head in response. To Lola, I said, "Would you sit next to me on the flight? Maybe you could give me some fashion and makeup tips. I admire you, Lola."

As I predicted, she fell for the flattery. "Sure, Bebe. We can talk about ideas for the shoot."

Oh, no, we wouldn't. Bradley had gone over with the Durden swimwear people exactly what they wanted: white-sand beaches, blue water, palm trees, and a fabulous girl in a sexy black bikini.

Everyone settled into their seats on the plane. Lola took the window seat, which was fine with me. Rain poured from the skies, quashing any wish I had to look outside during takeoff.

All our seats were in the front section of the plane, which carried a total of 115 people. Darlene had told me that earlier. She also said we'd be cruising at 610 miles per hour. It sounded way too fast to be safe.

I watched as people boarded the plane after us, hoping for a nun or priest for protection. Funny,

though, neither appeared to be taking a trip to Saint
Thomas. The majority were couples, young and old,
seeking an island paradise.

Across the aisle from me, Pierre sat next to Cole,
who was in the window seat. Pierre argued with busty
Peggy about how fragile his cameras were. She finally
wrapped his case in a blanket and took it to a special
compartment in the staff's area.

Gloria sat one row back, sulking. A vague feeling
of unease came over me. Did Gloria think Lola had
killed Suzie? Was that why she was surprised Bradley
had been arrested? Who *did* Gloria think had killed
Suzie? Would she tell me?

As the plane engines roared to life, I noticed with
pride that Darlene worked in a businesslike, hustle-
bustle manner, smiling and friendly with everyone, not
giving any particular passenger more attention than
another.

However, I did see her try to knock Peggy down
with the wheeled cart. I looked to the galley kitchen.
Darlene was snagging Peggy's stockings on a low
stainless-steel cupboard, and Peggy was opening a bottle of champagne directed at Darlene's eyes. The two
hissed what surely were insults at each other.

After the plane took off, Darlene served Lola and
me prime rib and champagne. I gave her a look when
she poured the champagne, slanting my eyes at Lola.
Darlene nodded. No alcohol for Lola.

However, despite my earlier warnings, the model
kept signaling for more champagne. When Darlene
ignored her, Lola snagged Peggy. "That other stewardess won't refill my champagne."

"I am so sorry. She's a fill-in, not very good at her
job. I'll take care of you," Peggy promised.

Darn Peggy! "Lola, should you be drinking the
night before the shoot?" I asked.

She waved a careless hand. "I've been dry for almost a week. I deserve some champagne. It won't
make any difference."

There was nothing I could do. Plan B: Maybe Lola

would get tipsy enough to confess, but not so drunk she'd ruin the photo shoot.

I counted three glasses of champagne that slid down the model's throat before Peggy took away our dinner plates. Lola hadn't touched her food.

"Thanks for sitting next to me," I said in a confidential tone, holding my half-full champagne glass in my right hand. "I'm looking forward to the photo shoot."

Lola lit another cigarette, then reached across me to accept a champagne refill from Peggy. Her fourth. "Not nearly as much as I am. Durden swimwear advertises in all the major magazines. My career will be revived."

I patted her arm. "Lola," I whispered, forcing her to move her head close to mine, "you're going to be bigger than you ever were before. I have Pierre eating out of my hand. He'll want to please me, and what will please me is you looking sexier than any movie star in these photos. Even Liz Taylor."

"Are you sleeping with Pierre?" Lola asked. "I think he's falling for you."

Oh, no. "Not yet, but it's only a matter of time, now that Bradley's been arrested," I fibbed, trying another tactic. "I've been more than a secretary to Bradley, if you know what I mean." Mentally, I thought I would have to buy a thick new notebook for confessions.

Lola smiled smugly. "Too bad about Bradley. I'm glad I have you on my side, Bebe. I warn you, though, Pierre can be intolerable with his French sensibilities." She finished her glass of champagne and signaled to Peggy.

"What can I get you?" she asked.

"I'm switching to Manhattans," Lola said to Peggy, who raced up the aisle to get the highball.

In the galley, Darlene knocked over the drink the minute Peggy mixed it. The two were at it again.

Lola said, "I'll be the top model in the city. What better way to celebrate than drinking Manhattans?" she asked, then giggled.

I giggled along with her, then whispered, "You're right on both counts, and I'm glad. I hated Suzie for dating Bradley. I'm glad she's dead."

Lola drank her highball. "You hated Suzie that much?"

I looked at her askance. "Are you kidding?" I leaned over and whispered in her ear, "I would have strangled Suzie myself if Bradley hadn't done it for me."

I sat back and waited. Lola's words were beginning to slur. I'd lost count of how much alcohol was in her system.

She tried to light a cigarette with unsteady hands. I immediately lit it for her. She took a drag, then absently let the cigarette burn in the handrest's metal tray. "Damn, I wish Bradley weren't the one arrested for the murder. He's too choice to languish in jail the rest of his life."

"So you don't think he was the one who actually killed her?" I asked, hoping my face reflected an admiration of Lola's intelligence.

She finished her drink, carefully put the glass on her tray, then licked her lips. She gazed at me, her head resting on the back of her seat. "I wanted Suzie dead, too, Bebe. Many nights I'd lie in bed thinking of how to kill her and get away with it. I didn't have a gun. I didn't want to shoot her anyway. Soooooo impersonal. Knives are messy, and I might have cut my hand."

"I agree," I whispered, daring at last to hope for that drunken confession.

Lola closed her eyes. "I dreamed of strangling the bitch, while telling her how much I hated her. It was important that Suzie knew I much I hated her, how she was a nobody from Omaha. I was the star model, not her. Never her. I wanted to wrap my hands around her neck and squeeze all my hatred into her and slowly watch the life go out of her. I needed Suzie to know who had finally triumphed. Oh, the pleasure . . ."

Chilled to the bone, I whispered, "You can tell me

if you took that pleasure, Lola. We're friends. I'll keep the secret."

My heart raced in my chest, waiting for her answer.

"Lola?" I whispered. "Tell me what Suzie's last words were."

Lola's head fell onto her shoulder.

Passed-out drunk, she slipped her hand out of mine along with my hopes for a confession that would clear Bradley's name.

Chapter Twenty-one

"And I told Lola all those lies! How will I ever get through confession?" I asked, and dropped my head in my hands.

It was a little after nine in the morning, and I had just finished bringing Darlene up-to-date about what had happened on the flight the previous evening.

"Cheer up, Bebe; you'll explain your actions by saying they were for a good cause, namely your hunky boss's life," Darlene reassured me. "We're here, and we can try again to get Lola to confess."

"I hope so."

Darlene gazed out at the ocean. "Can you believe the color of the water? It's the same color as that turquoise dress you're wearing."

"I've never seen anything like it," I admitted. "Daddy and Mama always took me to Virginia Beach when I was growing up, and I thought water couldn't get any bluer. I was wrong."

Darlene and I sat at an aluminum table in the casual, covered outdoor restaurant of our hotel, aptly named White Sands since it sat right on the beach. Crisscrossed wooden poles formed the structure, which was open to the little brown lizards that scurried about. Palm trees swayed among the lush foliage, and butterflies flew around the wild purple bougainvillea. Bradley could not have picked a better setting for the Durden swimwear shoot.

Once we'd landed on the island, the five in our party

had been driven in a safari taxi on a dirt road populated by donkeys and cows. All the stopping and starting because of the slow-moving animals, coupled with the disastrous day, had made me go straight to my room and to bed.

"Are you and Cole sharing a room?" I asked, rubbing my bare feet together under the table. Waiters swept the wooden floor, but the sand found its way back.

Cole sat in a white wooden beach chair at the water's edge. He'd traded his Stetson for a big straw hat, probably purchased from a street vendor. He was shirtless—I didn't want to look—and wore a pair of tan-and-white swimming trunks that came to his skinny knees.

"Unfortunately, we are," Darlene said, glancing down at her engagement ring with narrowed eyes. "We've been fighting ever since we got here. Last night I stomped off to the bar alone—remind me to tell you about that in a minute—and then this morning, Cole was mad as a hornet when I put on this bathing suit. He said it was something a prostitute would wear."

"That was mean of Cole! How dare he refer to you that way?"

I looked at her red one-piece suit. True, the sides were completely cut out, and there was a slit down the front with three orange ties for modesty, but it was no racy bikini. Though somehow, on Darlene, the suit emphasized her tiny waist and generous bosom. She just couldn't help but look sexy.

Darlene drank some coffee, then set the cup down in the saucer. She smiled. "The suit is called 'the She-Devil.' "

We burst into laughter.

Then she grew serious. "I've been doing some thinking, Bebe."

"Oh?"

"Yeah, ever since that talk you and I had. And I've come to the conclusion that Cole and I would never be happy together. I love Stu, and he loves me. All

that stuff about Peggy . . . I should never have believed her. Stu's a reformed stew-bum. I'm gonna do
my best to trust him. When we get back to New York,
I'll make it up to him. No more father figures for me."

I grabbed her right hand and squeezed it. "I am so
happy, Darlene! When are you going to tell Cole?
Can I watch?"

She giggled. "You are bad, Bebe. When the moment is right, I'll tell him. Privately. No sense arguing
with him on this perfect day."

Grinning, I popped a delicious slice of mango in
my mouth.

Darlene stuck her fork into a cube of fresh pineapple. "I'll give him the ring back—that's only fair—
but I'm keeping the diamond necklace."

"You'd better. I might want to borrow it one day,"
I said. "What was it you wanted me to remind you
of, something you wanted to tell me?"

Darlene finished her pineapple and nodded.
"Thought you might like to know that Lola got a second wind last night."

"What? Don't tell me—"

"Yes, ma'am, your star model was in the bar drinking again when I went in for my nightcap. She was all
over a cute local guy, and his hands were everywhere
on her. Lola didn't push him away."

"Oh, dear God," I said. "I'd better check—"

"Good morning, my lovely Bebe," Pierre said, arriving at our table. He bent and kissed my cheek, while
I shot a look at Darlene that begged her not to laugh.

Pierre had on the beach version of his city attire:
black short-sleeved shirt, black shorts, black socks and
shoes. The beret was gone, though, replaced by a
straw hat like Cole's.

"Hello, Pierre. You know Darlene."

"Ah, yes, our hostess on the plane," he said, and
raised Darlene's hand to his lips for a brief kiss.

She smiled, and Pierre took a seat next to me. A
waiter came and took his detailed order; then Pierre
said, "Bebe, the weather couldn't be better for our

shoot. You are my good luck charm. I'd like to start in an hour or so, as soon as I've breakfasted, and Lola is in makeup. Where is Gloria?"

Thinking this would be a good excuse to find Lola, I said, "Why don't I round everyone up while you sit here and relax?"

Pierre smiled. "You mean more and more to me every day. What would I do without you, my *chérie?*"

Darlene slid me a glance.

I felt uncomfortable and, if I were honest with myself, a tiny bit flattered by Pierre's growing feelings for me. Uncomfortable because I couldn't return his interest. Flattered since Pierre, Louis, and the young actor at the gala all helped my confidence that I was attractive to the opposite sex. Then there was Bradley. . . .

Gloria, wearing a loose cotton floral shift, plunked down her makeup bag with a thud. "Yeah, Bebe, what would we do without you?" she asked, and snorted a laugh.

Puzzled, I stood up. "Good morning, Gloria. If everyone will excuse me, I'll go find Lola."

"I'll go with you," she said. "I need to get her in makeup."

"Um, let me go up first, Gloria; then I'll come back and find you."

"Whatever floats your boat," she said, and sat down.

Dashing to the front desk, I finally convinced the native clerk to give me Lola's room number. Twenty-seven, just three doors down from me.

I ran up the wooden steps and knocked on her door. No answer.

I knocked harder, urgently.

"One minute!" called a male voice.

Had the desk clerk given me the wrong room number?

The door opened, revealing a deeply tanned young man with blond hair. Nice-looking, but tousled and shirtless, he wore a pair of white Levi's. "Hey, you woke me."

An American living off of sand dollars, I thought. Trying to avoid gazing at his naked chest, I stammered, "Is, um, Lola—"

"That her name?" He shook his head as if to clear it. "Wild woman. I gotta split."

He brushed past me, making tracks.

I pushed the door open.

Lola, naked, lay sprawled across the double bed on her stomach, snoring. I inched over and picked up a white sheet from the floor. Covering her to the neck, I bent down and touched her shoulder. "Lola, it's me, Bebe. Time to wake up."

Her thick blond hair lay across her face. I gently pushed it aside. "Lola, please wake up."

Her eyes opened a crack. Her eyelids were as swollen as a wet sponge, and she still had on last night's makeup, her black eyeliner smeared onto her bloated cheek.

Slowly she came awake, groaning. "I'm gonna be sick," she whispered, then scooted across the bed and into the bathroom.

I pressed my fingers to my temples as the sounds of last night's overindulgence met my ears. I went to the window and opened it, letting some fresh air into the foul-smelling room.

When all was quiet in the bathroom, I stood with my back against the wall next to the bathroom. Lola hadn't closed the door, and I didn't want to see inside.

"Lola, Pierre wants to start the shoot in about an hour. Why don't you take a hot shower while I go get you some coffee and the bikini you're supposed to wear?"

She mumbled something I couldn't understand.

"What did you say?" I asked.

"Aspirin," she moaned.

"Okay, I'll be back in fifteen minutes with coffee and aspirin. You'll get your shower while I'm gone?"

"Uh-huh."

Unlocking my door, I sat on the edge of my bed and allowed myself a good five minutes of self-pity.

Lola had been drinking on the plane despite my advice not to. But I had no idea she'd continue once we landed and get completely wasted. Her face! All bloated, eyes swollen and red. Maybe the shower, the coffee, and the aspirin would take care of it, I told myself. She would be a fool to ruin this opportunity. And I'd let Bradley down after he put his trust in me. I steeled my resolve. This photo shoot would be successful, no matter what.

I applied suntan lotion to my arms and legs, touched up my lip gloss, and got the Durden black bikinis out of my suitcase. There were two of them in different sizes. I'd have Lola put the larger one on first. Out of my first-aid travel case, I retrieved two aspirin.

Leaving my room, I secured a cup of coffee and headed back to Lola's room. I'd left the door unlocked and walked right in.

"Lola," I said, putting the coffee down on a small table, "are you feeling better?"

No answer.

I opened the bathroom door. She lay on the bathroom floor, snoring.

That was when I got mad.

Over the next forty-five minutes, I woke Lola, got her to drink some coffee and take her aspirin, then made her shower. I was nice about everything, but inside I seethed. By the time her hair was dry and she'd squeezed into the bikini, I wanted to scream.

"You're fussing over me, Bebe," she said, then stumbled as we walked out the door.

With horror I saw long red scratches down her back. *Pancake makeup,* I thought, *that should cover it.* "I'm counting on you, Lola, and we're late. Pierre is going to be furious."

"Screw him. I'm tired of his moods," she grumbled. "Hey, I didn't say anything about Pierre last night that I shouldn't have, did I? He's still gotta do this shoot with me."

"Pierre? No, you didn't," I said. With every step I grew more anxious. Gloria would have to be a miracle worker with Lola's makeup, and Pierre a genius with the camera.

We stepped outside, Lola complaining of the brightness of the sun, and found where Pierre had set up for the shoot. A white wooden beach lounger and a tiny round bamboo table had been placed near lush green plants and a low palm tree. From my Durden swimwear notes, I knew there were supposed to be shots of Lola frolicking in the water, reclining with a tropical drink, and sunbathing.

Pierre saw us first. *"Merde!"* he cursed.

"Oh, shit," Gloria echoed.

Lola put her hands on her hips. "What is wrong with you people?"

Pierre held Lola's chin in one hand. He examined her face intently before she swiped his hand away.

"There is nothing I can do. Nothing! She's been drinking. Her looks are ruined," he declared, and kicked a seashell across the beach. He walked a few feet away and assumed a tragic pose.

"Don't talk about me like I'm not here," Lola said. "Gloria will—"

"Gloria cannot fix that mess you call a face!" Pierre shouted. "And your stomach is hanging over the top of that bikini bottom!"

Darlene and Cole drifted over.

"If Gloria has *any* talent at all, she'll make me beautiful," Lola countered.

Gloria drew in a deep breath at the insult. "I'm sorry, Pierre. There's no way I can cover those bags under her eyes, not to mention her swollen eyelids. Maybe you can shoot her at an angle where her bloated face appears thin."

"Shut up, Gloria," Lola snapped. Then she turned her ire on Pierre. "You always have a love-hate relationship with your star model. You did with Suzie, with me, and with Kiki before us."

Pierre took an angry step toward Lola.

I put myself between them. I was supposed to be in charge here. "Pierre, I know you're upset, and you're perfectly justified. Lola, you should have gone to bed early and gotten your beauty rest. Now, why don't I take Lola back to her room, where she can rest for an hour with a cool cloth over her eyes."

Darlene said, "It sounds gross, but the cream people use for hemorrhoids can shrink the swelling around your eyes too. We were taught that in stew school."

"Darlene," Cole barked in a tone that dropped the eighty-something-degree temperature down to fifty, "I won't have you speaking of such personal things in public. And for Pete's sake, tie those things on the front of that bathing suit tighter. You're exposing yourself. No wife of mine—"

Darlene's freckles stood out like drops of red wine on a white-tiled floor. She stopped Cole before he could continue. "I'll say anything I want to say! And what I've wanted to say for a while now is that *I won't be your wife!*" She twisted her engagement ring off her finger and flung it at Cole.

The ring hit him squarely in the center of his forehead, then bounced down to the sand. He bent down, scrambling around trying to find it.

Darlene flounced off to the hotel.

"This is madness," Pierre said. "I have to wait for a drunken model before I can do my work. I'll never photograph you again after this, Lola."

Cole, ever the bearer of good tidings, said, "If you don't stop arguing, you won't get any pictures at all. Storm's coming in later today. Supposed to last through tomorrow. Lola looks pretty enough to me even without makeup."

She smiled at him and moved away from Pierre to help Cole look for Darlene's ring.

I couldn't believe what was happening around me. I felt the shoot slipping through my fingers, and me helpless to do anything to save it.

Added to that, Cole, single for all of two minutes, was flirting with Lola, and she was loving every minute.

"Bebe," Pierre said, "please make flight arrangements. I wish to leave at once."

"No, Pierre," I said, half pleading. "There must be a way to salvage the situation. Can't you give Lola some time? I'll help her get the swelling down. With your talent, I know we can work this out."

"Bebe, I would love to please you, but it's out of my hands. We need at least three hours to shoot, and that's only because I am so talented. I need a model in makeup right—"

He stopped and looked at me. "This is an important shoot for you, isn't it, my *chérie?* Whoever is your new superior at the agency will consider this failure your fault, won't they?"

"Yes," I said in a resigned tone.

"I have an idea."

My spirits lifted. "Tell me! I'll do anything to help."

"Excellent! Now go put on the bikini."

"What?" I said, not believing my ears.

Pierre ignored me. "Gloria, you will do Bebe's makeup. I want her to look light and fun. The perfect all-American girl."

"I knew it would come to this," Gloria mumbled.

"Pierre," I said, grabbing his arm, "I'm not a model, much less a *star* model. I can't do it. What about Darlene? She's sexy and beautiful."

"Darlene is too sexy and curvy for what Durden wants. You should know that. Don't you see? You will be something better than a star model: a fresh new face. You *are* beautiful, my *chérie.*"

Lola stood, wiping the sand from her hands. "This is an outrage!"

"Bebe's pretty, I guess, but not like Lola," Cole said.

"Leave us. Your opinion is not wanted here," Pierre told Cole. Then as if to himself, "Gloria's makeup will enhance her natural beauty, and I will make her an angel in a devil's attire. I don't know what that murderer was thinking to give Lola the assignment in the first place. Bebe has a sweetness that Lola could never project."

Cole pulled Darlene's ring from the sand and pocketed it. "Lola, why don't you let me take you back to New York? I can cheer you up if you like Broadway shows, eating out—"

"I'd love to, Cole. Since it's going to rain here, this place would bore me silly."

The two walked away.

My mind raced. Would my doing the shoot be better than coming back with no photographs at all? Maybe Gloria could make me pretty enough. What choice did I have?

Bradley's words came back to me. *Make me proud.*

"Okay, Pierre. But you'll have to give me lots of instruction," I said.

He clapped his hands together in delight. "Wonderful!"

I turned to Gloria. "Should I get the suit on first?"

"Yeah."

She started walking with me back to the hotel.

"Gloria, are you mad at me?" I said, finally bringing my feelings out into the open.

She snorted. "Little Miss Innocent, don't worry; I'll do my job. The photos will be gear. After all, you're going to be Pierre's new girlfriend."

"That's not true," I protested.

"Right. We have a professional relationship now, so act like it."

"I'm sorry that our friendship never grew."

Silence.

We were at the staircase leading to my room. Something else nibbled at the edge of my mind. "Gloria, what happened to Kiki?"

This time Gloria threw her head back and laughed. "Always good to know what happened to those who came before you." Then she looked me right in the eyes and said, "Kiki committed suicide. She jumped off the top of Pierre's building."

"How dreadful. Why did she do it?"

Gloria shrugged. "I don't know, Bebe. You tell me why people kill themselves. Or others."

Chapter Twenty-two

"I can't wait to see those pictures of you, Bebe. You have to get copies for yourself," Darlene said. "Bradley sure is gonna get an eyeful. I'm so happy I got to watch the whole thing." She burst out laughing.

I rolled my eyes. "Please. I'm afraid Bradley won't be happy."

We'd managed to get the shoot done, and with Darlene's pull at Skyway, all of us flew back to New York before the storm got too bad. As it was, I'd had my first experience with turbulence, and I hadn't liked it one bit.

To add to the tension, Pierre had sat next to me on the plane, trying to convince me to come work for him. He said he would welcome another assistant, and promised he could easily get me modeling jobs. When I'd reminded him I was only five foot seven, hardly tall enough to model, he scoffed and told me height rules were for runway models. I spent the flight being noncommittal and finally feigned sleep even when Pierre took my hand and held it against his heart.

Cole and Lola didn't join us on the plane. Either they were stuck on the island, or they'd taken an earlier flight. Darlene assisted the stews, glowing with happiness now that she was free of the domineering oil man.

Gloria sat across and down one row from me. Her head fell to one side the minute the plane took off. While she'd done my makeup, she had only given me commands like "turn your head to the left" and "raise your chin." I wanted to tell her that she was wrong; I wasn't planning a romance with Pierre, or a big modeling career. But then I figured Gloria wouldn't believe me, and I wondered again *why* she was so upset.

Once home, Darlene and I had slept until almost noon on Friday. Clad in our pajamas, we were now enjoying coffee and toast in the living room.

"I want to forget all about those photos, Darlene. I had to show my navel! Not even Annette Funicello does that. If Daddy ever finds out—"

"What will he do? Ground you for life?" She said, and laughed.

"You've met Daddy. He'll trot me to the closest nunnery," I said.

"Honey, he won't even recognize his 'Little Magnolia' in those shots. That one pose Pierre put you in, the one where you're lying on the beach lounger, one knee raised slightly, holding a piña colada with the little paper umbrella in it? Not his little girl," Darlene half sang.

I put my hands over my ears. "Stop!"

"Not to mention the one of you just out of the ocean, with drops of water glistening over your exposed skin, lying on the hard sand. Pierre had to adjust his shorts every few minutes—"

"Darlene!"

"Once he got you in the mood, you delivered a sexy mix of innocence and secret knowledge," she assured me.

"It's a secret, all right, even to me. I couldn't have done it without Pierre's instructions. I shouldn't have agreed in the first place. Durden will never accept the photos. I'll disappoint Bradley."

"Ha! Time will tell." Darlene shot me a sly look. "But you had a teensy-weensy amount of fun, didn't you?"

"I did it for Bradley, so the shoot wouldn't be a total failure," I said, and sipped my coffee.

Darlene smiled.

"Oh, all right! I had fun," I said, shifting position so that my legs were folded under me on the pink sectional. "Pierre made me feel cherished and beautiful."

"You are beautiful, silly," Darlene said. "Do you think you might accept another modeling assignment?"

I smiled. "If the circumstances were right, maybe. Pierre said he could get me assignments, and if Bradley fires me for not controlling Lola . . ."

"Nobody could have handled that drunk. Cole will keep her in alcohol and under his thumb. Lola's modeling career is over," Darlene said, lying down and propping a yellow satin pillow under her head.

"Gosh, let me call Danielle and see if Bradley is back at the office. That Pickering—the so-called lawyer—had better have gotten him out of jail," I said, and stood.

"You're not going into the office, are you? Even *I'm* exhausted."

"Let's see what Danielle says. Don't move."

Darlene yawned. "I won't. I'm going to close my eyes and figure out what to wear when I see Stu."

I went to the kitchen wall unit and dialed the office.

"Hi, Danielle, it's me, Bebe. We got our shots and came home last night because of a storm down in the islands."

"Wow, that was a fast trip. Are you tired? Or do you want to hear the latest?"

"Both," I answered. "First tell me if Mr. Williams is back in the office."

"No, he's not. We haven't heard from him since . . . well, you were at the reception," Danielle said. "No one has come to take his place either, like Debbie Ann keeps telling everyone."

I closed my eyes and leaned against the wall. Darn Debbie Ann! She believed Bradley was guilty and must have been gloating that *she* had inside information of the imminent arrival of his replacement. "Okay, give me the latest now."

"We've been bombarded with phone calls."

"Reporters?"

"Uh-huh. Four of them even came to the office, but I showed them the elevator fast. I treated them politely but firmly, like you taught me, Bebe."

"Thank you, Danielle. I'll speak with your supervisor when I can. I appreciate everything you've done."

"You're too sweet. I've learned a lot from you, and I can add my extra duties to my résumé."

"Slow down. I don't want you leaving us. You're a valuable person to have around."

She chuckled. "Okay, the biggest news—I mean, besides Mr. Williams not being here—is that I transferred a call from Precision Knives to Gina. They want to shoot an ad with Debbie Ann using their knives. The ad's supposed to run in newspapers across the state."

"Debbie Ann must be over the moon."

"She is! The shoot is scheduled for Tuesday on her set. I'm making a list of things you should know when you come back, but that's the main one. Are you coming in today?"

"No, I'm not. I'm confident you have everything under control, and I have some things to do," I said.

"Before you go, tell me something. Did you bring back anything pretty from Saint Thomas?"

"I didn't have time for shopping, but I found this huge conch shell on the beach. It's heavy, and you can hear the sound of the ocean in it. My roommate and I put it in the center of our coffee table. That and a slight sunburn across my nose and cheeks are all I brought back."

Danielle chuckled and we ended the call.

"You want more coffee, Darlene?"

"No, thanks."

I plopped down on the sectional. "Bradley's not at the office."

Darlene shook her head. "Finelli can't still have him in custody, can he?"

I bit my lower lip, reached up, and twirled a piece of my hair. "There's only one way to find out."

Darlene nodded. "I'll go with you."

Darlene and I exited the cab in front of the police station, me in a pale green suit, and Darlene in a short-sleeved lavender A-line dress that tied at the neck.

I opened the door to the station and almost cursed.

"You again?" Officer Lonegan said. He stood behind the desk looking more unkempt than he had last Sunday.

Darlene turned to me. "You know this person?"

"Who are you, Red?" the officer asked.

I answered. "She's my friend. Have you got Mr. Williams in jail?"

Officer Lonegan smirked. "Your boyfriend? That would be none of *your* business."

Darlene said, "Get Finelli out here then."

The officer's eyebrows came together. "Hey, missy, did you forget who's in charge here? I recommend you both take yourselves off. The detective's gone out for lunch."

"We'll wait," I said, and led Darlene to the long wooden bench behind us. We sat at the far end, away from the officer.

He picked up his newspaper, folded it, and said, "You can wait here all day if you want. All the same to me. But if either of you causes any trouble, I'll put you behind bars myself."

Darlene started to get up. I put my hand on her arm and whispered in her ear, "Don't let him rattle you. He's one of those people who've reached a certain age and are unhappy with their life."

We waited in silence lest Officer Lonegan overhear our conversation. Fortunately, only fifteen minutes went by before Detective Finelli entered the building carrying a deli bag and a bottle of Coke.

Darlene and I stood.

Finelli saw us and blew out a deep breath. "I have nothing to say to either one of you at the present time."

"What if we have evidence you might need?" I asked, knowing I didn't have evidence, only conjecture.

"As taxpayers in the state of New York, I think you are obliged to hear us out," Darlene said in her firm stewardess-controlling-an-angry-passenger voice.

"Cripes. Follow me. I know you won't leave until you've given me *your* ideas on *my* case," the detective responded.

He led us down the beige hall, past the desks of curious policemen—Darlene grinned—and into his small office. Motioning us to sit in the two chairs opposite his desk, he sat in a torn brown leather chair.

"What's the evidence, Miss Bennett?" he asked, dropping his deli bag and Coke on his desk and picking up a pencil.

"Do you still have Mr. Williams in jail?" I asked.

Detective Finelli leaned back in his chair, making it creak in protest. "I didn't realize I was giving you information."

Darlene said, "Maybe if we work together, Suzie's murder will be solved."

He looked at Darlene. "I've already made an arrest, Miss Roland. Are you telling me I can't do my job?"

"No," she said. "We just want to help you, because you have the wrong person in jail."

He pinched the bridge of his nose, then sighed and addressed me. "Look, Miss Bennett, I know you helped me on that other case, and that you recently fended off an armed robber with a bottle of mustard—"

"How did you find out about that?" I asked, surprised.

"Cops talk to one another," he said, and coughed. Or smothered a laugh. "The department doesn't encourage citizens to endanger themselves by getting involved in homicide cases. I've had a parade of people in here giving me their opinion on who killed Miss Wexford."

"You'll need to hear us out as well," I said bluntly.

Then I remembered how I had treated Finelli the last
time I'd seen him.

I leaned forward in my chair. "Listen, I don't want to
argue. I owe you an apology for insulting you when you
arrested Mr. Williams. I'm sorry I said that you hadn't
investigated the case properly. When I was growing up,
my parents taught me to respect the law and policemen.
You do have my respect."

Finelli spoke in a gruff voice. "Apology accepted.
In a way, I admire your spunk."

"Oh, thanks," I said, softening the words with a
smile.

"What about me?" Darlene asked.

"The department apologized to you after the Philip
Royal case was closed, Miss Roland," Finelli reminded
her. Then he said, "But what gets me is that the two
of you put yourselves in danger. And the chief doesn't
appreciate private citizens meddling in police matters.
You can see my predicament."

"We don't go randomly chasing crooks and killers,
Detective," Darlene said. "Last time I was defending
myself. Now you've got Bebe's boss in jail for strangling that slut Suzie. We had to get involved."

He sat forward and stared at me. "Miss Bennett,
last Sunday you promised me you wouldn't interfere."

"You're right. But I didn't say I wouldn't investigate." I gave him my most earnest expression. "I'm
going to confession this afternoon at St. Patrick's.
Now, please, eat your sandwich while we talk."

Finelli snapped his pencil down on his desk, then
reached for the white deli bag. He unwrapped a thick
pastrami on rye. "I'm listening." He took a bite.

"Thank you," I said. "Is Mr. Williams still in jail?"

I had to wait for him to swallow and take a long
drink from his Coke before he answered. "This is all
off the record, understand? I could lose my job."

"We agree," I assured him. "Do I look like the kind
of woman who would put two young boys' father out
of work?"

"You don't miss anything, do you? Pickering brought

Williams before the judge about two hours ago. Your boss is out on bail."

"Thank God," I muttered. "You know Jeff Granford threatened to kill Mr. Williams."

"I've got a team watching the Omaha boy."

"Good," I said, relief washing over me. "Do you believe Mr. Pickering has put a private investigator on the case?"

Finelli took another bite of his sandwich and wiped his hands on a napkin. After he swallowed, he said, "Williams was formally charged on Wednesday. Pickering probably didn't want to run up a bill with a P.I. until he knew the outcome of the grand jury hearing. Then his job was to get Williams out of jail, which he did. He'll probably hire someone now."

"Exactly as I feared," I said, furious at Mr. Pickering and determined to tell Stu how the lawyer had handled the case so far.

"Miss Bennett, Pickering is a rich trial lawyer with a high-profile practice. Speaking of which, I've had the chief breathing down my neck on this case because of the celebrity status of Miss Wexford. And from where I sit, Williams was caught red-handed."

I crossed my hands in my lap. "Mr. Williams was with Suzie the night she was killed. However—and this is the important part—he left her apartment for at least a half an hour. During that time, the killer strangled Suzie. When Mr. Williams returned he found her dead. Have you even tried to find a store clerk who could identify him and give him an alibi?"

"You talkin' about the chocolate syrup?"

I blushed. "Yes."

"Didn't your boyfriend tell you? He couldn't find a place nearby that sold the stuff. He didn't buy anything. Which means no clerk to ID him."

I wanted to scream.

Darlene picked it up. "We've got suspects, motives, and opportunity."

Finelli put down the sandwich and picked up his pencil. "Let's hear it."

"First of all," I said, "there's Lola—another famous model. Suzie pushed Lola out of the spotlight. I'm a witness to Lola stating that she could strangle Suzie. Those were her exact words the Thursday before Suzie's murder."

Finelli made notes.

"Next is Jeff Granford, Suzie's hometown boy-friend. I've spoken to him, and he lived in a fantasy world, where Suzie was concerned. And he's a bully. You saw him in action yourself at Suzie's memorial. He could have found out the truth about Pierre Benoit and Suzie—they were having an affair—or about Mr. Williams and Suzie. I'm going to find out his address—"

"Granford was questioned and released," Finelli interrupted. "Don't you go near him, Miss Bennett. He's violent. I called the Omaha police, and Granford has a history of beating women."

"There!" Darlene exclaimed. "With his temper, if he found out the truth about Suzie—he could have followed her around—it's an easy step from hitting to strangling."

"Says he was teaching a kid to box at the time of the murder," Finelli said. "Williams was caught at the scene."

"Jeff was teaching a kid to box at two in the morning?"

Finelli shrugged.

I made a mental note to follow up on that. "Then there's Pierre. He was very possessive of Suzie."

Finelli shook his head. "The photographer has a reputation with the ladies and was known to turn a blind eye to Miss Wexford's straying."

"Did you know he asked Suzie to marry him the night before she was murdered?" I asked. "And that she turned down his proposal?"

Finelli made no comment, but wrote on his pad again.

"Tell him about Gloria, Bebe," Darlene said.

I didn't speak.

"Bebe, you have to! I know you thought she was your friend, but look how she's treated you. Tell him what Gloria said about Suzie."

Reluctantly I conceded. "Suzie's makeup artist, Gloria Castellano, had hated her client for a long time. Gloria told me on more than one occasion that she could kill Suzie. After Suzie was murdered, Gloria was happy. She even said, 'Good riddance.'"

"You and Gloria aren't friends now? Why is that?" Finelli asked.

I shrugged. "Gloria got some idea in her head about me wanting to engage Pierre's affections and become a model. It doesn't make sense to me why that would bother her. Even before that, she turned chilly toward me."

"Miss Castellano came in on her own earlier this week." Detective Finelli held my gaze. "She told me who she thought had the most motive to kill Suzie. Someone who was in love with Williams. Someone jealous of Miss Wexford's relationship with Williams. Someone who had threatened to kill the model."

Silence fell.

I whispered, "You can't believe that *I* would take a human life."

While I sat stunned, Darlene shot to her feet. "How dare you, Finelli? Bebe would never kill anyone, and you know it! This just makes me think *Gloria* is the murderer, and she's trying to throw the spotlight elsewhere. Did she come to you *before* Mr. Williams was arrested?"

"Yes, she did. Sit down, Miss Roland."

Darlene sat. "Has Gloria come back *since* Mr. Williams was arrested to tell you he's *not* the killer, that Bebe did it?"

"No, she hasn't," Finelli said.

"Exactly where was Gloria the night Suzie was killed? Did you ask her?"

"She was out at a nightclub with a friend."

Darlene laughed. "Now that's a great alibi. *Nobody* in this case has a good alibi."

"Williams was at the scene of the crime. He was intimately involved with the victim. The murder weapon was something he bought for her."

"And you've got pressure on you from the chief. It doesn't matter if you've got the killer, just that you made an arrest." Darlene shot the detective a look of disdain. She rose and took my elbow. "Come on, Bebe. We should have known we couldn't work with the fuzz."

Darlene walked us out of the police station and hailed a cab.

"Bebe," she said over "Return to Sender" playing on the cab's radio, "stop worrying about what Detective Finelli thinks. Let's focus on our next move. We've got a lot of work to do."

I rolled down my window and let the spring breeze cool my face. "What are we going to do, Darlene?"

"Once I'm back with Stu—which will be tonight—he'll help us," she said with confidence. "There's got to be a way Stu can get to Lola, find out exactly where she was the night Suzie was killed."

"Okay."

"As for that lying bitch Gloria, you need to confront her. See if you can figure out why she wanted you put away. I don't buy that nightclub alibi for a second."

"Neither do I," I said. "I can't believe I never seriously considered her a suspect before."

"You trusted her too quickly. Gloria's one of our chief suspects now," Darlene said.

We reached our building. Darlene paid the cabbie. Behind her back I looked around for Harry, but didn't see him.

Upstairs, I called Danielle again and asked if Bradley had come in. He hadn't, but at least the staff would shortly know he was out of jail.

Darlene took the phone from my hands and called Stu.

I sat on the pink sectional, tired, confused, and feeling guilty that I'd posed for those photos in Saint Thomas.

"Stu's going to fix me dinner on his hibachi," Darlene said.

"I'll bet he was happy you called."

"Yeah. He's going to be even happier when I walk in wearing what I plan to wear," Darlene said smugly. "I have to shower and get ready. What are you going to do?"

"I'm beat. I need to type up my notes on the Durden swimwear shoot, but I think I'll go to the office tomorrow for that. I'm going to confession and Mass."

Darlene patted my shoulder. "Sounds like what you need is peace and quiet. Then we'll put our plans into action."

I left the apartment after donning an ivory hat.

The priest was kind, Mass filled me with hope, and I gave Harry two quarters upon my return home.

I couldn't eat. I drank a glass of milk and changed into a light nightgown. I pulled my secret steno pad out from under the cushion of the Banana chair. Spotting Bradley's blue scarf, I picked it up and carried it with me to bed, breathing in his lime cologne.

I flipped open to the page in the steno pad where I had listed my "fun things to do in New York," written while I still lived in Richmond. I hadn't had time to do many—take the ferry to see the Statue of Libery, go to the top of the Empire State Building, float a sailboat in Central Park. But I had attended Mass at St. Patrick's and window-shopped on Fifth Avenue. I crossed those off the list.

I looked down at the last entry I'd written since I'd arrived and met Bradley: Kiss one certain guy next to the clock in the lobby of the Waldorf-Astoria.

I closed the steno pad and tossed it onto the chair.

Would Bradley come into the office Monday?

Should I call him at home?

What if Debbie Ann was right, and his replacement was on the way?

Chapter Twenty-three

My eyes flew open. A great pounding on the apartment door had brought me to consciousness. Funny, I hadn't heard the intercom buzzer.

I threw on my robe and peeked in Darlene's room. Empty. Whatever she wore to Stu's last night must have been one hot number, since it was late in the morning and she still wasn't home.

Standing at the front door, I said, "Who is it?"

Daddy's voice bellowed from the other side: "Your parents. Open the door, young lady. This building has no security."

Uh-oh.

"Yes, it does. Someone else must have opened the building door." I undid the three locks on the door and swung it wide.

"Mama!" I said, throwing myself into her arms. She smelled like Shalimar cologne, her favorite.

Grace Bennett, my mama, was dressed impeccably in a two-piece, cocoa-colored, long-sleeved suit. Attached to her right shoulder was a big gold flower pin with a seed-pearl center. She collected pretty pins. Styled in short curls, her dark hair capped her head. I couldn't remember the number of times I'd gone with her to the same beauty parlor on Broad Street in Richmond, and watched her get her hair done.

She kissed my cheek, then held me at arm's distance—she was five foot two compared with my five foot seven. Her weight had climbed until she was now plump. "Let me look at my baby girl."

"Can we come in?" Daddy asked. "We spent all yesterday on the train."

"Sure," I said, stepping aside. "You came in last night?"

"Yes, dear. I'm so happy to find you in one piece." Mama smiled. "Earl, isn't this the cutest apartment? I do adore that pink sectional, Bebe. I remember when you wrote to us about it."

Confused and not fully awake, I asked, "Where did you stay last night? Why didn't you tell me you were coming?"

Daddy's face turned a scary shade of purple. A veteran of World War II, he walked around the small living room with a stiff, military bearing. He had iron-gray hair and dwarfed Mama with his husky six-foot-one-inch frame.

"Your mother and I hadn't heard from you since I called you Monday night. You told me that boss of yours, Williams, hadn't killed that fancy model. Then I read in Thursday morning's paper that the playboy has been arrested," Daddy said, taking his suit jacket off and tossing it over the sofa.

"We were so worried, Bebe," Mama said. "I tried to call you all day and night Thursday, but there was no answer. When your father decided to take the train and find out where you were, I came with him, though you know how I hate to travel out of Virginia and leave all my plants and flowers."

"Please sit down," I said. "I'm sorry to have worried you. There was a photo shoot in Saint Thomas, and I got to go along," I said in a cheerful tone.

Mama put her hand to her throat. "Aren't there wild natives and animals in those islands?"

Daddy said, "You flew on a plane again? And you've been working for that playboy Williams—I met him; I know what I'm talking about—with him being a murderer?"

I spread my hands out in front of me. "Saint Thomas was lovely, Mama, and I was only there one day. Darlene went with me. Mr. Williams got arrested because the case hasn't been investigated properly. His lawyer has already had the judge release him from jail." I stopped and smiled. "So where did you say you're staying?"

"All these hotels are the same," Daddy pronounced. "We're at that Legends Hotel where I was last time. Tomorrow being Mother's Day"—here Daddy shot me a meaningful look—"I thought they'd have a nice brunch for us after Mass."

I barely refrained from clapping my hand over my mouth. Mother's Day! I had completely forgotten.

Mama took my bare hand in her white-gloved one. "You'll change jobs now, won't you, dear? Or even come back home? I can't like the idea of your living in such a big city with all manner of criminals and a fast crowd. You have your reputation to think about, and you know what I've taught you over the years about a girl's reputation."

"Mama, I'm happy here," I said gently, looking into her brown eyes. "You know that. Mr. Williams is a good man, and Darlene is my very best friend. My reputation is fine, honest."

At that moment the key turned in the lock of the apartment door. Darlene bounced into the room, grinning. I took one look at her, closed my eyes for second, then opened them again.

She had on a wild, two-piece outfit, skintight, in swirls of yellow, pink, turquoise, and black. The top ended just under her bra. Her entire midriff was exposed, as the bottom half, a pair of pants, sat snugly on her hips.

Daddy and I stood up.

Darlene smiled at Daddy, then rushed over and balanced on her tiptoes to gave him a kiss on the cheek. "Hi, Mr. Bennett. And you must be Mrs. Bennett. You and Bebe look so much alike."

I saw Mama's gloved hands clasp together tightly,

never a good sign. "Yes, I'm Bebe's mother. You must be Miss Roland."

Daddy hadn't taken his eyes off her figure.

Darlene, oblivious to the reaction her entrance was causing, said, "Oh, call me Darlene, Mrs. Bennett. Bebe, you didn't tell me your parents were coming for a visit. We could have arranged for Broadway show tickets. Heck, it might not be too late. I can ask Stu."

"We're not here to be entertained. We're concerned about Bebe's welfare," Daddy said.

Darlene gave a lopsided grin, then put her arm around me and gave me a little shake. "Bebe's doing fiiiiine. She's a big girl now. You don't have to sweat it. Just the other day she was working a hot-dog stand for a friend, and this—"

Mama's gloved hand went to her heart. "Hot-dog stand?"

"Darlene! I don't think Mama and Daddy would be interested in that silly story," I said sharply.

She giggled. "You're right, Bebe. Well, I'm just here to change clothes. Stu is taking me out for lunch. I hope you all enjoy your stay in New York, Mr. and Mrs. Bennett," she chirped, then went into her room and closed the door.

I turned to my parents.

Mama's coral-colored lips pursed. Her hands were clenched so tight, I thought she might break a finger or, at the very least, split a glove.

Daddy opened his mouth to deliver what I was sure would be a scathing speech.

Quickly, I said the one thing that would defuse the situation. "Gosh, I sure am hungry."

Mama sprang from the sofa like a jack-in-the-box. "I'll make you breakfast, or lunch. It's after eleven, dear. What have you got in your refrigerator?"

I blocked her path to the kitchen. "Nothing, really. I, ah, planned to go grocery shopping today. And I had some notes to type up at the office about the photo shoot."

The latter was true. I did need to go to the office for about half an hour and type my report. Also, if I could slip away for a little while, I could pick up a Mother's Day gift for Mama.

Daddy patted his big belly. "Little Magnolia, why don't you put on one of your pretty suits, and we'll go out for lunch? Afterward you can go to the office, type your notes and your resignation, and then meet us at the hotel."

"That's a wonderful idea, Daddy," I said, and gave him a hug. Once he started calling me by my lifelong nickname, I knew he might be mad, but wouldn't get purple-faced again. "I'll turn on the TV for you," I said, switching on the little black-and-white TV. "And I'll hurry."

"Haste makes waste, Bebe," Mama said. "I don't want you slipping in the shower. And put on your red suit, dear. Red is your color."

"Yes, Mama," I said, and ran to get in the shower before Darlene claimed it.

Slipping into a seat on the subway, I breathed a huge sigh of relief. My parents and I had lunched on Italian food at Mamma Leone's. While everything had been delicious, my parents had each expressed their disapproval of New York in their own way.

I knew Mama would never ride the subway, so I'd had to perform the magic trick of obtaining a taxi on a busy Saturday afternoon.

Mama acted like she was Fay Wray in King Kong's clutches, saying she got dizzy looking up at the tall buildings. She covered her eyes as the cab wound its way through traffic, and once back on the street gripped Daddy's arm in case any ruffian dared attack her. Bless her heart.

Daddy assumed his fiercest expression, escorting what he considered his two weak females through the evil city.

I loved my parents, but I'd never feel free except

here in New York, and I couldn't agree to their repeated pleas for me to move back to Richmond.

Reaching the subway stop nearest Ryan, I climbed the steps and emerged into the sunny day. First, I thought, a present for Mama. I found a jewelry shop and bought her a gold rose pin with red-enameled petals.

Tucking the box in my purse, I walked to the Ryan building and entered the elevator.

The doors opened on seventeen, where the faint sounds of jazz met my ears. I walked slowly to my desk, placed my purse down, and went to Bradley's doorway. The overhead light was out, leaving his office illuminated by two windows.

There he was, looking sexier than I'd ever seen him, in the seating area to the right of his desk. He wore a pair of slim-cut black pants and a white, long-sleeved shirt open at the neck. The sliding door to his bar was open, and he sat drinking a martini while seated on the long blue mission-style sofa. On the coffee table in front of him papers were scattered in disarray.

"What are you doing here on a Saturday afternoon, Miss Bennett?" he asked, giving me the once-over.

I walked across his office until I was a few feet away from him. He stood, swallowed the last of his martini, and began making another.

God, how I wanted to throw my arms around him. I'd been starved for the sight of him! His blond hair, neatly combed, his long fingers, nails buffed to a shine, and those incredible blue eyes. Not to mention the open neck of his shirt, which allowed me a tiny glimpse of his chest.

He wasn't wearing an undershirt. I felt a little woozy.

"I came in to do some work," I managed, hoping he would not ask about the Saint Thomas trip.

He turned from the bar, fresh martini in hand, tapped a toothpick holding three olives on the rim of the glass, and ate one. "Dressed in that red suit?"

I tilted my head slightly, studying him. How many of those martinis had crossed his lips? He was always so cool, I couldn't tell if he'd had three or ten. "My parents are in town. We went out to lunch."

He raised an eyebrow. "You didn't mention they were coming."

"It was rather unexpected."

He drank half the martini, then licked his lips and let out a short laugh. "Daddy came to save his Little Magnolia from the big, bad monster?"

Hot, I felt hot, and wanted to take off my suit jacket. There was something so intensely intimate in being in that part of his executive office with him. Alone. On a Saturday. I unbuttoned my jacket and flung it on the sofa.

Standing there in a thin white sleeveless silk blouse, I forced myself to chuckle. "Are you making fun of my father?"

"Never. I don't want to tangle with the big guy again," Bradley said, and gave a mock salute.

The music ended. There was a clicking sound of the needle arm returning to its place. Bradley finished his martini and reached for the silver shaker.

My heart beating fast, I took three steps until I was but a foot away from him. "How many of those have you had?" I asked in a low voice.

He put the shaker down, kept his gaze on it, and said, "Enough to forget the sights and smells of that jail I've been in twice this week. Enough to forget the pictures I've seen of the electric chair."

"Erase that picture from your mind. It has nothing to do with you," I said, instilling my voice with confidence.

Still facing the bar, he glanced in my direction. He looked from my jacket on the sofa to my silk blouse. "Ever my champion, Miss Bennett. Maybe I'll get lucky and be sentenced to life in prison."

"They will never convict you because you're innocent."

He turned toward me and went on as if I hadn't

spoken. "I'd miss seeing you, kid, and hearing your honeyed voice. God, I love the way you talk." He closed his eyes for a moment and breathed in. "And that perfume. I told you never to wear it again."

Desire overcame me. I couldn't stop looking at him. The words *I love you* wanted to come out, but I forced myself not to say them. Instead I whispered, "Are you drunk? I can't tell. You're always so cool and composed."

Bradley closed the distance between us and ran his right thumb lightly across my cheek. "Yes, I'm drunk; that's it," he murmured. "That's why I'm going to do this."

All at once I was in his arms. He slanted his head, and his lips came down on mine, warm and tasting of liquor, gently, as if he were testing me.

To my embarrassment, my whole body trembled. I lifted my arms. My right hand stroked his neck, my left gripped his upper arm, and I kissed him back. Out of instinct or I don't know what, I ran the tip of my tongue across his full bottom lip.

He drew in a deep breath and crushed his lips on mine. I matched his passion, immersed in pleasure and wanting more and more.

And he gave it to me, our kisses intense and desperate, as if he would be taken away at any second and locked in jail forever. In the darkness behind my closed eyes, nothing existed except the smell of his lime aftershave, the delicious taste of him, the strength of his muscles, and the warmth of his hot mouth.

I went along when he moved us to the sofa, kissing all the while. His knee nudged me down, and then we were lying side by side, pressed against each other. My hand moved to that tiny area of bare chest, and I stroked his skin. Bradley leaned over me, ripped open the top third of his shirt, buttons flying, and my hand caressed his exposed chest.

I thought I'd die if he didn't give me more. A pain deep inside me began, one I'd never felt before. He laid his cheek against mine and then kissed my neck, whispering, "Bebe," in my ear before his mouth returned to mine. My blouse must have worked its way out of my skirt, because I felt his hand on my stomach.

I kicked off my pumps and ran my foot up his calf. He groaned, and I felt his hand on my leg. He moved my skirt higher and higher until his fingers found the snap of my garter.

Far away I heard laughter, but I didn't—I couldn't—care about anything except Bradley and what we were doing.

He must have heard it too, because he abruptly went still. He stopped kissing me, despite my murmuring, "No," in protest, and pulled my skirt down. He looked into my eyes and then slowly turned his head toward the laughter.

A male voice spoke, one I recognized and despised. Bradley's despicable cousin, who wanted his job.

"Back to your old tricks with company women, cousin? Isn't that what always gets you in trouble? You've been charged with murdering the last one."

"Get the hell out of here, Drew," Bradley ordered, his voice thick.

"I've come all the way from Chicago—"

"Out!" Bradley yelled.

"Okay, okay," Drew said. "Carry on; I'll be out in the waiting room."

I heard the door close.

Bradley looked at me and ran a hand through his hair. "Miss Bennett, I'm sorry. I shouldn't have let myself get carried away like that. You're very pretty, and—"

Frustrated as I'd never been in my whole life, I sat up, forcing him to do the same. "Don't you *dare* say you're sorry, Bradley. And stop calling me 'Miss Bennett' when we're alone."

"I'm not going to put you in a situation where you're alone with me again," he said, buttoning the few buttons left on his shirt and tucking it into his pants. "Obviously I can't be trusted. Of course I'd been drinking."

"That's a good excuse. Nothing would have happened had you been in your right mind," I said, fighting tears. Grabbing my shoes, I struggled to put them on. My heart still pounded, and that ache would not go away. Worse, I didn't think I could stand just yet.

"Kid, you're a good, sweet girl, and I don't want anything to hurt you," he said.

All my frustration manifested itself in anger. I struck out at him with words. "Oh, great. You can't even take responsibility for your own actions. Bradley, I can take care of myself. And by the way, the investigation is going well. I've narrowed the suspect list down, and hope to have your name cleared in the next few days."

He shot to his feet and stood towering over me. Pointing his finger at my face, he said, "I told you not to meddle, not to put yourself in danger. I told you I'd fire you if I found out you were investigating Suzie's murder."

That brought me to my feet. Looking him straight in the eye, I said, "So, am I fired for trying to help you, or maybe for what just happened, because you don't want to admit any feelings for me?"

We glared at each other.

"Yes, you *are* fired. I warned you. I'll write you an excellent recommendation," he said, and moved to his desk, fumbling for paper.

"Fine. I'll get my purse, and you'll never see me again. You can put that recommendation in the mail," I told him.

Head held high, I stormed out of his office, grabbed my purse, and walked past Drew to the elevator.

Mercifully, it came immediately.

In the lobby there was a ladies' room. I dashed in there, sat on a squarish green chair, and began to cry.

Chapter Twenty-four

When I returned to my apartment, I had to hurry and get ready to meet my parents at six. Darlene wasn't home, so I couldn't cry on her shoulder.

I had to wash off what was left of my makeup, then reapply it. My lips were swollen, and my chin sported a dark pink color. With heavy makeup on my chin, I put on a bright, floral sheath dress to distract attention from my lips. My hand trembled when I touched the garter snap that Bradley's fingers had been about to undo.

Like a chant going through my head, I kept thinking, *You've lost him forever. You won't even get to see him at the office.* Nothing would stop me from finishing the investigation, though. That night at dinner, sharp-eyed Daddy said, "Bebe, what's wrong with your lips?"

Mama chimed in, "Oh, dear, Bebe. Your father is right. Your lips are puffy."

I tried to laugh, but a squeaky sound came out. "It was warm in the office, so I went out and bought a snow cone."

Unable to eat, I pushed food around my plate, and struggled to chitchat with Mama and Daddy so they'd be reassured.

Once home, I sobbed my heart out.

Sunday wasn't any better. I'd slept about three hours the night before, and had to be up for the early

Mass at St. Patrick's. In church, I felt guilty for my actions the day before, but I didn't regret them. Then there was Mother's Day brunch at the Legends. Mama loved her pin and put it on immediately. The whole time, part of my brain kept replaying the scene on Bradley's sofa.

Upstairs in my parents' hotel room, while Daddy watched a baseball game on TV, Mama and I sat on the other bed. We chatted about hometown people, but she knew something was wrong. Thank God she didn't pry, because I would have broken down and told her everything, ensuring her horror and disapproval.

After dinner—another meal wasted on me—I hugged them each hard and said good-bye. I was even able to reassure Daddy that I no longer worked for Bradley Williams.

Entering my apartment, I was confronted with Stu and Darlene making out on the sectional. I ran into my room, flinging the door shut, and bent double on the side of the bed. Racking sobs overtook me.

Darlene came in and closed the door. "You look like hell."

I told her everything, down to the last detail, ending with, "And what must he think about me, behaving like a . . . like a—"

"Passionate woman?" Darlene supplied. "I'll bet you drove him out of his mind with desire."

I considered this. "He was . . . um, well, never mind. But he fired me. I'll never see him again. And he didn't take responsibility for being attracted to me."

"He's fighting it, I keep telling you. He'll call you, Bebe. Wait and see. Bradley won't be able to stand not having you in the office."

I wiped my eyes with a balled-up, mascara-blotted tissue. "He was able to stand it yesterday."

Darlene put her arm around me. "Just how far were you prepared to go, honey?"

I closed my eyes as a fresh wave of pain came over

me. "I don't know. The way I felt at the time, I think I would have done whatever Bradley wanted," I whispered, and felt heat come into my cheeks.

Darlene moved to the floor, crouching in front of me. "And Bradley knew that. He also knew *he* wasn't able to stop. He knows what would have happened if Drew hadn't walked in on you. *That's* why Bradley's mad."

"I'm not getting your drift," I said.

"Bradley is mad at *himself,* not you. He violated his male moral code against seducing virgins. When you think about it, Bradley's tipped his hand. He cares deeply about you, and he wants you in every meaning of the word."

"Do you think he loves me?"

Darlene paused, then said, "I think he's battling his own feelings. He's been a swinging bachelor for a long time."

I shredded the tissue. "He told me at the memorial service that he'd been lied to a lot by women. He said 'someday' he might get married."

"Wow. I'm surprised he opened up to you that much. The man is in torment, I tell you."

The phone rang.

Darlene grinned and got to her feet.

I grabbed her arm. "If it's him, tell him I'm unable to come to the phone and take a message."

"Why?"

I shook my head, tears falling again. "It's probably not him anyway."

"The phone's ringing!" Stu yelled.

Darlene ran into the kitchen. I looked for a clean nightgown.

A minute later, Darlene returned. "Guess who that was?"

Despite myself, I smiled. "Really?"

"Oh, yeah. Sounded like a wounded puppy. Wants you to call him back," Darlene said, waving a piece of paper with Bradley's phone number on it in front of my face.

I shifted my ivory cotton nightgown to my left hand

and took the paper. "He probably just has a question about the photo shoot. I'm not calling him back. He fired me. Let him figure it out."

"You're just as stubborn as he is." Darlene bit her lower lip. "Though, that might be the way to play it. Let him call again. Let him go into the office tomorrow and see your empty chair. Let him learn a lesson."

Bradley called again an hour later.

Darlene came to my door, grinning. "Oh, the poor baby. He asked if you had received his message, and I told him you had."

I sat in my nightgown on the floor next to my record player, listening to John Lennon singing about money on *The Beatles Second Album*. "What did he say then?"

"At first he was speechless. Then he said, 'Please ask her to call me; it's important.'"

I frowned. "I told you it's about the photo shoot."

Darlene slapped her hand on her thigh and laughed. "No, it isn't."

"Yes, it is."

"Okay, honey. Stu's going home now. He has an important business meeting in the morning; then he wants to take both of us out for an early lunch tomorrow."

"That would be nice," I said.

I waited until I heard the apartment door close before I came out of my room. All my crying had made me thirsty. I had grabbed a Tab when the buzzer from downstairs went off. The bottle almost slipped from my hand.

I rushed into the living room in time to hear Darlene speak into the intercom. "Yes, Stu, what did you forget?"

"Is this Darlene?"

Bradley's voice. He was downstairs! I couldn't see him like this: in my nightgown, my hair a mess, my nose and eyes red from crying. Still, a rush of elation went through me that he had actually come to see me.

I motioned frantically for Darlene not to let him in. She nodded her agreement.

"Yes, Bradley?" she said.

"I'd like to come up and talk with Bebe."

"Oh, geez, I'm sorry, but she's asleep," Darlene said.

"Please go wake her up and get her to either see me or talk to me over this damned intercom," Bradley demanded.

"I'll see what I can do," Darlene promised.

I let a full five minutes go by before I took over at the intercom. "Yes, Bradley?"

"Let me come up, Bebe. I want to see you," he said, his voice somber.

"That's impossible. It's very late, I'm not properly dressed, and I do have my *reputation* to maintain."

Darlene buried her face in the gold sofa cushion, she was laughing so hard. I was not ready to find the situation funny.

Neither was Bradley. "Bebe, we need to talk."

"We already talked. I have no intention of listening to you make excuses about what happened between us on your sofa. I'll mail you a report on the Saint Thomas shoot, even though I'm no longer employed by Ryan Modeling. Pierre Benoit has offered me a job twice. I assume the offer is still open. I'm going to see him in the morning."

Darlene fell to the floor laughing, both hands over her mouth.

"Bebe, don't do this," Bradley said. "Let me come up."

Darlene ran the first finger of her right hand around the pinkie of her left, meaning I had Bradley wrapped around my little finger. She scooted off to her room.

That ache started again, hearing the vulnerable tone of his voice. Vulnerable? Cool man-about-town Bradley? I softened my voice. "No. You're not coming up here. And *you* are the one who fired *me*."

"You can't go to work for Pierre, that lecher."

"I need a job," I said.

"You have a job, Bebe," he said. "You're my executive secretary."

Tears came to my eyes. I could tell he was very

close to his end of the intercom. It was as if he were whispering in my ear again. And, oh, dear God, he wanted me back. Kept calling me Bebe. Was on my doorstep despite its being almost midnight.

Bradley said, "You aren't fired."

I let a long minute go by. "I'll come in tomorrow morning, and we'll see how it goes on a trial basis," I told him.

"Thank you," he said.

"Hey, mister, are you talkin' to Miss Sweet Face?" Harry's drunken voice met my ears.

Uh-oh. Harry had better not say anything about how I loved one man. Bradley would know for sure it was him. "Bradley!" I said urgently.

"Yes?"

"Give Harry some money."

"This wino?"

"Miss Sweet Face has a lot of boyfriends. You one of them? Had a fella come get her a couple of nights ago. She had on the prettiest blue dress. She didn't see me, only had eyes for him."

Lord have mercy! Harry was talking about Louis.

"Bebe?" Bradley said.

"Yes."

"I gave the bum five dollars, okay? He's gone now. We'll talk about your association with this person in the morning."

"Good night, Bradley."

I drifted into Darlene's room. "I'm not fired, Bradley says."

Darlene grinned. "Told ya. Now, we have to plot your next step."

"What next step?"

"What you're going to wear tomorrow."

In unison we said, "The white go-go boots!"

I made Bradley wait Monday morning, arriving at the office at quarter after nine. Sauntering off the elevator, I lingered on the opposite side of my desk, pretending to read phone messages.

The truth was, I wanted Bradley to have a good look at me. I was wearing a pale pink sleeveless mini-dress that Darlene had brought back from London. The dress had tiny white fuzzy dots all over it, and featured a scooped neck with a white bow at the bosom. On my legs were white tights and those precious white go-go boots.

I'm not positive he saw me, though I heard him choke on his coffee.

It was Drew who spoke to me first. Coming around the corner, he plunked himself down in one of the waiting-area chairs. "Wow, great outfit. We don't have anything like that in our stores." He lit a cigar and stared at me.

"Perhaps because your chain of department stores hasn't caught up to the latest fashions from London," I said.

Drew crossed his legs, showing off his expensive leather shoes. He wore a flashy Italian suit, which didn't impress me. His face always reminded me of a fox's, angling in as it did from his wide forehead. His auburn hair added to the image.

"I'll have to get on that. You know, Bebe, you could always come out to Chicago and work for me," Drew said, his tone suggestive.

I went around my desk and sat in my chair. "I like New York, thank you."

Drew went on. "I'd like to take you and Debbie Ann. Man, that woman can cook. She's here working on her show—that would go over good in Chicago—and she made me a perfect omelet."

"Debbie Ann has had a tragic past," I informed him. "She lost both her husband and her son. Leave her alone."

He held up his hands. "I didn't come here to cause trouble. Uncle Herman wanted me to check things out."

I didn't answer. Instead, I remembered Uncle Herman's deadline for Bradley. His ten days would be up on Wednesday.

Glancing up from Danielle's notes, I caught Bradley

looking at me. He wore a slate-blue suit—which brought out the color of his eyes—with a goldish tie sporting square and circular blue swirls. No more mourning for Suzie, I thought.

"Miss Bennett, come in here please," he said.

Drew hollered, "Should I leave this time?"

Bradley bolted out of his office. "Drew, make no mistake. You are not to speak that way in front of Miss Bennett. Should you choose to test my resolve in this, you'll find yourself with a black eye. I'm fed up with your tactics. You come here, spying on me again, trying to find ways to make me look bad in front of Uncle Herman. I don't interfere in your business."

"That's because I run a clean operation."

Bradley grabbed Drew by his lapels. "Like hell you do."

As if no one had spoken, I placed a check made out to the Legends for Suzie's memorial reception at the edge of my desk. In a casual tone, I said, "Mr. Williams, you need to sign this. I'll take it over to the Legends myself, as I have an early business lunch at eleven."

The phone rang before he could reply. Instead, Bradley and Drew got into an argument over who was authorized to sign the check.

I picked up the receiver and chatted with a girl from Precision Knives about Debbie Ann's shoot tomorrow.

Bradley signed the check and held it out to me. Without touching his fingers, I accepted it. He returned to his office.

Drew went down the hall.

Ending my phone call, I started typing my notes on the Saint Thomas shoot, noting that Bradley was on his private line. Listening while typing, I figured out he was on the phone with his uncle, talking and drinking coffee I hadn't made for him.

He was still on the phone when I summoned Danielle to cover for me while I met Darlene and Stu for an early lunch.

At the restaurant, Darlene and Stu couldn't keep their hands off each other. Their happiness made me smile. I was able to eat a hearty lunch, which made me feel better. The meal, and the looks I got from men checking out my go-go boots, helped put me in a better frame of mind.

Darlene said, "Okay, now what are we going to do next to clear Bradley's name?"

Stu looked at me. "Bebe, what about Lola?"

I shook my head. "She's a suspect with a strong motive and opportunity. I'm sure she won't talk to me after what happened in Saint Thomas."

Stu grinned. "She'll talk to an adoring fan. Me. I'm good at getting what I want out of a woman. After all, I got the best girl in the world back with me," he said, and winked at Darlene.

She elbowed him. "Watch it, buster. And behave."

I said, "Thanks so much for your help, Stu. And Darlene, don't worry if you can't come with me on my appointment with Scott Roberts later today."

She waved a dismissive hand. "Honey, I'll be there."

I left them and returned to the office around one. Drew wasn't there. Bradley sat with his chair turned around from me, looking out the window. On his desk was a sandwich from the Automat.

Danielle and I went over phone messages before she returned to the typing pool. I had about three hours until I'd need to leave for my appointment with Scott Roberts. Out of habit, I brewed a fresh pot of coffee.

I finished typing my Saint Thomas report and marched into Bradley's office, laying it on his desk.

"If I hurt you—by firing you—it wasn't what I wanted," he said, turning to face me.

"I'm fine. You haven't eaten your lunch," I said, unwilling to reveal how much I'd been hurt. "Can I get you a cup of coffee? There's a fresh pot."

"That sounds great."

I returned with the hot mug a minute later. "I'll be

leaving today at four fifteen. I have another appointment."

"Are you going out looking for a job?" Bradley asked, his cool demeanor back in place.

"Actually this has to do with another matter," I said, and crossed my arms over my chest.

"Pickering hired a private detective. There's no need for you to investigate any longer." The last two words came out through gritted teeth.

"If you'll excuse me, I have lots of work to do," I told him.

"Just a minute. What is with you and that wino?"

I took a deep breath. "While I don't see why I have to answer questions about my personal life, in this case I will tell you. Harry is a friend. I try to help him when I can."

"You're always trying to help people, aren't you, kid?" Bradley said, picking up a pencil and holding it between his two index fingers. His voice dropped to a husky murmur. "I wish you could help me, stop me from wanting—" He broke off.

Wanting to kiss me again? My heart started that crazy beat. I chose to misunderstand him. "Don't worry. You'll be cleared of Suzie's murder."

With that, I strode back to my desk. Bradley and I didn't exchange another word for the rest of the day until I told him good night at four fifteen.

"Arrange to have someone cover for you during Debbie Ann's shoot tomorrow," he said. "I want you there. You know how to deal with Pierre." A bit of sarcasm laced his last words.

"Fine," I said, and went downstairs, breathing a sigh of relief. Obviously he hadn't read the Saint Thomas report, which described how *I* had ended up being the model.

Outside, Darlene waited for me in the sunshine. "How'd it go?"

I popped on my shades and filled her in while we tried to get a cab.

She said, "Sounds like Bradley's a man with a lot on his mind. Betcha you're number one."

I twirled a piece of my hair. "Yeah, right. Men may be easy for you to charm, but not for me."

A cab stopped and we got in. I had Scott's card in hand, and gave the cabbie the address.

"You're in training, Bebe," Darlene said. "As for Scott, we're trying to find out if he really has nude photos of Suzie, right?"

"Yes. Louis gave me the idea that Scott had that type of photos. I thought Scott might be blackmailing Suzie. If she was paying him, he's off the suspect list. If she wasn't, maybe the two argued and he killed her. My only concern is how we're going to convince him to talk."

Darlene laughed. "You keep forgetting I'm a Texas girl. Don't you worry. He'll talk."

Scott Roberts's business turned out to be in a brownstone in a residential area. He gave me an ice-cold look, but admitted us. Like Pierre's place, the first floor served as a studio, with cameras and umbrella lights set up.

Three female models—all long-haired blondes with bangs, blue eyes, and skinny figures—wore matching outfits: a sleeveless black chiffon dress that broke into pleats at the bottom. Round white collars circled their necks with a white daisy in their centers. Each girl's hair had been pulled to one side in a low ponytail, secured with a fabric daisy pin.

A lone dark-haired male model, dressed in a black velvet suit and ruffled shirt, sat at a white cloth-covered table set for four.

They were passing a pipe among them, smoking hash. One of the girls held out the pipe to Darlene. She reached for it, but I put my hand on her arm. "Darlene," I hissed.

"Sorry. I was just trying to fit in." But her gaze turned wistful as the pipe went on to the next person.

Scott looked at me without interest. "I can't use you. I told you that at Suzie's memorial."

Darlene said, "Then why did you make an appointment with her?"

He shrugged. "Couldn't appear nasty in front of the Thom McAn guy. You can go now, both of you."

I moved close to him and spoke in a low voice. "I don't think so. You see, I couldn't care less about being a model. I want the pictures and the negatives of the nude photos you have of Suzie Wexford."

He stared at me with those freaky eyes. "What makes you think I'm going to discuss Suzie with you?"

Darlene opened her purse. "This does, honey."

To my horror, a small gun lay in Darlene's purse.

Scott's face went pale. "Come upstairs."

As we made our way up, I whispered, "Do you always carry that thing around, Darlene?"

"No, the gun usually stays in my panty drawer, but I had it with me today because of Scott. I told you I can protect myself."

Reeling from the thought that Darlene kept a gun in our apartment, I blinked twice when Scott flipped the light on in a small room with a desk and lined with filing cabinets.

"Show us the pictures," Darlene commanded, the gun now in her hand.

With an angry movement, Scott unlocked a file cabinet and pulled out a set of photos. He shoved them at me.

So there really were nude pictures of Suzie! I flipped through two of the shots, my eyes going wide at the sight of her naked body.

Darlene took a quick glance. "Ha, natural brunette."

"Why did Suzie pose for these?" I asked.

Scott shrugged. "Look, most girls who get off the bus wanting to be a model end up doing nude shots."

"But I thought you encouraged Suzie to move here based on candid pictures she sent you from Omaha."

"True. I knew she had potential and thought she could go far. It was Suzie who wanted the nudes done in case her career didn't take off as she'd planned."

"And you enjoyed obliging her," Darlene said.

"I've found that having those types of pictures can be, shall we say, *beneficial* to a photographer."

I stared at Scott. "What I want to know is if you killed her."

He laughed. "The two of you are crazy. Right in your hands, you've got proof of why I'd never kill the two-timing bitch. Suzie left me for Pierre, but she paid me *good*, in money and in bed."

"Blackmailer."

"As I told you, nude shots are useful."

"Did Suzie threaten to stop paying you?" I asked.

Scott gazed at me with disgust. "You're not going to pin her murder on me, baby. I can show you my canceled checks to prove that Suzie had paid me through the end of this year."

"Let's see them," Darlene ordered, her gun still pointed at him.

Looking over the documents he produced in short order, I could see he was telling the truth. In 1963, Suzie had paid him five hundred dollars a month regularly. In January of this year, she'd paid him six thousand dollars.

"All right. I believe you were blackmailing her and she paid, so you had no reason to kill her. Give me all the pictures and all the negatives," I said.

"Come on, baby, can't we make a deal?" Scott whined. "I'll give you half of what I get for selling them to *Playboy*."

And have Bradley's name—sure to be included in any article about Suzie—dragged through the mud again? "I could just take what I have here to the police. I know Detective Finelli personally. He'd charge you with blackmail. Now, would you rather do as I say or have me pay a visit to the detective?"

Scott sighed. "What difference does it make to you if I sell the pictures to *Playboy*? I told you I'd give you half the money."

"This is the difference: Suzie paid you not to sell those pictures. Suzie is dead, and even she doesn't

deserve to be humiliated now. Finally, you should earn
your money by finding the next top model and making
her a star," I finished.

Darlene waved the gun at Scott. "It's very quiet."

Cursing bitterly, he handed over the photos.

I tucked them in my purse. "Now write a statement
saying you will never sell or give away any nude photos of Suzie Wexford and sign it."

"Why? You have everything," Scott replied tersely.

"I don't trust you."

Grabbing a piece of paper and a pen, Scott wrote.

He thrust the document in my hands and I read it.
"I'm satisfied now."

He narrowed his eyes at me. "You know, I could
go to the police myself and tell them you forced me
at gunpoint to turn over personal property."

Darlene and I laughed, knowing the coward would
never go to the police.

He went red. "What are you going to do with the
shots?"

I tilted my head. "We have a fireplace."

Darlene agreed, "That will do."

"Crazy women, burning a pile of money," he spat.

Darlene forced him to walk in front of us as we
descended the stairs to the first floor. We made our
escape outside, and ran to the nearest subway stop.

Once underground, I caught my breath. "We're
down to four possible killers: Lola, Gloria, Jeff, or
Pierre. I'm seeing Gloria and Pierre tomorrow. Jeff's
address was in the phone book."

"You're not confronting Jeff alone," Darlene said.
"Let's come up with a plan for him later. I'm going to
Stu's. He'll give you a report on Lola in the morning."

I went home, hid Scott's letter, and lit the fire.

Chapter Twenty-five

I arrived at the office before nine Tuesday morning. I wore a short knit dress, white on top, turquoise-and-white-checked on the bottom. My go-go boots looked fab with the outfit.

The first thing I did was put on a pot of coffee.

Bradley hadn't come in yet, so the second thing I did was refresh my pink lip gloss.

Debbie Ann's photo shoot for Precision Knives was set for eleven. I managed to return phone calls and type a letter before Bradley emerged from the elevator, Drew on his heels.

"Good morning," I said. "Do you want coffee, Mr. Williams?"

"Please, Miss Bennett." He entered his office, took off his suit coat, and sat in his chair. Drew lingered at Bradley's doorway.

"Hey, Bebe, would you bring me a cup?" he asked.

I walked past him and snatched Bradley's mug from his desk. Fixing his coffee the way he liked, I indicated the Styrofoam cups next to the coffeepot. "Drew, everything you need is right there."

Before he could answer, I entered Bradley's office and put the hot mug in front of him. Taking a few steps back, I made sure Bradley could see my outfit. I figured I'd done my job when his gaze went over me; then he quickly averted his eyes.

"Thanks, kid. We've got a busy day. You don't have any outside appointments, do you?"

"I'll be here all day."

From behind me, Drew strolled in with his coffee and sat down on the sofa. "Good coffee, comfortable couch, pretty girls . . . I'd like to be in charge of Ryan."

Bradley swung around in his chair, facing his cousin. "Get out of here, Drew."

From the doorway a male voice said, "Excuse me for interrupting, but I need to see you, Bebe."

God bless Stu! Handsome and exuding power, he filled the door frame.

"Hi, Stu," I said and gave him a blinding smile. "Come on out to my desk."

Stu knew how to play the game. He put his arm around my shoulder and hugged me so hard that my right foot came off the ground.

I sat at my desk—in full view of Bradley—and crossed my legs. "What happened with Lola?"

Stu crouched down, grinning, and spoke softly. "I know you're anxious to hear, and boy, do I have a doozy of a story for you."

"I'm on the edge of my seat."

"Be careful you don't fall off when you hear what I've found out."

"That bad?"

"Yes. I posed as a modeling agent interested in representing her. Lola was flattered and welcomed me inside. She drinks like a man, Bebe. I swear she had five glasses of scotch. Come to think of it, she had been drinking before I got there."

"That's Lola."

"Drinking is only one side of her. I stroked her ego, told her how she wasn't getting the assignments she deserved. She decided I was her new best friend and spilled the beans. She complained about Suzie, how she took all her work." Stu paused. "Brace yourself, Bebe. Here's where you might fall off your chair. Lola confided she's been working part-time for Fran Bitsy."

"Who?"

Stu sighed and rubbed his forehead. "Fran Bitsy runs a group of high-class prostitutes in New York."

I gasped. "Why would Lola do such a thing? And how could she keep it a secret?"

Stu put his hand on mine. "Bebe, Lola is not only an alcoholic; she's a gambler. Las Vegas is practically her second home. She told me how everyone in the Rat Pack knows her. I saw her at Pierre's gala hanging on Frank Sinatra. Anyway, Lola has deep gaming debts, and the casinos threatened to cut her off about six months ago."

"So Lola contacted this woman and started to—"

"Yes. Lola was with a very well known, very married Broadway star the night of Suzie's murder. I verified it with Fran myself."

"You *know* this woman?"

"Yes. Wealthy men and celebrities all over Manhattan know Fran, or know of her. She has a solid reputation for being discreet. That's why Lola hasn't been found out," he said. "It doesn't mean anything that I know who Fran is, Bebe. You know there's only one doll for me."

Whispering, I said, "Do you think Bradley knows Fran?"

Stu's gaze met mine. "He probably does, but Williams isn't the type to seek those services."

"How do you know?"

"Male intuition?"

"Okay." I swallowed. "This means Lola didn't kill Suzie."

"Right. Now, what else can I do to help?"

We stood. "Nothing, Stu. I can't thank you enough for everything."

"No need," he said, wrapping me in a big hug. "I consider myself in your debt for helping me square things with Darlene."

Stu released me, and I saw Drew and Debbie Ann standing down the hall watching. My gaze shifted to Bradley. He crunched a piece of paper into a ball.

Stu and I smiled at each other and said good-bye.

I worked hard until near the time of Debbie Ann's

shoot. Then I called Danielle to cover for me, and took the stairs up to the eighteenth floor. Inside Debbie Ann's kitchen, Gloria knelt on the floor rummaging through her big makeup case. She hadn't even stopped at my desk to sign in!

Debbie Ann was talking to her assistant, Nellie.

"None of the girls here are as attractive as you, Bebe," Drew said close to my ear, startling me.

I moved away without answering him. Drew was nuts if he thought I'd move to Chicago for him.

Nellie scurried off to the elevator, which also brought Bradley. Nellie jumped back at the sight of him. He ignored her, and the suddenly chilly atmosphere, and stepped onto the set.

To my surprise, Louis appeared out of nowhere and greeted me warmly, taking my hand and giving it a squeeze. "Hello, Bebe. You look ravishing, as always."

"Louis, what are you doing here?" I said for his ears alone. "There's no Burma-Shave shoot today."

He raised a hand to my hair, pushing a strand behind my ear. "I asked Gina if I could play a husband in the background of Debbie Ann's ad. She said no, but I knew you would approve."

Jerk! "You're wrong, Louis. You can't use me to get modeling gigs. Gina and Mr. Williams schedule the models. Now please leave the set."

A wounded expression on his face, he said, "If that's what you want, surely. How about dinner one night this week? You pick the day."

"No. We won't be going out again," I said, and walked toward the kitchen.

"You liked it when I kissed you," he said, loud enough for everyone to hear.

Mortified, I turned and opened my mouth, but Bradley had Louis by the arm. He said, "Do you want me to escort you to the door, or should I call security?"

Louis snatched his arm away and stalked off to the elevator.

I entered the kitchen, bracing myself for another nasty encounter. Debbie Ann fussed around, waiting for Gloria.

I took a deep breath and stood over Gloria. "I want to talk to you," I said.

No response.

"Gloria, I'm speaking to you."

She rose and faced me. "You. Pierre will be here any minute, if that's what you're wondering."

"Actually, what I'm *wondering* is why you told Detective Finelli that I killed Suzie Wexford."

We stared at each other. I had no intention of backing down.

"You make me sick," Gloria spat. "When you couldn't get anywhere with your boss, you decided Pierre was the better catch."

"Pierre is not the issue here. Answer my question: Why did you lie to Finelli?"

"Look at you, dressed like that. You're no better than Lola or Suzie. I saw you allow Lola to drink on the plane so that Pierre would have to use you to model that skimpy black bikini. You and Pierre were real cozy on that beach in Saint Thomas."

Why was Gloria going on about Pierre? "Where were you on the night Suzie was murdered?"

"Me! I was on a date with a medical intern. Finelli has checked out my alibi. What's yours? You told me you hated Suzie. You wanted her dead. I think *you* killed her!"

"How could you—"

"Enough!" yelled Pierre.

The Frenchman stood at the edge of the set. He'd heard everything, as had Bradley, Drew, and Debbie Ann.

Pierre crossed to Gloria. "How dare you speak that way of Bebe?"

Gloria's voice rose. "Go ahead. Take your new girlfriend's side. You always pick the wrong girl! It should have been *me* all this time, but you never noticed how much I love you. How it's been me who's stuck with you all these years. But you couldn't love me. All you saw was that I'm chubby and don't have a pretty enough face."

"You foolish girl. You'll do Debbie Ann's makeup because I won't have Bebe's shoot ruined, but after this, you will work for me no more," Pierre announced dramatically.

Gloria narrowed her eyes at him. "That's fine with me. I don't need you or want you, Pierre. You have a love-hate relationship with all your women. Just look at your history: Kiki threw herself off a building rather than be with you. Lola drove herself to drink. Suzie's dead—"

Pierre slapped Gloria.

Bradley stepped forward as if to intervene, but I shook my head at him.

"Pierre," I said, "I started all this by confronting Gloria. Please apologize to Gloria for hitting her."

"No. It is Gloria who must apologize to us," Pierre said, his face red.

Gloria said, "I didn't say anything that wasn't true. I'm leaving. Sorry, Debbie Ann."

Debbie Ann hovered in the corner, twisting her apron, for once not relishing this glimpse into personal matters.

Bradley spoke. "Gloria, if you leave without doing Debbie Ann's makeup, you will not work for Ryan Modeling again. Do you understand? Debbie Ann needs you; the agency needs you to fulfill your obligation."

Debbie Ann found her voice. "Please stay, Gloria. All this unpleasantness has made me quite upset. I don't think I could bear a stranger doing my face."

"I'll do it for *you,* Debbie Ann," Gloria finally agreed.

I rubbed Pierre's arm and looked into his eyes. "Please, Pierre, we need your talent. You want to make the folks at Precision Knives happy, don't you? A great ad photographed by the best in the business."

As quickly as his temper had flared, Pierre relaxed under my soothing words.

"On one condition, Bebe," he said.

"What?"

"That you will have dinner with me tonight at Sardi's."

Gloria laughed. "One of Suzie's two favorite restaurants."

"That would be lovely, Pierre," I said quickly before an argument could flare again. While I didn't like leading Pierre on, I needed to spend time with him. He and Jeff Granford were the only suspects left.

"Can we get to work here, everyone?" Bradley snapped.

Pierre glared his disgust at Bradley.

"Pierre, what time will you pick me up?" I asked, hoping to divert him.

"At seven thirty, *chérie.*"

"I'll be ready," I said, then gave him my address, which he wrote on the back of one of his business cards.

"You're not going back to your desk now, are you? Someone needs to oversee the shoot," he said, as if Bradley weren't a few feet away.

"I'll stay," I told him, causing Bradley to head for the elevator.

When the shoot was finished, successfully in my opinion, I returned to my desk.

The first thing I saw was Bradley's closed door.

"How'd it go, Danielle?" I asked.

"Fine. I typed some letters for you."

"You're swell. I'm calling your supervisor right now to praise your hard work."

"Thanks, Bebe. Mr. Williams sure was mad when he came back downstairs."

"Really?" I asked.

"Uh-huh. He slammed his door so hard the coffee-pot rattled."

"Men," I said, and rolled my eyes. Danielle chuckled and returned to the typing pool.

Was Bradley mad at *me*? Jealous about the male

attention I'd received today? Had he heard Gloria's comment about me posing in the black bikini?

I dialed Mrs. Seeds's extension and explained in detail what a valuable employee Danielle was to the agency. Mrs. Seeds listened and we hung up on excellent terms.

Then I dialed Detective Finelli's number.

"Finelli."

"I'm glad I caught you, Detective."

"Miss Bennett. It's gotten so I recognize your voice."

"That's nice, isn't it?" I proceeded to explain *almost* everything that had happened with Lola, Scott, and Gloria. He acknowledged me with a grunt here and there.

"Interesting, Miss Bennett. Who's at the top of your suspect list now?"

"I'll tell you if you tell me if there was a diamond engagement ring found in Suzie Wexford's apartment," I bargained.

A sigh came from the other end of the line. "Lots of jewelry, no diamond ring."

A shiver went through me. Pierre had lied when he said that Suzie had accepted his ring.

"Miss Bennett?"

"Pierre Benoit and Jeff Granford are my main suspects. Pierre has a temper, is known for having unstable relationships with women, and he lied about being engaged to Suzie. Assuming he was jealous enough over Suzie's dating Mr. Williams, he could have gone to her apartment and murdered her." The more I talked about it, the more Pierre seemed like the killer.

"Possibly."

"Then there's Jeff Granford. We've already discussed his motives: jealousy, his feeling of ownership over Suzie. I haven't had time yet to go down to his apartment and question him. I guess I'll do it tomorrow."

Finelli's voice grew stern. "I wouldn't advise you to go near Granford. I mean it, Miss Bennett."

"Why don't you take these men in for questioning?" I asked, desperation in my voice.

"I've told you, the department is working the case."

"How? You arrested Mr. Williams. That's all I've seen you do. And now I'm going out tonight on a dinner date with Pierre, who could be a killer."

"I'd advise against that."

"Yet you won't lock Pierre and Granford up like you did Mr. Williams," I argued.

"Put on your party dress, Miss Bennett," Finelli said before hanging up on me.

Party dress it was then.

Chapter Twenty-six

"Don't argue with me. You're wearing it," Darlene said.

We were in my room in front of the full-length mirror. I had on a pale pink silk shantung A-line dress, sleeveless with a scooped neck. The top of the dress had clusters of silver beading ending with pink beads at the Empire waistline.

"Darlene, I appreciate your offer to let me borrow your diamond necklace," I began, practically drooling over the expensive, glittering stones. "But—"

"But nothing. You're going to Sardi's! You must wear diamonds," Darlene insisted, moving my hair to one side and clasping the necklace around my throat.

I looked in the mirror and gasped. "Oh, my."

"See, Marilyn Monroe was right. Diamonds *are* a girl's best friend."

"What if someone tries to rob me and take the necklace? And I don't have a wrap that goes with this dress."

"Stop! You'll be with Pierre—"

"Who's probably the killer—"

"And Stu had the necklace insured for me."

I blew air into my bangs. "Thank heavens. I feel like a princess in these."

"Cole was good for something," she said.

We laughed and I said, "That's naughty," which made us laugh harder.

The buzzer sounded.

Darlene grinned. "Right on time. Order the filet mignon and get Pierre's confession. Good luck, honey."

I took a deep breath. "I have to clear Bradley, Darlene, I just have to. But I feel bad misleading Pierre this way. He's truly interested in me—"

"Sshh. Don't get tears in your eyes now. You'll do your best. Pierre's a big boy. He'll get over any feelings he has for you. Have you done anything to lead him on? What if he really is the killer, Bebe?"

"No, I haven't encouraged his personal attentions. It's been business and Bradley. That's how I'm justifying this date with Pierre."

"Good girl. If you can't get him to confess, we'll simply put him in one of my girdles and hold him hostage until he breaks," Darlene said, and grinned.

"Good idea!"

Downstairs, Pierre kissed both my cheeks. "I have never seen you more beautiful, my *chérie*. You were born to wear diamonds." Then he bent and whispered in my ear, "And I want to be the one to give them to you."

"Pierre, you're so kind," I said, figuring I'd have to update the "Confessions" section of my notebook for lying.

"I could give you everything you ever dreamed of, Bebe," he said, opening the cab door.

Maybe he could, but not in the way he thought. If Pierre confessed to killing Suzie, Bradley would not be railroaded into jail. Bradley's freedom, the clearing of his name—that was what I wanted more than anything.

Pierre had left his beret at home. I caught myself staring at his thin brown hair. No wonder he covered it up. He wore a black suit, black shirt, and a black tie.

We chatted about Saint Thomas on the cab ride over to Sardi's.

"Your photos are magnificent, Bebe. They bring out your irresistible combination of innocence and sensuality. The Durden people will be happily surprised—

as I have been, to find someone so soon after Suzie's death."

"I hope the Durden people are happy." Bradley, though, would have a fit.

"I have arranged for a messenger tomorrow to bring the photos to whoever is in charge now at Ryan," Pierre informed me.

Oh, boy. Maybe I could intercept them, send them straight to the Durden people myself without Bradley ever seeing me in that black bikini.

Excitement took over when the cab pulled in front of the restaurant. A big green neon sign proclaimed SARDI'S, and in smaller letters, RESTAURANT, and COCKTAILS.

Inside I was dazzled by the gleaming wood, the famous celebrity caricatures, and the hearty greeting Pierre received by the maître d' who guided us to an elegant table for two. People nodded at Pierre and he smiled back, but he stopped for no one.

Once seated, I became conscious of people staring at me. Did they think I was Pierre's new girlfriend? Pierre certainly thought so.

After consulting at great length with the waiter, who brought the wine list, Pierre decided on a French champagne. I didn't even want to think about what it cost.

Following Darlene's suggestion, I ordered the filet mignon from my menu, which did not list prices. I loved being a woman dining in an expensive restaurant, not worrying about prices!

Pierre chose cannelloni au gratin, Sardi's specialty, which turned out to be a French crepe with sherry sauce.

We chatted about New York. I couldn't hide how much I loved the city, all the places I had yet to see, and Pierre approved. "Virginia bored you. I can understand."

I felt decadent in Darlene's diamonds, drinking the most delicious champagne and eating the best food I'd ever tasted. In order to get Pierre's confession, I allowed myself to become a little tipsy, but not so much that I didn't feel in control.

Just about to launch into my questioning, I saw something that made my eyes widen. Bradley and model Evelyn Miller were being seated at a table across the aisle and two up from Pierre and me. Bradley, in a white dinner jacket that almost made me faint, sat facing me, though he didn't look my way. I fixed my gaze at the napkin in my lap, not sure whether to smile or go over and punch him. He had overheard my plans to dine here with Pierre and had come to keep an eye on me. Didn't he think I could take care of myself?

Bradley's entrance did not go unnoted by Pierre.

"Mon dieu," he sneered. "Cannot I go anywhere without that man reminding me of Suzie's murder? We shall ignore him and take pleasure in this time together."

I was going to have to play along with him. "Speaking of Suzie, what was Gloria talking about today when she said you had a love-hate relationship with your girlfriends, Pierre?" I asked innocently, running my tongue across my upper lip.

Bradley opened his napkin with a loud snap.

Pierre reached his left arm across the table and took my free hand. "I'm a passionate man, *chérie.* You know that."

I kept my hand in his. "But I don't know how bad your temper can be. I'm afraid."

"How can I reassure you? I will give you an example of my feelings." Pierre scowled. "I could not like what Louis said about kissing you. Is it true?"

"It was nothing. He merely brushed my lips."

"I shall never photograph him again," Pierre announced.

As angry as I was at Louis for trying to use me to get ahead at Ryan, I said, "Don't do that to him, Pierre. I'm not going out with him again."

Pierre swallowed champagne, his thumb moving over the back of my hand.

I slanted a glance at Bradley. He held a martini, the sight of which brought back the last time I'd seen him drink one—in his office—and I felt myself blush.

"Ah, there is that pretty color in your face, Bebe. Do not return to Ryan. Come to me," Pierre said slowly and seductively, not even bothering to mention a job.

Daddy would have beaten Pierre to a pulp if he'd heard him.

Here we go. "Pierre," I said, instilling my voice with confusion, "how can I? I must know a man's history with women before I can make a commitment. Please try to understand. I've had a sheltered upbringing."

A gleam entered his eye. "And you have not dated much, nor had a lover?"

I gasped. "A lover? Certainly not."

Almost, though.

His fervor grew; I could see it shining in his eyes. "What do you want to know about me, *chérie?* Did you read my biography at the gallery showing? It was there I first noticed you."

Liar. He'd had eyes only for Suzie and the other celebrities. "Yes, I read it. I'm impressed with your ambition, and how you've overcome horrible odds," I replied. That much was true. "Tell me, at Debbie Ann's shoot today, Lola mentioned someone named Kiki."

I saw Evelyn bang her fist on the table to get Bradley's attention.

Our waiter chose that moment to clear our plates and hand us the dessert menu.

"Order the New York cheesecake, Bebe," Pierre suggested.

"I couldn't eat it, but thank you."

"If only one bite crosses your pink lips, I shall take great delight in watching you savor the richness," Pierre cajoled.

"Very well," I replied. When the waiter left, I said, "We were talking about Kiki."

Pierre released my hand and sat back in his chair.

"How can I explain Kiki? She was eighteen, wild, and lived for cocaine and parties."

"Cocaine? Oh, dear," I sympathized, trying to hide my shock.

Pierre looked away. "Part French, part Italian, she was like no one else. Her beauty lay in the wildness, the free spirit that shone through the camera lens like a mermaid luring ships to shore."

High drama there, I thought. "Did you argue?"

"Of course. I wanted her off drugs, but I couldn't tame her. She broke my heart when she took cocaine and went nightclubbing, not coming home for days. Then one evening I returned late from a dinner with friends. There were policemen, an ambulance—" He broke off, tears in his eyes.

"Kiki was dead?"

He nodded, pulling his handkerchief out of his suit coat pocket and wiping his face. "She had fallen off the roof of our building. I know people say she killed herself. It's not true, Bebe. Kiki had pots and pots of flowers on the roof. We used to go up there and talk, look at the stars. I believe she went to the roof to wait for me and fell. The coroner told me she had cocaine in her system."

"What a tragic accident," I said, thinking Kiki and Pierre might have had an argument, and he pushed her. "What about Lola?"

Pierre leaned closer to the table as the waiter brought our cheesecake and coffee.

Picking up his dessert fork, Pierre waved it in the air. "That one. You know her. Who could get along with that drunk? She used me. Our relationship was short, a year perhaps. Then Suzie came into my life."

While Pierre savored another bite of cheesecake, I dared a glance at Bradley. He had another martini in his hand. Evelyn didn't appear to be happy. Although I could make out only her profile, she spoke angrily to him, while Bradley was the picture of cool.

I took a bite of cheesecake, which was delicious. I licked my lips, then noticed both Pierre and Bradley staring at me. I marshaled my forces and went in for the attack. I faced Pierre. "I can understand why your association with Suzie was one of love-hate. She was a beautiful woman, but cared for no one."

Pierre set his fork down. "What do you mean? Suzie told me she loved me. She brought out more passion in me than has any other woman."

"I'm sure Suzie loved you. In her way. But over time, a man of your intelligence, your sensitivity, must have realized she was only using you, like Lola had."

Tiny beads of perspiration broke out on Pierre's forehead.

"Suzie wasn't loyal even before she met Mr. Williams. Is loyalty something you don't require in a relationship, Pierre?"

"Of course I demand loyalty," he responded.

I nodded. "Then I can understand why Gloria said you had a love-hate relationship with Suzie. It was an open secret that she still saw Scott Roberts, her old photographer."

Pierre lifted the almost empty bottle of champagne from the ice bucket, poured the remainder into his glass, and drank it down.

"Then there was her other boyfriend—you know, Jeff Granford, the guy who followed Suzie to New York from Omaha."

"That madman!" Pierre declared.

"True. But can you blame him? He told me at the memorial reception that Suzie was promised to him. They met whenever they could and talked about their plans to get rich from Suzie's modeling, then return to Omaha and raise a family. Come to think of it, Gloria mentioned Suzie's meetings with Scott and Jeff."

Pierre pounded his fist on the table.

Bradley rose.

Evelyn stood too. I heard her say, "You're not paying any attention to me." Then she slapped Bradley across the face and stormed out of Sardi's. Bradley sat down and ordered another drink.

I had to keep my focus. I put a hand to my heart. "You knew about all this, didn't you, Pierre? Gosh, I hope I haven't said too much."

Pierre's right hand balled into a fist. "I knew."

"You fought with Suzie about her boyfriends, I'm sure."

"Yes, but I couldn't stop her cheating. Then Williams came along. I thought I would lose her forever," Pierre said, his expression clouded with anger. "I bought her a four-carat-diamond engagement ring. Never had I married before, but I felt if Suzie were my wife, she would be faithful."

"Gloria told me Suzie didn't accept your ring during that Friday night at dinner. Gloria said that you were never engaged," I said softly.

"Gloria has a big mouth," Pierre said with contempt. "Suzie would have said yes had it not been for Williams." He turned and glared at Bradley, who saluted the photographer with his martini glass.

Pierre had just admitted he'd lied at Suzie's memorial, when he declared to one and all that Suzie had been his fiancée. I reached across and took Pierre's hand. Holding it tight, I said, "You must have been awfully hurt when Suzie turned down your proposal. After all you'd done for her, all you'd put up with from her."

He whirled to face me. His eyes blazed with anger. "I made Suzie a *star*. Scott Roberts could never have done that for her. Suzie should have been grateful, been loyal, obeyed me."

"You're right. You fought about it during that Friday-night dinner when you proposed."

"Yes," he said, his voice inflamed with passion. "We argued all evening, especially about Williams. Then we made love, and when I woke she was gone. She had the Mustang assignment, and Ford had hired their own photographer."

I lowered my voice. "You loved Suzie dearly. She was the most important woman in the world to you. You desperately wanted her to marry you, give up Mr. Williams."

"Yes," Pierre said, shaking with emotion, dragging his

hand away from mine. "Suzie called me late that Saturday, and told me she was exhausted, and felt a cold coming on. She said she was going straight to bed."

I coughed. The same excuse she'd given Bradley the night before. "But you couldn't stand being away from her, could you? Late Saturday night, you went to her apartment, and you found her awake and nude. Did she tell you it was Mr. Williams she was with? That he'd gone out and would be returning?"

"What?" Pierre demanded.

"Pierre, don't you know that if you want me to trust you, then you must trust me? Knowing Suzie was with another lover, after you had made your beautiful marriage proposal, surely threw you over the edge."

He looked at me, a mixture of shock and anger twisting his features.

"You're a passionate man. Suzie had hurt you again. This time she wasn't going to get away with it. You reached for the scarf and wrapped it around her neck—"

Pierre leaped to his feet, upsetting his chair. His nostrils flared with fury. "How *dare* you even suggest such a thing?" French curses fell from his mouth for everyone to hear.

I saw Bradley stand.

A hush came over the room. People were staring.

Pierre walked around to my side of the table, his eyes black and thunderous. He bent and spoke right in my face. "Suzie told me you were in love with Williams. I couldn't fathom a playboy like him having any interest in a piddlin' girl from the South. You're trying to clear *his* name by accusing *me*."

"No, I—"

"You are dead to me, as is your agency." He pitched his napkin over my cheesecake, and stalked out of Sardi's.

Talk resumed in earnest across the room.

Trembling, I finished the last of my champagne, peeking over the top of the glass at Bradley. He was seated again and giving orders to a waiter.

A feeling of total failure washed over me.

A different waiter appeared at my table and righted the empty chair. He held a small silver tray with a single glass of champagne. "Miss, the gentleman over there," he said, indicating Bradley, "sends this with his compliments. He asks if he may join you."

"Thank you," I said, accepting the glass. "He may."

The waiter nodded at Bradley, who picked up his martini glass, sauntered over, and sat in Pierre's chair.

Taking a sip of my drink, I realized it was not champagne. "Why, Bradley, how did you know Canada Dry is my favorite?"

"Just a lucky guess, kid. Nice rocks around your neck. Pierre give them to you?"

"What difference would it make to you if he had?"

Bradley sipped his martini. "You just told me the French lecher didn't give them to you. I must be paying you too much if you can buy them on your own."

"They're Darlene's," I said, leaning across the table.

Bradley's blue gaze met mine. "You've got that perfume on again."

"What are you going to do about it? Break into my apartment and steal the bottle?" I narrowed my eyes at him.

He ran his fingertip slowly around the rim of his martini glass.

Suddenly I felt uncomfortably warm. I drank the cold ginger ale. Tension had filled me when I questioned Pierre. Now another kind of tension began to build while I stared at Bradley.

"Louis certainly likes to brag about his conquests." I rolled my eyes. "He disgusts me."

"So you didn't like kissing him?"

"None of your business."

"Will you be living at your apartment much longer?" Bradley asked. "Holding hands with New York's most famous photographer in one of New York's famous restaurants. The society pages will be all over the story. Won't you have to marry Pierre to protect your reputation?"

"I most certainly will not marry Pierre," I hissed.
"And don't *you* talk to me about my reputation."

His gaze roved lazily over the bust of my dress.

I looked down and felt heat burn my cheeks. The
heavy beading at the top of the dress had pulled it
down when I leaned forward. I sat up straight, bringing a slow smile to Bradley's lips.

The waiter returned. "Would you like anything
else, miss?"

"Yes, a glass of champagne, please."

"And you, sir?"

"Nothing for me, thank you."

"You haven't eaten anything," I said.

"I don't like dining alone, and you've already had
dinner."

"Guess you'll have to make yourself a peanut-
butter-and-jelly sandwich when you go back to your
bachelor's lair."

"That's right. You were at my town house once.
Pity I was already occupied. By the way, what did
Gloria mean at Debbie Ann's shoot when she said
that you couldn't 'get anywhere' with me?"

I turned my head to the side, but I knew it was not
enough. The red of my skin probably started at my
toes and went to my hairline. I flipped my hair in a
gesture of unconcern and turned to face him. Avoid-
ance of the question seemed best. "You might as well
know, I couldn't get a confession out of Pierre," I
said, and sighed.

Bradley threw back his head and laughed. Then,
looking at me, he said, "You tried your hardest,
though. I watched you work, kid. I have to admit, it
was impressive."

"Are you laughing at me? Here I am, trying to
save—"

The waiter reappeared. He placed my champagne
in front of me, and discreetly put a closed black book-
let at my elbow.

Oh, dear God! Pierre had left me with the bill.

I took a big swallow of champagne.

Bradley slid the bill over to his side of the table with one fluid move of a slim finger. He opened it and signed his name. "I'm sure you were discussing Ryan business. The agency will take care of this."

I tried not to appear relieved. "Actually, we did discuss business."

Bradley slanted his body toward me. He placed his right hand over my champagne glass. "What about when Drew flirted with you? He wants you in Chicago with him."

"I love New York."

"I suppose you do. You've made a lot of close friends since you moved here, like the guy who groped you right outside my office this morning."

"That was Stu, Darlene's boyfriend, and he didn't *grope* me; he gave me a hug!"

I tried to push his hand away from my champagne glass. To further my mortification, I succeeded only in knocking the glass and the contents onto the white tablecloth.

Bradley stood. "Let's go, Bebe."

I got to my feet, feeling woozy. Bradley wasn't going to know about it, though. He might try something with me.

Or I might try something with him.

I giggled.

The maître d' said, "Good night, Mr. Williams."

"Good night," Bradley said.

Outside, I shivered without a wrap.

Bradley put his arm around me. He kissed the side of my head. "Come on, Bebe, we're going home."

Home? Home to his house?

A black car pulled up, and Bradley held the back door open for me. We entered, and I immediately missed having his arm around me. "Much better than a regular cab," he murmured in the darkness.

"Comfortable," I said softly. Why didn't he touch me?

I couldn't bear being alone with him like this.

I loved Bradley. He might be sent to prison! His uncle

might take away Bradley's job and give it to Drew or someone else. Hadn't he threatened to do just that if Bradley didn't clear his name in ten days? Tomorrow would be the tenth day since Suzie's murder.

"Are you still cold? You're rubbing your upper arms," he said.

I loved his voice. "I'm fine, Bradley."

The car rolled to a stop.

"We're here."

I glanced outside. Harry lounged on the stoop of my apartment building. Bradley wasn't taking me to his house for a night of love after all. *Damn him!*

"If you'll excuse me, Bradley, you are sitting in the seat closest to the curb," I said, trying to keep my voice emotionless. "Thanks for the ride."

He didn't budge. "I couldn't let you go home by yourself wearing that necklace, kid."

"You're such a gentleman," I said, then began to open my door, anxious to get away.

He leaned across me. He took my hand from the door handle and held it in his, staying very close to me. I looked at his lips, mere inches from mine.

He put his hand in my hair, and gently pulled me to him.

Thump. Thump. Thump.

Bradley and I turned toward his window.

Harry's face peered inside. Though muffled, his voice came through. "Hey, mister, what are you doing with Miss Sweet Face?"

Bradley eased back into his seat. "This is your wino, I believe." He opened the door, and we both got out. But Bradley only whispered, "Good night," before re-entering the car, which drove away.

Harry scratched his head. "He wasn't the one, was he?"

"Yes, he was," I said, handed Harry two quarters, and went upstairs.

Trying to keep myself from going insane over Bradley, I thought about Pierre. Something he'd said niggled at me, but I couldn't think what it was.

Chapter Twenty-seven

Wednesday morning, I entered Ryan, put my purse on my desk, and went directly to the coffeepot. My mouth tasted like yesterday's dishwater, my eyes were full of sand, and my body might have been run over—twice—by a garbage truck.

That's the way I felt after last night's failure with Pierre, the champagne I'd consumed, and about four hours of sleep. Earlier this morning, while dressing in my apple-green suit, I'd told Darlene everything.

"Honey, from all you've told me, I still think Pierre's the killer," she had said.

"I do too, if only we can prove it. I guess I'll go by Jeff Granford's at lunchtime to make sure we've covered every base."

"Not without me, you won't." Darlene proclaimed. "He's like a cobra ready to strike. I want this mess finished by the time I leave Saturday afternoon."

I looked up from attaching my stocking to my garter belt. "Skyway's given you a flight assignment?"

Darlene nodded. "Rome first, and I have a full schedule for the next month. Stu's going with me. We'll be at his place tonight, making plans."

Staring at the coffeepot, willing it to drip faster, I thought about how much I'd miss Darlene. She might not be the only one leaving my life for a while. I took off my shades and squinted at the office light, trying hard not to think about how this might be Bradley's last day at Ryan.

"Miss Bennett," Bradley called from his office.

I moved to his doorway. "Coffee is almost ready."

"Good. Please bring me a cup, and then I want to talk to you."

I carried his filled mug into his office and gave it to him. Holding a cup for myself, I dug in the pocket of my suit.

"Here," I said, laying Suzie's gold bracelet on his desk. "I found this in Pierre's bedroom. Suzie won't need it now."

"In Pierre's bedroom?" he asked ominously.

I sat down and drank some coffee. "Please, not today. It was all innocent. He wasn't even in the bedroom at the time. I was just—"

"Putting yourself into a dangerous situation," Bradley said. He picked up the glittering gold piece and said, "Why don't you take it, kid."

"No, thank you. I'd rather not have Suzie's hand-me-downs."

Bradley put the bracelet in his suit coat pocket. He *would* wear my favorite suit today—the medium-blue one made of silk.

"Drew's coming in after lunch to take my place," Bradley said. "I know you don't like him, but do your best."

"I'll do my best to make Drew miserable every day he's here." Tears replaced the sand in my eyes.

Bradley pointed at me. "Don't make me ruin my handkerchief. Pickering will—"

"Mr. Pickering, yes, he's swell," I said.

Bradley drew in a deep breath. "You won't have work from me today, so try to clear your desk—" He broke off and looked toward the doorway. "Can I help you?"

A skinny guy with SPEEDY DELIVERY stamped on his navy shirt stepped forward. "I have an envelope from a Mr. Ben something for Mr. Williams."

"Oh, I'll take those," I said, jumping to my feet and holding out my hand.

"Supposed to give them directly to Williams and get his signature," the dufus said.

Bradley stretched out his arm. "I'm Williams." He signed the messenger's pad, making him disappear. "These must be the Durden photos from Saint Thomas."

"Here, let me have them and I'll send them off to Durden myself. You don't need to concern yourself with trivial matters right now," I said, placing my coffee cup on his desk and holding out my hand.

Bradley ripped open the envelope. "Wait a minute. Didn't Gloria say you had posed—" He broke off, taking pictures out of the envelope one at a time and tossing them on his desk.

There I was in that tiny bikini, giving my best Sophia Loren imitation. I'd never looked better, but there was a lot of skin showing.

I tried to come up with an explanation. "Lola got drunk, and we had no one else. I only did it to save the shoot."

Bradley's astonishment, obviously genuine, grew until he reached the last of the photos and looked at me. His voice was cold and filled with contempt. "I must say, you're an enigma, Miss Bennett. Never, in my wildest imagination, would I have thought you would pose wearing less than we see on America's beaches, and more like what men view in *Playboy*."

My heart hammered in my chest.

Bradley scooped up the photos and returned them to their envelope. "Your father would gun me down in the street if I allowed these photographs to be printed in magazines distributed nationally. I'll call the Durden people right now and tell them the shoot will have to be redone. Close the door on your way out."

I picked up my coffee cup and did as he asked, making my way to my desk. My blood pounded, my face grew hot with humiliation, and I felt as if I'd just lost something precious. Bradley had never looked at me with such *disappointment*.

My fingers automatically reached for the mail. I opened letters and invoices, stacking them into piles, all the while feeling a deep sense of shame.

Around ten, Debbie Ann came in holding a newspaper. She stopped at my desk.

"Hi, Debbie Ann."

"Bebe, how can you look down in the dumps when you're mentioned in the society section of today's *Times*? Actually, the reporter didn't know your name, but he described you well, and said you had dinner at Sardi's last night with Pierre. Didn't you see it?"

I shook my head. "I don't have time to read the society section of the newspaper, Debbie Ann. Besides, I don't know any of those people."

"My dear, if you're going to live in New York, you must familiarize yourself with our luminaries. I'll leave this with you. Perhaps it will cheer you. Whatever is wrong?"

I twirled a piece of my hair, ready to pour my heart out to her, but I didn't think she'd have a sympathetic ear. Debbie Ann was a caring person, but so opinionated. I said, "Oh, it's nothing that won't be fixed. When two people care about each other—" I broke off, blushing.

"I see. You know what? I think I'll go whip up some cookies. I have some cookie dough in the freezer," Debbie Ann said, patting me on the shoulder. "While I don't want to ruin your figure, I think we can make an exception today."

I managed a smile. "Thanks, Debbie Ann."

She signed the talent sheet and disappeared into the elevator.

The phone rang half an hour later. "Ryan Modeling Agency, Miss Bennett speaking."

"Finelli here."

I sat up straight. "What have you got? Something on Pierre?"

"No. I assigned three officers to check out Granford's alibi."

"Did they find out Jeff lied? Did they get evidence that he killed Suzie?"

"Sorry to disappoint you, but just the opposite. I've got two witnesses who can vouch for Granford boxing with a kid named Shelton late into the night Suzie Wexford was murdered."

"They were boxing after midnight?"

"The kid goes to high school, then works as a waiter. Doesn't get off work until eleven thirty or later. Granford's broke, needs the money. Before you ask, I verified with Granford's bank that the guy is living on nothing. Miss Wexford probably helped support him. Now that we've cleared him, he'll probably go back to Omaha."

"Thanks, anyway," I replied, despair washing over me.

"Got any new leads for me?" Finelli asked.

"No, but I think Pierre is the killer," I said, and hung up.

I sat staring into space. I needed to call Darlene and tell her I wouldn't need her to go on a Jeff Granford mission. I'd get the energy to do it in a minute.

"Bebe?"

Debbie Ann stood next to my desk with a paper Dixie cup full of what looked like white wedding cookies. "Those are like the ones my mother makes at Christmas," I said.

She smiled. "They're small. I brought you half a dozen, so you can nibble on them throughout the afternoon. If you want to talk, I have some time."

I accepted the cup and dug for a cookie. "Thanks for the offer, Debbie Ann. I may go home early today." Anything to get away from that crushing look of disapproval on Bradley's face.

"That's sensible. It can't be pleasant working for a murderer. I'll never understand why you've stayed this long. At least his replacement has finally arrived."

I popped the cookie into my mouth so I wouldn't

have to answer. The powdered sugar melted on my tongue, and the cookies were yummy. "These are delicious, Debbie Ann," I said.

"I'll be on my set if you want any milk to go with them," she said, and went to the elevator.

I popped another cookie in my mouth and dialed home.

"Hello."

"Darlene, it's me. More news."

"Uh-oh, I don't like the sound of your voice."

"Finelli's cleared Granford. We don't need to pay the boxer a visit."

"Damn Finelli!"

"It's not his fault Granford is innocent. There's also more bad news."

"What? Speak up, it sounds like you're eating something."

I swallowed my second cookie. "Sorry. Bradley saw the Saint Thomas photos and flipped. In a bad way. He was disgusted with me, Darlene."

"What exactly did he say?"

"I can't talk about it now," I said. "I'll tell you later. I'm so tired and down, I want to come home and crawl under the covers. Drew's going to be here all afternoon. I don't think I can take it."

"Get that girl from the typing pool to cover for you and leave. You'll only get more upset as the day goes on, and when the time comes for Bradley to go—"

I rubbed my left temple. "Gosh, I hadn't even thought of that moment. Dear God. Bradley's shut his door. I've got to finish some work, then let Danielle have her lunch. Maybe after that I'll come home."

"Good. Honey, I'm going to head over to Stu's house. You call me if there's anything you need, okay?"

"Yes. Thanks, Darlene."

I dialed Danielle and asked her to cover for me after she'd had lunch. She said she would, but that it might not be until two, because they were swamped in the typing pool.

Throughout the morning, Bradley's door stayed shut.

Around one, Drew swooped in like a vulture. "Hey, baby. Ready to start work for your new boss?"

"Temporary boss," I replied, and popped another cookie into my mouth.

"I'll win you over, baby. Soon you'll be eating cookies out of my hand," he promised, entering Bradley's office and closing the door behind him.

I felt queasy just looking at him.

In fact, by the time Danielle finally arrived to relieve me at close to two thirty, I felt dizzy from nerves, exhaustion, and lack of sleep.

I grabbed my purse, my cup of cookies, and took the elevator to the lobby. I had no idea when I'd see Bradley again. Days? Months?

I rode the subway home, trying not to cry. The noise of the train sounded loud in my ears, and the masses of people began to blur together. I wished I could shake the dizziness. Plus, now I could take only shallow breaths. I needed sleep.

As I entered my apartment, it was all I could do to close and lock the door. With difficulty I changed into a short, sleeveless cotton nightgown, leaving my suit lying across my bed.

About to leave the room, I spotted Bradley's scarf on the Banana chair. I grabbed it and held the soft wool close to my face. I opened a window in the living room and lay down on the sectional, out of breath. I tried to sleep, but instead developed a terrible headache.

I looked at the big conch shell on the coffee table next to where I'd dropped my purse and the rest of Debbie Ann's cookies. As pretty as the shell was, I decided to give it away. It only held memories of that trip to Saint Thomas, and the mistake I'd made. Bradley was right: I should never have posed for Pierre. I had been so darned concerned about not disappointing Bradley, I'd ending up doing just that.

My stomach rolled. I needed to take some aspirin for my headache. I pushed myself off the sectional and stood. The room tilted. By holding on to the sectional, then grasping the door frame to the kitchen, I managed to reach the aspirin on the counter. My heart beat hard in my chest. I thought about calling Darlene, but I didn't want to interrupt her time with Stu over something that would pass with sleep.

The phone rang.

Bradley!

"Hello," I said, surprised that my voice sounded like I'd been running.

"Bebe, dear, this is Debbie Ann. I heard you left the office. I've been worried about you. My show ended moments ago, and I called you first thing. Are you all right?"

I leaned against the wall for support, closing my eyes in an attempt to stop the dizziness. "I have a terrible headache, I'm dizzy, and I feel a little nauseous. I'm going to take some aspirin."

"Heavens, sounds like a flu coming on. Is your roommate helping you?"

"No, she's not here," I mumbled. "I think it's the strain . . . Suzie's death . . . Mr. Williams . . . Pierre . . . I need sleep."

"Give me your address, Bebe, I'm coming over. I don't like the way you sound," Debbie Ann commanded.

"I'll be fine," I said, and gasped for breath. "Need aspirin and sleep." I slid down and sat on the floor.

"Listen to me, Bebe. You're a young girl without a mother nearby to take care of you. Of course I don't *have* to come over, but I want to. I have a strong pain reliever, and I am no stranger to illness. You might have to see a doctor, and mine would make a house call if I asked him."

"Okay," I said and gave her my address. "Buzz me when you get here."

"I'll be right there."

I took shallow breaths after talking to her. Was it the flu, or was I having a nervous breakdown? I couldn't even return the receiver to its cradle. Instead I left it on the kitchen floor and crawled over to the door. With effort I lifted myself enough to unlock it, and then sat down underneath the intercom to wait for Debbie Ann.

When the buzzer sounded, I pressed the button for the downstairs door to open, then crawled over to the sectional. I didn't want Debbie Ann to see me on the floor. She might do something rash like call an ambulance.

I had just lain down, clutching Bradley's scarf, when Debbie Ann came in, still in TV makeup, her lips very red, wearing a striped shirtwaist dress. I moved my legs to make room for her, and she sat down near my hips.

"You don't look at all well, Bebe."

"Think I need a doctor?" I got out, finding it harder to breathe.

"If only you'd eaten all the cookies I laced with cyanide it would all be over. I wouldn't have had to risk coming over here. But no one will remember an ordinary woman like me."

My head swam. "Huh?"

Debbie Ann's red lips curved. "You'd be in heaven now, following a rather unpleasant death, I admit. I despise rodents and always keep rodenticide." She laughed. "You are a rodent, are you not, Bebe? Toying with things weaker than yourself."

She pulled something thin, sharp, and shiny from her black pocketbook and held it over me. "If only I knew exactly where to place this, you wouldn't have to suffer. It's just as well. Messy stabbings happen frequently in New York."

"Why?" I couldn't understand. Debbie Ann was going to kill me? Poison. The cookies were poisoned.

Her face turned into a mask of rage. "You filthy girls and my Petey. None of you are good enough for him. Do you think I don't know what you've put him through, Bebe? He fancies himself in love with you and you've played with him, hurt him. After last night, I begged him not to see you anymore, but Petey wouldn't listen, said he'd win your love."

"Petey?"

"Pierre, you fool, my son. We changed his name when we moved from West Virginia. He always cries on his mother's shoulder, and I take care of him, all to his good. I knew you'd have to die when he told me how much he loved you, but that you'd turned on him and tried to make him say he'd killed that hussy Suzie. He's forgiven you already and is determined to make you his."

Piddlin'. A Southern phrase Pierre had used at dinner last night. That's what had bothered me. And the photograph in Pierre's bedroom of a family with the mountains in the background. "Pierre's parents . . . dead," I got out, forcing back nausea.

"I saw the talent in Petey, the greatness. I knew he'd be our ticket out of poverty if we moved to New York and Petey made a name for himself. His father thought I was crazy. I killed him first, making it look like a suicide, so Petey wouldn't be angry. Then Petey and I were free. Now we're both successful, and I won't let *any* woman hurt him or interfere with his greatness."

Through the dizziness, the headache, the nausea, I began to comprehend. Terror gripped me.

"Petey . . . a good photographer," I said, breathlessly. I had to be strong. I had to save myself.

"He's the best," Debbie Ann snarled. She relaxed her arms for a moment, lowering the thin blade. "We contrived that story about his being French. So much more high-class than West Virginia. The orphan angle coaxed people into feeling sorry for him. He honed his craft from them, until we were ready to take New York."

"You did," I said, buying time like they always did on TV.

She laughed. "Both of us did. But where I was able to avoid the pitfalls of the chains of marriage, Petey was an idiot when it came to models. At first there was nothing serious, nothing for me to worry about. But as he got older, Petey started having long affairs that only hurt him and distracted him from his work. I tried to tell him, but he wouldn't listen to me."

"Kiki?"

She gave me a withering stare. "You know even more than I thought. No girl who took cocaine was good enough for my son! She was out of her mind with the drug, so surprised to learn Pierre really had a mother, so willing to show me her pretty flowers, so easy to push off the building."

I tried not to reveal my horror. "Lola."

Debbie Ann *tsk*ed. "She was no threat. Drunken whore. Petey and I talk about everything—well, almost everything."

Pierre didn't know his mother had killed! Suddenly, through my dizziness, my pounding head, came one word: "Suzie."

Debbie Ann's features contorted. "That lying, whoring bitch! Petey and I fought constantly about her. I hoped Williams would take Suzie away from Petey, but their affair had the opposite effect on him."

"How?"

"Suzie had my boy under her control. *Her* control! Petey bought her a ring, intending to marry that trash. I kept a constant watch on her, waiting, waiting for the right opportunity. When I saw Suzie and Williams go into her apartment building, I followed dressed as a cleaning woman. When Williams left, I knocked on the door. Suzie opened it, naked. I could have strangled her with my bare hands, but instead I saw the scarf. The one the newspaper said Williams gave her. Petey believes Williams strangled Suzie."

She broke off and tilted her head at me. "I'm glad you've kept me talking, Bebe. You've served me well." She placed the knife back in her purse.

Relief swept me. She wasn't going to kill me.

"You're in love with Williams. I know, because ever since you came to Ryan, there's been gossip about the two of you."

Her hand darted out and she snatched Bradley's scarf from me. She twisted the blue wool until it was tightly wound. "Two women strangled with scarves from Williams. How utterly perfect."

"Scarf. Not. Bradley's."

She laughed. "Your Bradley will get the electric chair for double murder. My Petey will never come under suspicion. We'll go on, mother and son. I'll help Petey get over his grief."

At those words, a current of adrenaline shot through me.

I reached out for the conch shell on the coffee table, grabbing it just as she wrapped the scarf around my neck.

With all my might, I let the heavy shell come crashing down on her head.

Stunned, she slumped over on top of me. I gripped the shell, but Debbie Ann's weight crushed the breath from me.

The front door swung open.

"Bebe!" Bradley yelled.

"Gun. Darlene. Underwear." The room went black, then came into focus again.

Debbie Ann regained consciousness. She pulled the knife back out of her purse.

"Drop it, Debbie Ann, or I'll put a bullet through your back," Bradley commanded.

"You're the one who's going to die!" she screamed at him, her head turned away from me.

I brought the shell down again. This time when it made contact it shattered.

She fell to the floor.

Bradley rushed over. "Darlene had these in her drawer too," he said, holding out some handcuffs. He snapped them on Debbie Ann's wrists.

Then he gathered me up into his arms. Carrying me into the kitchen, he bent down, holding me close, and picked up the phone. "Hang on, sweetheart; you're going to be fine."

"Sorry. Photos. Forgive me," I said, and once again the blackness rushed toward me.

Chapter Twenty-eight

Two days later, Friday, the doctor let me out of the hospital. I'd had to have my stomach pumped, and all sorts of nasty injections, but I was completely healthy again. The doctor said I hadn't had a lethal amount of poison in my system, but if I had eaten all of Debbie Ann's cookies, things might have gone a different way.

I didn't remember Bradley calling the ambulance or much about my first night at the hospital. One of the nurses told me later that he stayed until four in the morning, when the doctor finally declared I was out of the woods.

Bradley called me Thursday afternoon and asked if he could visit, but I told him I'd rather wait to see him when I was home again. Actually, I didn't want him to see me without makeup in an ugly hospital gown. That could leave a lasting impression on a man. Darlene, who'd been with me most of the time, agreed.

Instead, Bradley sent me a dozen pink roses with a card that read, *Meet me at Tiffany's at noon on Saturday.*

At first, visions of us picking out my engagement ring flashed in my head. Then I realized Bradley would never propose marriage that way. Darlene had said, "He's probably going to return Suzie's bracelet and buy you something."

Also on Thursday, Detective Finelli visited.

"Landed yourself in the hospital this time, Miss Bennett," he said gruffly, dropping a box of chocolates on my tray. "Those aren't poisoned."

"You're so kind, Detective. Tell me everything."

"While you were dying, Pickering called Williams and instructed him to hurry to my office. Williams rushed in and the two of them met with me. Pickering had done a background check on Pierre Benoit per your boss's request. Williams hadn't seen it yet."

"Pickering found out Pierre is a phony?"

"Yeah, his name is Peter Benson, and another of his girlfriends, Kiki, died under questionable circumstances. Her death was ruled a suicide, but we're reopening the case."

"Debbie Ann told me she pushed Kiki off the roof of Peter's building."

Finelli pulled out his notepad and wrote. "Williams flipped out, saying that you had gone home sick. Took the two of us to calm him down. Pickering went on to say that Peter's mother is actually Debbie Ann Allard, aka Debbie Ann Benson. Her husband, Chuck Benson, shot himself back in the fifties. At that point, with Williams breathing down my neck, I called the Charleston, West Virginia, police. A detective there said they had suspected Chuck Benson may not have been the one to pull the trigger, but without proof they couldn't hold Debbie Ann in the state."

"Debbie Ann told me she killed her husband."

Finelli jotted down more notes. "Williams and I took a patrol car, lights flashing, and sped to find Mrs. Benson at Ryan, but she was gone. Your boss was like a wild man, Miss Bennett. He told me he intended to go to the photographer's studio immediately, yelling that either Peter or Debbie Ann was the killer and that you could be in danger. Your boyfriend looked like he would have a stroke at any minute."

"He's not my boyfriend," I murmured, imagining Bradley acting like "a wild man" over me.

"So you say. I went with him for Benson's protection. When confronted about his background, Benson

first tried to deny it, but Williams had the papers
from Pickering."

"What did Pierre—I mean Peter—say then?"

"First he cursed Williams for invading his privacy
and demanded to know why he wasn't in police custody for Suzie Wexford's murder. Then, under pressure, Benson admitted he and his mother had
contrived the story of his being from France, but insisted they'd done no harm. Benson said they came
to New York so he could make a name for himself
and that his mother was the only woman in the world
he trusted. He asked us not to reveal their little
deception."

"So Peter had no idea his mother had murdered
anyone?"

"Not a clue."

"I hope you didn't tell him his mother murdered
his father."

Finelli shook his head. "No. I didn't know she had
at that point. I only knew that the West Virginia police
suspected her."

"Good."

"Instead, I grilled him about Kiki's and Suzie's
deaths, telling him he was the connection between the
two women, both of whom were now dead. He furiously denied killing anyone. Williams pointed out that
Benson had lied about his identity, and that now he
was lying about killing Suzie. The two men almost
came to blows. That's when I called for backup. Officers arrived at the scene and took Benson to jail."

"Is he still there?"

Finelli held up his hand. "Do you want the whole
story or not?"

"Yes!"

"With Benson safe in the slammer, I was telling
Williams that I would put out an APB on Debbie Ann
Benson when he shouted your name and shot out of
there like a man on fire. He could run in the
Olympics."

"Really?"

"Yeah. Williams saved you from Debbie Ann. You'd blacked out when I got there. When I told Debbie Ann we had her son in jail on suspicion of murder, she broke. I've got a full confession for Suzie Wexford's murder. Sheesh, that woman went on and on about how I'd ruined her plans for a future with Benson in the French Riviera."

"What will happen to her now?"

"Life in prison is my guess. New York frowns on frying women."

"She deserves it. And Peter?"

Finelli shook his head. "He's had a mental breakdown, doesn't believe his mother did anything wrong. We took him to a private institution at her insistence. The man is traumatized."

"I feel sorry for Peter. What about Mr. Williams?"

"The case against your boyfriend has been dropped.

"Thanks, Detective. I knew you'd see the light about Bradley," I said, and smiled.

Finelli rubbed his crew cut. "When I go to church this Sunday, I'm going to pray that no one connected to you is ever murdered again, Miss Bennett."

Darlene and Stu brought me home from the hospital Friday afternoon. Stu left us alone on this, Darlene's last night in town.

I put the Beatles on my record player and flopped down on my bed.

Darlene went through my wardrobe. "Let's see, a trip to Tiffany's at noon. He'll probably buy you lunch afterward."

"That would be delicious. How about the boots?" I asked.

Darlene shook her red curls. "No. They're stuffy at Tiffany's." She pulled out a cherry-red dress. "This one."

Although not a mini, the dress was sleeveless and had four round cutout circles between the collar and the bust. When I had first tried it on, I had been pleased by the way the dress curved in at my waist.

"Red is supposed to be my best color."

"It was your red suit that drove Bradley to get you on that sofa."

"Groovy," I said, and grinned.

We chatted until the album ended; then Darlene said, "We should both get some sleep. I'm leaving early in the morning, so I won't see you."

She gave me a big hug and I hugged her back. "I'll check on you, honey. The airline lets us call home."

"That would be super," I said.

At the doorway, she turned back. "You know, I just realized Bradley had his hands on my panties."

I threw a pillow at her and yelled, "What were you doing with handcuffs?"

She laughed and laughed.

Saturday I took special care with my hair and makeup. When I slipped on the cherry number, I smiled with evil glee. Neutral stockings and black T-straps completed the outfit. In the bathroom I sprayed myself with My Sin, and then put on pearl earrings just to confuse Bradley.

I bounded down the steps and out into the sunshine. Thanking God I was alive, I darted down to the corner and waited for a cab. I didn't want to go underground on such a beautiful day.

Saturday midday traffic held me up. My watch read ten minutes after twelve when the taxi dropped me at the corner of Fifty-seventh and Fifth Avenue. I paid the driver and joined the throngs of people on the sidewalk.

Through them, I saw Bradley, dressed in a mod combo suit, lounging in front of Tiffany's.

Telling myself to be cool, I walked closer. His tight pants were black. His suit jacket was a gray, light blue, and white plaid. He wore a white shirt with a narrow pale blue tie.

I tried not to fall into his arms.

"Hi, Bradley," I said, trying not to burst out laughing with delight.

His blue gaze ran the length of me and back up, stopping at the cutouts of my dress. "Hi, Bebe. Let's go inside," he said. "That's an unusual dress you have on."

I smiled as he held the door for me. "Thank you."

A portly, balding, middle-aged man met us at the bracelet counter. "May I help you, sir?"

Bradley pulled out Suzie's gold bracelet and a receipt.

I turned discreetly away, acting as if I were giving Bradley privacy, while I strained my neck to see the diamond engagement rings.

The clerk's next words snagged my attention. "Mrs. Williams, would you like to select another piece?"

"I—"

"She's not my wife. Miss Bennett is my executive secretary," Bradley said, looking in the display case.

The clerk regarded me askance. "Oh, pardon me," he said in a snooty voice.

I gave him a flirty look and ran a finger around one of the cutouts of my dress. He turned beet red.

"Bebe, how about a gold cross?" In an aside the clerk couldn't hear, Bradley added, "A cross around your neck might remind me what kind of girl you are."

"No. No crosses," I said hastily. "I have a family one at home."

"Okay. Oh, I have it. Bebe, how about a gold charm bracelet? You don't have one, do you?" Bradley asked.

"Um, no—"

The clerk pulled the bracelet out for me to inspect. Then he reached into a drawer underneath the counter and placed a gold typewriter charm on a turquoise velvet pad.

"Hey, that's perfect, Bebe. Try it on, with the typewriter charm, of course," Bradley said.

I longed for something more intimate, more romantic.

Before I could say a word, the clerk closed the bracelet, charm dangling, around my right wrist.

Bradley took my hand in his and examined the shiny gold piece. Then he bent and whispered in my ear, "This will remind us of how we first met."

My heart melted. No way could anyone rip the bracelet from my wrist. "Bradley, I love"—I cleared my throat—"it. May I keep it on now, please?"

He winked at me. "Sure, kid." Then to the clerk, "But we would like a box for it, for when Miss Bennett is not wearing the piece."

How did he know I wanted one of Tiffany's famous pale turquoise boxes? I sighed.

Back on the sidewalk, Bradley hesitated. "It's a beautiful day."

"Yes," I said, transmitting vibes that said, *Let's spend it together!*

He turned to me abruptly. "Are you hungry?"

"I haven't eaten all day."

"You've just gotten out of the hospital! Where would you like to go for lunch?"

Your town house. No! I pushed that thought from my head. "What about the Waldorf-Astoria?" I said, remembering my neglected list of things to do in New York, specifically the last entry.

"Great idea. The Waldorf isn't far from here, but we could try to get a cab if you don't feel up to walking," Bradley said.

"I'd love to walk," I chirped.

"I like a girl who isn't afraid of a little exercise. Here," he said, walking around to the street side. Then he held out his arm for me to hold. I took it, feeling the muscles underneath his suit coat.

I felt blissfully happy, alive in the city of my dreams, on the arm of the man of my dreams. And the Tiffany's bag in my hand.

We walked down Park Avenue in comfortable silence. I happily thought I'd escaped any lecture on my investigating.

I was mistaken.

The Waldorf was in view when Bradley said, "You know you almost died."

"No, I didn't. The doctor said I didn't consume a lethal dose."

"But had you eaten all the cookies, you would be dead."

"You would have saved me."

"Like you risked your life trying to save me? I told you to leave it to Pickering."

"Are you saying you're not grateful for all I did?"

"You're a very frustrating person, twisting my words around. Of course I'm grateful. It's just that I don't want you to be in danger ever again."

"Have you heard from your uncle Herman?"

"Yes, he called me from Palm Springs, all apologies."

"Good."

"I saw that bottom painting at your apartment. The one you signed. That's not you."

I smiled. "No, it's not."

"I want your promise, Bebe, that you won't do any more snooping."

We walked into the Waldorf lobby.

"As long as no one close to me is charged with murder, my investigating days are over."

"I'll hold you to that, Bebe, I mean it."

"Yes, Bradley."

"That dress isn't very modest, either."

"You don't like it?"

"I didn't say that. And another thing—"

I had guided him over to where I wanted him. "What's that?"

He faced me. "I told you not to wear that perfume again."

I looked up at him from under my lashes. My hands moved to rest lightly on his chest. "Why? What kind of effect does it have on you?"

"This kind," he murmured, and put his arms around me and kissed me, a long, slow kiss, which I returned with enthusiasm.

There, under the clock in the lobby of the Waldorf-Astoria.

Look for Bebe Bennett's
next mystery adventure in the
1960s-set Murder A-Go-Go series
Secret Agent Girl
Coming from Signet
In April 2007

When Bebe's boss, Bradley, on whom she con-
tinues to have a huge crush, is put in charge of
the famous Merryweather Toy Shoppe, he as-
signs Bebe the task of making sure the fortieth
anniversary party at the flagship store in New
York City goes smoothly. But the store's mascot,
Mr. Skidoo, nastily insults all the other store
characters, and Bebe herself, before turning up
dead, a toy pirate knife stuck in his chest. Inspired by the popular *Man From U.N.C.L.E.* TV
show, Bebe dubs herself Secret Agent Girl and
sets out to unmask the murderer . . . and to win
Bradley's heart once and for all.

Introducing the new
Murder A-Go-Go Mystery series
by Rosemary Martin

It's a
Mod, Mod, Mod, Mod
Murder

Bebe Bennett is set to take 1964 New York City by
storm. She's got her own apartment, a fun
roommate, and a great job as secretary to dreamy
Bradley Williams, vice president of talent for Rip City
Records. But when a British pop star is murdered,
she'll have to venture into the dark side of
the swinging city to expose a killer.

"*THAT GIRL!* MEETS MISS MARPLE...YOU'LL
HAVE A BALL." —JERRILYN FARMER

"BEEHIVE HAIRDOS, JACKIE O CLOTHES, BRITISH ROCK STARS...AND
MURDER. WHAT FUN!"
—KASEY MICHAELS

"ROMANCE, CHARM, ORIGINALITY, AND PLENTY
OF DIPPITY-DO." —HARLEY JANE KOZAK

0-451-21470-6

penguin.com

Read the award-winning
Bubbles Yablonsky
series by
Sarah Strohmeyer

It doesn't help that her name's Bubbles. Or that she's a gum-snapping hairdresser. Or that she's saddled with a sleazy ex-hubby, a precocious daughter and a shoplifting mother. What can a beautician do to add new highlights to her image? Now, with a well-muscled photographer by her side, Bubbles is playing star sleuth.

BUBBLES UNBOUND
0-451-20844-8

BUBBLES IN TROUBLE
0-451-20850-1

BUBBLES ABLAZE
0-451-21217-7

BUBBLES A BROAD
0-451-41177-3

BUBBLES BETROTHED
0-451-21568-0

Available wherever books are sold or at
penguin.com

Just Murdered
by Elaine Viets
0-451-21492-7

When Helen gets a job at Millicent's Bridal Salon, she doesn't expect to get caught up in a fatal trip to the altar. But when the mother of the bride ends up dead, there are as many suspects as guests—including Helen.

Don't miss the other
Dead-End Job mysteries:

Shop Till You Drop   0-451-20855-2

Murder Between the Covers
                              0-451-21081-6

Dying to Call You   0-451-21332-7

Available wherever books are sold or at
penguin.com